What They Couldn't

What They Couldn't

Isabella "Pansy" Alden

Anglocentria
Aurora, Colorado

This is a work of fiction. Names, characters, places and incidents are products of the author's imagination or are used fictitiously. Any resemblance to actual persons, living or dead, or to events or locales, is entirely coincidental.

A Note from the Publisher . . .
What They Couldn't was originally published in 1895. This edition has been reproduced with every effort to retain the flavor of the original with minor changes to update spelling and punctuation. You'll find this book reflects many of the feelings and attitudes prevalent at the time of its original publication. It may contain references that reflect mores and opinions that directly conflict with today's prevailing sentiments.

WHAT THEY COULDN'T.
Copyright © 2014 by Anglocentria, Inc.
P.O. Box 460458
Aurora, CO 80046-0458

ISBN: 978-1-940896-45-8

ALSO BY ISABELLA ALDEN:

As In a Mirror

The Browns at Mount Hermon

By Way of the Wilderness

Cunning Workmen

Doris Farrand's Vocation

Eighty-Seven

From Different Standpoints

The Hall in the Grove

Her Associate Members

Interrupted

Jessie Wells

Links in Rebecca's Life

Lost on the Trail

A New Graft on the Family Tree

Pauline

Unto the End

Wanted

What They Couldn't

Workers Together; An Endless Chain

The Chautauqua Series
Four Girls at Chautauqua
The Chautauqua Girls at Home
Ruth Erskine's Crosses
Judge Burnham's Daughters
Ruth Erskine's Son
Four Mothers at Chautauqua

Marjorie's Story
Making Fate
Overruled

The Bryant Family
Miss Dee Dunmore Bryant
Twenty Minutes Late

The Endeavor Books
Chrissy's Endeavor
Her Associate Members

The Randolph Family
Household Puzzles
The Randolphs

The Remingtons
Aunt Hannah and Martha and John
John Remington, Martyr

You can learn more about Isabella, read free novels and stories, and view a complete list of her published books at:

www.IsabellaAlden.com

CONTENTS

THE GAME OF HALMA

In this novel, the Cameron family plays Halma. Halma was a Victorian board game, much like Chinese Checkers. Played on a checkerboard, the object was not to capture an opponent's pieces but to hop over them in an effort to be the first player to get to the opposite side of the game board.

1. FAMILY PROBLEMS

The Camerons were moving. That was their chronic condition; at least so the neighbors thought; and really it did seem as though they were always either just trying to get settled in one home, or planning to break up and get ready for another.

"We move and *move*," would Lucia say, "and never get anywhere. I wish father would make one grand move, out West, or down South, or anywhere besides just here. I should like to go a thousand miles away, and begin all over again."

"That would take money," the elder sister, Mary, would reply. "Ever so much money. When do you suppose father would get enough together to take a journey, to say nothing of taking all our belongings along?"

"It costs money to move from one end of the town to the other," would Lucia retort; "a ruinous amount; those furniture vans charge just frightfully. I don't wonder that father was pale this morning, and couldn't eat any breakfast after settling with them. If we had all the money that we have spent in breaking up, and moving, and getting settled again, my! I'd furnish this house anew from attic to cellar, and take a journey into the bargain. We might go in emigrant wagons, and camp out at night. I've read about people doing it, and having great fun. Oh, dear, I wonder how it feels to go to places, and have what one wants, and never think or care how much the whole costs."

The conversation, if conversation it can be called, was sure to end with some such sentence, and a sigh; albeit the sigh was a light one, for Lucia was young, and the cares of life sat lightly on her as yet.

Perhaps she, in common with the entire younger portion of the family, felt them more heavily this morning than ever before. Someway, this move had been the hardest; the last one always, was, the Camerons declared; and in their case it was truer than it may be in many, for each time they moved into a smaller and more inconvenient house than the last one was; and each time the strain of getting settled, and of learning over again the lesson of doing without, was increased by the fact that, as Lucia expressed it, there were more things to do without, each change they made. The air of the new house was surcharged with groans and regrets and queries. How were they ever, to get along with one less sleeping room? Where was Mac to be put when he came home? Mac and Rod just despised rooming together. Moreover, the room was so small that those great tall fellows couldn't be expected to endure it. And a house without a china-closet in the dining-room! Who ever heard of such a thing? Nor did it lessen the gloom of the occasion to be told grimly by Mary that most of the china was smashed and did not need a closet. Truth to tell, some pieces of the smashed china were so choice and so beloved that the mistress of this new home sat down in the disorder and cried over her loss.

"Mother gave me that set when I was married," she said, her lip quivering, "and to think not a whole piece is left to me now!"

Mary Cameron tried to be sympathetic, but it was hard work. There were so much more important things than old china. There, for instance, was the new silk dress which she had been promised this fall. Didn't she make her old white dress do all summer, saving for that pale green silk which she meant to have? She did not share Lucia's anxieties in the least about the boys; she even declared with curling lip that she saw no reason why Mac and Rod should not share the family straits, as well as to have all the trouble fall on the girls.

It may be necessary at this point to explain that the Camerons were not poor people in the sense which they may seem. Mr. Cameron's salary was two thousand a year, and was paid in regular quarterly installments, as sure to come as the sun was to rise. There are people to whom such a state of things would mean wealth. The Camerons were not among them. Given, a family of grown sons and daughters, six in number, all of them with expensive tastes and desires, three of them still in expensive schools, none of them having ever learned even the initial letters of the art of true economy, and it will readily be seen that to make ends meet, even on two thousand a year, may become a difficult task.

Not that the Camerons did not consider themselves economical. It was a word they hated, yet it was continually on their lips; and there were undoubtedly ways in which they economized. The difficulty was that they began at wrong ends. The very house in which they had just slept through the first night, and awakened in the crisp October morning to wrestle with boxes and bales and bundles, was an illustration. Two rooms smaller than the last house, and into that they could barely crowd; a house whose plumbing was doubtful, whose gas-fixtures leaked, whose water-pipes were always out of order, whose kitchen was dingy to the last degree, whose dining-room was narrow and dark, and whose hall was a miserable little square, from which Lucia said one must retreat to out-doors if one wanted to change one's mind and turn around. And it was seventy dollars a year more rent than was the large, roomy, sunny house on Seventh Street, a house which actually had a cherry tree all its own, and a robin that built its nest there every spring; and a bit of a side yard to put the tree in, and a dry cellar, and no steps down from the dining-room to the kitchen. Yes, the house was for rent, they could have had it as well as not; in fact, the owner urged Mr. Cameron to take it, and promised to re-paper the two front rooms up-stairs if he would. Why did they not? Why, because it was on

Seventh Street and not on Durand Avenue. To be sure the house they had taken was at the extreme lower end of the avenue, where none of the people lived whom they knew, even by sight; but nevertheless it was Durand Avenue, and the Camerons, even without discussing it, had known to a woman that of course they could not go down on Seventh Street to live.

"Nobody lives there," they said.

Now, Seventh Street was one long row of dwelling-houses on either side; neat, trim-looking houses, always tenanted, so, of course, somebody lived there. You must judge what the Camerons meant. Because the cherry tree house was larger, and was on a corner, and had the dry cellar, and some other special advantages, it rented for more than the other houses on the street, and was consequently occasionally vacant for a few weeks at a time, looking for the person who could afford to pay that amount of rent, and yet who would be willing to live on Seventh Street. You think, perhaps, there was a nuisance of some sort hidden away around the corner? Or at least that the place was inconvenient of access? Nothing of the sort. The lower end of Durand Avenue was but a block away from a suspicious vacant lot where nuisances did sometimes congregate, but the corner house on Seventh Street stood high and dry, and had only rows of neat and comparatively new dwelling-houses all about it; and the Centre-street line of cars which connected with almost every downtown line in the city, wound around that very corner. Oh, do not ask for any explanation as to why some

5

people could not live on Seventh Street; the Camerons knew, without reasoning, that it could not be done.

There were other things they knew. This unfortunate year it became absolutely necessary to have a new carpet. There was no dissenting voice, save from the boys; they declared that they did not see but the old carpet was good enough. But the boys were away in college; only home for vacations, and were having, the girls said, every earthly thing they wanted, and didn't care how shabby the folks at home were so that *they* had plenty. The boys' opinion was counted out. Mr. Cameron, accustomed to leaving all such matters to his wife and daughters, said only, if they must they *must,* he supposed, but he did not see where the money was to come from. However, Jamison & Burns would wait for their pay. So the new carpet was bought. Axminster it had to be. To be sure, it cost more than a body Brussels; and Mrs. Cameron, who remembered the days when body Brussels carpet was quite the thing to buy, voted in its favor, but she was tremendously overruled. "Nobody uses body Brussels in their parlors any more. It is simply for sitting-rooms and bedrooms." Mrs. Cameron argued vigorously, but submitted at last.

"It is good economy to get the best while you are about it, I suppose," Mr. Cameron said with a troubled face, on being appealed to. Somewhere in the dim recesses of his memory he had stored away certain aphorisms of that kind which he brought out on occasion. Nobody explained to him that good body Brussels had far more enduring qualities than cheap Axminster, so called.

It is not even certain that any of this family knew the fact.

It was in the midst of the miseries of getting settled that there came a letter which all the family, Mr. Cameron excepted, sat down in the half-regulated sitting-room to discuss. More or less excitement was evidently felt concerning it. Mary was the first to express herself, her cheeks unnaturally flushed the while. Mrs. Cameron was re-reading the letter.

"I must say I think Mac and Rod are two of the most selfish creatures I ever heard of in my life. Dress suits indeed! Why, they are nothing but boys!"

Mrs. Cameron glanced up from the letter. "Don't be absurd, Mary. I believe you think boys never grow up. Mac is twenty-two, the time when most boys consider themselves men."

"It is the time when most boys are thinking about supporting themselves, and not depending on their fathers for dress suits and everything else. I say it is selfish. Sending for more things just now, when we are moving, and doing without everything we can to help along. Look at those curtains—darned in half a dozen places. I have been ashamed of them for the last six months. Suppose I say we must have new ones? I'm sure they would be as important as dress suits for the boys, and a great deal more sensible."

"Still, Mary," interposed Lucia's quieter voice, "they say they cannot attend the president's reception without them."

"Then I should think it would be a good plan for them to stay at home. The idea that college boys cannot appear at a reception unless they are dressed in the extreme of fashion! I cannot go to Mrs. Peterson's dinner-party next week unless I have my new silk dress that was promised me. Suppose I say so? At least three tongues would begin to tell me how entirely suitable my old blue dress is that I have worn wherever I've been for the last year. But because it is the boys who want things, we girls must give up, of course."

Lucia laughed over this. "There is some truth in what you are saying. We have been giving up things for those boys ever since they entered college. If they appreciated it, I should feel differently; but they take it so entirely as a matter of course, that I must say it is discouraging."

"Well," said Mrs. Cameron, "do you want us then to write to the boys that they cannot have dress suits, and must stay at home from the reception?"

This was putting the matter blankly. Evidently, the sisters were astonished; they were not accustomed to such direct questions from their mother. Neither of them desired to have such word sent to the boys. If it were true, as the boys said, that all the students in their set wore dress suits, why, certainly their brothers must have them. It was really a foregone conclusion, as they expected their mother to understand. It was hard that they could not have the privilege of grumbling, since they were to make the sacrifice. It was a curious development of this entire family that they did their giving up with grumbling. It was true, as the girls had said, that much had been sacrificed for their brothers. Mr. Cameron, who in certain respects was something of a cipher in his own home, constantly allowing himself to be overruled, and led whither his better judgment did not approve, could yet be firm on occasion. He had, as Mrs. Cameron expressed it, "set his foot down," that both his boys should have college educations. He was not one of those who deemed the collegiate education as important for the girls as the boys, although he had done his best for his daughters. The two elder ones had been sent to excellent and expensive schools; and Emilie, the youngest, was still a school-girl. The father had had pride in his daughters' acquirements, but he had had determination in regard to his sons. They were smart boys; they made fair records for themselves in preparatory schools, even excelling in certain studies; and to college they should go.

It had been, and was still, a hard struggle. College life proved to be a much more expensive thing than it had been when Mr. Cameron was a young man; and his sons were not of the sort to carefully curtail their expenses, although they thought they were models of prudence. The dress suits which had suddenly appeared before them as necessities will serve as illustrations of their mode of thought. Necessities were what other people in their set had. To have remained quietly away from dress occasions because to have what they judged to be suitable attire would burden the people at home was thought of, but cast aside as impracticable. It would be a discourteous way of treating the invitations of the faculty. To join the few quiet, scholarly students who frequented such places conspicuous in the suits which they wore for best, was not even thought of at all by the Camerons. Their home education had developed no such heights of self-abnegation as that. It would be worse than living on Seventh Street.

Neither, strange to say, would Mary Cameron, who grumbled the loudest, have had them do any such thing. No one understood necessities of this kind better than she.

"Why, of course not!" she said in answer to her mother's question. "They will have to have the suits, I suppose. All the same, I think it is mean in them to send, doing it in such a lordly way. Why can't they at least show that they appreciate the sacrifices we shall have to make to gratify them?"

"I don't see anything very lordly about the letter. Mac writes that they cannot go to the receptions without dressing as others do, and of course, they can't. You are always hard on your brothers, Mary."

"I? Hard on them! Who gave up a silk dress for their sakes, I should like to know? Talk about their having to dress like others when they appear in society! How do you think I will look in that horrid silk which I have worn until people can describe me as the girl in the old blue dress?"

"Oh, Mary!" said Lucia. "Do give us a rest about that silk dress. I am sure if you never mention it again, we shall none of us ever forget that you were going to have one and didn't! We have heard so much about it."

Lucia spoke laughingly—she generally did—nevertheless there was a sting in her words. Perhaps that phrase will describe the Cameron habit. They stung one another. From the mother down to even Emilie, who being only fifteen could still be told on occasion to say no more.

They loved one another, this family—not one of them thought of doubting it. In times of illness it would not be possible to conceive of tenderness and self-abnegation greater than theirs. Long nights of weary watching were as nothing; long days of patient, persistent, gentle care-taking were matters of course; yet directly the invalid took on once more the appearance and habits of health, the stinging process commenced. It was as if the stock of patience which had seemed inexhaustible during illness had suddenly frozen, and left only irritable nerves over which to tread.

Not that the Camerons were always in ill-humor; far from it. They had their merry hours and their good times together. It was only that the too excitable nerves lay always near the surface, and would not bear so much as a pin prick. Those dress suits were really more than a pin prick. Sixty additional dollars when the family purse was strained already to its utmost, was no small matter.

"I declare," said Mr. Cameron at the dinner table that evening, leaning his weary head on his hand, and giving over the attempt to eat the not too inviting dinner which had to be served in the kitchen as the only spot available, "I don't know how to raise the money. The boys did not say anything about it when they went away, and I tried to plan for everything that would be wanted before Christmas. One would suppose if it were such an important item they would have remembered, and spoken of it. When I was a young fellow, if I had a decent suit for Sunday, and a half-way decent one for every day, I considered myself well off. The boys had entirely new suits throughout only six weeks ago."

"It isn't that their clothes are worn out, Edward," said Mrs. Cameron, her tone showing that her nerves felt the pin-pricks. "They must wear what others do if they mingle with them, of course. Don't you understand? Rodney says all the fellows, except two or three who are being helped through college, wear evening dress at the receptions. You wouldn't want your sons to appear different from the other respectable young men, I suppose, would you?"

"I don't know," said Mr. Cameron, and he tried to let a faint smile appear on his face to lessen the seeming harshness of the words. "I would like them to appear as honest men if they could; and I don't know how they are to have new suits this fall unless I borrow the money, with no prospect of paying for it so far as I can see. I don't know but they would better join the two or three who are being helped through college. That is what it will amount to in the end."

"Oh, nonsense!" said Mrs. Cameron; and her voice was unmistakably sharp. "What is the use in talking such stuff as that? We are not paupers. A man who gets a two-thousand-dollar salary ought to be able to furnish his children with clothes, without having a fuss about it every time they need a pocket-handkerchief."

"I know it," Mr. Cameron said; and he wore the perplexed look his face was sure to assume when any phase of this subject was before them. "I don't understand how it is. When I sit down with pencil and paper and calculate the year's expenditures, so much for living, and so much for extras, it all seems to come out reasonably well; but when we get to the end of the quarter, we are behind every time; and something will come of it one of these days. I can't see how it is going to end."

"I'll tell you what, father," said Emilie briskly. "I'll leave school, if you will let me. Then there will be no bills to pay for all sorts of extras; music, you know, and books, and everything. That will make quite a difference in a year's time."

It was a fortunate diversion; the entire Cameron family laughed. Emilie was, sometimes merrily and sometimes a bit sharply called the family dunce. She hated study, and cared almost nothing for music, and would have been only too glad to be relieved from the burden of both. The intensely personal reasons for her magnanimous offer were so entirely apparent that it needed no other answer than a laugh.

It cleared the atmosphere somewhat, albeit Mr. Cameron sighed almost immediately. But he said as he arose from his barely tasted dinner, "Oh, well, we shall pull through somehow, we always have. I'll ask Hosmer to let me have a little advance. The boys have got to be like others, I suppose. Get the letter written, some of you, and I will have the money ready for the first mail tomorrow."

2. Trying to "Belong"

It was while they were piecing the dining-room carpet that the next subject for discussion and annoyance came before the Camerons. Those two words, "discussion" and "annoyance," might almost be called the keynotes of their lives, so frequent had they become; the one seeming to be a sequence of the other. It is very probable that sewing on the old carpet helped to irritate the nerves; it is not particularly soothing work, and Lucia hated sewing.

"I wish we had sold this old thing to the rag man," she said gloomily. "The last time we patched it, I remember we said it would not hold together for another move."

"Then you would have had bare floor for the dining-room, I can tell you," said Mrs. Cameron. "I am not going to ask your father for another thing this fall that can be done without. He hasn't slept for two nights, worrying about the extra money needed for the boys."

"What is the use in father's worrying? That will not pay any bills. I should think it would be a good deal more sensible for him to get his sleep, and save his strength."

"Don't criticize your father," said Mrs. Cameron sharply; "I will not bear it."

The poor wife criticized him herself sometimes with great sharpness, and in the presence of his children, but she would not permit them to follow her example. Like many other nervous, overstrained women, her thought of the husband of her youth was always tenderness, but her words to him were often tinged with whatever feeling rasped the hour.

"Why, dear me!" began Lucia. "What did I say? I am sure that I pity father as much as anybody can, and I think—" Here Mary's entrance from the kitchen interrupted the sentence.

"Mother," she began, "Betsey says she cannot make another pudding until she has a new pudding-dish; the old one leaks."

"Then we will go without pudding," said Mrs. Cameron with emphasis. "I am not going to get a new pudding-dish nor a new *anything* for Betsey. She is careless with the dishes or they would last longer. She is always wanting something—asked for a new bread-bowl only this morning."

"Well, mother, the bread-bowl got broken in the moving. It wasn't Betsey's fault. I do not think she should be made to suffer. You packed the bowl yourself, you remember."

"For pity's sake don't talk about the bread-bowl! It is quite likely I remember that I packed it without being told. If you had not hurried me almost to distraction over that last load, I could have packed it more securely."

"I'm sure *I* don't want to talk about bread-bowls," said Mary, bringing needle and thread and preparing to do her share of the long seam which was to be sewed in the mended carpet. "I have something of more importance to say. I saw Jessie Lee just now when I was sweeping the leaves from the porch, and she says the Denhams are going home next Tuesday. What shall we do about that?"

"Congratulations to Mrs. Lee would be in order, I should say," replied Lucia. "I hope we shall never have any friends who will think it their duty to make us as long a visit as the Denhams have been making."

"Long as they have been here," said Mary, "we have not invited them even to lunch with us, and we have been everywhere with them. Three times out to formal dinners, four or five times to lunches, and to evening gatherings innumerable. Mother, we shall certainly be obliged to have them here, shall we not?"

"Oh, dear me!" said Mrs. Cameron; and she dropped the patch she was deftly fitting into the carpet, and looked her utter dismay. "Mary Cameron, what can you be thinking about, with all that we have on hand now!"

"I am thinking about the fact that the Denhams are going on Tuesday, as I said, and that there are just four days left in which to show them any courtesy; unless, indeed, we have lost all sense of propriety, and are going to let them leave without having received any attention from us. You have been out to dinner once with them yourself, mother."

"I know it," said Mrs. Cameron, her face a study. "I wish we hadn't accepted one of their invitations, for I really do not see how we can entertain them now."

"I don't know why not. We can't give a party for them, I suppose, as we really ought to do. We are under obligations to so many people that I am ashamed to meet some of them; but we are equal to a plain lunch I should hope. Russell Denham is going back to college as soon as he has taken his mother and sister home; and Mac and Rod will be with him a good deal this winter, I suppose. They wouldn't like it if they knew we had not shown their friends any attention."

"Oh, well! I suppose we shall have to do something; but I declare it worries me dreadfully, so unsettled as we are, and this little bit of a house to have company in. I wish we didn't have anything to do with society."

"We have extremely little," Mary replied coldly. "I sometimes think with Emilie, that it would be better if we just said squarely that we are nobodies, and do not expect to be invited, or to belong."

The mother winced. She wanted her children to "belong;" her ambition for them in society, and everywhere else, was limitless.

"Of course, we must do something," she said briskly. "What shall it be? We can get up a lunch, as you say, more economically than a dinner or a regular evening gathering. It would be less burdensome to your father, too, for they will know that he cannot get away from business for luncheon, and he is so tired nowadays that he shrinks from seeing company. But you must be content with having everything very simple. We cannot undertake any expense, remember."

Their ideas of simplicity would have bewildered some people. A lunch without salads was not to be thought of, of course; and chicken salads were the best. No matter if chicken was very expensive just now, it did not take a great deal for a salad. Then oysters were just getting nice, and, after the long summer, seemed so new; raw oysters were the very thing with which to begin a lunch. Served on the half-shell and properly garnished, there was no simple dish which looked more inviting. As for the creams, they must have them from Alburgh's, of course. Oh, positively, there were none fit to eat after having had his. No matter if he did charge seventy-five cents a quart; it would be much better not to have cream at all than to have an inferior quality. They could afford to pay a little extra for creams and ices, because they would make their own cake. Very few of the girls did that when they had company. They just ordered from some first-class caterer. Lucia sighed, and wished that they could afford to do so; it would be only pleasure to have company if they could give orders as other people did, and have trained servants to attend to everything at home. At the mention of servants, Mrs. Cameron could not suppress a groan of anxiety. How could they hope to serve guests properly with only Betsey to depend upon? She was a new recruit, and a cheap one, therefore, not much could be expected of her.

"I shall just have to stay in the kitchen and attend to things myself," she said. "That will be the only way to avoid distressing failures; and as it is, I tremble for the serving. I wish I could be in two places at once."

"Oh, mother!" said Lucia, dismayed. "You cannot be in the kitchen. What a ridiculous way to have company, with the lady of the house invisible! Mary, you surely do not think anything of that kind can be done?"

"It is like everything else," said Mary drearily. "Of course we cannot have company like other people; we never can. We have been invited and *invited,* just as I said, until I am ashamed to meet my acquaintances, and yet the very thought of paying some of our obligations sets us all into a tremor. If we could hire a professional waiter for one day to help Betsey out, we could hope to have things decent."

Mrs. Cameron caught at the idea. Perhaps they could do that. It would not be such a very heavy expense for one day—a part of a day, indeed. They would save the price of it in the end, because professional helpers knew how to manage without spoiling anything.

It was curious what a relief this professional assistant was, and how many things grew out of her proposed services. It was Mrs. Cameron herself who said that since they were to have help, she did not know but they would better make it an occasion for asking a few others. The expense would not be materially increased, and, as Mary said, they were indebted to so many people. There were the Westbrooks, for instance, and the Overmans, and Mrs. Lorimer. Why not make a clean sweep of it and ask them all?

"But, mother, think what it will cost to get ready for so many," objected Lucia. "What will father say?"

"It would not cost so very much more," Mrs. Cameron argued, strong for the time being in the thought of that professional helper. "We shall not have to pay any more for help than we would if we had just three or four; and I really do not see how we can have anybody without inviting those I have mentioned. We have been entertained by them so many times."

It was too true; and there were found to be others quite as alarming as the ones mentioned, until Mary, who finally went for pencil and paper, and began to consider them numerically and systematically, declared that it was not possible to get along without inviting seventeen.

"Then we might as well make it nineteen," said Lucia composedly, "and ask that Miss Landis and her brother. We shall never have a better opportunity to return their kindness."

"The idea!" said Mary. "Why in the world should we ask them? They will not know a person who will be here, and we know them very little ourselves."

"I can't help it. We can make them acquainted with the others. They have certainly been very kind to us. We never had *neighbors* before, in our lives. They must be from the country, they have such friendly, uncitified ways. I like them very well indeed, and I think it would be bad manners, to say the least, to have company and not invite them when they are almost in the same house, one may say, and when we have all been in there to have tea with them."

Lucia may or may not have understood what a troublesome subject she had introduced. To Mary it seemed to be a positively irritating one. She expressed herself so decidedly, and with such annoying sharpness, that Lucia, who at first made it as only a passing suggestion, grew obstinate, declaring that she had had nothing to say about the other guests, and it was strange if she could not select two. Then Mary replied that of course, if Lucia had adopted Professor Landis as her particular friend, nothing more was to be said. She had not imagined so great a degree of intimacy on such short acquaintance. Then Lucia, her face aglow with indignation, appealed to her mother as to whether it was necessary for Mary, because she was less than two years the elder, to insult her in that manner.

Mrs. Cameron hastened to the rescue, assuring both girls that she was ashamed of them. Why couldn't they talk things over together without always having some sort of a fuss? As for the Landis young people, she thought it would be very proper to invite them. They were not exactly in their set, perhaps—she thought with Lucia that they were probably from the country—but they were nice, pleasant persons, and had been very kind and thoughtful to them. Two more would make very little difference, and their father would be pleased to have them show kindness to his neighbors. He had spoken of them several times. It ended by an invitation being sent to the Landis brother and sister, and to several others whom it became imperative to remember. It is quite safe to say that not a Cameron among them had any idea whereunto this thing would grow or they would certainly not have begun. Mr. Cameron was bewildered.

"I thought you said—" he began to his half-distracted wife when she essayed to explain, "that we would make a special effort to economize, to help meet the extras for the boys and for the moving?"

"Well, I wonder if I am not doing it?" she replied irritably. "You know very little about it, Edward, or you would understand that I am straining every nerve. I ironed all the afternoon in order to save extra help. Betsey would never have gotten the ironing done if I hadn't. She is a stroke of economy herself. I never had such poor help. Oh, nobody knows how I twist and contrive in order to help! It is hard to have to be blamed when I am doing my best."

"I am not blaming you, Rachel," Mr. Cameron said, and he tried to speak quietly, "I am only asking questions. I don't understand. We all felt, I supposed, the need for special care this fall, and here we have a party on our hands! There has not been a season in ten years when we could not have afforded it better."

"A party!" repeated Mrs. Cameron in intense annoyance. "Now, Edward, I call that being very disagreeable. I have explained to you that it is only the plainest possible luncheon served to a few of our most intimate friends; and I told you the special necessity of it at this time, too. I don't believe even you, careless as you are, would be willing to have the Denhams leave without showing them so much attention, when they have been here for two months, and have been more intimate with our young people than with any others. Russell Denham has certainly paid Mary a great deal of attention. I think she is interested in him. It is for her sake that I want to be courteous. I thought you would appreciate that." A little note of injured innocence was added to the tone.

Mr. Cameron still tried to understand.

"Why not invite the Denhams and the Lees in to have a comfortable, quiet dinner with us, and make no fuss about it? If the young people enjoy one another's society, I should think that would be a pleasanter way to secure it, and the expense would be less, certainly, to say nothing of the work. You are hardly able to take any more care upon yourself."

"Oh, Edward, you don't understand such things! One would suppose you were from the country yourself to hear you go on sometimes. Fancy Mary singling out the Denhams from all her acquaintances, and inviting them to a family gathering! I should not like to have her even know that such an idea had been mentioned. It would be the same as asking the young man if he did not want to belong to the family. There is nothing special between them, Edward, and, of course, we do not want to act as though we expected there would be."

"Well, well!" said Mr. Cameron. "There is no use in talking about it, I suppose. I was brought up in the country, and I wish sometimes that I still lived there. I like country ways best. We had a friend in to take supper with us whenever we wanted to, and thought nothing of it. What I want to know is how much this thing is going to cost. I want it in black and white." He drew out notebook and pencil, and looked determined. "Come, now, I'm not going to run into a thing in the dark; at least, I'll act as though I meant to be honest, just as long as I can. How many people are there to be?"

Mrs. Cameron hesitated and faltered. "Why, the girls thought they ought to ask the Porters if they did the Lees; and I myself suggested the Overmans, we have been there so much. And Lucia thought our next-door neighbors, the girl and her brother, ought to be asked— you know they had us in there for tea that first evening we were in the house, and were very kind. You spoke of offering them some attention."

"How many does it all make?" asked Mr. Cameron with the air of a martyr.

"Why, I think it counts up twenty-three. I'm sure I did not imagine when we began, that there would be half so many. But the girls feel really embarrassed about accepting invitations and not making any returns."

"Twenty-three outsiders and four of our own make twenty-seven; and cream to be ordered from Alburgh's I suppose? Yes, I was sure of it. Seventy-five cents a quart; say two gallons, that is the least you can get along with; eight times seventy-five, that makes six dollars just for cream! What next?"

That inexorable pencil scribbled and figured; and Mrs. Cameron, growing each moment more perturbed, made reluctant admissions to searching questions, and at last in a shamefaced way admitted that they could hardly hope to get through with the plainest possible luncheon for less than an outlay of thirty dollars, including the extra help which it was necessary to have.

"I would get along without that if it were possible," she explained humbly. "I am willing to work my fingers to the bone in order to give the girls half a chance in the world; but I know perfectly well that Betsey will blunder in some way if I leave her to herself for a moment; and I *can't* be in two places at once."

"Exactly the price of one of the dress suits," said Mr. Cameron, re-adding his hateful figures. "Now put down ten dollars for the things we have forgotten, and for the smashes in crockery and the like that will result, and for the new things here and there to be added, and we shall do well if we escape with forty dollars. Doesn't that seem rather hard on our creditors, Rachel? We are a hundred dollars behind this quarter already, you know."

But at this point Mrs. Cameron's nerves would bear no more. She sank in a limp heap on the chair before

26

which she had been standing, gathered her housekeeper's apron to her eyes, and cried outright. Mr. Cameron looked appalled and helpless. His wife rarely cried; almost never in his presence. He essayed to comfort, bunglingly yet sincerely. He didn't know much about such things. Of course she was doing the best she could; he was sure of that. The girls must be like others, he supposed. She must not think he meant to blame her. He was harassed about money a good deal of the time, and it made him less careful of his words, perhaps, than he ought to be. She was not to worry; and, of course, she could not give up the scheme now. He did not mean that—in fact, he did not mean anything. She must not think any more about it, but just go on as she had planned.

He went away looking troubled. Something he must have said to cause his wife's tears. A man was a brute who made a woman cry; and infinitely more a brute when that woman was his wife, the mother of his children. But what had he said to bring the tears to Rachel's eyes? He had seen them a trifle red on rare occasions, as though something might have troubled her; but he did not remember ever before having seen her break down in a burst of weeping. He ought to be careful. Perhaps this eternal fret and worry about money matters was making him hard. He did not want to be a man who seemed to think only of money. When he was young he had never expected to develop into such a man. There were many things he had thought in his youth which had not matured with his years. And he sighed heavily, and asked himself, as he had done a hundred times in the last few years, whether there were not some quick way of making money. There were Jones and Osborne who were making it by speculating. Only the other day Osborne told him about gaining a thousand dollars in a few hours of time. And Osborne had no family to support. What would *not* a thousand dollars be to him, with sons and daughters to think about! If he only had a little money to start with, there was no reason why he should not be as successful as Osborne or Jones.

All the way to the office he thought about it, and tried to contrive ways of securing a few hundreds with which to try his . . . skill. He hesitated for a word and finally chose *skill*. He did not like the sound of *luck*.

It was not the first time that the harassed father had thought in these lines. That man Osborne was always offering to invest for him in a way that would bring at least twelve percent—Oh, twelve percent was nothing!— in a way that would be sure to double his money in a few years' time.

3. Burns and Heart-burns

Through trials manifold the Cameron family pressed their way to the day of the luncheon party. What they endured from incompetency and accidents and unforeseen complications cannot be put on paper. Unless you are the mistress of a home limited as to room and dishes and means, and are trying to entertain twenty or thirty people in the space designed for ten, you will not be able to understand or appreciate the situation. A hundred times before the climax was reached, did Mrs. Cameron wish she had let the Denhams go on their way unentertained. She even had occasionally a wild wish that something very unusual would occur; if, for instance, one of them could fall ill, just on that fatal day, and be *very* ill for a few hours, so that the imperative necessity for recalling the invitations would be manifest, and then recover rapidly without any unpleasant consequences, what a relief it would be. She would be quite willing to be herself the victim, if Providence would so order. Nay, as she struggled on with her mighty problem of salads and sauces and expenses, she grew so weary that it seemed to her a sharp illness which would compel her to lie still for hours, yes, even for days, was the only comfortable thing which could happen to her. Nobody sickened, however, and the fatal day arrived.

Betsey, poor blundering mass of good-natured stupidity, had been doing her best; but to the over-strained nerves of the Camerons, it seemed as though she actually tried sometimes to be stupid and slow and exasperating. They ceased trying to speak to her in other than a sharp, irritated way, which of itself, if they had but understood her, deprived poor Betsey of what wits she had. It was annoying, certainly, to have her slam the oven door quite shut when she was told to leave it ajar, and thereby ruin one entire mass of cake on which Mary had spent her strength and endurance. It is perhaps not to be wondered at that she spoke so emphatically to Betsey as to make that young woman appear before her mistress with red face and angry eyes, to declare that she would not be imposed upon another minute, she would "just quit, so there!" Then a soothing potion had to be administered, for to lose even Betsey at such a crisis as this was not to be thought of.

That "professional helper," who was such a tower of strength in perspective, needs a word of comment. He came at the appointed hour; but his importance was something phenomenal. Mrs. Cameron, who was utterly unused to masculine help in the kitchen, and who, whenever she had thought of this addition to her forces, had produced before her mental vision a smiling-faced, deft-handed young woman who would know just what to do without being told, and who yet would do her bidding on occasion swiftly and well, felt utterly cowed before the majestic personage in immaculate necktie, who gazed about him on the diminutive quarters where he was expected to reign, with something very like a sneer on his face, and asked where the trays were, and if they had none larger than that, and how many sets of spoons were there, and where were the relays of napkins to be found, and where were the coffee spoons, and the oyster forks? Where *were,* indeed, all those fine, queer-shaped, costly little extras which he was accustomed to see? The Camerons did not possess them.

Mary, as she listened to the professional's abundant questions, realized perhaps as never before what poverty meant; and felt for a moment the utter folly of trying to do what they could not. Never mind, it must be lived through now. The guests were almost at the door; it would never do to flinch. She helped her mother answer the embarrassing questions as best she could; she put on an air of superiority, and tried to give the majestic person an order or two; but faltered, and crimsoned to her very forehead, when he only stared, and told her he "couldn't do that sort of thing, of course;" he had never been in the habit of doing it; she must call upon some under-servant.

After that, Mary went to receive her guests, leaving her mother to cope with the important stranger. There proved to be a number of things for which he had been depended upon that were entirely out of his province; and at the last moment Betsey had to be further bewildered by receiving minute instructions concerning matters of which she was as ignorant as a child.

"I shall have to stay out here and direct things," declared Mrs. Cameron in excited tones to her two elder daughters, as they lingered for a moment in the kitchen for a last word together before the ordeal commenced. "There is no use in trying to plan differently; that horrid fellow—" As she spoke she looked about her nervously to make sure that he was far enough away at the moment not to hear her opinion of him, and sank her voice to a whisper, "—that horrid fellow will do only the things which have been expected of him before; and they are very few indeed apparently; and he asks for some new-fangled dish or spoon or fork every minute. I wish he were where he came from! I could get along better without him. But I shall have to stay and watch Betsey; she doesn't know the ice-pitcher from the cream-jug today; she blunders all the time."

"Oh, mother, don't do that! Let her blunder. Let them both manage. The fellow will behave better perhaps when we are all away. Tell him to direct Betsey. Whatever you do, don't stay in the kitchen and leave us to look after the guests. That is something I have never seen done; and when father isn't here either, it will look horrid. I think father might have come home for a little while."

"Well, he couldn't," said Mrs. Cameron sharply; "and once for all, Lucia, stop criticizing your father. You do altogether too much of that sort of thing, and I tell you I will not have it."

The voices of coming guests broke up this family conclave suddenly. Lucia went to receive them with a heightened color on her cheeks. Her mother's reprimand hurt. She was fond of her father, and knew she had meant only to express a desire for his presence among their guests. Mrs. Cameron returned to her arduous duties, resolved to put everything in as good train as she could, and then leave the helpers to themselves, since the girls felt so badly about her not being in the parlor. She would do almost anything rather than add to their annoyance.

The guests were very gay. They had no anxieties concerning the feast, and were prepared to enjoy themselves. Most of them were old acquaintances, accustomed to meeting one another at all sorts of gatherings. Had the Camerons been at their ease they might have enjoyed the hour which intervened before lunch was announced. As it was, visions of Betsey's blundering, or of Selmser's obstinacy, kept constantly floating before their mental vision. It was a relief when the summons to the dining-room came; at least the suspense would soon be over now.

But it was not; it seemed to draw itself out endlessly. Whether his majesty, called Selmser, essayed to teach them the folly of trying to serve so pretentious a luncheon with their resources, or whether he was so carefully trained to run in a particular groove that he really could not step out of it, will not be known. Certain it is that the courses were so long in being served as to lead one almost to forget what had last appeared. Several of the guests had no forks for their salads until after the others were ready for the next course. This, Selmser explained afterwards to the annoyed hostess, was unavoidable because there were not forks enough for the different sets; some had to be washed and waited for, a thing unknown before in all his experience of serving. It seemed also to take an unaccountable time to replenish the cream-pitchers and cake plates; and when the coffee and chocolate began to come in so slowly that part of the company sat with empty cups before the other part had been reached, it was with difficulty that Mary Cameron restrained herself from rushing out to the kitchen to express her mind to both Betsey and his majesty. It is perhaps a pity that she did not. For some unknown reason Selmser had at that moment rebelled; the ices needed his attention, he declared, and Betsey must serve the rest of the chocolate. In vain she protested that she could never carry that great awkward tray; it would slip out of her hands, she knew it would. He assured her that she would have to carry it if it went; and added that she would better step lively, for some of them would be getting too old to drink it by this time, he should think! What could they expect, with a houseful and only one person to do it all? So Betsey, who had all day been honestly doing the best she could, seized the chocolate-pot in both her red, nervous hands, and made a dash for the dining-room. She might have done well, but for a miserable mend in the dining-room carpet, covered for this occasion by a rug from one of the chambers. Over this rug Betsey stumbled; her feet had not grown accustomed to expecting it at that place. A moment more and there was a confused mass of Betsey, chocolate-pot, rug, and a scalding hot fluid. The pain which this latter occasioned rose above every other consideration, at least for Betsey, and she howled.

There were people present who had been acquaintances of the Camerons for years, but someway it was Dorothy Landis who sprang to Betsey's assistance. It was her brother who said kindly to Lucia, that although he was only a teacher, he had once been a medical student, and knew exactly what and how to do for a scald; they might safely leave Betsey's hand to him. Meantime, Dorothy Landis had with haste and skill assisted in removing the *debris*, and had accomplished one thing more for which Mrs. Cameron's heart went out in gratitude.

"Let me open this side window and call our Annie; she is really very good at serving table. I thought of offering to lend her. I wish now we had yielded to our neighborly feeling." While she spoke she raised the sash and called. In a very few minutes Annie came, white-aproned, low-voiced, swift and silent of movement, the very perfection of a maid. From that moment the table service went on smoothly; even his majesty seeming to discover that in the keen-eyed, swift-moving Annie he had met his peer.

"If only that Landis girl had offered her before!" It was Mary Cameron who thought this, feeling almost indignant the while over such a breach of neighborliness as the delay suggested. Nor did she at the moment realize that had the offer been made before, it would probably have been declined with stiff dignity, and have been commented upon as a specimen of country ignorance.

It was all over at last. The chocolate stain had been washed out as well as it could be, Emilie lamenting the while that it covered the only bright breadth of carpeting in the room. The "picked-up" dinner had been served by the united efforts of the weary mother and her equally weary girls, Betsey being still in the depths of misery with her scalded wrist and hand. Emilie had vexed them all, and brought a sharp reprimand on herself, by announcing suddenly at the dreary dinner, that the chickens for the salad cost two dollars and forty cents; the grocer called to her and gave her the bill as she passed; and that "hired fellow" threw a whole nice bowl full of it away; and did they know he broke the largest meat-dish?

"Do for pity's sake let us eat a few mouthfuls," Mary had said angrily, "without having bills and broken dishes thrown at us."

Then Emilie had told her that she was cross, and that she was most of the time. She saved all her pleasant words for other people, and never had any for her own folks. Of course, the mother had to interfere then; and because she was overtired she did it sharply, bidding the fifteen-year-old girl hold her peace. If she had no better words than those to speak, they did not want to hear her speak at all. It cannot be a matter of surprise under the circumstances that the girl revenged herself by murmuring that one who had such examples to follow as were given her ought not to be expected to speak pleasant words. Then the entire family had a diversion. Mr. Cameron, who had been unusually silent even for him, suddenly made a remark:

"I had a letter from Aunt Eunice this morning."

This in itself was a somewhat surprising announcement. Aunt Eunice, his only sister, a maiden lady, was not given to letter-writing. The few letters which her brother had received from her in the past half-dozen years had been written for the purpose of giving some family news. Very brief letters they were. Mary remembered two of them. One received three years ago ran thus:

Brother Edward,

James died last night. I suppose you cannot come to the funeral, being so far, and there is no need. We shall bury him on Thursday.

Your sister, Eunice.

37

Another received later, ran:

> *Brother Edward,*
>
> *Johnson has foreclosed. We shall move, of course.*
> *Hannah did her best, but she is only a woman and*
> *had sharpers to deal with. We shall manage, I dare*
> *say. I am letting you know because I said I would, not*
> *because I expect anything.*

"Hannah" was her sister-in-law, the widow of the "James." Aunt Eunice's expectations had been fulfilled. Her brother could do nothing for her, save to write a sympathetic letter and bewail the fact that the hard times and a large family to support made it impossible for him to come to the rescue. The girls had thought their aunt's letters "queer," not to say heartless.

"Only three lines to tell father about the death of his brother; and no particulars!" Lucia had said, and added, "Imagine my writing to one of you announcing the death of Mac or Rod in any such fashion!" She had shivered as she spoke the words, and Mary had said:

"Don't! What is the use in imagining anything so horrid?" Yet both of them had quarreled with their brother Rodney that very afternoon, and did not speak to him for twenty-four hours! But the small knowledge which they had of Aunt Eunice made them wait for their father's news with expectancy. She and her sister-in-law had kept together and "managed" as best they could since the death of the husband and brother.

"Well," said Mrs. Cameron, after waiting a moment for the expected news, "what has moved her to write a letter? Is there anything special?"

"Yes, there is. Hannah is dead."

The girls exchanged glances of amusement, and Emilie giggled a little. It struck her as amusing that this relative was never heard from except through the agency of death. "Hannah" was only an aunt by marriage, and one whom they not only had never seen, but had never heard much about. It was not to be expected that they would care very deeply; though their father shot an annoyed glance at them.

"Poor thing!" said their mother, meaning Aunt Eunice. "She will miss her sadly I suppose, they have been together for so long. She will have some of Hannah's nieces come to live with her, will she not?"

"No," said Mr. Cameron, "she cannot live on there. What Hannah had was an annuity; it stops at her death. She wants to come here."

Undoubtedly he meant his sister Eunice, and not the aunt who had changed worlds; but the Camerons could hardly have looked more startled had they supposed he meant her.

"Here!" repeated Mrs. Cameron amazed and dazed. "Why—how could she?"

There is something peculiarly trying to some nerves in this repetition of the last word they have spoken. It always tried Mr. Cameron, he could not have told why. Moreover, the question was inane.

"She could come on the cars of course, just as any other person would," he replied, more testily than he was in the habit of speaking.

"Well, but, Edward, I don't understand. She doesn't mean to come here to *stay,* of course. Why should she be at the expense of taking so long a journey when she has but little means?"

Mr. Cameron pushed away his plate, with the remains of the luncheon still remaining as they had been served to him, and gave his attention entirely to his wife.

"Why not?" he asked. "Why should she not come here to stay? I am the only brother she has, the only near relative living. She is without means of support, and by the death of her sister-in-law is left desolate. What more natural than that she should write to me and propose to come to my home?"

"For pity's sake!" said Mary.

"Oh, dear!" said Lucia.

And Mrs. Cameron said, "Edward, how *can* we do it? You know we just manage to live, as it is, and Rachel is coming home in a few weeks. That will be another one to feed and clothe. How is it possible for us to take care of your sister?"

"I don't know," said Mr. Cameron doggedly. "I know how it cannot be done. If we are to give lunches, and buy new carpets and china and even silver in order to do it, we must let our relatives go to the poorhouse I suppose."

"Oh, father!" said Lucia; while Mary spoke rapidly and in excited tones:

"I must say I don't think that is quite fair. We haven't had any company before to speak of in two years; and father talks as though we gave lunches every other day. As for new carpets, we had to have that one; the company had nothing to do with it. Three pieces of china to replace broken ones, and a half-dozen plated spoons, was every article that we bought on account of the company; and we had to manage in a way that will humiliate us forever, in order to get along without the things which with other people are matters of course. I am sure *I* do not want any more company. I thought today if I lived through the humiliation of this attempt I should never ask to make another. Hereafter I am going to decline all invitations, to be spared the mortification of never being able to return courtesies."

"Mary!" said her mother as soon as her voice could be heard. "Mary, hush! You forget yourself."

But Mr. Cameron had already attained to the self-control which he usually had.

"I am hard on you, I suppose," he said wearily. "I am harassed to the point of despair in many ways. I know you have to do without many things that others have, and it humiliates me that it is so. But I do not know how to help it. I do my best. I must write to Eunice, I suppose, that we have no place for her. If she cannot find a home among any of her old acquaintances and work for her board, she must go—*where* shall I say?"

The sudden revulsion of feeling in his family, if he had not been accustomed to it, would have astonished him.

"Oh, father!" Lucia said. "You wouldn't do that!"

"Father!" said Emilie. "That would be perfectly dreadful. Why, she is our own auntie!"

Among the girls poor Mary was the only silent one. She was struggling to keep back a rush of tears, and could have spoken no word, whatever had happened. Nor were the tears pushing their way for her own sake. She was already utterly miserable because of the way in which she had spoken to her father. She had not meant to censure him. She was often so grieved for his embarrassments as to lie awake at night wondering what could be done. It was terrible in her to add to his burden by speaking as she had. Mrs. Cameron glanced at her and was sorry for her.

"I don't see, Edward, what is to be gained by talking in that way. The girls do not mean to complain. They are generally very patient, I am sure. Mary has, of her own accord, given up things which she was to have in order to save expense. As for Eunice going to the poorhouse, that is nonsense! She will come here, of course, if there is no other way. We shall manage it somehow."

"Of course," said Lucia quickly. "Mary and I wouldn't think of having anything else done, would we, Mary? She can have the room that Rod and Mac were to have. They won't be home until the holidays, and some way can be planned for them."

"And I can leave school now certainly," chimed in Emilie, triumph in her voice. "If I give up my music it will save thirty dollars a term. I think it is dreadful to spend so much money just on piano lessons. Thirty dollars is worth saving, isn't it, father?"

But even this offer could not lighten the harassed father's burden. Perhaps he realized better than—in the excitement of the moment—any of the others did, what a burden he was about to add to the family through his maiden sister. Still, what else was to be done? It was hard on a man if he could not make room in his home for his only sister.

After the first exclamations, they had all known how it would end. Not a Cameron among them would have had the father do other than write by the morning's mail to Aunt Eunice to come to them as soon as she could make arrangements to do so. Nevertheless, they left the dinner table that evening so overwhelmed with this new calamity as to almost forget even the trials of the luncheon party.

1. O Wad Some Power

"O wad some power the giftie gie us,
To see oursel's as ithers see us!"

That last sentence does not apply to Mary. Aunt Eunice's coming was dreadful enough, but it could not overshadow the miseries of that humiliating luncheon. When the hated dishes were fairly out of sight for the night, the girl threw a light wrap about her, and went out to the side porch to be alone with her gloomy thoughts.

The evening was crisp even for October; so much so that Lucia called after her, that if she was going to "moon" out there, she would better put on a heavier shawl. She vouchsafed no reply to this, and felt sure that the light wrap which she had chosen would be all-sufficient. To be sure, her hands were cold; she could feel that they were like ice, but her head was hot and throbbing, and to get where it was cool and still and dark had become her necessity.

Let it not be supposed that Mary Cameron was so weak a young woman as to have worked herself into this state of misery over the annoyances and embarrassments attendant upon the day's experience. It was trying, of course, to have had a series of mishaps, and finally an accident—all of which were the evident result of incompetent help and insufficient means; but such possibilities had been taken into consideration when the lunch was planned, and the girl had strength of character to rise above such petty trials after the first excitement was over. There was a deeper cause for her gloom. There had come to her that day a revelation concerning the character of one of her guests; one which, though slight in itself, revealed much to her, and hurt her as she had not before understood that she could be hurt. It was when Betsey lay prone upon the floor, "howling," as Emilie expressed it, "for all she was worth," and the distress of the hostess was at its climax, that Mary's eyes chanced to make a swift journey to the corner where Russell Denham was enjoying himself with a charming young lady at either side. Of course, their attention was arrested by the accident—as whose was not, thanks to Betsey's effective voice?—but it was the look on Russell Denham's face which lingered with Mary and stabbed her. An unmistakable smile disfigured his handsome features.

Now, it is supposable that a man may smile, even under such circumstances, if he have no special interest in the immediate sufferer—certainly Betsey's appearance and tones had their ludicrous side—and it was not probable that she was very seriously injured; but there are smiles and *smiles*. This one had in it a hint of a sneer; an amused sneer it is true, but still a sneer; not so much at Betsey, as over the whole miserable attempt at doing things as other people did, and failing. At least Mary, though she tried her utmost to do so, could not translate it otherwise. It was almost as though she had heard his voice in amused sarcasm turning the whole thing into ridicule.

In vain she told herself she was unjust, unreasonable, to so translate a passing glance on the face of a man who spoke not a word; but in her inmost heart she felt that the smile was not one which would have lingered on his face had he been in hearty sympathy with the people who were trying to entertain him. The contrast between his manner and that of Mr. Landis, for instance, was sufficiently marked to impress itself upon her. It was of no use to tell herself that Mr. Landis was officious, that it would have been in better taste for him to have kept his seat, and appeared not to notice the accident, as the other well-bred persons did. Mary Cameron knew she was not true to her own convictions when she did so. Poor Betsey was at this moment blessing the man for his prompt and efficient help. Still it was folly to contrast the two. Not every young man is an apprentice in a drug-store long enough to know how to succor scalded hands. She did not know anything about it, but she presumed this was the case with Mr. Landis. Certainly she had not expected nor desired Mr. Denham to rush to Betsey's help. But—yes, there came constantly back to her that tantalizing "but." It stood for so many things. He had not even said to her the well-bred nothings with which the others had made their adieus: "Such a charming time," "So sorry that poor girl had to hurt herself," "The only mar to a pleasant occasion."

"A unique lunch-party," Russell Denham had said as he extended his hand; and there was still that lurking smile which she hated, curving his lips. When Jessie Lee had essayed to express civilly her regret that poor Betsey had suffered, he had said gaily, "Oh, we cannot afford to regret that; it added a touch of uniqueness to the whole. I assure you she looked quite picturesque reclining there; it was after the manner of an Eastern salaam," and he laughed again; while his sister added:

"There was an Eastern howl at least. Wasn't she terrific, Miss Cameron? I knew by the strength of her lungs that she could not be fatally injured."

It had all been hateful. It was not so much the words as the undefined subtle something behind them which Mary Cameron felt; the something which made her ask herself now, as she threw back even her small wrap and let the night wind blow about her throbbing temples, what Russell Denham had meant by the attentions he had lavished upon her during the past two months. Why had he several times in a marked manner singled her out from others, and given exclusive thought apparently to her, since he could wear that smile and speak those indifferent words when he must have known she was suffering humiliation?

Only a night or two ago he had said to her, "To think that I have been lingering here for more than seven weeks when I half expected to limit my stay to as many days! I am afraid you do not understand who is to blame for this dereliction from duty." And he had looked at her in such a way that she could not but understand that he was casting the sweet blame upon her. Then immediately he had added, "I confess that they are the shortest seven weeks of my life; but perhaps they have seemed long to you; sometimes I fear so."

She had been on the eve of confessing that they did not, that she had enjoyed them more than she was wont to enjoy the society of her friends; but that irrepressible Emilie, who was always where she ought not to be, had burst in upon them at that moment with some gay news gleaned from "the girls," and they two had chattered together constantly thereafter, so there was no opportunity for reply. As she thought of it now, was she glad or sorry that she had not told him she had enjoyed the weeks? What might he not have said in reply? But then, if he meant none of it—and could he have meant anything and have smiled and sneered as he did today?

The blood seemed to roll in waves over her face as she wondered if he had insulted her by saying soft nothings to her! He was not a boy to play at offering special attentions, as some idiotic boys might do, just to see if they knew how to use the language of their elders.

True, he was on the eve of a return to college; but it was for a post-graduate course, and taken because he was fond of study, and had abundant means and abundant leisure. He-was twenty-six. She had discovered it when they were comparing dates in regard to certain past experiences. "Why, I was at that very concert!" he had said, in almost boyish delight. "I remember it was my twenty-fourth birthday, and I indulged myself in a rare musical treat in order to celebrate the event. To think that you were in the same row of boxes and I never knew it! How shall I account for such unparalleled stupidity on my part?"

Even while she laughed gleefully over his pretended disgust at not recognizing a person of whom he had never even heard, she had felt at her heart a little thrill of satisfaction. Then he was twenty-six years old now, and she had but passed her twenty-fourth birthday. An eminently proper age were they for being intimate friends, even the most intimate. He had seemed younger than that; she had thought him possibly a trifle younger than herself, and had caught herself wondering whether people would discover it some day, and make unpleasant remarks thereupon. No, they were neither of them young simpletons playing at life. It made the pain all the sharper for Mary Cameron to remember this.

She had not been a girl who was especially fond of the society of young men. She had almost no intimate friendships with them. Lucia was inclined to have at least half a dozen very good friends among "the boys;" friends with whom she corresponded in a happy-go-lucky sort of way, writing when she felt like it, and when she did not, letting weeks, even months, slip by with an occasional statement that she supposed she ought to answer Charlie's letter, or she was afraid Dick would think she had forgotten how to write; but Mary had not interested herself enough in any of their acquaintances to write to them, save when business or some courtesy called for it.

She had often wondered whether she were different from other girls; why they cared, some of them, so much for the attentions of the young men of their set, and whether she ever should care in the least about these things. Perhaps her very indifference heretofore made the sting deeper when she discovered that she had grown to have a feeling which, to say the least, was not indifference for this young man who could smile when she was troubled, and who was going away tomorrow, and had left her that day with a genial, "Well, I suppose this is good-bye? You will hardly allow me to call in the morning, since I must leave at twelve. The Eastern princess will demand some of your morning perhaps? I shall not soon forget my pleasant visit to your city."

Did he really mean that that was good-bye? She had thought that even letter-writing, of which she was not fond, as her brothers could testify, would be pleasant, if the letters were to be addressed to him. But he made no mention of letters, although when he offered to mail for her one evening a letter to her brother, he had glanced at the address and said, "Has it become natural for you to address letters to the university, so that your friends who beg for them one of these days will not have to wait for you to get in the habit of it?"

She had laughed in reply, and also blushed, as she remembered that his post-graduate course was to be taken at the university where her brothers were.

After that she had expected to be asked to correspond with him, and had gone over in her mind the reply she would make. She blushed under cover of the darkness as she thought of it now. Aside from the fact that her interest in this man had been unusual from the first, and had steadily increased with acquaintance, it was humiliating to have it seem as though her friendship had been trifled with. In truth, she did not admit it, after a little. It suggested itself, and she put it away as unworthy of her and of him. No opportunity had offered itself for him to say the words he meant to say. That ridiculous affair of Betsey and the chocolate had made it impossible to plan for any real conversation afterwards.

Then Emilie was at hand, of course; she always was when she was not desired. Girls of fifteen ought to be sent to boarding-school until they could learn common-sense and good manners. Mr. Denham would call in the morning, despite his hint to the contrary; she had not told him he could not. From nine until twelve was ample time for a call, provided he wished to make it. Or, even if he should be detained from that, he could write; she had not told him she would not address letters to him. It was foolish for her to condemn him as a trifler merely because he had laughed when she did not feel like it. The quiet and coolness of the front porch suggested this train of thought. Was it fortunate or otherwise that she could not hear a conversation which was taking place at this moment at the extreme upper end of Durand Avenue? Russell Denham was taking his sister home from an evening visit, and the two were discussing the luncheon-party.

After a moment's silence the young man broke forth afresh, prefacing his sentence with a light laugh. "What a ridiculous tableau that whole thing made! The howling girl with chocolate pouring serenely over her, the faces of the guests, and above all the faces of our hostess and her two older daughters. It would have been more humane not to have laughed, but really I don't see how a fellow was to prevent it. The whole thing matched somehow."

"Matched what, Russell?"

"Why, the effort at style and elegance; and the effort to appear at ease when the entire family were undoubtedly far from ease. One could see that affairs were in jeopardy all the while. Miss Cameron conversed with one eye on the kitchen door, so to speak, even before the luncheon was announced; and even that rollicking Miss Lucia was subdued and nervous."

"Yet the Camerons are used to good society, and always have been; we have met them everywhere."

"They are more used to going than to entertaining evidently," said her brother. "The question is, why could they not have been content with an effort which was within their means, and in correspondence with their surroundings? A man would have known better than to place himself in a position where such embarrassments as they labored under were possible. Fancy waiting ten minutes by the clock for an extra spoon for the coffee!" Whereupon he laughed again.

"Do you know," said his sister, "that you relieve my mind immensely? I really thought, or feared, until today that you had a very special interest in Miss Mary Cameron. I am sure you have shown her more attention than is your habit, and it seemed to me several times that I joined you when you were on the verge of a conversation which might end dangerously."

Mr. Denham did not laugh this time; instead, he was silent for several seconds; then he said in a changed tone, "To be entirely frank with you, Miss Cameron has interested me more than young women generally do. Possibly, had I not been strangely interrupted more than once, I might have said something which would need to be repented of. I have not been entirely sure of my own mind at any time, but I thought perhaps on a closer acquaintance I should grow to be. I will confess that the farce we have been through today opened my eyes somewhat to her true character, and—well, to speak plainly, frightened me. It is a very little thing, you think, to accomplish so serious a result; but look at it. The Camerons are poor, much poorer even than we are; and you know very well that at home we never indulge in this sort of thing. The father is working on a salary; not a very large one either, and just at this time he is decidedly embarrassed. Young Holcombe was speaking of it today: he told me that Mr. Cameron has asked the Hosmers twice lately for an extension of time. He looks harassed and worn. Under such circumstances his daughters might be excused from entertaining guests one would think. Or, if they considered that impossible, why not, as I said, have given us a simple cup of chocolate and a biscuit, or cracker, or whatever you call those little things which people serve? Their dishes would have gone around for such an entertainment, which they manifestly did not for this spread. I frankly confess I was disgusted with the whole thing. I could not help realizing that in my mother's house nothing like it could ever have occurred. I hate to see people undertake what they cannot carry out. I own it is queer that it should have given me such a revulsion of feeling as it did, but I came away from there telling myself that I could not afford to be interested in a girl like that. My income would never justify it. Anyone who tries to make a dollar look to her friends as though it was ten dollars, and she had plenty more in reserve, I am afraid of."

"Yet you have the name of being very lavish with your money, Russell. That Mr. Stuart who sat beside me at table hinted that you were a subject of envy on that account among his gentlemen friends."

"Oh, that is because I have arrived at the age when a man is generally in business for himself, and am still studying. I cannot go around the country telling everyone to whom I am introduced that what money I have is bestowed upon me by the most eccentric of uncles, who made it impossible for me to use another penny after my education is completed; and that I am hard at work planning ways and means to get a living after I have secured as good an education as the money will give. Professor Landis whom we met today, and whom, by the way, I like better than any of the other fellows, told me I was right in believing that it would make a great difference with my prospects as a teacher if I took a thorough postgraduate course. I grant you that, thanks to my whimsical uncle, I am sailing under what might be considered false colors; but I am doing it honestly and mean to tell the exact truth to whomever is intimate enough with me to have a right to it. I thought I should have told Miss Cameron before this, but I have decided that I probably never shall."

"Well, but, Russell, are you not a little severe? I am not fond of Mary Cameron, but I ought to want justice done her. Perhaps she is the creature of circumstance. The lavish effort at expenditure today may not have been in accordance with her ideas or wishes. All mothers are not like ours; and although she is the eldest daughter, younger ones sometimes have more weight in the home than their elders."

"No," said her brother emphatically. "I have been all over that ground. Mary Cameron was the moving spirit there today. The anxious way in which her mother's eyes constantly sought hers to see if things were going to her mind, and the deprecating manner in which she appealed to her when they went wrong, would have been pitiful if it had not been exasperating. It told the entire story. I could fancy Mary getting into a storm of determination to carry her point, regardless of results. She is not a meek and quiet spirit. In fact, I thought she had an independent spirit at first, and admired it; but instead, she is one of those who *must* ape society ways of doing things, whether they be reasonable ways or not, even though she adds to her father's burdens, as the smallest expenditures must at present. To have a social hour with her friends and give them pleasure was not her aim today, but to show the Overmans and Westbrooks, who are worth hundreds of thousands, that she can make as expensive a spread as they can. And even that failed, you see; she could not do it. No, I am quite decided that I was mistaken in her character, and that my expectations, which at present are represented by zero, will not admit of my further cultivating her friendship."

His sister laughed cheerily. "Your tone as well as words show that you do not care. The impression which she made has evidently not been a very serious one. I am glad of it. As I said, I have not been drawn to her; and it is a great comfort to think that I need not oblige myself to like her for your sake. But I hope the poor girl has not become too much interested in you for her peace of mind."

"Oh, not at all," her brother said quickly. "Miss Cameron's weaknesses do not lie in that direction; and, of course, I have not made my possible thoughts concerning her plain to her. I think she likes me very well, and might have learned to like me better perhaps, but that is over."

Nevertheless, as he left his sister at the door of the library with her girl friends, and went on up to his room, he sighed and said to himself, "Nettie knows very little about it after all. Mary Cameron came nearer to touching my life than I had supposed any woman could. Heigh ho! 'Trifles light as air' accomplish strange results sometimes. Who would have supposed that a luncheon party, gotten up regardless of expense, and calculated to impress us with a sense of position in life, should have had such a peculiar effect on me? I wish I had gone to Boston yesterday as I ought, instead of lingering here purely for the sake of having another visit with her. Then I might have—or no, of course I don't wish that, because then I should have—*Do* I wish it, I wonder? Oh, get out of the way! I don't want *you* at least."

The very last sentence was addressed to the cat, who came purring about him ready to be played with. With regret be it stated that he kicked her, not seriously, but unmistakably. Assuredly Russell Denham was in ill humor.

5. IN THE GLOOM

The twilight deepened and the evening grew more chill. Mrs. Cameron put her head out of the door once and said, "Mary, I think you are imprudent; it is really quite cold." Still the girl lingered. She was not crying; she had no desire to cry; but it seemed to her that she could not go into that well-lighted sitting-room and listen to Emilie's chatter about the guests and the luncheon and Aunt Eunice. Neither could she go to her own room; for Lucia would be sure to follow quite soon, and there would be her tongue to endure. If Lucia said anything about Russell Denham tonight she did not know what would become of her. She could not endure the thought of the family wondering that he did not come for a farewell call, or asking if he meant to call in the morning. A quick, firm step sounded on the pavement— there had been many since she stood there, but there is a difference in footsteps. These demanded attention. They grew slower as they neared the little gate which shut her in from the street. They lingered at the gate, and a clear voice said, "Good evening." For a moment Mary Cameron's heart had seemed to stand still. Could this be *he,* come after all to tell her good-by? Then it went on again in dull thuds. It was only their next-door neighbor, or, as Lucia expressed it, the one who lived almost in the same house.

"Good-evening," he said; and his hand was on the little gate, although his own gate was just the other side of it. "Are you enjoying the darkness and stillness? Isn't there a restful hush over the world tonight? I think I like dark nights almost better than moonlight ones. At least, they certainly have their charm." He had come up the steps as he spoke, but Mary had no words for him about the beauty of the night. She wished he would go away and leave her alone.

"I have not mistaken the house," he said, and she could feel that he was smiling; "although they are so close and so exactly alike that one might readily do so. Do you like twin houses, Miss Cameron?"

"No," she said coldly. "I don't think I like 'twin' anything. It seems to me that houses and people would do better not so close." She made a mental reservation in favor of Lucia and McLloyd who were twins, though she found herself thinking that even they would be better friends if they were not in some respects so much alike.

"I think I agree with you in the main, at least about houses. It is the misfortune of the city that it forces itself upon its neighbors, leaving no green and quiet spaces between."

The girl had absolutely no words for him. She did not mean to be ungracious, or, rather, she did not mean to show her ungraciousness; but she had said too many sharp words to Lucia about this man, and he was too distinctly associated with her day's mortifications to be other than disagreeable to her now. She had even sneered at his profession.

"I presume he teaches spelling and arithmetic in one of the ward schools, and therefore expects to be dubbed 'Professor' on all possible occasions. Those small teachers are always jealous of titles."

This she had said, not having any knowledge of his position or desires, but simply on general principles, and because she felt at the time like saying something disagreeable. Lucia seemed to her to have taken up those strangers in an unaccountable manner. What if they did rush in and have all the family come over for a cup of tea the evening they arrived at their new home, belated and damp from the dreary, autumnal rain, and very weary? It was kind, of course. Who denied it? But the very act showed their country breeding. People in cities did not offer strangers who moved next door to them cups of tea. But people in cities are supposed to know how to treat their callers, and it was no part of Mary Cameron's intention to be rude to the young man who had stopped in a friendly way to speak to her. She simply could not think of a civil commonplace to say. He relieved her embarrassment.

"I had it in mind to ask a question or two today, had the opportunity offered. My sister and I are comparative strangers in the city, you know, and I believe you are old residents. Some of the churches near us have been closed since our coming. What can you tell us concerning them? Is there one where we are needed?"

"I haven't the least idea," said Miss Cameron promptly, glad of a subject upon which she could speak glibly. "We have no more knowledge of this part of the town than entire strangers have. Our own church is away uptown at Fountain Square."

"But you do not expect to continue your connection with that church now that you have come to this part of the town, I presume?"

"Why not? We have not thought of such a thing as making a change in that respect. We are sufficiently homesick now, without adding to it unnecessarily."

"I beg pardon; I had supposed the distance would be an objection."

"Oh, not at all. The cable takes us quite to the doors. It connects with the Central Avenue one, you know." Then, feeling that the occasion demanded so much courtesy from her, she added with an attempt at graciousness, "If you and your sister are fond of good music you will hear none finer in the city than at the Fountainsquare Church. They spend thousands of dollars every year on their choir. They are also quite attentive to strangers—have pews set apart for their use. You might like to go there evenings occasionally."

"No," he said quietly; "I think we will find our corner nearer home. There is a little church on Smith Street, just out of Durand Avenue, which interests us. The pastor is absent, in attendance upon his father who is ill, I understand; but the people are very cordial. If it shall prove that we are as much pleased with the pastor as with his flock, I think we shall decide for that church. To tell you the truth, we had hoped that you would join us there. The church evidently needs help, and affords a splendid opportunity for work. They have a Christian Endeavor Society which could be made a power in the neighborhood."

Mary Cameron received a fresh accession of dignity. The man actually wanted to patronize them, and get them into that little hive on Smith Street, which already swarmed with people, judging from the crowds of children who blocked the streets on Sunday mornings surging out of their Sunday-school.

"We haven't the slightest idea of making any change, as I said," she replied coldly; and she wished he would go home. It was growing chilly; she began to realize it. Did he expect her to invite him in to a family chat? She did not mean to do it. Certainly she was not going to show him to the parlor, and undertake to entertain him; and it would hardly do to call Lucia to the task and then vanish. Why could he not see that she wanted to be alone, even though she came to the front doorsteps to secure the opportunity?

He seemed to have no idea of going. He leaned against the railing which separated his home from theirs, and looked up at the far-away stars in silence for a moment, then said suddenly:

"Miss Cameron, do you ever feel—I hardly know how to express it—perhaps I will say, *homesick* for a visit with Jesus Christ? Not for communion with him through prayer—of course, that is always open to us. Isn't it wonderful, by the way, that it is? Suppose we had to wait for times and occasions? Suppose, for instance, you and I could not speak to him tonight, no matter how great our need, but must wait until tomorrow, or next week, or next month, for a certain date to arrive? Why, one would hardly dare to live! But I am not speaking of that which is already ours; I mean a real human longing for the visible presence of my friend Jesus. The desire to clasp his hand, and hear his voice, and walk with him, perhaps arm-in-arm, down the busy streets, and converse with him as friend to friend. Do you ever have such desires, so strong that they seem to fairly clamor for satisfaction?"

Miss Cameron was very much startled. Was her next neighbor a lunatic? What a strange, irreverent way to speak of Christ! Certainly she never had such desires. On the contrary, the very suggestion of them made her feel afraid. It would be to her a terrible thing to meet face to face with Jesus Christ! She did not think people ought to talk in that way. Nobody did who was entirely sane, she believed.

"I don't think I understand you very well," she said hesitatingly, and her hand was on the door-knob; she had thrown off the night-latch when she came out. The utmost she wanted now was to get in, out of reach of the voice of this strange man.

He took his eyes away from the stars and looked at her. "I beg your pardon," he said, recognizing the tremor in her voice; "I was simply thinking aloud, as I do sometimes with my sister Dorothy. And I thought, too, to be entirely frank, that your face today had a look of unrest, as though you needed the familiar companionship of which I speak, and longed for it. Do you not think we keep our infinite Friend too far away, and forget that he is interested in the veriest trifle that pleases or disturbs us? That is why I sometimes fancy, in my folly, that it would be better if we could see him for a little, and clasp hands with him, even though he had to go away again tomorrow. I am afraid I have always envied the disciples. I could bear the sight of the cloud, I think, which received him, if only I could have had three years—yes, even three days—of visible presence to remember forever. Which shows, by the way, what poor, selfish creatures we are. While I was enjoying his companionship, what would my brethren only a few miles away do without him? And, as he has arranged it, we have him always, each of us, if only we could realize it."

Miss Cameron had never been so uncomfortable in her life. Never, in all the twenty-four years she had lived, had she heard from mortal lips such sentences as these. Christians she had met, of course; she hoped they were none of them heathen! But the Christians she knew had common-sense, and did not rave in the darkness about impossible and really terrible ideas.

At any risk she must get away from him. If he thought her rude she could not help it.

"I think I must go in now," she said hurriedly; "it is growing very chilly. Do you—will you—come inside?"

She hesitated and stammered over the simple invitation, in great fear lest he should accept it. He could not resist a smile in the darkness at her expense, it was so evident that she wanted to be rid of him. He made his adieus with all speed after that, and Mary Cameron returned to the family room to be stormed with questions.

"What was she doing out there in the darkness so long?"

"Wasn't she chilled through? It was the coolest evening they had had."

"Tomorrow she would have a stiff neck and a sore throat, and wonder where she took cold."

"Who was out there with her? Surely they heard voices."

"I know," said Emilie the irrepressible, "it was Mr. Denham come back to say good-bye. I knew he would find his way around here again. It would have saved him lots of car-fare if he had stayed when he was here. Why in the world didn't you come into the parlor? It is lighted and deserted. I should think it would have been a great deal pleasanter than out in the dark and cold."

"Was Mr. Denham there, Mary?" the mother asked. She spoke gently, yet with an undertone of curiousness in her voice—yes, and of satisfaction.

The poor, sore-hearted girl resented it all. They would be glad to be rid of her. They were watching to see what possible chances there might be to that end. They had discussed her prospects and hopes, probably, while she was out there in the darkness and loneliness. She could not bear it.

"No," she said, her voice high-keyed; "he was not. Why should you think he would be? Is it possible that I cannot be out of the room a few minutes without having my affairs discussed and my actions commented upon? I think Emilie ought to be taught not to meddle with matters which do not in the least concern her."

"My patience!" said Emilie. "Did anyone ever see a crosser creature? If Mr. Denham knew what he was about he would take care how he had anything more to do with you. I think somebody ought to warn him."

"Emilie!" said the mother in great severity, "I am ashamed of you. How can you be so disagreeable? Apologize to your sister at once."

But the sister had fled. She wanted no apology. She wanted only to get away out of sight, where she might pour out her heart's pain undisturbed.

It was hard enough to be left in solitude on this evening which she had thought would be made bright with the companionship of one who sought her company above all others; it was horrible to be made the gazing-stock of even her own family. She over-rated the state of things, of course. The over-sensitive always do. The merest passing mention had been made of her fondness for the front porch that evening, then the family had returned to the all-absorbing theme of Aunt Eunice. There was need for planning if she was to become for any length of time a member of their family. Mary and Lucia shared each other's room, not because of any special fondness upon their part for each other's society, but because space had been scarce.

In the other house there had been a tiny room, or what they had called such—in point of fact it was only a good-sized closet opening out of Mrs. Cameron's room—which had been declared to be just the thing for Emilie. She had rebelled a little; had said it was nothing but a clothespress, and she was tired of being tucked away anywhere, and she was old enough she should think to have a decent room, and what was the use of their keeping a spare chamber always in immaculate order, with the best things in the house in it, for nobody to use? She was sure they rarely had company. But at the same time there had been enough of the child about her to be secretly glad that mother's room opened into her "closet," and that on dark nights when the wind blew, she had only to listen to hear her father's regular breathing.

There were times when it gave her a delightful sense of security, and made her even take the closet's part when Mary occasionally argued the propriety of her taking the spare room to herself and letting Lucia and Emilie share the other. That this had never been done was because that guest chamber, with its well-bred air of being always ready, was really dear to Mary's heart. But the Durand Avenue house had no convenient closet, and it had distinctly one less room to plan with, and Rachel was coming home. This gave to Emilie, for a time at least, the luxury of "a whole room" to herself, as she delightedly expressed it. For to Mary the well-understood peculiarities of Lucia were more endurable than the unknown possibilities of Rachel, and she distinctly refused to share a room with the latter.

Now the question was, what should be done with Aunt Eunice? Should they put her with Emilie, thus giving her tacitly to understand that they had no guest chamber and were incommoding themselves to receive her? They discussed this carefully, the mother and Lucia giving little heed to Emilie's groans the while. She was still regarded as a child who must do as she was told. Rachel was not coming for at least six weeks yet, and who knew what might happen in that length of time? But there were objections to the plan. Mrs. Cameron did not quite like to voice them. In her heart she said, "If anything should happen that Rachel did not come as soon as she was expected—and a girl who was away in California with cousins might have occasion to change her mind—then Aunt Eunice would be settled with them, and feel that she was not in anyone's way.

If, on the contrary, they should give her the boys' room, always referring to it as such, when the Christmas holidays began to draw near, it would be apparent to any reasonable creature that there was no place for Aunt Eunice. They could hardly be expected to turn their own sons out of the house in order to make room for their father's sister! Mrs. Cameron said this over to her own heart, in order to arouse the proper feeling of indignation; but she found that she did not like to present the argument about rooms aloud, even to Lucia; so she represented the great discomfort there would be to a middle-aged woman in having a young, careless girl like Emilie always with her. It would really be inhospitable.

"And the great discomfort it would be to me!" Emilie chimed in. "You don't any of you think of that."

These sentences had been interspersed with wishes from the mother that Mary would not stay out in the chilly air so long, and occasional wonderings from Emilie as to who was out there with her. Mother and daughter had both laughed at Emilie's pathetic reference to herself, which was often the only reply the girl received; and then Mary had come in from the porch and concocted out of nothing, as has been shown, her theory of having been discussed all the time she had been away.

Young Landis, not finding his sister Dorothy visible anywhere, went from his neighbor's porch to his room, and sat down to consider what had been said. He looked grave and disappointed over it.

"I did her no good," he thought; "not the least in the world. The poor creature carries unrest and dissatisfaction written on her face so that he 'who runs may read.' How very plain it is that she is not acquainted with Him whom 'to know aright is peace.' And I did not help her. Instead of being plain and direct in what I had to say, I went off on some ideas of my own which she did not understand any more than if I had spoken Sanskrit. I might have known that she wouldn't. I actually frightened her. To think of Jesus Christ as a personal Presence is terror to her. How few there are who seem to know him aright! I wonder if he feels it as we feel the indifference, the positive slight, of those with whom we would be friends? Think of him stooping to win us by every gentle, tender word in our language, and we indifferent! Sometimes it passes belief that he can endure this sort of thing much longer. Sometimes it is the strongest mark of divinity which I recognize, that he does so endure through the ages. Fancy a young woman having so little to occupy her precious Sabbath time, that she is willing to spend two hours, to say the least, in going and returning from Fountain Square in company with crowds of Sabbath-breakers bent on reaching a like locality, for a different reason from hers! Though, when one thinks of it, her reasons for going seem not to be very definite. She does not impress one as deeply attached to her church. It would almost seem as though she sought it because it was located at Fountain Square. Now, brother Landis, that is a charitable conclusion! No doubt she does feel at home there, and desolate here. Apparently I am not the one to help her into a happier frame of mind." And he laughed outright over the girl's manifest desire to be rid of him. "I ought to have let my sweet little saint Dorothy undertake that task. But the girl looked so utterly miserable today. I wonder what it is? Certainly the accident, awkward as it was, cannot account for so much unhappiness. Ah, well! I cannot carry my neighbor's burdens. But I confess to an unusual desire to help this girl. Perhaps it is because she seems in such dire need of help. I wonder if the people who are striving after a place and name in this world, and failing to reach them, are not more to be pitied than the people who are content down where they are? That is a question in social ethics to consider. To answer it in the affirmative would upset all the theories of philanthropists the world over. Oh, the world! When *will* it learn what it needs?"

6. "Isn't She a Terror!"

Aunt Eunice was duly watched for and met at the station; met several times, in fact, by anticipation, and at various depots. On two occasions Mr. Cameron lost his lunch entirely in order to be in time for a train on which it was thought she might arrive. And after all this she came at an hour when she was not expected; rattled up to the door near midnight in a cab, and made her voice distinct to all the anxious ears which were hovering about upper windows, while she had a parley with the driver about the unreasonable sum which he wished to charge her. Because it was characteristic of Aunt Eunice, it shall be mentioned here that he did not receive the fare he called for. But this beginning did not prepossess the Camerons in her favor.

"Listen to her!" exclaimed Emilie with a very distinct gurgle of laughter. "She is telling him that he ought to be published in all the papers, and that he will find he has tried to cheat the wrong woman this time!"

Emilie was the only one who laughed. Mary was indignant.

"Why doesn't the creature come in and let father attend to the cabman!" she inquired angrily of no one in particular. "It wasn't enough for her to appear at an unearthly hour of the night, after being waited for at every depot in town, but she must arouse the neighborhood with her tongue."

"Father!" said Emilie with another giggle. "He stands at one side, vanquished. She has already told him to go away and let her alone; that she knows how to manage a cabman she guesses; if she doesn't, he can't teach her."

"Do let us go back to bed," said Lucia, shivering under the light wrapper she had hastily thrown about her when the bell rang. "If I had imagined it was she, ringing so furiously, I would have stayed there in the first place. I thought of Mac and Rod, and a telegram. We can survive until morning without seeing her, I think. Emilie, come away from the window, and close it; you would laugh if a madman were out there, instead of a mad woman."

"I am going down," said Emilie, dashing into her own room to make a rapid toilet; "mother may need some help in looking after her, she is in such a belligerent frame of mind."

Perhaps this, too, was characteristic; it was often Emilie who went down to give mother a little help in emergencies. To be sure, she got no credit for it with the family. Emilie's curiosity, they said, would take her out of bed into the most disagreeable places, if there were anything new to be seen. But the mother or Betsey often had the benefit of snatches of help from her.

———◆———

It was a cold morning; cold enough to make everyone realize that November had come, and meant to be severe and surly. The Camerons were in the sitting-room, variously employed. Mrs. Cameron was busy with a roll of garments which had arrived by mail from the boys. They did not know what was the matter with them, Mac wrote, except that they seemed to need mother.

"If they were my boys," said Aunt Eunice, gazing with severe eyes on yawning rents in the garment being held up for inspection, "they would know what was the matter, and get a lesson to remember into the bargain. Things don't tear like that unless they have awful jerks getting them off. Boys ought to learn how to take off their clothes decently before they go away from home."

"All boys are careless sometimes, I suppose," said Mrs. Cameron coldly. She had been known to tell her sons that never were there two such careless creatures born, she verily believed, but she was not pleased to have such an idea even hinted at by another.

"Yes," said Aunt Eunice grimly; "and that is the way to make them so. From the time they get on roundabout jackets until they are married and have families of their own to look after, they hear it everlastingly said that 'boys must be boys,' and 'boys are born heedless,' and all that sort of thing, until they get a notion that they are of no account unless they pull and haul, and tear around like wild animals, and destroy more things than they use. I haven't any patience with that kind of bringing up."

"Aunt Eunice, how many boys have you brought up?" asked Lucia, looking up from the cow she was carefully daubing into her painting.

Aunt Eunice's sallow face grew slowly red as she replied, "I haven't brought up any, as I suppose you know very well without my telling; but I was brought up to be respectful to my elders, which is more, I should think, than can be said of some."

"Lucia!" said Mrs. Cameron, warning and distress in her voice; but Lucia's only reply was, "Dear me, mother! I only asked a question."

"Mother!" said Emilie, rushing into the room from the outside world somewhere, and speaking eagerly—in fact Emilie Cameron generally rushed to and from all places, and always spoke eagerly. "Mother, the class begins tonight, and I haven't got my ticket, or shoes, or anything. Can't I see about them right away?"

"I must have a talk with your father first, Emilie," said Mrs. Cameron, looking more distressed. "I haven't had a moment when I could mention it."

"But, mother, I tell you they begin tonight. If I lose the first lesson, I might as well lose the whole; they will all be ahead of me."

"Then you would better lose the first lesson," said Mary, quickly. "I don't see how father can afford the money for that class this fall."

"Now, Mary Cameron, you only say that to be hateful. You know you told mother you thought I might better give up my music than my dancing lessons."

"Dancing lessons!" repeated Aunt Eunice in impressive tones. "A granddaughter of Daniel Cameron! Well, well! What next, I wonder?"

"Emilie," said Mrs. Cameron with decision, "I wish you to let that subject entirely alone until I can talk with your father. I thought you had more sense." She shot an annoyed glance in the direction of the newcomer as she spoke; and Emilie, who had forgotten her in the excitement of the moment, went slowly from the room murmuring something which it is thought was not complimentary to Aunt Eunice. That person knitted hard and fast on a stern gray sock she was fashioning, and did not speak for several minutes. Then she addressed Mary, who was sewing braid in elaborate design on something white and silky.

"What is that you are making?"

Mary explained that it was a new front to wear with an old dress, to brighten it up.

"Humph! I should think it would disfigure it. Putting beads on in all sorts of shapes, exactly as the squaws do. They used to come to our back door by the dozens, rigged up in bead-work; but I did not know that civilized women copied their fashions. I should think you were too old to wear such things."

Here Lucia laid down her paint-brush to laugh immoderately.

"I'm not seventy yet!" said Mary, bestowing an indignant glance on Lucia.

"No; but you are twenty-four years and two months. I kept a record of my brother's children in my Bible, and I know to a day how old each one is. It seems to me that a young woman who has reached your age shouldn't waste her time on such follies. What do *you* do with all your time? Do you teach, or what?"

This last question was evidently addressed to Lucia, and had reference to her painting.

"'What,' I guess," she answered, laughing, and added, "No, ma'am; I never had the misfortune to be obliged to teach anybody. I paint for my own amusement."

"Humph! I hope you find yourself amused. That cow you are making don't look any more like a cow to me than it does like a rooster, and I have been brought up with both of them all my life. Our minister used to say he thought people ought not to spend time painting pictures unless they could make money by it, or had a special genius in that direction. I shouldn't think you have the genius if I am any judge."

"People do not usually put on spectacles, and move as close to oil-paintings as they can get, in order to judge of their merit," said Lucia, trying to defend her cow. "They have to be viewed at a distance."

"I should think likely! And the greater the distance the better the view. Why don't you two young women go to work and earn some money for your father? He says he has hard times to make ends meet, and I don't wonder, I am sure. Before I was Mary's age, I had earned two hundred dollars for my father, teaching in district schools, and boarding around. I *worked,* I tell you. I hadn't any time to waste on sewing beads to wear around my neck. And as for Lucy—"

"My name is Lucia, Aunt Eunice," interposed that young woman.

"Oh, well, *Lucia,* then. I don't see any sense in such a name. Plain Lucy used to be good enough for your ancestors. You were named after your Aunt Lucy Edmonds, weren't you? A body would think to read over your names that you had lost all the *y's* out of the language down this way. Spelling Emily '*Emilie*'! I ended it in a good honest *y* in the family Bible; and so I did yours. What is Rachel doing?"

This sudden change of subject was addressed to Mrs. Cameron, who made haste to explain. "Why, Rachel, you know, went back with her Aunt Kate, six years ago, and has not been home since."

"Not in six years!"

"No; it seems a long time, doesn't it, to give a child? Edward and I have seen her since, but the children never have. It was a sacrifice, of course, but my sister Kate seemed to need her, and begged for her; she had no daughters of her own. Then, at that time, they could give her advantages which we could not. We let her go only for the winter, we supposed; but in the spring my sister wanted to take her to the mountains, and it seemed an opportunity for the child. During the next winter Kate lost a son, and we couldn't deprive her of Rachel then. In the early spring they went to California for my brother-in-law's health; and after he died, of course, Kate needed Rachel more than ever, and they were so far away, too. For one reason and another, she kept staying on, until it is now nearly six years. But we are expecting her home very soon. My sister Kate died in the spring, you know. Rachel would have come then, had there been a suitable escort for her; but her cousins wanted her to stay, dreadfully; they missed their mother and felt all broken up. Yes; she is with the cousins. There were two boys; they are both married and have pleasant families, and Rachel is naturally attached to them. But John, the elder, is coming East in about six weeks, they think; and Rachel is to come home with him."

"It is a dreadful long time to give up the care of a child," said Aunt Eunice. "I don't understand how you could do it."

"We have to do a good many things which we think we can't," said Mrs. Cameron, sewing vigorously on the patch she had set in Mac's garment. "My sister Kate was lonely; both her boys were away at school, and she took the greatest fancy to Rachel, and begged for her; and as I had three other daughters and two boys all at home with me, it did seem selfish."

"It is a wonder she did not want one of the older girls," said Aunt Eunice. "I should have thought they would have been of more use to her."

"Yes," said Lucia; "I have often wished she had wanted me; she lived then where there was a fine art-school, and I might have learned how to paint a cow."

"She wanted Rachel and nobody else," said Mrs. Cameron. "She had lost a little daughter a year or two before, and she fancied that Rachel looked like her. I suppose that accounts for the great affection she had for her from the first."

"Did she leave her property to her?"

Mrs. Cameron shook her head, and sighed. "She had no property to leave. They used to be in good circumstances; quite wealthy, indeed; but my brother-in-law was unfortunate in some way. He speculated, I believe, and lost heavily; then he was ill for a long time, and they traveled, and used up a great deal of money; so that when he died, there was barely enough to support my sister and Rachel during her life. The boys are in good business; but they are young, and have growing families, and, of course, not much to spare. Kate left Rachel the most of her clothes, and her watch, and such things, but no money, or barely enough to bring her home; she is saving what she had, for that purpose. No, we didn't send her away from home to secure a fortune; if we had, our sacrifice would have been in vain. As it is, she was a great comfort to her aunt all her life, and we cannot regret having spared her to her."

Mrs. Cameron meant every word of this. Nevertheless, it had been a sore trial to her when the brother-in-law lost his money. She could not help commenting severely at the time on his folly in allowing himself to get entangled with speculations. Also she could not help admitting to herself that if it had been Mary or Lucia who had been chosen, with the advantages which her sister Kate had offered, they were old enough to have profited more by it than Rachel had probably done; she was only eighteen now. It cannot be denied that, much as the *mother* in her wanted to see this member of her flock, she had wakeful hours over the problem of how they were to properly clothe another young lady.

Aunt Eunice had a way of turning suddenly from one topic to another, apparently entirely irrelevant. She took one of those flights now. "Where do you go to church?"

The merits of the Fountain Square Church were carefully pointed out to her.

"How far away is it?"

They really did not know; it was quite a distance. Well, couldn't they guess it? Was it half a mile, or a mile, or two miles? What did they mean by "quite a distance"?

Lucia stayed her brush to count the squares. "Why, it must be about four miles."

"For pity's sake!" They didn't mean that they walked four miles to church!

Walked! No, indeed. Who had thought of such a thing?

Well, then, how did they manage? They didn't keep a horse, Edward told her. Did they have to do with those precious cabmen, like the one who tried to cheat her out of fifty cents?

"Why, Aunt Eunice," said Mary, speaking for the first time since she had been compared to a squaw, "we know you have lived in the country all your life, but surely you have heard of horse-cars, and cable-cars, and such conveniences!"

"Oh, yes," Aunt Eunice said. She had heard of them, and traveled in them too; but she didn't suppose that respectable people went to meeting in them. She knew James used to think they were as Sabbath-breaking an institution as he knew anything about. Once he was offered some stock in them, and he wouldn't take it, because he said a man who made his money by trampling over the Sabbath as they did, couldn't prosper.

"That is probably the reason that he died poor," said Mary.

Aunt Eunice's sallow face flushed, and her gray eyes flashed. "No, it wasn't any such thing; it was because he trusted one of your rich, fashionable men too much, and got cheated. James was always anxious to think that folks were better than they were; that was about the biggest fault he had. Oh, we had considerable knowledge of what was going on in the world, if we did live out West. You are not very well acquainted with the West, I guess. The electric cars passed our door, but we didn't ride in them on Sundays."

Here Lucia indulged in another laugh. "Why, Aunt Eunice," she said, "that is the queerest idea I ever heard of! They are necessities in cities. How would people get to church, or to Sunday-school, or anywhere, without them?"

"Don't you have any churches within four miles of you?"

"Oh, yes, of course; but they are not the ones that we want to attend."

"Exactly; then that isn't necessity, it is notion. Not that there is any argument in what you said, however you fix it. I suppose if we really couldn't go to church without breaking one of the commandments to do it, the Lord would contrive to get along somehow without our being there. Are you two girls church-members?"

Another startling transition! The girls exchanged glances, each wishing that the other would answer. At last, Lucia, ashamed of the silence, admitted that they were not.

"Well, why aren't you? That seems queer business. One wouldn't think you were the grand-children of Daniel Cameron. Your father joined the church when he was thirteen years old; and a nicer, more faithful boy in church and Sunday-school I don't believe there ever was. Aren't none of you young folks church-members? The boys are, I should hope."

Mrs. Cameron felt obliged to answer this.

"No, McLoyd and Rodney are good boys, quite as good as some church-members I could mention. They have never given us cause for special anxiety; but none of our children have felt called upon to unite with any church. That isn't everything, Eunice."

"Of course not. Who ever thought it was? But it is what one might expect from Daniel Cameron's grand-children. Edward must have changed a good deal since he was a boy. I hope he doesn't often rush off as he did this morning."

Mrs. Cameron could not help a sigh of anxiety as she replied to this last remark.

"He is nearly always in a hurry; he has to work very hard—too hard for his strength. But we were later than usual this morning. We delayed breakfast in order to let you rest after your journey."

"I! Goodness, I was up and had my windows open airing my room a full hour before your bell rang. Nobody has me for an excuse for laziness, I can tell you."

Perhaps sufficient illustration has been given to suggest the general character of the new inmate of the Cameron family. A stern, strong-minded, rigidly upright, narrow, Christian woman. One who for years had carefully repressed anything like tenderness in her disposition, and judged her neighbor rigidly by the rules which she thought she applied to herself. One consequence of her training was that she failed in the very things which she most desired to accomplish. Perhaps above all other interests she truly desired the advancement of the Kingdom of Christ in the world, and perhaps it is not extravagant to say that she never spoke to a person on the subject without antagonizing him or her. It will readily be seen that her effort with the Cameron girls was not one calculated to win. She was not more successful with the father.

"Edward, what time do you have family worship? You flew off this morning without seeming to remember that there was such a thing; but I presume you do not live like heathen always. What is the supposed hour?"

"To tell you the truth," said the much embarrassed man, "we have not been having family worship of late years. As the children grew up, they were irregular about getting down to breakfast, and I was always in a hurry, and so—well, the fact is, we dropped it."

"Dear, dear!" said Aunt Eunice. "What next, I wonder? And you a son of Daniel Cameron! What would father say, do you suppose? I must say, Edward, I am disappointed. I judged from all I heard about your family that you were not what you used to be; but I did not suppose you had gone back on your early training like that."

"Isn't she a terror?" was Emilie's query, as she sought her elder sisters' room to relieve her mind. "Did you ever realize before, what an affliction it was to have Daniel Cameron for a grandfather? Poor father was utterly squelched tonight. I haven't seen him look so miserable since Rod got into his last scrape. I'm going to write to the boys, and tell them Aunt Eunice wants to know if they are church-members!" Whereupon she threw back her head and indulged in a merry laugh.

"If she is a specimen of the average church member," said Mary, "I hope I may be kept from ever joining their ranks. Of all the disagreeable, meddling old cranks I ever heard of, I think she is the worst. How we are ever to endure her until Christmas I cannot imagine."

And at that very moment the "disagreeable, meddling old crank" was on her knees, praying earnestly and most sincerely for her brother and his family, that they all might be turned from the error of their ways.

7. A "PECULIAR" MAN

Professor Landis was moving about his room, making ready for the day's duties. The university where he was engaged during the day was a long distance from Durand Avenue, making it necessary for him to take lunch downtown; so he must make ready for an all day's absence. His sister Dorothy, whose hours were earlier than his, had departed in the eight o'clock car; so he was practically alone. This being the case, he indulged himself in his favorite pastime of singing as loud as his lungs would permit. As he moved leisurely about, doing little last things, he let his splendid bass voice out in full power, so that it rolled through the quiet house like a trumpet. He was mistaken in supposing that he had no listeners. Said Aunt Eunice, on the other side of the dividing wall:

"Do hear that man roar! It is to be hoped that the rest of the family are deaf and dumb."

"There is no family," said Emilie, to whom was often left the duty of replying to her Aunt Eunice's remarks.

"You don't mean to say that he lives in that big house all alone?"

"It isn't very big; it is as like ours as two peas in a pod. And his sister lives with him; but she teaches, I guess. Anyway, she goes off early every morning, with her arms full of books; so he is alone except for the girl in the basement. He often roars around like that. I like it. I think his voice is splendid."

"And what does he do for a living?"

"Why, he teaches too, somewhere. At least we think so. They call him Professor Landis."

"Humph! And so he and she live all alone. I suppose they are orphans; I should think it would be cheaper to board, especially as they have to keep a servant. But I suppose they both get good salaries and choose to live it all up. That is the way young folks do nowadays. When I was a girl we lived on as little as we could, and saved the rest, or spent it on some of the family who needed our help. Mercy! I don't like his voice; it sounds like distant thunder."

Entirely unconscious of criticism, Professor Landis paused long enough to look thoughtfully at a bit of paper on which was written a couple of names, then placed it in his diary, and began on the last verse of the hymn he loved:

> "If our love were but more simple,
>   We should take Him at his word;
> And our lives would be all sunshine
>   In the sweetness of our Lord."

Then, his own preparations completed, came the last thing before leaving the house. This professor of Latin dropped on his knees and prayed. If people who wondered at some of his ways could have heard that prayer, it would have given them a hint of the motive power of his life. It was not a lengthy prayer; manifestly the words were spoken by one who was very familiar with the Friend whom he addressed. There was no introduction, nothing of the usual formula of prayer. It would have given a listener the impression, which would have been a true one, that the man had prayed before this same morning, and now was only claiming a parting word before he went out into the world. He asked for a special blessing on the scholars who should that day come under his care; that his influence in the class might be such as would some way hint of the Leader whose colors he wore. He asked for two or three, individually, referring briefly to the reason why they lay so close to his heart. More than that, he asked for the right word to say to any whom he should chance to pass, to and from his duties that day. He remembered those to whom he would have no chance to say a word, and begged that if possible, by look or smile, or courtesy of some sort, he might help to make their day brighter and better. In short he asked to be Christ-like that day.

Happy the mother who can send her boy out from home each morning to the care and influence of such a teacher. He is subject to a thousand temptations and strains which she does not and cannot understand. She will never know, perhaps, how much she owes to the influence of the thoroughly consecrated teacher, or that it is because of him that the boy bears the strain. Never mind; God knows. It was the living up to the spirit of such prayers as these which made of Professor Landis a man whom some called "peculiar." He had heard the name applied to him; and, while certainly he did not seek to win it, yet he was in no wise disturbed thereby. In truth, he liked the word. As often as he heard it, there came to his heart the memory of the strong old words of promise: "Now therefore if ye will obey my voice indeed, and keep my covenant, then ye shall be a peculiar treasure unto me." This young man frankly confessed to his own heart that he coveted for himself that promise. His exalted ambition was to be a peculiar treasure to the Lord Christ.

It was the spirit born of intimate companionship with this Friend of his which led him, as he stood on the platform of the crowded streetcar beside the red-faced, gruff-voiced driver, to say pleasantly, "It is too bad to crowd you so that you cannot have room for your stool. When we get the cable on this line you will have it easier, will you not?"

"Humph!" the man said. "More like, I won't have it at all. A lot of us fellows will get turned off then, and have to lie idle for a spell, and live on nothing while we're doing it. That's the way them new-fangled things always work."

Perhaps a dozen times before, in the course of the previous two weeks, had this street-car driver whose heart was sore over expected trouble for himself and family, made a similar comment concerning the new arrangements which were being watched for eagerly by the passengers. A dozen times had he received either no reply at all, or a good-natured, "Oh, maybe not," or a half-sneering, "You fellows always look on the dark side, don't you?" and then a dismissal of himself and his trouble from their minds. But the thirteenth time he mentioned it Professor Landis was the listener.

"Is there fear of that?" he asked. Then followed question and answer in rapid succession, until the young professor, who had never met the man before—he having been temporally transferred to that part of the line—knew more about his affairs, it is quite safe to say, than did any of the men for whom he had been working for a year or more. Also, the professor had gotten out a little book, and noted down name and residence, and an item or two about the man's boy who was ill, and made, in curious little characters which the man could not have read had be been given opportunity, certain suggestions to himself for future use; and then had said:

"The next corner is mine, Mr. Styver. I am coming to see that boy of yours on Saturday if I can; my time is full until then. Meantime, here is my card; and if your fears are realized about being discharged, bring that card to my address on any day after five o'clock, and I will see what can be done towards getting you work. Now, will you give the boy this little book from me, and will you keep this one yourself, and take a peep into it at some odd moment?"

The books were not three inches long, either of them. The boy's had one or two bright pictures in it, and some cheery words. The man's was a collection of very carefully chosen and most striking Bible verses, which Professor Landis had arranged for his use. The driver, who was known to his portion of the outside world as "No. 17," looked after the young man curiously as he sprang from the car and went with rapid strides down the street.

"He's a *chap*, he is!" he said to himself, as he strained his eyes to see what would become of the strange man. "I never hit on his like before. I'm blest if I don't keep the little book, and take a look into it, too, jest for his sake." And he put both of them carefully away with the card which had been offered first.

One other incident occurred during the progress of that car downtown which deserves to be chronicled. Aunt Eunice Cameron was also one of the passengers. She had hailed the car at a crossing between it and another line, and she left soon after Professor Landis did. Now, Aunt Eunice was a tract distributor; one of the kind who are, after their fashion, "instant in season and out of season," and are always rebuking, reproving, and exhorting the world. As Aunt Eunice brushed past the driver she said, "Here, sir, is a tract for you. If you will read it, which I don't suppose you will, it will do you good."

"You're right there," said Mr. Styver. "I won't read a word of it, nor keep it neither. I know your kind, and I've got no use for you." Thereupon he threw the meek little leaflet after her. Another specimen was No. 17 of the total depravity of mankind. What is the use in trying to do good in the world, if this is the result? If people could only be induced to undertake the work that they could do, instead of being apparently possessed of Satan to be forever dabbling with that which they cannot do! As for sincerity, not Professor Landis himself was more thoroughly in earnest than was Aunt Eunice.

That gentleman stayed his steps just at the door of the Public Library, and held out his hand to a young fellow of perhaps nineteen—unmistakably a country youth, who had not been in town long enough to wear away a certain rusticity of manner. His face this morning wore a gloomy expression, and his heavy eyes told a story which would probably have filled his country mother's heart with anxiety.

The face lighted just a little under Professor Landis's cordial greeting.

"Ah, Ben, good-morning. I have been hoping I should meet you. We missed you last night."

"Did you?" said Ben; and he smiled grimly, the look on his face suggesting that he felt tempted to add, "I don't believe a word of it!"

"*I* certainly did," said Professor Landis, moved perhaps by the look to drop the plural form. "I was much disappointed. Were you engaged at the store?"

"No, sir." Ben would have liked to say that he was. He hesitated; but the Professor waited, with those steady, inquiring eyes fixed on him. "I went somewhere else," he said at last.

"To a better place, Ben?"

The blood crept slowly into the sun-burned face. "A place where the most of them were better pleased to see me," he said with a slow laugh. Then, after another pause, "It is of no use, Professor Landis. I can't feel at home in the places where you want me to go. The folks wear different clothes from mine, and act and talk different. I don't know how to do it, and I don't want to be stared at, nor laughed at, nor patronized. There are places to go to where folks aren't so particular; and where some of them, at least, don't know any more than I do myself."

"Good places, Ben? Places which you like to describe in your letters to your mother?"

Again the red showed plainly on his face, and the answer came slower than before. "They are not the worst places in the world, by any means. Some of the boys are real kind, and often there isn't much to find fault with."

"In the opinion of mothers do you mean?"

Ben laughed faintly. "Mothers are very particular," he said.

"Yes; they are. Good mothers always are; and good sons like to honor even their notions. You and I ought to remember that. I have been separated from my mother most of the time for five years; yet I leave undone to this day certain things which I would like well enough to do, and in which I see no danger, because I am sure they would distress my mother. As it is, she feels, I believe, that she can absolutely trust me."

The younger man looked up at him with a gleam of appreciation in his eyes. Evidently he admired the character which he made no pretence of imitating.

Professor Landis changed his position so that his hand could be rested familiarly on Ben's arm; then he said in winning tones, "Ben, my boy, I wish you would make up your mind to be a little more independent."

The boy started, and looked puzzled. Clearly, if there was anything on which he prided himself, it was independence. That he was not able, as he expressed it, "to hold up his head with the best of them," was the main reason why Professor Landis found it so hard to win him to places where he might have been helped.

"I mean it," the professor said, smiling. "If you were able to rise superior to the question of dress, and to the fact that you, being still quite young, do not yet know all the customs of society, and determine to mix only with people who could help you in these directions as well as in some others, and whose acquaintance it would be an honor to have, it would make a radical difference in your life."

"Oh!" said Ben. "Well, now, Professor Landis, that isn't so easy a thing to do as it sounds. You folks who have lived in cities all your lives, and had things, and been to places, and all that, don't know a thing about it. If folks were all like—well, like you," raising his head with a determined air, as though resolved that it must be said, "it would make a big difference. But to feel that you are making mistakes all the while, and that you don't know what to do with your feet or your hands, and that you haven't got a thing about you which is up to time anyhow, and to hear a giggle every now and then behind your back, and see pretty near a sneer before your eyes, isn't the pleasantest experience in the world, I can tell you. Folks who must go somewhere or freeze aren't to be blamed for choosing decent loafing places instead of such gatherings, I think."

"Didn't I admit that it was not easy? I said it required independence of spirit above the average; I thoroughly mean it. It is true I do not think the giggles nor the sneers are by any means so numerous as they seem to you; although I admit that even in what is called good society, one comes in contact with some underbred people who indulge in both. What I deplore is the fact that Benjamin Reeder, a young man whose mother and father depend upon and trust, has not independence of character sufficient to pass these experiences by with the indifference which they deserve, and make the most of his opportunities in spite of them. Last evening, for instance, at the church social, we had some very choice people present, whose acquaintance it is decidedly worth one's while to make; but the young man of whom I speak lost the opportunity, and if I am not greatly mistaken, spent the evening in a way which he will not describe to his mother when he writes that long letter for which she waits. One of these days the young man's heart will ache because of the places he left blank in those letters. Be sure she notices the evenings about which he is silent; I am afraid she even cries over them. It is a way mothers have; and the days will surely come when he cannot reach her with letters. If I were he, I would make them wellsprings of joy to her while I had her."

Evidently he knew his boy. Ben Reeder's eyes drooped and dimmed. He had not been so long away from the country home that his heart had ceased to beat the faster at the sound of his mother's name; and there were times, at least, when he wanted nothing in life so much as to please her.

The two men were moving slowly down the street together now. Professor Landis had gone as far in this direction as his work led him; but no matter, the Master's work seemed to call him a few steps farther. He saw the impression he had made, and waited in silence for a moment. But his next sentence was a mistake.

"Did young Myers stop for you last evening?"

Ben's face darkened. "Yes, sir, he did; and if you will be kind enough to let him know that he needn't try to patronize me anymore, I'll be glad. I think likely that is the reason why I finally gave up going. I can't stand his airs nor his advice. He told me last night that if I'd wear a different necktie I would look less queer; he even offered to lend me one of the right kind. I came pretty near kicking him downstairs to pay for it. My necktie may not be just the right shape, but it is my own, and was bought with honest money. I don't want to rig up in any borrowed finery. Besides that, there isn't a worse giggler in the crowd than this same Myers. I don't want to have anything to do with him nor his kind. He and that Miss Hudson that he goes with so much were giggling for all they were worth the other night at the concert. I knew it was about me; anybody could see that at a glance; and I suppose it was my necktie that tickled them, though what is the matter with it, I'm sure I don't know. It is new and clean; and there were ten thousand others like it in the store where I bought it; so it must be in fashion for somebody."

And then Professor Landis knew, by a bell which began at the moment to twang, that he must leave this part of the Vineyard and make haste to other work.

"I am sorry," was all he had time to say to Ben; then he went swiftly back over the ground which he had slowly traversed, thinking deeply as he went. Not only had his question been a mistake, tossing Ben's thoughts suddenly back upon his own uncomfortable experiences, but evidently his experiment with young Myers had been, also. Myers was one of his students; a merry-hearted, good-natured sort of a fellow, who had never so much as thought of doing or trying to do for others. Though a young man of means and of assured position, these seemed of so little consequence to him, that it occurred to his Latin professor to send him in search of Reeder, in hopes that his free-and-easy ways might put the boy more at his ease, and that he himself might get really interested in the effort, and begin to think of something besides his own amusement. He had shown him carefully, he thought, the sort of boy Reeder was, and the sort of help he needed. Neckties, though unmentioned, were certainly among the list of things wherein help was needed, but what a disastrous way to undertake it!

"That hardly seems like Myers," he said to himself, going over Ben's story. "He seems to care extremely little about dress and conventionalities of that sort, and yet to be thoroughly posted. But I am distressed that I sent him after Ben. If I could have gotten the foolish boy to the social last evening, I could have introduced him, I think, to one or two persons who might have helped him. I wonder if Miss Hudson's influence over Myers is calculated to destroy what little there may be in him to be used for service? Both of them among the 'gigglers'! Poor Ben!"

And through the disturbed brain of this Christian worker there ran a phrase somewhat after this fashion: "For neckties and giggles 'shall the weak brother perish for whom Christ died?'"

8. A Lesson in Fanaticism

It was later in the day by several hours when Professor Landis finally reached the Public Library, whither his steps had been tending when he met young Reeder. In fact, the working hours of the day were over. It had been an unusually busy day in the university; but the professor who had gone to his duties from his knees had not for a moment forgotten Whom he served, and had kept that part of the service uppermost. In consequence of this, who shall be able to estimate the work he had done that day? Work of which even he had no knowledge. In fact, his part was only to drop the seed. He had not been able, even with other crowding cares, to keep young Reeder out of his thoughts. He was troubled for the frank-faced boy who had a mother in the country watching hungrily for each mail, in the hope—oftentimes, he feared, the vain hope—that she might hear from her boy. There were rumors, which he trusted did not reach the mother, that would have given her some definite anxiety. Not that Ben Reeder had gone far astray; many people would not have thought him astray at all. In fact, among his associates he was called "the deacon," because there were so many things he would not do. But Professor Landis had high ideals; and he believed that mothers were "very particular," as Ben put it.

Still thinking of Ben, he almost ran against Miss Cameron as she stood at one of the tables turning over a pile of books which had been brought her.

"I beg your pardon," he said, and then scrutinized the girl's face closely. It always arrested his thoughts, because there was unrest written on it so distinctly. His acquaintance with the Camerons had not progressed rapidly. Miss Cameron had so manifestly desired to avoid his company that Professor Landis had hesitated, since the night when she all but sent him away from her porch. He told himself then, that perhaps he would better leave her entirely to Dorothy; she was evidently not one whom he could reach. Yet as often as he met her in street-car or on the street, her face would always oblige him to leave other thoughts, and wonder if there were really nothing he could do for her.

Today came in force the very impression which he had had several times before, concerning her. The girl was brooding over herself; some trouble, real or fancied, was eating her strength away. If she could get interested in someone else, someone whom she could help, would it not help her? He thought of Ben Reeder. Had the two an idea in common on which one could seize? Oh, she could undoubtedly do much for Ben—this girl who had brothers, and so understood boys and their needs and temptations; this girl who had a home to which she could occasionally invite the homeless boy. But would she? While he decided to sacrifice a little more time in order to see whether this latest idea would develop, he began a desultory conversation with her, watching for the right opening for his thought.

"Do you come here for books, Miss Cameron? Comparatively few people seem to have found this branch of the library. I find it much more convenient than the one farther uptown. Are you looking for anything special? Perhaps I can aid you." This as she pushed the pile of books impatiently from her and drew a catalogue nearer.

"Nothing special. I am looking for something which I care to read. No, you couldn't help me. I want an unmitigated novel. I do not suppose you allow such wickedness on your lists."

"Are novels wicked?" he asked with a smile.

"I suppose so; from the standpoint of particular people. Everything that is interesting is more or less wicked is it not?"

"That depends. I know some interesting things which I would not enter in that list. What sort of novels do you like, Miss Cameron?"

"The unmitigated ones, as I told you. I like to read about real people; not the affected effigies which they put into the 'goody' books."

"Howells, for instance?"

Miss Cameron made a gesture of disgust. "No, indeed. I never read Howells if I can find anything else to pass the time. He is much *too* real. There are troubles enough, in the commonplace line, of one's own, without wading through his books, which sound as though he had merely written out what he saw on the street."

"That strikes me as one of the finest compliments to Howells's genius that I have heard in some time. But since you evidently do not like 'real' things after all, tell me if you ever indulge in one of my favorites. Do you read Miss Warner?"

If her face had shown disgust over Howells's name, how shall its expression now be described? "You cannot mean the old-fashioned Miss Warner, with her interminable 'Wide, Wide World' and 'Queechy' and 'The Hills of —' something or other!" she said.

"Ah, but I do! She is the very Miss Warner, with her 'Say and Seal' and her 'Old Helmet,' and all the other creations of her earnest brain. I am glad to find you familiar with her."

"I am not. You give me too much credit. It was a spasm of my childhood, long since passed. Professor Landis, it is not possible that you can intend to seriously commend her writings!"

"Why not?"

"Because she is not worthy of it. From a literary point of view, which I supposed a teacher would feel bound to consider, I am sure she is of no account; and as for her characters—because I do not like the hopelessly commonplace realism of Howells, it does not follow that I can be satisfied with the impossible immaculateness of her everlasting hero or heroine. It is the same person always, whether in masculine or feminine dress, and the most improbable one imaginable."

"I have heard that criticism before. It never strikes me as quite fair. It ignores the possible design in the author's mind."

"Oh, her design was to make all the money she could, I suppose; but it really surprises me to hear you commending her. Gentlemen generally appreciate the weakness of her characters."

"Do you think them weak? I frankly affirm that I do not."

"But, Professor Landis, isn't marked unnaturalness an element of weakness? The literary critics all say so; and Miss Warner will bear off the palm for that characteristic, I am sure. Did you ever meet such a being, for instance, as her wonderful young man? Never mind whether his name be John, or Winthrop, or Mr. Rhys, he is the same person. Do you know him, Professor Landis?"

"I admit at the outset that I have never met him; but may I ask you one question? Are the characters you have mentioned better than the Pattern?"

"The pattern?" she repeated in genuine bewilderment. This young woman was so unused to meeting a religious thought in ordinary conversation that her mind did not take in his meaning.

"Yes, the Lord Jesus Christ. He came among us for that purpose, among others, you remember. Has Miss Warner succeeded in imagining a human being superior to him?"

"Of course not. But she has tried to make a human being like him; and that makes the whole unnatural."

"I beg pardon, but what is a copy worth unless one strives to attain to it? Let us suppose an artist with a perfect model, quarrelling with it, wishing to clip off a bit of the ear, or the cheek, or the forehead, because he cannot hope to copy it in absolute perfection."

"I do not think the cases parallel, Mr. —I beg your pardon—*Professor* Landis. The artist struggles after perfection, but does not expect to attain; and when occasionally one poses as having done so, we naturally dislike him."

He made no reference to her marked use of his title, but passed it by as of too little consequence to notice, and gave himself to her illustration.

"In life, I grant you that such is the case. But have you not touched upon the special realm of religious fiction? Should it not be the aim of the Christian writer to portray, so far as he or she may be able, characters as they would be if the Lord Christ had all the power over their lives which he ought to have? In other words, must not religious fiction, in order to have the right to be, deal with humanity, not so much as it is, but as it might be if it would? Not that we would have all fictitious characters of that type. If I remember correctly, some of Miss

Warner's creations are intensely human; but the power of
her work to me is that she tries in each book to present
one person, at least, who has reached the place spiritually
which we all believe that those who profess to follow
Christ ought to reach. It is not the impossible, after all,
which she represents, but the unusual."

Miss Cameron made that peculiar gesture of hers
which meant dissent and slight annoyance.

"I am not fond of religious fiction," she said. "I prefer
authors who leave it out of their thoughts entirely, as not
suited to fiction, and deal with life as they find it."

"Ah, but do not such authors deal with life as they
find it? I grant you that those who ignore it are
numerous. One may revel in fiction for a lifetime, and not
so much as suspect that there is such a factor as
Christianity at work in the world; but isn't that, after all,
the most unnatural of all forms of fiction? Are not the
great facts of human sin and human suffering present
everywhere to be accounted for? Is not death a real and
fully illustrated power in our very midst? Isn't this life at
its best very short? Shall we talk about that being natural
writing which ignores these three great elements that
sooner or later enter into all our lives?"

"It is not ignored," said Miss Cameron, speaking
indignantly. "What can you mean? Some of the finest
passages of modern fiction have to do with sin and
suffering; and as for death—tragedy, I am sure, has a
prominent place in all great novels."

"Granted; but isn't it ignoring a subject to present only the bare outlines of facts, and dwell upon the results without an attempt to reach to the cause or the remedy? Without even a hint, indeed, that a cause is known or a remedy suggested? Nothing is more bewildering to me in modern fiction, than the coolness with which men and women write volume after volume, ignoring the one great, ever-present, ever-working Factor in human history. The reverent student of history sees nothing plainer in every volume he reads than God's hand, shaping, controlling, guiding. The great writers of fiction seem to a great extent to have forgotten Him. So entirely has it become the custom to ignore Christianity as a powerful agent in human affairs, that certain critics have given themselves to criticizing the few who remember it. I recall reading but a few days ago, a book review written in a semi-commendatory tone, in which the writer, having found some points which he was kind enough to approve, added: 'To be sure, her characters have an astonishing way of changing their natures all of a sudden, and growing surprisingly patient and forgiving and the like; but this is pardonable, perhaps, in fiction, and the tone of the whole is helpful.' I have not quoted literally, but that is the idea. I remember it distinctly, because it was reviewing a book with which I happened to be familiar, and I realized that in just so flippant a way as that, the tremendous fact of conversion had been disposed of. Doesn't that seem very strange to you, Miss Cameron? We live in a world which witnesses every day to these marvelous changes; men who have been in the depths of drunkenness or worse—if there is a worse state than that—men and women who have been all that is low and vile and terrible, become suddenly new creatures, with changed appetites and desires and motives, and the fiction-writing world looks on and smiles, and writes its stories of human lives, and is silent about the greatest event which can happen to any life."

"Still, some people do not believe in these things," said Miss Cameron. It was a weak answer, and she knew it; but he had paused suddenly in his outburst, and was looking at her as though he was waiting for a reply.

"That is not true," he said quickly. "I beg your pardon. I mean that there are facts in the world which reasonable beings do not deny. No one in his senses, for instance, who is at all cognizant of events as they are occurring in our large cities, but must admit that there are men and women who a year ago were fair representatives of all that is evil, and who today are living earnest, worthy lives; and if they choose to inquire into the facts, they can learn that these changes were sudden; not that the lives became in a day as distinctly changed as they are now, but that the desires and inclinations were changed, oftentimes in a moment; and they can learn that without exception these people who have been so changed, attribute it all to the power of one Jesus Christ. Also they know, all of them, that they live in a land which acknowledges in its civil government, in its schools and colleges, in its very dates even, the power of this same Factor. Why, in fiction—which professes to represent life as it is—do they think it natural to utterly ignore Him, or in their reviews of those who do *not,* speak of his work almost with a sneer?"

Despite her want of interest in the speaker, Miss Cameron could not but be interested in his theme. She was a thoughtful girl, in certain lines. She was capable of understanding intelligent conversation; and the humiliating fact was that she had belonged all her life in a social circle where, by common consent, anything serious or earnest in the way of conversation was purposely put aside. For a young woman who was not by nature flippant, this was hard. She gravely considered what had been said to her, and admitted that there was truth in it.

"Still," she said thoughtfully, recalling the belief, or rather the unbelief, of some of her favorite writers of fiction, "if people are not believers in Jesus Christ, how can they write of his work?"

"But, my dear Miss Cameron, Jesus Christ is a *fact* in history. Sane people cannot ignore him. He lived and died; nothing that we have to do with in the past is more certainly attested than this. He is to be accounted for in some way. It is folly for writers of fiction, above all others, to ignore him; for whether they like it or not, he has had more to do with life in the present and in the past than has any other name in history. If they are to write of things as they are, or were, with any show of sincerity, they must have to do with him. But I ought to beg your pardon. I did not mean to give a lecture on fiction. I have had to give two lectures in class today, and seem to have gotten into the mood. I had it in mind to speak to you on an entirely different subject, one which has occupied my thoughts much today. Miss Cameron, if you could help a human being who is in need of help, I am surely right in thinking you would like to do it, am I not?"

She was on her guard in a moment. This fanatical young man, who wanted even novels to be impossibly good, should not inveigle her into any philanthropic scheme.

"Perhaps so," she said coldly; "though I consider the 'if' with which your sentence began an important one. I do not believe I can help anybody. I am not one of those persons of whom you have been speaking; and I do not know how to be of use in the world, even if my tastes lay in that direction, which they do not."

"Do you mean that you are not personally acquainted with Jesus Christ?"

The color flamed into her face. She had never in her life before been spoken to directly on this subject. The manner in which it was now done struck her as strange. Certainly she knew a good deal about Jesus Christ; she had heard of him since her babyhood; she used to kneel beside her crib and lisp his name. "And this I ask for Jesus' sake," was as familiar to her as her own name; yet she did not feel acquainted with him, and she was a truthful girl.

"I suppose I am not," she said, trying to smile; "but that seems a strange way of putting it."

"It is really the only way of putting it, Miss Cameron. Believe me, one cannot have an actual personal acquaintance with him without having it color one's life, permeate one's desires and motives, change one's nature indeed. I wish that I might be permitted to introduce him to you. I can recommend him as the truest, wisest, most faithful friend and helper that human being ever knew."

"I do not understand you," she said coldly; "and I will confess that that sounds to me like fanaticism."

"Yes, I have no doubt it does. That is because you and he are not friends. He does not force his friendship, Miss Cameron; but how can you help desiring it? However, there is a sense in which that has not to do with the work of which I was speaking. It is only common human kindness of which I am in search. There is a young friend of mine, a mere boy indeed, scarcely twenty, who has recently come from a country home. He has been well brought up, and has a good mother; but he is having his first experience of city life. He finds himself bewildered; accustomed in the country to associate with the best people, and to feel on terms of equality with them, he discovers himself to be quite alone here. He has become identified with a church, because his mother wished it; that is, he has rented a sitting in its gallery, and is, or was, reasonably regular in attendance; but he has no at-home feeling anywhere. His clothes are not quite what he finds other young men wearing; his manners are not the same as theirs. These things he feels, but does not know how to correct. What he needs imperatively and very soon is friends; women with whom he can feel at ease, and who in a hundred little indescribable ways can help tide him over a dangerous period in his life into safe waters. Do you get the idea? I have longed for a home which had a mother in it, and safety and kindliness. I find it difficult to express just what I want; but it is something which true women can give to boys younger than themselves, and I am not sure that any other human beings can. I have tried young men, and they are partial failures. It is a curious fact that boys will take from a woman whom they respect the help which they will not allow one of their own sex to give. It is very commonplace help for which I am seeking. If Ben knew how to enter and leave a room; how to conduct himself in accordance with the common courtesies of life; what it would be proper and improper to do at a well-appointed table—oh, a score of things which people are supposed to breathe in unconsciously, and which they do, more or less, in cultured atmospheres. It is these common and, in a sense, unimportant things that are shutting Ben out from the companionship which he needs, and forcing him almost into a companionship in which he feels at ease, but which will injure him and hurt his mother."

Why was he telling all this to her? He actually questioned it himself, even while he talked. Certainly she had not given him reason to hope that she could or would do anything for anybody. Yet there was a sudden softening of her face even while he waited, and the eyes which drooped from before his gaze were misty.

A vague wish she felt for the moment that she were the sort of woman which he seemed to fancy her—a woman who could do kind things in the world, helpful things. This country boy, for instance, who felt out of place in the city. She had had something of the feeling; there had been circles in which she had felt quite out of place, not because she did not know how to act, nor what it would be proper to say under given circumstances, but because her dress was not such as made her feel at ease among the other guests. Oh, she could imagine very well what it was to Ben! She would really like to help him, but how could she? What would Lucia think, or her mother for that matter? And what was there she could do anyway? Rod and Mac had never felt the need of any help from her, had never sought her in any way. She knew no more about boys than did other girls who had not brothers. It was absurd to think that she could do anything.

The hour for closing the library had arrived, and nothing had been accomplished. Professor Landis could only apologize for monopolizing her time, and then both had to leave without the books for which they had come a long distance. They separated at the door, for Mr. Landis had an errand in another direction. He walked away with a grave face, telling himself that he feared it had been a wasted hour. Of what use to talk about poor Ben to a young woman who did not know any way of peace for her own feet to tread? If he could only help this girl who seemed in such sore need of help! He wondered why it should be so difficult to say the right word to her. He had told her he wished she would allow him to introduce his Master; but he had not done so. Instead of attempting it, he had drawn her thought away from her own sore need, and talked of Ben! Well, perhaps he was not the one to influence her; but in that case, why was she so often in his mind?

9. HOME THRUSTS

As for Mary Cameron, her homeward walk was an exceedingly disturbed one. Try as she would to put some of the sentences which had been spoken away from her, they clung. She had affected to be skeptical over certain statements which Professor Landis had made, but in her heart she knew she believed them.

She had not lived an utterly blinded life thus far. Limited as was her practical knowledge of Christianity, she could call to mind remarkable changes of character in persons known to her; yes, and sudden changes. Was not Tim Nolan in the old days one of the trials of her uncle's life? Did he not at least three times a month appear at the office with bleared eyes and blackened face, and humbly confess that he had been "at it again"? Was he not discharged regularly once a month, and hired again because he confessed such penitence and made such strong promises, and because her uncle was sorry for his wife and children, and could not help a lurking feeling of interest in Tim himself? Had there not come a week in which he lost all patience, and declared that he had now discharged Tim Nolan for the last time; that he had been on a spree for five consecutive days, and was in worse condition than ever before; that it was worse than useless to try to do anything more for him; and demoralizing to the other men to keep giving him chances? And then, did not Tim Nolan appear to him one morning with clean-shaven face, and clothes neatly mended, and with a look in his eyes such as had not been seen there before, and beg for one more trial, promising that if he failed this time he would not ask again for mercy? Had they not laughed at their uncle for being too credulous and tender-hearted, in that he tried him again, after all?

And then, oh, marvel of marvels, Tim Nolan stayed! He took no more "sprees;" he lost no more time; he passed directly by the saloon where his earnings had been regularly spent; he went to church and to prayer-meeting; yes, more than that, he *took part* in the prayer-meeting!

They had laughed about it at the time, they girls, it seemed so absurd to think of Tim Nolan having anything to say that was worth saying. But their uncle had unwittingly spoken the truth; he never discharged him again. Tim had been suddenly, mysteriously, completely changed. The things which he used to love he apparently began to hate. The companions whom he had sought but the week before as friends, he began to shun as enemies. And when he was asked, as some of the curious asked him, to give a reason for this strange change, he was wont to say solemnly:

"One night the Lord Jesus Christ came to me, and got hold of me somehow, and I ain't the same man I was; nor ain't like to be."

Tim Nolan was a living witness to her conscience that the words which had been spoken to her about Jesus Christ that afternoon were true. Moreover, she could recall other instances, some of them quite as marked as this. Changes which had been marveled over in her circle of friends. There was young Dr. Powelton; a cultured, scholarly skeptic. Sneering in a gentlemanly way one day about the "superstitions of modern religion," the next, on his knees in the presence of some of those before whom he had sneered, vowing allegiance henceforth to Jesus Christ. Yes, and keeping faith with him! Being from that hour so changed a man that they could but speak of it for a time, whenever his name was mentioned.

"Without exception people so changed attribute it to the power of Jesus Christ." This was what Professor Landis had said, and it was true. There were witnesses enough known to her, and always the same Name to stand for! Yes, it was folly to ignore such a power in the world as this. It was silly to write books about life, and pass in silence a force which was able to pervade all life.

As her judgment made this admission, there came to Mary Cameron for the first time a vague longing to realize that force in her own nature. What a thing it would be to be suddenly changed! To begin tomorrow morning, for instance, and show by her life that she was another person. It is true the change would not be so marked as in Tim Nolan or in Dr. Powelton; but Mary Cameron, being an honest person, told herself frankly that there was opportunity enough for change in her, that would be noticeable. She knew herself to be growing steadily in irritability. Each day it became more difficult to keep even a show of patience with Aunt Eunice; and Lucia had always aggravated her in dozens of petty ways. As for Emilie, everyone knew how utterly unendurable a girl of fifteen or sixteen could be on occasion. Yet there are people who manage to live in peace, even with such provocations.

She went swiftly back over the recent past, and could not recall a morning for days, hardly for weeks, in which something rasping had not come up for conversation; something which had led her to say words for which she was sorry a moment afterwards.

"It is all Aunt Eunice's fault," she told herself bitterly. "A saint from heaven could not have patience with her." Yet no sooner had she admitted the thought than she was obliged to add to it that they had been far from peaceful before Aunt Eunice's arrival. In short, it was the habit of her life to differ with Lucia, and discuss the most trivial things until they came to sharp words, especially if Emilie were at home to aggravate her. She was even sharp to her mother, and spoke often to her father in a way which she did not herself approve. Oh, there certainly was opportunity for great improvement in her outward life.

There were also other ways in which she admitted that she would like to be different. Professor Landis was fond of the word "peace." He had it often on his lips. He seemed to think it possible for one to be always at peace, no matter what the outward circumstances of life might be. *Was* it possible to have such a friendship with this One who seemed so mysterious to her, and over whose name Mr. Landis's voice lingered with reverent love— such a friendship as would calm all the turbulence of life, smooth out the crooked ways, atone for slights and disappointments and discouragements? She did not believe it; yet might it not be worth trying for? There was a power about it all which she did not understand, which she had never felt. What if she should decide now and here to give herself to this new life? She had ceased praying long ago; rather, she had ceased observing the outward form, save as she bowed her head in church with the others; but it is doubtful if her thoughts roved more freely there than they had in her earlier days, when she went down on her knees before retiring, and thought she prayed. It seems a startling thing to say of a fairly well-educated young woman in this Christian land, of a believer in, and outward supporter of, Christianity; but I suppose it is true that she had never prayed.

She weighed the possibilities now, much as she might have weighed the question whether she should or should not go to the lecture that evening. Should she take a new stand; begin to pray, to read her Bible, to go to church regularly, and to prayer-meeting, and honestly try to follow Christ? She had never given it careful consideration before, but why should she not? She was tired of all her surroundings; nothing in or about her home or her life was quite as she wished it. Why not have it utterly different? In short, why not try Christianity for all it was worth? She did not settle the question; but as she applied the latch-key to their own door, she *almost* thought she would.

Matters inside offered abundant opportunity for the exercise of any new virtues she could command. Betsey, whose duty it was to attend to the furnace during the day, had evidently forgotten it, and the sitting-room was cold. Aunt Eunice, wrapped in an ugly shawl, was shivering over the register and grumbling about trying to get warmth out of a "black hole in the floor."

"There isn't any fire here," she exclaimed, as Mary opened the door.

"Of course not," said Lucia coolly. "The fire is in the cellar, Aunt Eunice, not in that 'black hole.'"

"Well, I tell you, there isn't a speck of heat coming up; and it is as cold as a barn here. It always is, for that matter. I wonder we don't all get our deaths; and we shall before the winter is over."

"Why, Aunt Eunice, it was only this morning that you complained of the room being as hot as a furnace, and said it was so more than half the time."

"Well, that is just what I say now; it is always either too cold or too hot, never a decent, reasonable fire. What is the use of catching me up every word I say, like a pert girl as you are? Who is going to fix the fire? That is what I want to know. Your father is upstairs; why don't you call him, and tell him that the fire has gone out?"

"It is Betsey's business to attend to the fire," said Mary with dignity. Already she felt her half-formed resolution slipping away. She was cold, and the dimly lighted room looked very cheerless; and both Aunt Eunice and Lucia were evidently in ill-humor. What was the use in trying to be anything but miserable?

"Oh, *Betsey!*" echoed Aunt Eunice spitefully. "The things you expect of that girl she couldn't get through with in a day, if she was as smart as she is dull and stupid. I don't wonder she never gets her work done, I am sure. You put too much on her. If you two girls would stop your everlasting puttering over paint and embroidery, and do something, your mother wouldn't have such a hard time of it, and Betsey would stand a chance of getting her own work half way done. I never in my life saw such management as you have here! How Edward endures it I don't know. He was brought up very differently, I can tell you. The Camerons always had things in systematic order at their house; and each had his or her work to do."

"I wish our names were Rafferty instead of Cameron!" said Lucia, as she went hastily from the room; and she banged the door a little.

The atmosphere did not brighten as the evening drew on. They gathered presently at the dinner table, but Mr. Cameron was even more silent than usual. In fact, there was such an utterly miserable look on his face that the girls hesitated to address him, and their mother had evidently been crying.

"It is some money matter, of course," said Mary to herself; and it irritated her to think that they must always be haunted by that merciless fiend, Poverty.

Aunt Eunice harped upon the extinct fire, and upon the folly of expecting a blundering girl like Betsey to start it again, until Lucia, darting an angry look at her, asked if she didn't think it her Christian duty to go down and help Betsey, or perhaps make the fire in her stead. Somebody ought to adopt that girl, she affirmed, and send her to boarding-school. She was evidently out of her sphere in the kitchen; overworked and ill-treated, according to Aunt Eunice's views. It would be a virtuous act to report her to the society for the Prevention of Cruelty to—"Which, Aunt Eunice, Animals or Children?" she finished, turning toward her with a wicked smile on her face. "Betsey is rather old to be called a child; and it is only four-footed animals that the other society attends to, isn't it? I confess I don't know how to manage it."

It was mirthless fun. If Lucia had not been troubled over the question of what fresh calamity had disturbed her father and mother, she would not have indulged herself in it. Aunt Eunice deigned no reply. Even the semblance of conversation was dropped after that.

Mary, who had faint memories of her half-formed resolve hovering about her, fell to wondering what— suppose she were that changed person of whom they had talked that afternoon—would she do to brighten the gloom of this dinner-table. Suppose she were capable of making gentle, cheerful replies to Aunt Eunice, and of telling some pleasant bit of news, which would cheer her father, and of winning Lucia into a more amiable frame of mind? Something of that kind she felt sure one of Miss Warner's "goody" characters which she had criticized would essay to do. Well, would it not be a laudable act? Yes, but the trouble was, it could be done only in books. That was what she had meant to express to Professor Landis, the fact that it was only *book* people who succeed in doing these things.

Then her thoughts wandered to Ben Reeder. What was it that Mr. Landis wanted her to do for him? "A girl with a home" indeed! What good would a visit to such a home as theirs was tonight do to a lonesome boy? A well-lighted, well-warmed saloon, where the people were good-natured, would perhaps be preferable. As for her mother—she stole another glance at her downcast face. What could she have been crying about? What extra thing had happened, and they not told? They were treated as children; things which they ought to know kept from them. She was growing irritable again, less sure of her wish, even, to make that radical change in her character.

Into the midst of the silence and gloom of this dining-room came Emilie with the whirr and bustle peculiar to her, letting in a rush of cold air as she came, which caused Aunt Eunice to shiver, and draw her shawl closer about her. Emilie paid not the slightest attention to the gloom which enveloped the family.

"I've had such a lark!" she said, tossing schoolbooks and wraps in a promiscuous heap, and taking her place at the table. "Nannie Fuller and I have been away down to the skating-park. Oh, there are such lots and lots of people there this afternoon! The first really good skating of the season, they say. There are some new people, college boys I guess, splendid-looking fellows, and they skated exquisitely. I was just dying to skip in and join them. Father, I really must have a pair of skates. I would rather go without shoes than skates."

"You may have to do both," replied the father, with no lighting up of his worn face. But Emilie had already flitted to another subject.

"Why, Mary Cameron, have you reached home? I didn't expect you yet for hours. Did you come up on the car? What a commonplace way to finish a special afternoon! I thought you would walk. It is quite the fashion now for very particular friends to take long walks, when they have important matters to settle."

"What particular folly is uppermost with you just now?" asked Mary, in her coldest and most indifferent tone.

Emilie laughed gleefully. "You should have heard Nannie take off the scene; she is a perfect mimic. She told to the life just how Professor Landis gesticulated in the more exciting parts; and if you could have seen her draw herself up and pretend to look at him before she made reply, you would have thought it was your very self. I never saw anybody like Nannie for describing scenes."

"What is all that?" asked Lucia, growing interested, while Mary looked bewildered and annoyed. What *was* that silly girl talking about!

"Why, Nannie had been to the library, the branch one, you know, over on Duane Street; and there it seems she saw Professor Landis—and who should be his companion but our Mary! Nannie said it was as good as going to the play to watch them. Of course, she was not near enough to hear what was said, and she wouldn't have listened if she had been; but she said she did not need to hear in order to enjoy it. They talked for *hours,* and were both just as eager and interested as they could be. It was great fun to hear her tell about it. She took Mary off to the life. There they were, she said, surrounded by books, and neither of them looking into one. She came away and left them there; but her cousin Robert joined us while she was telling me about it, and said he could add the last chapter, that the librarian actually had to tell them that it was time to close that part of the building; and they went away without a book, after spending the afternoon there!"

"Really!" said Lucia, joining in the burst of laughter with which Emilie finished her sentence. "I should think that the parlor would have been a pleasanter place than the Public Library for a confidential interview. Still, I am thankful to have something accomplished. Are you to be congratulated, Mary?"

What was there in such utter nonsense to make Mary Cameron's eyes blaze with anger? The girl was too refined by nature to enjoy this species of amusement, and to do Lucia justice, she rarely descended to it; but Emilie was at the age and had such intimacies, that her temptations lay in just this direction. As a rule, her older sisters bore her attacks with at least outward indifference, and contented themselves by calling her a simpleton; but one glance at Mary's face this evening would have shown that she was in no mood for trifling.

In truth, the girl's heart was still sore over the continued absence and silence of Russell Denham. Six weeks since he had left her with that gay farewell, and not a word had she heard from him. For the first few weeks she watched the mails with an eagerness of hope and a sickening of suspense such as only those who have been through like experiences can understand. Not a small part of her humiliation had grown out of the fact that her family were more or less disappointed, also. Her mother, even, had questioned her closely, and been betrayed into expressing surprise that she did not hear from Mr. Denham; and Lucia had not failed to characterize him as a "flirt," declaring that she considered a female flirt despicable enough, but when a *man* descended to it, no words were equal to his description. She and Mary had had more than one sharp exchange of views concerning him; Mary invariably taking the position that he had shown her no more attention than was common among ladies and gentlemen. In her heart she did not believe this, but not for the world would she have admitted it in speech.

Emilie's giddy nonsense might not have hurt her so, had she not caught that sudden gleam of interest on her mother's face; a look which said as plainly as words could have said, that to know that one of her daughters had definite plans for the future would be a relief. Poor Mary resented this. She knew, it is true, that it was only the grind of poverty and the uncertainty of the present which made her mother think much of such possible provisions; she knew that the mother would not have been dazzled by any prospects which did not touch the inmost affections of her children; but, nevertheless, it was bitter to feel herself watched and commented upon; to feel that that silly Emilie looked upon her as growing very old, and wondered among her mates probably, as she did openly one day at home, whether Mary really would be an old maid like Aunt Eunice; to feel that even her father speculated as to the possibility of having one person less to provide for in the near future.

As has been said before, there was less of this feeling than Mary imagined. She had grown morbid over it, because there had been more or less speculation as to Russell Denham's intentions, and more or less satisfaction looked if not expressed when his attentions became somewhat pronounced; but there was no such continuous espionage upon her friendships and movements as she chose to think. Still, it was all these things combined which made Emilie's folly seem like gross and premeditated insult. Her response was prompt and emphatic.

"Emilie Cameron, what do you mean by making such an utter fool of yourself, not only, but dragging in your family as well? And Lucia, instead of rebuking, has to help you along. I must say, I think I have borne enough of such coarseness at the hands of both of you. If it has come to pass that one cannot meet the most commonplace of acquaintances in a public building and exchange a few words of conversation with him without being caricatured by idiots, I think it is time that something should be done to keep them from roving the streets. As for Professor Landis, you may insult him to your heart's content for all I care; he is nothing to me but an acquaintance from the country, with whom I try to be civil when I come in contact with him by accident. Make all the fun of him that you choose; but in future I advise you and Nannie Fuller to leave me out, or it will be the worse for both of you."

Then this angry young woman arose abruptly and left the room. "My patience!" said Emilie, looking after her with a half-scared, half-amused face. "She is as mad as a March hare, and at what, I should like to know? What do you suppose she will do to Nannie and me? Kill us? She looked fierce enough to, didn't she?"

Said Aunt Eunice, "You girls do beat all for quarrelling that I ever heard in my life. The three of you can't be together for fifteen minutes without having some sort of a rumpus. I should think your father would go raving crazy."

He looked at that moment more like fainting. He had toyed with his knife and fork, but eaten almost nothing; now he pushed the untasted coffee from him, and rising with slow step, like an old man, he, too, left the room.

10. "How Will it All End?"

The tumult of indignation in which Mary Cameron went to her room continued far into the evening. Lucia came up soon after dinner, and made ready for a lecture which was in the immediate neighborhood. Earlier in the day the girls had agreed to go with Emilie, who had been requested by one of her teachers to attend; but Mary, in response to Lucia's reminder, said shortly that she had changed her mind. Lucia hesitated, and nervously moved sundry articles on the dressing-table, while she decided how to say what she meant to say. At last it came abruptly:

"I wish you wouldn't mind Emilie's nonsense so much, Mary. She doesn't mean anything but fun; and in what I said, I was just trying to lighten the gloom a little. Father is awfully worried about something, and I wanted to divert his thoughts."

"You took a very strange way to do it," said Mary in her coldest tone; "but never mind. You need not offer any apology; I ought to be quite used to such experiences by this time. Emilie needs to be rebuked, not encouraged. You need not wait for me, as I most decidedly am not going out."

Then Lucia went away, wishing that she had left Mary to indulge her ill-humor without trying to propitiate her. As for Mary, her disagreeable words had hardly passed her lips before she would have recalled them if she could. She realized the hatefulness of her character, at least to some extent. In the light of the talk which she had had with Professor Landis her shortcomings were more marked than usual; at the same time, she could not rise to a real desire to make herself better. Instead, she yielded to the inclination to brood over her annoyances and Emilie's rudeness until, as has been said, her indignation rose. The truth is, she was one of those unfortunate persons to whom a laugh is worse than a blow. To feel that Emilie's companions had made her the subject of their keen wit set her blood boiling.

Into the midst of her gloomy and angry thoughts came a sound which suddenly held them in check. Her room was directly over her father's; and when the register was open, even conversation in the room below could be distinctly heard. What came to Mary at this time was an unmistakable groan from her father's lips, and then the words: "I believe I would rather have heard of his death." Then her mother in strong, sharp tones, "Edward, I should think you would be afraid to talk in that way. I know it frightens me to hear you. I tell you, you are hard on the poor boy. If anything will drive him to desperation, it will be the way in which you write to him tonight. I wish you would not write at all; let his mother do it."

It seemed to Mary that her heart suddenly gave a great throb, then stopped beating. What had happened? Either Rod or Mac was in trouble of some sort. Father and mother were always brooding over something which they did not explain, and now some terrible thing had come and she was ignorant of it. She would not endure it another moment. She would claim her right as the eldest of the family.

She rose up quickly, her limbs trembling so that they all but refused to support her, and made what speed she could to the room below. Entering without the ceremony of a knock she broke forth:

"Mother, I want to know what has happened. I heard you and father talking, and I know there is something wrong with the boys. I think it is unjust and cruel to keep me in ignorance. What is the matter?"

"Hush!" said Mrs. Cameron. "Nothing very dreadful is the matter, only your father is worn out, and excited over trifles."

Mr. Cameron interrupted her gravely, "Rachel, nothing is gained by trying to gloss over a wrong. This is not a trifle, and we injure our own consciences by trying to make it appear so."

He sat at his writing-desk, paper before him, pen in hand; but he had written no word on the page, and his face looked drawn and haggard, quite as though he needed to be in bed instead of trying to write.

"Nonsense!" said Mrs. Cameron, with the sharpness of a heart that was desperate. "I tell you, you are making altogether too much of a boyish act done on the impulse of a moment. See if Mary will not tell you so."

"Mother, *what is it?*" said Mary, almost stamping her foot in her excitement and anxiety to learn just what had happened. Mrs. Cameron made haste to answer.

"Nothing serious at all, I tell you. McLoyd found himself short of money and in need of certain things in haste, so instead of delaying to write home for funds, he has sent an order to the store where he has been in the habit of shopping, and has had the bill charged to his father, as was natural enough, I am sure. If a boy cannot depend on his father to that extent, it is hard."

"And has he written about it?" asked Mary breathlessly.

Before Mrs. Cameron could reply, her husband, shading his face with his hand, spoke in a low, humiliated tone, "No, Mary, he has not. No good will come of our trying to hide our eyes to the truth of this matter. The facts are these: It is six weeks since McLoyd ordered the bill of goods from Dunlap & Pierson's, a place where I never trade if I can help it, and never had a penny's worth charged. No word has come to me in the meantime of any such transaction. The first I learn of it is a bill presented to me today."

Mary caught eagerly at the suggestion which this offered. "Then I should say it was a wretched forgery. Somebody has been playing sharp with the boys. I wonder you would think that Mac would do such a thing! But it is just like some unprincipled college boy. I should send the bill to Mac at once, and get him to ferret out the mischief."

Slowly, as one convinced against his will, the father shook his head.

"That will not do, Mary. You may be sure I did not believe such a story about my boy without proof. I went at once to see Mr. Pierson; and he showed me two letters from McLoyd, describing carefully the sort of cut there must be to the vest, and the shade of the neckties. It is the old temptation, you see—clothes. The boys knew that I could spare them no more funds for such a purpose, so they have taken matters into their own hands. Both Rodney and McLoyd have replenished their wardrobes in this way. The bill is over sixty dollars, Mary."

While she listened, Mary's face had alternately flushed and paled. She stared at her father, and scarcely heard the eager words which her mother poured forth.

"What if it is? Sixty dollars goes a very little way toward supplying the necessities of two young men. And Mac always liked the goods best at Dunlap & Pierson's; I have heard him say there was a style about them which could not be found elsewhere. They have felt it absolutely necessary to have the things at once, and have taken the liberty to send for them in their father's name, because they knew the firm would be sure of him. I must insist that I don't think it is such a very great liberty to take with a father. To be sure, they ought not to have done it;

but they are young, and cannot be expected to think ahead very much."

Then Mary spoke, her voice low, her words studied.

"Father, I suppose it is as mother says, that the boys did not stop to think how it would look to us. They know we have always raised the money for their needs somehow. Perhaps they have in mind a way of earning enough to pay the bill, and only borrowed your name for a little while. Businessmen do that sometimes, do they not, as an accommodation?"

She hardly knew what she was saying. She knew very little about business matters, yet enough to feel that probably her words were weak; but there had come to her a great longing to say something soothing to that terribly crushed father, who sat with his head bowed on his hand, and with a strange, gray look on his face that seemed to age it infinitely.

The mother bestowed a grateful look on her eldest daughter, and spoke quickly. "Of course, there is some such explanation without a doubt, as I have been trying to make you understand. You see how the matter looks to Mary. You have always said that she had a clear brain. She does not see anything so very crushing in this. I tell you, you do very wrong to work yourself up over it in this way, as though it were a criminal matter. Some real trouble will come to people who persist in making mountains out of molehills."

"It being dishonorable and dishonest," said Mr. Cameron, his voice low, but terribly distinct. "I do not *want* to think of it for a moment as otherwise. I do not want the temptation of thinking that it can be considered anything else by honest people. The boys will not be helped but hindered if we gloss over a sin."

"Oh, dear!" said Mrs. Cameron, wiping the quick tears from her eyes. "You will drive the boys to desperation if you write to them in that spirit. What is a father for, but to overlook the mistakes of his children? I don't say they did right; but I say, as Mary does, that they did not think there was anything very wrong about it. Why, an acquaintance might take that amount of liberty if he felt sure of being able to pay in a short time; and I presume the boys have their plans. They are probably quite sure of winning the money prizes that will be declared in a few days."

After that, Mary, feeling her utter inability to make any further suggestions, or to administer comfort in any way, slipped quietly out and went back to her own room. Once there, she closed and locked the door, slipping the little bolt after she turned the key, as though she would in this way shut out even the thoughts of others and be more utterly alone than it is possible ever to be.

She was in a tumult of pain, humiliation, indignation. Which had the uppermost place in her heart? It was all very well for her to try to smooth over this astounding piece of news before her father—he needed all such helps—but in her heart she called her brother's action by its true name. It was bitter to have to admit it. A Cameron stooping to a dishonorable, nay, to a dishonest, act! They had been poor; they had resorted to all sorts of trying devices to make the yearly income meet the yearly demands; but the name, as far back as any of them knew, had never been sullied by a breath of dishonesty. Oh, they were in debt; but it was what Mary with flushed cheek and a curious pain in her heart called "honorable debt." Her father had explained to each creditor that he was a little behind this quarter; that he would divide among them what he had, and that by next quarter he hoped to be able to pay the entire sum. And they had been kind, and had assured him that they had no fears; his name was sufficient guaranty for honorable dealing. But Dunlap & Pierson had never been among her father's creditors, and the boys knew it. They knew, also, that the firm was the most expensive, not to say extravagant, in their prices, of any in the city. Oh, as her father had said, nothing was to be gained by mincing matters. The boys had been "dishonorable and dishonest." She winced over the words. She felt sure that she could have struck an outsider who had dared to use them, yet to her own heart she would speak truth.

What was to be the end? Boys who began in this way went often to utter ruin. She had read about and heard about a great many. Debt and dishonesty were the two potent factors in their ruin, of this she was sure; but no thought that any such experience could touch the Cameron name had ever before occurred to her. At that moment she thought of the "transformed lives" about which Professor Landis had talked that afternoon; the men who, almost as one might say, in a moment had changed natures. She remembered her own illustrations which had come to corroborate the truth of his words; and she found that she actually *craved* such experiences for the boys.

Suddenly she seemed to awaken to the thought that the boys were not all what they might be. They had been selfish and careless of the comforts of others; this she had known—at least, she had often so accused them—yet these had seemed very trifles when her brothers were away from home, and she thought about them tenderly. Now she felt that they, like herself, had dwarfed lives. Ay, and they had temptations which she had not realized before, and were yielding to them. How would it all end?

While perplexities and sorrows of this character were wearing the hearts of the Cameron family, Professor Landis, a self-constituted guardian of the young man Reeder, was not having a prosperous time. In addition to the fact that this servant of Christ felt himself in a measure responsible for every soul with whom he came in contact, he had a slight acquaintance with Ben Reeder's family. He had seen and talked with the hard-working, heavily burdened father, and the meek, anxious-eyed mother who waited back in their country home for news from Ben. They were prematurely old, these two. A wretched mortgage, which would have been as a mere toy to a man of capital, was yearly sapping away their energy and courage. They might almost of late years be said to live for the purpose of gathering together and hoarding enough money to meet the semi-annual payments. No; they lived for one other thing, their boy Ben. There were other children, older and younger than he, but Ben was the only boy; and someway their hopes of release from the burdens which had all their lives oppressed them were centered in him.

"I'll pay off that old mortgage when I am a man, and be done with it," were the words the boy of twelve had spoken, drawing himself up proudly, and looking at his mother in such a way that she took heart, and snatched him to her side, and kissed him hungrily as she said: "I believe in my soul that you will!"

The feeling thus planted grew with the years, until it became natural for the girls to refer with fond hopefulness to the time when Ben would be old enough to help them out. Meantime, two older sisters married and went away from home; not far away, within driving distance, indeed, of the old homestead. They married poor men, and simply continued the struggle for existence in other homes, instead of the one in which they were reared. So near were they, and so exactly were their lives a repetition of the lives of their parents, that it hardly seemed as though a break had been made in the family; but when Ben went away, it was another thing.

Ben, when barely nineteen, had an opening for business come to him from the great city. Professor Landis, whose father's farm was not far from the Reeder homestead, had seen Ben occasionally during his summer visits home, and had heard of the family burdens, and the family hopes as centered in the boy. It was he who had secured the opening; and great had been the excitement of the Reeder family when Ben departed cityward. Desolation is no word for the feeling which he left behind him. The married sisters, when they drove over for an hour's visit with their mother, lamented his absence as loudly as did those left at home.

"Boys are missed so much more than girls," they said. "They are noisier, and take up more room somehow." And then they all fell eagerly to telling one another what a splendid chance Ben had; and how lucky he was to get it these hard times; and how kind it had been of Professor Landis to speak a good word for him; and what a thing it would be when Ben got into business for himself, and got ahead enough to pay that dreadful mortgage! And they talked loud and laughed nervously over small nothings to cover up the quiver in their mother's voice, as she said that sometimes she felt that if they could only have Ben home again, just as he was, she would be willing to go on paying interest on the mortgage to the end of her days. After all, the city was a great, ugly, dangerous place, and she didn't know —

They were not afraid for their Ben, they interrupted her to say. But in their hearts they were, these married sisters. Their husbands knew a little more about city life than they did; and the things they told them made them drive over home oftener, and ask hungrily for letters from Ben. Then they every one—parents, daughters, and sons-in-law—took to reading surreptitiously and with bated breath all the terrible stories of accident and pain and crime with which the city weekly paper seemed suddenly to teem. Was the world wickeder that year than ever before? It certainly seemed so to the Reeder family.

Something of all this Professor Landis knew, and it increased his sense of responsibility for Ben Reeder. He had been instrumental in bringing Ben to the city. Often he regretted this. Often he had reason to fear that the city was going to prove too much for the country-bred boy whose feet had never been firmly set on a solid foundation. Viewed as a study, Ben Reeder was interesting. He had lived his nineteen years without great temptations of any sort. The home atmosphere from which he came might be clouded with anxiety, but it was loving. It had been a pleasant place to Ben all these years. There had been saloons in the village, but Ben lived two miles out and rarely went to the village of evenings. On the few occasions when he was belated, the lights of the saloon did not look so cheery to him as that which glowed in the open fireplace at home, where he knew mother and father and the girls were waiting to hear the news. The saloons had not tempted him. He heard nothing about them, thought nothing about them. Neither, alas, did his father or mother.

When Mr. Reeder was asked to sign a paper protesting against some flagrant nuisance in the village, he always signed it, and always remarked complacently: "These things don't come very close home to me. My boy doesn't belong to the people who find their level in such places."

The consequence was that Ben went to the city with only the force of habit to hold him in check. And that splendid factor, Habit, found itself a mere reed when it had to be used as a central force. In the city all things were very different. There was no wide fireplace with its splendid back-logs; there was no cozy tea-table with something warm for Ben because he had been out in the cold. Above all, there was no mother sitting, mending, and smiling at the stories he had to tell, and admiring his feats of industry and strength. In the city there was a cold, dreary, fourth-story back room shared with an uncongenial fellow-boarder. There were dismal breakfasts, and greasy, half-cooked, insufficient dinners, and no companionship.

The bright lights of the saloon appealed to him. The boys who were no better dressed than he, and knew no more than he, appealed to him. They were friendly and cheery, and made him feel at home. And the Smith boys, the worst of their set, were the most friendly. More than anything else, Ben Reeder needed the atmosphere of a home to surround and envelop him; and whatever else there was in the city, there seemed sometimes to be no *homes*. Certainly the boy from the country found none, and could not help almost laughing at Professor Landis's earnest attempts to make the tall, dark, solemn-looking city houses into homes.

Still, though he laughed, the good-natured boy made occasional efforts to meet his helper half way; not so much for his own sake, be it confessed, as for the helper's. It was a pity to disappoint Professor Landis when he really seemed to care; and for that reason Ben went occasionally to a church social or Christian Endeavor gathering, and tried to mingle with well-dressed people, and make himself believe he felt at home; and nearly always went back to his fourth-story room in a rage, telling himself that he would not be caught in a scrape like that again.

Professor Landis could not blame him. Matters connected with those socials did not move according to his ideas. Even the best-intentioned people did not seem to know how to make the evening pleasant and helpful to a certain class. The socials fell on an evening when Dorothy Landis was unavoidably engaged elsewhere, so that tower of strength was denied her much-perplexed brother.

11. "Out of His Sphere"

Despite Ben's resolve, he had promised, under pressure, to be present at another of those trying ordeals called socials. Professor Landis was more eager for this than usual, because he knew the Smith boys had other plans which would not be helpful to Ben. A few days preceding the social, he learned to his delight that the long absent pastor had returned. His pulpit had been supplied for several months, while he traveled with an aged and invalid father who needed his care. The supply was an old gentleman who was unable to do any pastoral work, and who had been seen only from the pulpit on Sundays. It was therefore with great satisfaction that Professor Landis was introduced one evening to "our pastor, the Rev. Mr. Edson," and found in him a young, energetic-looking man, who greeted him with heartiness, and promptly expressed his pleasure in the fact that the professor and his sister had decided to cast in their lot with them.

"He will be just the man to win Ben," Mr. Landis reflected, and noted with satisfaction that he had arrived in time for the social.

On the afternoon of the following day, Professor Landis, having a leisure hour, resolved to call upon the pastor, and give him a little of young Reeder's history, and a hint as to the influence of the Smith boys and their set. On his way thither he fell in with Ben himself, and conceived the idea of taking him captive for the call. It was no new work to the professor; he had been for years acting in unison with his pastor. The two had worked together with mutual pleasure, and nearly every time they met had exchanged views in regard to the special ways of reaching and helping certain ones whose names were on their list. Professor Landis had sorely missed this friendship in his new home, and had looked forward eagerly to the return of the pastor. He rejoiced in the thought that the man was in his early prime, and full of vigor and enthusiasm. Now here was Ben, and across the street could be seen from the study window the outline of the pastor's head. There was no time like the present. He would take Ben in, and let the pastor captivate him; then, at some other opportune moment, he could give him such points as might be helpful in the study of the boy's character.

"Ben, my boy," he said, laying a friendly hand on that young man's shoulder, "I want you to turn back with me and make a call. Mr. Edson has arrived, you know, and I am going to run in and make his acquaintance. I met him at Dr. Preston's, so I can introduce you; we shall both find it pleasanter this evening for having had this chat with him."

Ben demurred; he wasn't dressed for calling, although, truth to tell, he had on at that moment his best suit of clothes. He never made calls, he shouldn't know how to act. These and a dozen other trivialities were overruled. The professor had a good deal of influence over Ben, at least when he was with him; and they mounted the steps of the manse together, and were presently shown into the pastor's reception-room.

"Good-afternoon," he said, holding out a cordial hand to welcome Professor Landis. "You are just the person I want to see. There are two points in which I fancy I shall enlist your interest." And then Professor Landis presented his companion.

A swift, well-bred glance from head to foot, which was felt, rather than observed, and the keen-eyed pastor had gauged Ben Reeder's position in the world.

"Ah, indeed," he said carelessly, "a Sunday school pupil of yours, Professor? Glad to meet him. Be seated. I was looking over the announcements about the approaching ball-game when you rang. Unusual thing, is it not, in this region, to be able to have a game so late in the season? This one will be an exciting affair. The boys are well matched on both sides. I told my father he must let me get off in time for the game. I had missed two, and it wasn't within the bounds of reason to expect me to sacrifice another."

He laughed of course, as he spoke. It was partly mere talk, yet he was evidently excited over the coming contest, and quite in earnest in his determination not to miss it.

"You are fond of athletic sports, of course," continued the pastor. "All professional men are, I believe, in these days. A great change, my father says, since his time. Oh, I do not play very often, because I have no time for the drill; pity, too. Sometimes I think I will take time and let some of the work wait; but I attend the match games as often as they are within reach."

Professor Landis explained that the duties of his profession kept him occupied quite often during the hours of a baseball contest, and added frankly that in the neighborhood from which he had recently come, the game had become so entangled with liquor and gambling that he had been compelled to withdraw all recognition of it, even as a looker-on.

"Oh, no!" said the clergyman quickly. "That is not the way. We do not want to withdraw from such gatherings, but to hold on to them, and throw our influence on the side of good morals."

"True; but when one's influence fails to work the desired reform, one must take care how he is counted on the wrong side, you know. When it reached the point with us that a booth was set up on the ball-ground where choice wines and liquors could be bought, and when the gambling spirit ran so high that it was considered a matter of course, some of us felt it necessary to withdraw."

The clergyman laughed lightly. "Oh, well," he said, "it will not do for us to be too straight-laced. The boys *will* indulge in some of these doubtful things; they mean no harm. They have a booth on our grounds where all sorts of improper things can be bought. I don't patronize it, and they know that I don't. But I am on hand at their games, and they expect me as much as they do the players. You must go to the contest, Professor. You have probably hidden yourself among your books until you have forgotten how to be merry. We'll show you how. Well, never mind; we might not agree on all these points, though I shall convert you, I am sure. You are much too sensible a person to hold to narrow views. We mustn't run away from the world entirely, you know, because it does some things we don't happen to fancy. The world is a jolly good fellow, after all. Here is something which will interest you," whereupon he plunged eagerly into a description of certain lectures which were soon to be given by eminent speakers; lectures on highly literary topics such as only scholars could appreciate. There had been some difficulty in securing them for the season, and the clergyman dilated upon it, and his important and complicated part in accomplishing it.

Under other circumstances Professor Landis would have been much interested. As it was, he could only remember that poor Ben did not even know what the subjects meant, which rolled so glibly from the tongue of the clergyman. He made an effort to express his interest briefly, and turn to some topic which might have a bit of common ground. It was all in vain; throughout the interview the minister as persistently ignored Ben as though he had been a mere speck on the wall, and persisted in bringing forward topic after topic for conversation which it was manifestly impossible for him to be interested in, or even understand.

Professor Landis arose at last, disappointed and bewildered. What did the man mean? Did he not understand that Ben was one of his flock? As for Ben, it was with difficulty that he could restrain his feelings while in the minister's presence. As soon as the door closed after them he gave vent to what was apparently an uncontrollable burst of laughter.

"I hope you'll excuse me," he said, as soon as he could speak, and he was still laughing, "but it was so funny to see you trying to make that man know that I was there at all; and you did fail so entirely, even though I did my best to help! I coughed twice, and knocked the big brown book off the table, but that last was an accident."

Then seeing that Professor Landis did not join in the laugh, but on the contrary looked grave, and perhaps slightly disturbed, he essayed to turn comforter.

"Never mind, Professor; it isn't in a man like him to care for a fellow like me. If I were a book bound in calf, say, or even a great ball, it would be another thing; but being nothing but a blundering boy, what could you expect? Don't you see how it is? I don't belong in the same world, and there is no use of putting me into it. If you would make up your mind to give a fellow up, you would be more comfortable; and so would the fellow."

This last, in undertone, evidently not intended for his companion's ear; but he caught the muttered words and smiled, and rallied himself.

"Ben, my dear fellow, that is nonsense. I hope you do not desire me to give up your friendship because we have called upon a man who was preoccupied, and persisted in continuing the trains of thought which he had evidently been indulging when we interrupted him. Mr. Edson has just returned after a long absence, you remember, and he hasn't gotten into line yet. I presume he is a good deal worn—constant attendance upon an invalid is very wearing work—and professional men rest their brains and bodies by these athletic games, you know. Then he feels responsible for the course of lectures he was describing, and, of course, must push it on all possible occasions. By evening he will have gotten settled, and will be ready to interest himself in people. He must be fond of young people, for he is himself young, and you know what a large company of them attend his church. Do you take the south-bound car? I must go the other way. Well, you will remember to call for me tomorrow evening, will you not?"

"Oh, yes," said Ben with a toss of his head and a half-annoyed laugh. "I've given my word, and I'll be there; but I'd rather be hanged! I tell you now, honestly, there won't be any pleasure nor comfort for me at that place, and I don't understand why you want to push me in. There are lots of young people, but you know as well as I do that they are no more like me, the most of them, than that minister is; and I'm thankful to say I can't see any resemblance between us."

Professor Landis laughed, and lifted his hat for good-bye, being glad as he did so that there was no time for words. He would not have liked Ben to know how utterly that minister had disappointed and dismayed him. It had been an unusual experience. He had always heretofore found in ministers his heartiest supporters in his efforts to win young men. And this man's work had seemed always to lie in the direction of young men who needed to be won away from themselves and their companions and surroundings. As he sat in the corner of the car, being carried downtown, Mr. Landis did what he seldom allowed himself to do; he went over the interview with the pastor, step by step, and worried over it.

Why had a man who had to do with a church made up so largely of young people, been so unwise, so actually rude, in his dealings with one of them? True, he might not have realized that Ben attended his own church. He asked if he were a pupil of his. Perhaps he had heard of his scholars at the Lower Mission, and supposed Ben to be one of them; but even in that case, the Lower Mission had no church organization, and Mr. Edson was as much the pastor of that flock as any man was. Besides, without regard to church or Sunday school, Ben was a boy who either belonged to the fold of Christ or needed to be drawn thitherward. Why had not the heart of the young man responded to this possible opportunity, and greeted him as a brother? He had made excuses for him to Ben. What else was there to be done? But really—and here this Christian worker pulled himself up sharply. Was he going to condemn a man, and a minister at that, because he was not always ready for work and watchfulness? Had he not himself been off guard times enough to be patient with the obtuseness of others? It was himself who was to blame, for rushing the young man in, uninvited, without knowing whether the time was opportune or otherwise. If he had gone alone to make his call, and talked of Reeder and his temptations and needs, it would have been another matter. Whereupon he resolved that if he could possibly make time for it, he would look in upon Mr. Edson during the next day, and explain why he felt especially anxious that Reeder should enjoy the church social.

Having settled this, he was the sort of man who could *make* time on occasion, and by four o'clock of the following afternoon he was again in the pastor's study. Mr. Edson was as glad to see him as he had been the day before, and quite as eager to talk. This time it was the Choral Union which filled his thoughts. The cantata of Esther was to be rendered, and Mr. Edson had been appealed to as a tenor.

"It is old music," he said, "that old favorite revived, you know, and will not need much rehearsing on my part. I think I will help them; and I promised to look out for a bass voice. Are you not just the one, Professor?"

"It would be quite out of the question for me," said Professor Landis quickly. Then he plunged headlong into the subject which had brought him to the study. There was no use in waiting for favorable openings. "By the way, Mr. Edson, the young man I brought in with me yesterday is a particular friend of mine; and I am looking for friends of the right stamp for him." Then he described as briefly as he could Ben's environments; making much of the mother and father whose hopes centered in him.

The minister listened somewhat absently; he even turned the leaves of a new magazine while he did so. Once he interrupted to ask, "Why didn't the fellow stay at home and help his father and mother where he was? These country chaps are always running away to the city and ruining themselves, when they might at least help support the family at home."

"That is true, on general principles," said his caller; "but in Ben's case it would hardly apply. His father is a carpenter of the ordinary sort, and there is not work enough in the town where he lives to employ him. He has a little place, with an acre or two of land; but there is a mortgage on it which is sapping the energies of the family. Ben has ambitions, or had, concerning that mortgage. The best thing for him to do, seemed to be to get employment which would bring in a little ready money for the family, and with the hope of laying up something for the debt. I secured the situation which the young man now holds, and so feel an added responsibility for him."

"Ah!" said the minister. "They are great bores, aren't they, these responsibilities? Look here, this is a clever sketch, is it not? One can almost see that ridiculous old fellow trying to pose as an orator!" and he held up the magazine at which he had been surreptitiously looking.

Professor Landis gave it a passing glance. "Fairly well done," he said. "Now about the church social. I have got Reeder to promise to accompany me there. I had a special reason for desiring it this evening, above others, because—"

Here he bent forward and gave a rapid, vivid picture of the peculiar temptations which were likely to coil about Ben on this evening, unless his friends were on the alert; and his earnest desire that influences might be brought to bear upon him, through the people he should meet, which would tell for his future.

Mr. Edson put down his magazine and listened at last; but on his face was a disturbed, not to say annoyed, expression.

"My dear friend," he said, as his caller reached a period, "it is evident that I must make a confession to you. I am not the sort of hand-to-hand workman which you suppose. There are clergymen who can do that kind of thing, but I am not one of them. There is a sense in which I am out of my sphere in this church, though of course I do not say that aloud. I do not expect to be here long. It is a good place to study in, because the demands of society are not what they would be in an uptown church; and I expect, of course, to do my duty as long as I am here; but my forte lies in preaching. The church is very full, as you see. I have crowded it ever since I have been here. You have noticed, perhaps, that since *my* coming a different class of people, those more like yourself, have been drawn in. I feel that my influence is among all such. The perpetual rush after bad boys and rough boys, and uncouth, hoydenish girls, which some pastors keep up, is not in me; and I honestly wish I could say that my church was not the place for such. I said I did not expect to remain here long; that, of course, is entirely between us, and it may depend upon what I am able to accomplish with the church. If I can gradually gather about me those whom I feel I can benefit, who are sufficiently intellectual, for instance, to be helped by my style of preaching, and those whose pocketbooks are sufficient to afford me a decent salary, why I shall remain. I am not such a stickler for location that I care a great deal about its being farther downtown than some other churches. The streets nearest us are being peopled by a very fine class; and there is no reason in life why they should waste their time in riding uptown to church, if a church to their mind can be found and sustained nearer by. But in order to get them in and make them comfortable, we must not give too much attention to the other class, who are at present quite too numerous. The plain truth is, Professor, that we ought not to expect boys like your young *protégé*, and men like yourself, for instance, to be fed from the same pulpit. The boy is right: there ought to be some church where both pulpit and pew would be more entirely on a level with fellows of his stamp, and where they could feel at home. I believe in mission churches most heartily, but I am not calculated to run one. I have spoken very frankly to you, confidentially indeed; for I know you to be in a sense an outsider, with no lifelong associations here to run against, and I feel the importance of explaining to you that I actually do not know how to reach young fellows like the one you brought to see me yesterday. I would like to do it if I knew how, but I do not. It is absurd to suppose that the sermon I am now at work upon, for instance, can interest him. I am sure it cannot; and it is my misfortune that there will be dozens, almost hundreds, in the audience, of whom the same might be said. But I preach for the few, you understand, with the hope and belief that the character of the food offered will draw others of like tastes. I am sure you get my meaning, Professor."

"Yes," said Professor Landis, rising, "I think I do. Still, I hope you will remember my boy tonight, and give him a greeting."

Then he went away; walked the whole length of the square before he remembered that he had intended to take a car at the other corner, and as he roused himself to the present, said with a long-drawn sigh, "The man is right; he is out of his sphere."

12. A New Departure

The institution known as a church social is capable of a variety of forms. The one which Professor Landis had with infinite pains persuaded Ben Reeder to attend was different from any of his former experiences. Evidently it was held at one of the homes which Mr. Edson believed he had drawn to his church. There were a number of invited guests who did not know his church, and who believed, apparently, that they had been invited to a full-dress party. Moreover, the original members of the flock, in anticipation of such an experience, had done what they could to make their attire festive, and to give a general air of society life to the entire gathering. The result was that in a more marked sense than Professor Landis had supposed it possible, his *protégé* felt out of place and miserable. In sore disappointment and dismay, this Christian worker looked about him for an ally. The pastor on whom he had hoped to lean was absorbed with the younger members of a new family who lived, he had informed the Professor in hurried undertone, in "one of those handsome houses away up the avenue, and had been twice to church." They were wealthy and cultivated; by all means they must be held for the church around the corner. "Come and be introduced."

Professor Landis had excused himself on the plea that a friend was waiting for him in the hall, and promised attendance later; then he had gone in haste to where Ben was standing, leaning drearily against the wall, listlessly watching the still coming guests, although the hour was already late enough for him to wonder if he could not be allowed to slip away. He had done what he could to make himself smart; there was even a rose in his button-hole; but his face was uncomfortably red, and his very hands looked self-conscious.

Mr. Edson, who had hurriedly passed that way but a moment before, had not even recognized him by a nod. To do the man justice, his ignorance was not feigned; he did not remember some faces well, and no thought of Professor Landis's *protégé* had entered his mind as he passed the uncomfortable boy.

"Come with me to the library," said the Professor, slipping his hand through Ben's arm. "I want to show you a famous picture which hangs there. It has a history, and I know you will like it. I fancy you are fond of stories, are you not?"

"I'm fond of anything that will take me away from that corner where I have been leaning until I have bored a hole in my best coat, I guess. I say, Professor, haven't I done penance long enough? I can be good for some time, perhaps, if you'll only let me get away from here."

"Ben, I am looking for the coming of some friends whom I would like to have you meet. I think they must be here very soon."

"If they aren't," said Ben significantly, "and I have to wait for them, I guess I'll make my plans to stay to breakfast; because it's a good deal later than it was!"

"Oh, Mr. Landis!" called a lady at that moment. "Come here, please; we need your assistance very much."

"Go on," said Ben, letting his arm drop. "I'll wait for you in the library. No, thank you, I'm not going into that crowd of women. I'd rather wait three hours for you."

Very reluctantly his companion turned from him. One of the ladies held an open book over which two others were leaning, and an eager discussion was evidently being carried on. It did not seem courteous to ask them to wait, and Ben had already slipped away. The library was apparently deserted, and the lonesome boy dropped into a chair with a sigh of relief. At least he was not in the way here; and there was a chance for him to get his troublesome feet tucked under the window drapery; at that moment someone spoke to him:

"I wonder if this is Mr. Reeder, Professor Landis's friend?"

"That is my name," he said, springing to his feet in astonishment; "and I know Professor Landis."

"Then let us consider ourselves introduced. I am Miss Cameron, and there is scarcely a person in this house whom I have met before. I heard Professor Landis mention you once as a young friend of his, and saw him with you just now, so I determined to claim acquaintance."

Mary Cameron's intimate friends would have been amazed at her gracious tone and winning smile. What new departure was this, as unlike her as possible? Truth to tell, she was somewhat surprised at herself. She had declined the invitation to the social when first given, but after consideration had suddenly resolved to go. If they *must* live in this part of this city, it would certainly be well to have some speaking acquaintances. She had exchanged calls with the daughters of the hostess and knew them to be unexceptionable; she had not been out in company for several weeks, and was bored with the common-places and wearinesses of her life. Lucia was housed at home with toothache, and felt unamiable and selfish; and Aunt Eunice was always in the sitting-room evenings. To escape anywhere would be a relief. With no better motives than these, she had come to the church social. Her dress was severely plain, and simplicity itself. She had by no means chosen her best attire. Her idea of the congregation on Smith Street was that it was crowded with common people; and although the Kinkaids had opened their house for the evening to entertain them, of course the people would remain common. It was embarrassing, and in a sense disappointing, to find herself mistaken.

Mr. Edson was apparently right about the class of people whom he was drawing to his church. These were certainly well-bred, and, if they had not been too much dressed for a church gathering, would have commended themselves to Mary Cameron as cultured. They had not, however, the best culture. They seemed to be well acquainted, to enjoy one another's society, and to give exceedingly small attention to strangers. The result had been that Miss Cameron felt more alone than she had ever been before. She had not even met Professor Landis yet. It was perhaps the feeling of loneliness which gave her a sudden sense of sympathy with Ben Reeder.

Moreover, she had not forgotten Professor Landis's appeal to her for help. Being a new experience, it made a deep impression. Help of that sort, at least, had never before been asked of her. During the time which had intervened since her conversation with Professor Landis, Mary Cameron had done much thinking. The shadow of disgrace which she could not help feeling had fallen upon them through the action of her brothers, had made her shrink from the company of her acquaintances, and spend most of her time alone. She was haunted by the fear that people, old acquaintances of Rod and Mac, had heard of their act. Such stories, she believed, always leaked out somehow, and were always exaggerated. What if they were discussing her brothers and blaming them, and commiserating the family, and wondering whether the bill could be paid by the already overburdened father, and wondering if there would be more bills of a like nature in the future? In these and a dozen other ways she had tormented herself.

Her father and mother, after the first outburst of misery, seemed to have settled down to face the inevitable. What had been written to the boys, Mary did not know; nor did she understand how her father had managed the bill.

It was paid, he assured her; but he had not chosen to be more explicit, and had looked so worn and burdened that she had not liked to question. Thereafter, by common consent the subject had been dropped. Lucia knew nothing of what had occurred, nor, of course, did Emilie. Mary rejoiced over this fact, but all the more felt the necessity of doing her brooding in secret. It was all these things which helped her to remember Ben Reeder. Professor Landis was looking out for him, trying in all ways to help him. If a good and true man, such as the professor evidently was, had interested himself for her brothers, would they have been different young men from what they now were? Not that they were in any sense on a level with Ben Reeder; she could not help curling her lip even in the privacy of her own room over such an idea. The boys were splendid fellows; but then, there *were* young men who would not have done what they had, who were superior in many ways to them. She admitted it to herself; she would not have borne a hint of it from another.

Professor Landis had said that boys could be helped by women older than themselves. She cast about their circle of acquaintances to see if there was one woman who had possibly been helpful to her brothers, and smiled in a sarcastic way at the thought. There were numberless young women, some of them older than the boys, who had been glad, apparently, to receive their attentions, to help them spend money for concert and lecture tickets, and creams and caramels, and what not—but as for helping them! Well, why should she blame them? She had never helped anybody either; and she had attended many lectures and parties with young men. Still, she had never been among those women who sought friendships with persons younger than themselves. Perhaps if she had, she might have accomplished a little good in the world. Somewhat to this young woman's bewilderment she found herself at times yearning to accomplish good. When had she ever thought of such things before? Possibly you understand the subtle mixture of motives which made her suddenly resolve to introduce herself to young Reeder. It was a sudden resolve. Nothing had been further from her thoughts until she saw him dropping into the library chair in a bewildered attitude, having been apparently deserted by his one friend.

Her friendly way of introducing herself had been diffcrent from Ben's former experience with city ladies, and made him feel on familiar terms. He resolved to be entirely frank with her.

"I want to get out of this awfully," he said. "It is nothing but a horrid bore. If you are a friend of Professor Landis, I wish you could coax him to let me alone. I mean about such places. He does it for my good, you know; but upon my word, it will be bad for me. If I have to go to many more of them to please him, I think I shall go hang myself, to be rid of it all."

She laughed amusedly. She had never heard a society young man go on in this way. "Don't you like church socials?" she asked.

"I hate 'em!" said Ben with energy, feeling an immense sense of relief in being able to give vent to his feelings. "I hate this one the worst of all. They haven't had eating in the others, but they have even added that horror to this one."

Miss Cameron laughed again, in genuine merriment. "What is your objection to eating?" she asked. "I thought young men were always ready for refreshment of that sort."

He shook his head with a serio-comic air. "Not in such places. If they had some of mother's doughnuts to give a fellow, and her and the girls to wait on him, why then—" His voice choked in spite of himself, and he came to a sudden halt, while a mist gathered in his eyes. A moment before he would have scoffed at the idea of his being homesick, but the mention of his mother's doughnuts had been too much. Miss Cameron was interested and touched. She had not known that boys away from home felt like that.

"There is nothing here half so good as your mother's doughnuts, of course," she said gently, more gently than some people knew she could speak; "but the coffee is very nice, and there are some dainty little cakes which fairly melt in one's mouth. You must be sure to try them before you go."

He shook his head. "It isn't the *things*," he said, speaking disdainfully as one who resented both his own weakness and the idea that this woman should suppose that he cared only for doughnuts. "It's the everlasting style they put on; the not knowing whether it is the big spoon or the little spoon you must use, or whether you ought to let them both alone and take the coffee with your fork! And whether you must swallow things when you hate 'em, because everybody else is doing it; and whether you take two kinds of things or only one. You see, the whole jumble is what bothers me."

It was partly fun now; he saw that he was amusing her, but that it was sympathetic amusement. In truth, she was very sympathetic. She knew all about spoons and forks, and the small conventionalities of society life; but could she forget how great had been her embarrassment over the absence of many of these society extras on the day that hateful luncheon was served?

"The array must be bewildering," she said cheerily, "to one who has lived a pleasant home life heretofore, and is just beginning to belong to the big world; but, after all, it is very easily managed after a little experience. Suppose you take me out to the refreshment room, and let me pilot you through its mysteries. I want you to try those little cakes, and I promise to explain just how many may be eaten at once." Her eyes were dancing with amusement; but all the time there was that note of cordial friendliness in her voice, born of an honest desire in her heart to be useful to this country youth.

Ben Reeder was quick to feel the difference between her manner and the cold and formal civilities he had heretofore received from the women who belonged to this new world. Professor Landis's words about having independence enough to take help where help was offered also came to aid him, and he surprised himself by frankly accepting the suggestion.

Fifteen minutes later, Professor Landis, having escaped from the young ladies with inquiring minds, was seeking everywhere for his *protégé,* in distress lest he had escaped and sought the Smith boys after all. He came upon him at last, to his utter astonishment, in the room where refreshments were being informally served. He was holding a cup of chocolate, but giving amused attention to his companion, who was apparently describing something in an animated way; and the professor's astonishment was no whit abated to discover that the speaker was Miss Cameron.

"I cannot tell you how much I thank you," he said to her nearly an hour later, when Ben had at last been permitted to take his departure. His eyes had been bright with interest when he came to say good-night, and his words had been hearty.

"Upon my word and honor, Professor, I've actually had a good time. That I should live to confess it! That woman is tip-top. She puts me awfully in mind of my sister Sarah—that is, I think she is some like what Sarah would have been if she had had chances, you know. Church socials and that sort of thing." His gray eyes twinkled with fun. "You know what I mean, don't you? It seems as though she was like our kind of folks that had been with the other kind long enough to learn all they knew, and yet hadn't forgotten her common sense. The way she put me through out there at the supper-room was a caution! I know which fork is which, Professor, and spoons too. They can't stump me with them again."

"When did you meet forks and spoons under formidable circumstances?" asked Professor Landis, with a laugh almost as hearty as Ben's own.

"Why, that little Darlington fellow that you introduced me to tried to take me up and couldn't. He had me go home with him to dinner one night. It was raining cats and dogs; and I had to wait for a package to take back to the office, or I wouldn't have done it; and I got all tangled up among the forks and spoons and things, and his face got red as a beet because I used the wrong ones, and his little sister laughed outright. I've been afraid of 'em ever since—the forks and spoons, I mean; and six or eight different kinds of napkins; but she straightened them out. I say, Professor, why haven't you given me a chance with her kind of folks before?"

No wonder the Professor was grateful. And to think that it should have been Miss Cameron! He was a good deal bewildered. Had his entire estimate of the girl been at fault, or was she playing a part? If she was, it had certainly been a very kind, friendly part, and had put Ben more at his ease than he had ever seen him. He wondered whether it would do to tell her about the "sister Sarah," and "our kind of folks," and decided that it would not. But the voice was very pleasant in which he said, "I cannot tell you how much I thank you. You have given my boy a pleasant hour tonight; and it was just when I was at my wits' end how to hold him longer, though there were special reasons why he ought to be held. You have done a very kind thing tonight, Miss Cameron."

He could not be more surprised than she was with herself. Why had Ben interested her so much? He was a new experience in every way. A bright, merry boy, who had evidently looked up to her with admiration as to a superior being, and been ready to follow her lead, yet he had been as original and entertaining as any one she had ever met. If that was the way to "do good," she was sure she did not object to doing it.

There was nothing to thank her for, she told Professor Landis. The hour she had spent with his *protégé* had been the pleasantest one of the evening. His eccentricities had amused her.

"He is a good-hearted boy," she said, her face softening at thought of some of his half-merry, half-serious, and wholly tender words about his mother. "It is only the exterior that needs polish. He is coming to call upon me, Professor Landis. I have promised to play some pieces for him which he used to sing for his mother, and a new one that he is learning to surprise her when he goes home."

And Professor Landis, who had really taken this boy to his heart, and troubled over him more than he himself realized, felt such a sudden sense of relief at the thought of this home opening to him, that he could not help putting intense feeling into his words, as he said, "God bless you, Miss Cameron."

It was certainly pleasant to discover one's self to be of use.

13. "A Good Fellow in Every Way"

There were other experiences connected with that eventful social which need to be chronicled. It was after Ben Reeder had departed, and Mr. Landis was wondering whether he could be spared to do likewise, that he was waylaid in the hall by a new acquaintance.

"I say, Landis," said Mr. Kennedy, seizing his arm familiarly, "I want an introduction to the lady with whom you were just speaking. I have noticed her several times this evening, and asked two others to oblige me, but they were not acquainted with her."

Mr. Landis hesitated, and there was a slight trace of embarrassment in his manner. "I will ask if I may do so," he replied at last. "She is not an intimate acquaintance, and I am not privileged to take liberties." Then he passed on quickly, unable to overcome a feeling of annoyance.

He had met Mr. Kennedy but once before, and had not been prepossessed by his manner. Why, it would perhaps have been difficult to explain. He was not accustomed to people who addressed him as "Landis," or who seized hold of him in that off-hand manner; but these were certainly not reasons on which to base any opinion of character. Still, he tried to be conscientiously careful of his introductions. There were responsibilities enough without assuming such as these; but when one was asked . . .

He sought his host and questioned.

"Kennedy? Oh, he is a fine fellow, a nephew of Dr. Eustis Kennedy on Boulevard Avenue. He is on here from New York on business for his firm. A good fellow in every way, I presume."

Mr. Landis came slowly back in search of Miss Cameron. "You will remember I do not vouch for him, Miss Cameron. He is an entire stranger to me, but he asked for an introduction."

Mary Cameron smiled coldly. He seemed to her unnecessarily particular. She did not believe in treating people as suspicious characters until they could prove the contrary.

Mr. Kennedy was evidently pleased with his acquaintance. He devoted himself to her during the remainder of the evening, up to the moment when she disappeared within the dressing-room to make ready for her waiting father. During this time he had asked and received gracious permission to call at the Cameron home, Miss Cameron being more suave than usual, in order to mark to herself her disapproval of Professor Landis's evident coldness of manner.

"He wants his boy Ben patronized in every possible way," she told herself; "but when one comes who is on the same level in society with ourselves, he must needs explain who is his grandfather, and how far back the family can be traced before one may be friendly with him!"

Nor did it atone for his caution, to realize what her conscience told her, that it was character and not position which Professor Landis required in his friends. Of what use to be painfully particular, even about that? Why inquire into one's exact past, root out every little fault and failing, and make them an excuse for withholding one's friendship? She felt sure that Professor Landis would be just that sort of man, and she resented it.

Poor Mary Cameron was sore-hearted about character in these days. It was something new to have to wince over the possible stains in the Cameron name.

The Christmas holidays had come and gone, and her brothers had spent them away from home for the first time in their lives. No one but the father knew just what sort of a letter was sent them, but, whatever it was, they had resented it; had written loftily—that is, McLoyd had. The younger brother did not write at all. He had assured his father that he was not aware that he had committed so heinous an offence. Other boys, his classmates in college, shopped on their father's name whenever they chose, and their accounts were always honored, and no questions asked. They had been very careful. He and Rod, had gone without many things which to others in their set were considered necessities, in order to save their father from unnecessary expense, but they certainly had not understood that they were expected to go without clothes! Perhaps they would better both leave college without more ado, and get positions as day laborers or something of the sort, if their father really could not afford to let them appear like others. As for coming home for the vacation, since they had apparently so disgraced themselves and the entire family, it was not probable that anybody would want to see them. They both had invitations to spend the holidays with classmates, and had decided, in view of the last letter they had received, to accept them.

Over this letter Mrs. Cameron had shed bitter tears. Her boys were her idols. To live through Christmas and New Year without them seemed more than her much-enduring heart could bear. She blamed her husband with bitterness. She told him it was no wonder the boys felt as they did, after the letter he had probably written. She gave no heed, or at least apparently no credence, to his earnest attempt at explanation. He had not written bitterly, he assured her. He had spoken of their act as it deserved, spoken truthfully; he did not dare do otherwise; but he had told them that he did not believe they would have done it had they stopped to think, and that he forgave them, and would pay the bill, and never, of course, let any outsider know it was contracted without his consent.

"Oh, yes!" she had replied. "You spoke 'truthfully,' no doubt! You made them angry with your cold, hard truths, and you have driven them from you and from their mother. If they go wrong now, you will have yourself to thank."

Some of this talk had been in Mary's presence, Mrs. Cameron having so far forgotten herself as to ignore it. The result had been curious. Mary, the only one of the girls who had been made acquainted with the real reason for the boys' absence during the holidays, had found her sympathies being drawn in two opposite directions. There were times when she felt that her father had done just right. Who would speak plainly to the boys if he did not? Of course they ought to be reproved, and sharply, for taking matters into their own hands in that way. It was absurd to say that they had done it thoughtlessly. Whatever thoughtlessness any of the Cameron family might be guilty of, surely there was no excuse for their spending money without due consideration! It had never been plentiful enough, at least since they children were grown, to warrant any such proceeding. This she said very distinctly to her mother, calling forth a burst of tears, and the statement that the boys never had any help or comfort in their sisters. She did not know how it was, some brothers leaned upon their elder sisters and were guided by them, but her girls were more interested in other people's brothers. This was hard, and she did not mean it. She was sure that the brothers were tenderly loved, and she did not understand enough of what their sisters might have done to intelligently reproach them; yet the accusation stung. Mary was beginning to realize that there was truth in it. She did not admit it, however, to her mother, but replied with cold dignity; after which each went to her own room and was miserable. But there were other times when, in the bitterness of her disappointment at not having the boys at home for the holidays as usual, Mary blamed her father and let him know that she did.

"You are mistaken, Mary," he said to her one day, "in supposing that I was severe with the boys—as I see you do. I could not tell them other than the truth. You would hardly have had me commend them for their act, I suppose; but I assured them that if the thing never occurred again, it should be forgiven and forgotten, and that I would pay the bill just as soon as I could."

"I scarcely see how you could have said more," was her hard reply. "Fathers forgive and forget even grave crimes, do they not? At least, we read in books about the infinite patience and forgiveness of good fathers, and to use the same language to the boys as you would had they been guilty of forgery, or something equally dreadful, must have been hard to bear."

Then the father had sighed and turned away, feeling that there was no sympathy for him anywhere; and he questioned with himself as to whether his standard of morals was too high for this present world.

Then Mary, in her efforts to make amends to her mother for the lack of sympathy she had shown, and the words which ought not to have been spoken, essayed, the next time they met, to comfort her by regretting in unsparing terms the letter which had kept the boys away. If father had let one of them write, instead, all would have been well. Men do not know how to deal with such things. She wondered at father for not knowing that the boys would have been much better managed by their mother. Whereupon Mary, in her turn, was dismayed and vexed to be answered coldly to the effect that her father probably knew what was best to be done without asking advice from his children. He had always been a good and self-sacrificing father, she was sure. There could be no reason why his children should suppose that he had suddenly failed them. As to writing a harsh letter to the boys, she had never believed that he did. Harshness was foreign to his nature, and Mary would oblige her by not adding to her burdens at this time by censuring him.

Perhaps it is not to be wondered at, in the midst of all these conflicting views that Mary was bewildered and sore-hearted, and at times more unreasonable than ever before. It was the restlessness which had grown out of this state of things which helped to send her to the church social; and it was a curious desire to experiment and learn whether there was really anything which she could do to help a boy, that had led her to introduce herself to Ben Reeder. Perhaps there was never a girl more ready to be influenced, either for good or ill, than was Mary Cameron just at this time. But for Lucia's and Emilie's unfortunate teasing in connection with Professor

Landis, she would have allowed herself to enjoy his society and be influenced by his words; but the feeling that Emilie at least was on the alert, and would be likely to watch for ways to amuse her young friends at their expense, held this self-conscious woman from the help of which she was in such need. If thoughtless girls could only in some way be made to realize the mischief which their tongues may do in the name of "mere fun," what a blessing it would be to the world.

Mr. Kennedy was a different type of man from any who had heretofore crossed Miss Cameron's path. Lucia had more than one gentleman acquaintance who pleased themselves while with her by little special attentions, and sudden graceful turns in their sentences calculated to impress her with the fact that she was more interesting to them than was any other human being; and Lucia accepted these gaily, for what they were worth, and knew too little about the truest refinement to understand that she thereby brushed some of the bloom from her life's fruitage. But Mary's innate sense of honesty had instinctively repelled all such friendships. Most people were apt, when with her, to express only what they meant. Either Mr. Kennedy was an exception, or he meant a great deal for a new acquaintance. Mary Cameron, who was, as has been said, sore-hearted, and half afraid of her friends, welcomed this new peculiarly deferential manner as something unusually pleasant.

When Mr. Kennedy called, which he did as soon as propriety allowed, the good impression which he had made was deepened. He was certainly very agreeable, and more gentlemanly, Emilie declared, than any man she had ever seen, except Professor Landis. Mr. Cameron, who rarely commented upon the guests at his house, said that the young man had a head on his shoulders, and probably knew how to use it; he was connected with a leading business firm in New York.

"Dear me!" said Emilie, "I wish he would fall desperately in love with me, and ask me to elope with him. It would be so nice to get a little money into this family. I shouldn't much care how it came, so that we got it."

"Why need you elope?" asked Lucia. "If you could only bring the first mentioned wish to pass, couldn't the rest be carried out in a respectable manner, befitting the Cameron grandfather?"

"Oh, I don't know!" laughed Emilie. "I suppose there would be some bothersome hindrance about my being too young to know my own mind, and all that sort of thing. But I'm not, I can assure you. My mind is to have money, all I want for myself, and plenty to spare for all the rest of you; and as I said before, I am not particular how I get it. I would even allow a husband to be thrown in, if there were no other way."

"In my day," said Aunt Eunice severely, "girls hardly into their teens did not jest about love and marriage and matters of that kind. They had too much self-respect."

Emilie giggled. "I did not say a word about love," she declared; "it was *money* and marriage, Aunt Eunice. And you may depend upon it that if I find, upon diligent inquiry, that Mr. Kennedy has plenty of money, I'll do my best to coax him to decide for one of us. I don't particularly care which one, so that it is in the family."

It seemed not worthwhile to anybody but Aunt Eunice to make any reply to such bare-faced nonsense; but she continued the argument, if argument it could be called, provoking by her very gravity more daring nonsense still from the giddy girl, who finally verged so near the impudent that her mother had to silence her.

Mary, however, remembered and thought seriously over one or two of her sister's sentences. Money was what the family sorely needed. Her father's air of settled anxiety, and her mother's alternate fits of melancholy and nervous unrest, emphasized this thought daily. Retrenchment was, more than ever before, the order of the household. Emilie's expensive music lessons had at last been given up, to her great delight; and even the dancing lessons were threatened, but the child was so miserable over yielding those that her mother had not the heart to insist. She economized in whatever ways she could, or thought she did; but to a student of even ordinary economy the number of daily leaks which were allowed by these people, who did not know how to economize, would have been amusing if it had not been pitiful. Mary, as she went over in her weary mind the condition of things, admitted with Emilie that a wealthy marriage to a good, careless man, who would be willing to lavish much money on his wife, and care little as to what became of it, would be a great blessing to the family. And if this Mr. Kennedy was—she broke off there to say to herself indignantly that, of course, no respectable girl would marry for money. But then, he was very pleasant, all the family liked him, and if he really cared for one, what would prevent one's learning to be quite fond of him?

As the days passed, there grew to be more occasion for thought of this character, for it began to be increasingly apparent that Mr. Kennedy *cared,* and for Mary Cameron herself. His attentions, which were at first distributed with great cordiality among the entire family circle, not excepting Aunt Eunice, gradually centered so much that Emilie began to say with an air of great apparent relief:

"I do believe it is to be a rich brother-in-law instead of a husband! How nice! I shall like it ever so much better. They always give candies and things to young sisters-in-law. I've read that in books ever so many times; and those he gave me last night were delicious, Huyler's very own. I was the envy of half the girls in school today on account of them."

For some reason not understood by herself, Mary was not disturbed by all this. She made no attempt to check Emilie's exuberant satisfaction; and to her frequent reference to Mr. Kennedy's propensity for bringing her candies, made no other comment than that if she ever should be in a position to bestow gifts, she should remember how easily Emilie's tastes were satisfied.

Nor did she, amid all these pressing possibilities of her life, forget the boy whose gratitude she had won at the social. At last Ben Reeder summoned courage to make the call which, somewhat to his astonishment, he had promised. He found Mary at home, in the family sitting-room, which was, in fact, the back parlor; and because the piano was there she determined to entertain her caller in the presence of the entire family. Ben was at first much dismayed at meeting not one, but five ladies; and Mary exerted herself to the utmost to make him feel at ease. Lucia, at an utter loss as to why he had come, was interested in his frank, boyish face, and seconded Mary's efforts. The result was that Ben laid aside his embarrassment, and before the evening was over showed his bright, fun-loving spirit and his genial good sense to such advantage that one and all declared after he had gone that he was really very pleasant and bright, if he was a country boy.

"He reminds me of a boy I used to know, ever so far back, when I was a boy myself," said Mr. Cameron, with a pathetic little sigh which was apt to accompany any reference to his early life. "Where did you pick him up, Mary?"

"He was at the church social which was held at the Kinkaids', you remember. The pastor of the church is interested in him, I believe, and wanted to help him through the dangers of city life. I promised to play his songs for him if he would call. He has a pleasant voice, has he not? He would really make an excellent singer if his voice could be cultivated."

She hurried over the explanation. There was in her mind an unaccountable aversion to mentioning Professor Landis in connection with Ben. Of course it was the pastor of the church who was mainly interested, she told herself; pastors always were. It was probably he who had set Professor Landis on the boy's track. How else would a teacher come in contact with a boy who was a clerk in a store, and had never been to anything but a district school? At all events, she was not going to set Emilie off with some of her nonsense by admitting that Professor Landis had asked her to be kind to Ben. No comment was made on her explanation, save by Emilie.

"I think better of that Mr. Edson if he has really taken time to think of a boy from the country," she said complacently. "I didn't suppose he ever brought his lofty mind down to such trifles."

"Why, Emilie," said her father, a little amused, as he always was by this youngest daughter's comments, "what do you know of Mr. Edson?"

"Not much, father; and I can't say that I want to. He seems—well—*stuck up*—there are no other words that will express it. I was in Hartenburg's the other night when he came in with Miss Kinkaid. They stopped at the notion counter, where I stood talking with Nellie Evans. He chattered away to Miss Kinkaid like a magpie, and never even noticed Nellie, though she is a member of his church. After they had gone out I asked her if that wasn't her pastor, and if she hadn't been introduced to him. Oh, yes, she said, she had been introduced five or six times. Somebody was always introducing them; but he never remembered her for all that, unless he happened to see her in the Bible-class. I shouldn't like such a minister, father. Nellie Evans is as good as Miss Kinkaid, if she does have to sell crimpers and things to her behind Hartenburg's counter."

"Oh, well," said Mrs. Cameron, feeling that she ought to apologize for a minister, "a young man like him cannot be expected to remember all that swarm of young people, without years of practice."

But Emilie nodded her head sagely as she said, "I'll venture this yard of crochet that he remembers Miss Kinkaid wherever he sees *her*."

And Mary, a heightened color on her cheeks, wondered if he really was interested in Ben Reeder, and whether she had been quite as truthful as usual.

14. A New Game

Not only Mr. Kennedy, but Ben Reeder, came again. They met one evening in the Cameron back parlor. Ben had arrived first, and was domiciled with the family, having a good time, when Mr. Kennedy was announced.

"May I not join the circle?" he asked, as the parted curtains revealed Emilie in the act of initiating Ben into the mysteries of Halma. "It looks very homelike in that room."

They made a place for him around the center table. Ideas of economy had drawn this family closer together than had been their habit of late years. The winter was a cold one; and the furnace, after the manner of those eccentric creatures, frequently chose the back parlor as the room into which it delighted to pour its heat; therefore, the back parlor was by common consent chosen for the family room. Then, one drop-light could be made to do for several things, and Mrs. Cameron fell into the habit of bringing her work to it. It was Mr. Cameron's custom to give his evenings to the daily papers. Often, of late, he brought pencil and paper instead, and figured over weary lines of figures, apparently in a hopeless effort to make their sum less. The girls chose the room because their own was cold; and, having nothing in particular to do, they toyed with bits of fancy work, and rejoiced when the bell announced a possible relief. Even Ben Reeder had been welcomed with smiles. He was bright and good-natured, and brought news sometimes from a part of the world about which they knew little, and over which Emilie, at least, was curious.

On the evening in question, the entire family was present; Aunt Eunice with her interminable knitting, Lucia trifling over her crochet, and Emilie, whose books had been dropped that she might instruct Ben in the game. Mr. Cameron had his columns of figures, but put them aside when Mr. Kennedy was announced, and welcomed him with a look of relief.

With a heightened color on Mary's part, but a resolute air, Ben was introduced. Of course, Mr. Kennedy would wonder how a boy like him came to be at home in their circle, but it could not be helped. She would not copy what she despised in others, and ignore him. Apparently there was no need to worry over the result. Mr. Kennedy accepted Ben without a questioning glance, and included him in the conversation. A little later, when Mary was at the piano, and Mr. Kennedy had been turning the music, she took occasion to give the explanation which she thought was due.

"Our young guest is new to city life and ways, Mr. Kennedy, as I suppose you have observed. The truth is, he is a homesick boy who has few friends worthy of the name, and some enemies in the guise of friends."

"And you are trying to supply him with the one, and hold him from the other? I understand," said Mr. Kennedy, with a lighting up of his handsome face. "That is certainly kind, and is the sort of thoughtfulness which I should expect, especially from you. I appreciate it more than you think, perhaps. I was a homeless boy myself once."

Then Miss Cameron's truthfulness came to her aid. At least she could not listen to commendations which were not her due.

"You give me too much credit, Mr. Kennedy. I am quite new at any such attempt, and should never have thought of it had it not been suggested to me by another person."

He laughed lightly. "You have not a very true estimate of yourself, I think. I have observed it before. However, it is a failing so rare that one is tempted to admire rather than quarrel with it. I like your boy's face. It will give me pleasure to second your efforts in any way that I can."

Evidently this was not mere words. They went back, presently, to the circle around the table; and Mr. Kennedy drew his chair near to the players, and supplemented Emilie's careless teaching, devoting himself to the side of the learner with such skill that Ben was the winner.

"If you are fond of games," he said, while Ben was rejoicing over his victory, "come and see me some evening, and I will put you in the way of having one which is even more interesting than Halma."

"What is it?" Emilie asked, jealous for her favorite; but Mr. Kennedy's attention had already been called elsewhere, and he did not hear the question.

After that evening the friendship between Mr. Kennedy and Mary Cameron made rapid progress. On some pretext or other he managed to be with her a part at least of every evening. He took her to choice concerts and lectures. He took her one moonlight evening on a wonderful sleigh ride behind two swift-flying ponies. He took her to the Art Gallery to examine a certain rare picture which they forgot to examine, so absorbed did they become in each other's society. It was but the evening before Mr. Kennedy must return to New York, and he did not know when it would be his privilege to visit her city again, he told her. In fact, it depended upon her entirely whether he should ever care to come again. After that, how could they remember the picture? They were late in getting home, and Mrs. Cameron herself opened the door to them.

"Oh, mother! Are you still up?" asked Mary, and something in the tone of her voice made her mother turn and look closely at her.

"Is Mr. Cameron up also?" asked Mr. Kennedy eagerly. "Is he in the back parlor? Then may I not go in at once and have a few minutes with him? Consider, Mary, how little time there will be tomorrow."

He gave himself consent, being apparently too eager to wait for a demur; and Mrs. Cameron wondering, yet understanding, followed Mary into the dining-room, whither she had escaped.

"Oh, mother!" she said, her cheeks aglow. "He does rush things so! What made you let him talk to father tonight?"

"He did not wait for my permission. What is it that he wants, daughter?"

"Oh, *mother!* Don't you know? And yet it is all so sudden I do not wonder at your question."

"I understand," said Mrs. Cameron, all the mother in her heart coming into eyes and voice. "Oh, it is not so sudden to me. I have seen for days that he meant to get my girl away from me if he could. I am only half glad, Mary. I do not know that a mother could be expected to be more. It is in the nature of things, of course; but you are the oldest, you know—it will be the first break. Mary, you are sure you are doing what is the best for your happiness?"

"Oh mother! I am not sure of anything. It is sudden to me. He took me by surprise. I thought he liked me, a little; but one can never tell. I have thought—" She came to a sudden pause, the color flaming over her face. She had almost said, "I have thought so before of one other

person, and it meant nothing." Why should she think of
Russell Denham now? Assuredly she did not want to call
him to the remembrance of her mother. She went
upstairs in a fever of excitement; refusing to wait and see
Mr. Kennedy again as Mrs. Cameron suggested; refusing
to give her mother any more words.

"Tell him I had to go to my room," she said, pausing
half way up the stairs in answer to the appeal for a
message, at least, for Mr. Kennedy. "I will see him in the
morning at whatever hour he can come. I could not wait
tonight, it is so late. Mother I *can't*. I don't want to see
him again; I want to think."

"Think!" repeated Mrs. Cameron with a troubled
look. "It seems to me that the thinking should have come
before." But she spoke to herself; Mary had fled.

The next day the entire Cameron family were in a
state of subdued excitement. Indeed, on Emilie's part, the
word "subdued" does not apply. She was wild with
delight. "The very brother-in-law I would have selected
from the whole United States, I do believe," she declared.
"I used to think I liked Professor Landis better than any
other gentleman, and I think I do yet; but I am saving
him for myself, and Mr. Kennedy comes next. Such jolly
times as he will give me when he is once married and
settled down! I do hope, Mary, you are not going to keep
him waiting long. You can't. Long engagements are gone
entirely out. It is the style now to be married within a
very few months after the formal announcement is made.
When will it be, Mary?"

"I haven't the least idea," said Mary with composure. "What a ridiculous child you are, Emilie! I don't believe you will ever grow up."

"Oh, yes I shall. I shall blossom into young ladyhood now in a night. I shall have to, to keep Lucia company. What is the good of being a young lady when there is no chance for fun? Now I shall have a rich sister to visit; and she can make parties and things for me, and dress me to fit the occasions. Won't it be jolly?"

Amid the laughter that the girl's manner more than her words called forth, Lucia said: "I think that the prospective brother-in-law ought to be warned. If he were a millionaire he would hardly be equal to the demand which you could make. How do you know you are to have a rich sister?"

"Why, of course I am. Mr. Kennedy is a nephew of the Kennedy tribe, and they are all rich. He is a member of their firm, and so of course he has lots of money. That is the only drawback to Professor Landis. Professors are always poor, aren't they? They are in books—'poor but learned' you know. I don't know how I'll manage that, for I always thought I should never marry a poor man. Mary, you will have a carriage right away, won't you? And ponies, and a coachman? I always thought a coachman belonging to a family would be the height of bliss. And make him wear livery, too. You might use mother's coat-of-arms. Wouldn't that be fine?"

For almost the first time in her grown-up life, Emilie's nonsense did not jar on her sister's nerves. On the contrary, she enjoyed it. The girl was absurd, of course; but there was an underlying truth in her fun which soothed Mary Cameron's heart. She had come to the rescue of her family. This genial, merry-hearted young man, who had lavished money on her so freely during their short acquaintance, would be almost sure to let her do as she would with large sums. What would she *not* do for the girls whose lives had been so cramped for the lack of a few dollars; for the overburdened father, whose constantly increasing anxieties had eaten like a canker into her heart; for the mother who had sacrificed in many ways for her, as Mary knew well, though she had never acted as though she did; above all, for the boys, who were held away from their home because of poverty. She felt sure she could manage it so that the remainder of their college course need not be crippled in such petty ways as it had been heretofore. Oh, it was blissful to think of all the joy she could pour into this home life. She who had in her secret heart longed to do something for them all, and had felt so impotent that it had kept her irritable and unlovely—they should all see now how much she loved them, and how royally she could show it. During this entire first day of her engagement, this thought remained uppermost.

At three o'clock Mr. Kennedy hurried away to catch a New York train. There were no tears to mar the closing minutes of his stay. He was coming back so soon, and was such a short distance away at any time, that it did not seem worthwhile to be gloomy over his absence. Besides, there was no time. While they stood at the window watching him run for his car, having waited with an assurance characteristic of him until the very last moment, a messenger-boy arrived with a dispatch from the long-delayed Rachel, announcing her coming on the four-fifty train. Whereupon the family excitement was turned into a new channel. The daughter and sister who had been absent for so many years as to seem almost a stranger to the younger ones, and whose probable coming had been heralded and deferred so many times as to give them almost the feeling that she would never come at all, was now unexpectedly at the very door.

"The idea!" said Mrs. Cameron. "On the four-fifty train! Why, there will barely be time to meet it. Your father will have to be telephoned at once. Run, Emilie, and attend to it; and tell him to be sure to go himself, for I cannot, and none of you girls would know her."

"Not know our own sister!" Emilie exclaimed. "How absurd that seems! I believe I should know her by instinct. Why, we would know her from her photograph, of course."

This probability was discussed; and it was finally agreed that since Rachel had not even sent them a photograph in two years, and was at the age when two years make great changes, it was hardly to be supposed that she would be recognized. Emilie finally gave up the desire she had to meet her at the train; doing it, however, in a characteristic manner.

"After all, I don't believe I want to meet her. It is awfully poky standing around a railway station with a stranger. One never knows what to say; and if you have thought of something and shouted it out, it isn't heard in the din, and by the time it is repeated it sounds so silly you are vexed with yourself for having said it at all. I'll wait and welcome my lady at home. It is queer to be half afraid of my own sister; but that is exactly my state of mind."

It was the unexpressed state of mind of every one of them, the mother not excepted. Six years make such differences, even with one's own children.

At eight o'clock of that same evening, the newcomer was alone in the back parlor, which had been lighted brilliantly in honor of her home-coming. The family had been together there since dinner, and but a moment before had scattered. Mr. Cameron had reported that he must go out to a Board meeting, much against his will; Mrs. Cameron had been summoned to the kitchen with a view to the morning meal; Lucia had been obliged to accompany Emilie to the latter's dancing-class; and Mary had excused herself for a few minutes on the plea that some last arrangements for the new sister's comfort were necessary. They had all, despite their best intentions, treated her as though she were a guest; a loved and honored guest, indeed, but still it was not an ideal homecoming. The truth is, it had not been possible to be quite natural. Even Aunt Eunice seemed to have been stirred out of her usual grim calm. "Poor child!" she had said, when she greeted Rachel, and then her eyes had grown suddenly dim. After dinner she went directly to her room, no one knew wherefore.

So Rachel was for the moment alone. She arose from her easy chair, and wandered into the shadows of the long front parlor where a single gas jet burned faintly. She found her way to the low, wide mantel, leaned her arm on it, bowed her young head upon her arm, and thought. It would be very strange to let the tears come, now that she was really at home, but they were very near the surface. She had parted only that day with cousin John, and cousin John had been her brother for six years.

Just at that moment came Mr. Kennedy from the car at the corner, and sprang up the steps of the Cameron home. The curtains had not been drawn; and he saw, or thought he saw, Mary Cameron leaning in a dejected attitude against the mantel, her face hidden on her arm. It was reasonable to suppose that she was being desolate because she missed him. He would give her a surprise, if it could be managed skillfully.

"I will announce myself," he said to the astonished Betsey, when she answered his ring; for Betsey, with the rest of the family, believed this man to be well on his way to New York. "Your mistress is in the front parlor, I notice; and you need not mention my coming to the others—that is a good girl." He emphasized his direction by something hard and shining which he slipped into the girl's hand, and she went smiling away. If he wanted to see Miss Mary without being bothered by the others, why shouldn't he?

He went swiftly and silently toward the bowed figure robed in black, as he had seen Mary that day, and as, in the dimly lighted room, he believed he saw her still, bent over her, and kissed lightly the fair outline of cheek which was all of her face that was visible. Then there was a sudden uplifting of a haughty head, and a pair of cheeks that blazed, turned toward him, while a strange voice said: "What does this—?" and stopped, and began again on the instant:

"Can this be—you cannot be—one of my brothers, Rod, or Mac?"

Mr. Kennedy, who was at first dumbfounded, was a quick-witted man, and took in the probable situation.

"I beg ten thousand pardons," he said, "and I hardly know how to explain myself unless you have heard of me. You are Rachel Cameron, I am sure; and I thought you were your sister Mary. Have you been at home long enough to have heard of Willis Kennedy? No? Then I must explain further. I am neither Rod nor Mac, but I am, nevertheless, entitled to a brother's consideration. Your sister Mary is my promised wife; but I assure you, I did not intend to claim relationship in such wild fashion. I thought to take her by surprise."

The color slowly faded from the fair face, and Rachel gave him the benefit of a very frank, bright smile. It would be absurd to be dignified with even a stranger under such circumstances.

"I understand," she said, in a voice which was singularly pure. "I have been at home for a few hours only, not long enough for confidences, unless they are surprised out of one. But I am very glad to extend a sisterly greeting, if I may," and she held out her hand, "and then to call my sister."

"She is not expecting me," he explained. "I am supposed to be nearing New York at this moment; but I missed my train—lucky fellow that I nearly always am!—and cannot get away now until midnight. There were some tiresome complications connected with the delay, telegrams to send, and replies to wait for, or I should have been here sooner, in time to welcome you, perhaps. I have the advantage of you, Miss Rachel, having heard you mentioned frequently, but I was not aware that you were expected today."

"Upon my word," muttered this young man as Rachel Cameron, having lingered to respond to his explanations, went finally in search of her sister. "Upon my word, she is as delicious a specimen as I ever struck; has the air of a queen, and can be as gracious as one, and as indignant! How her beautiful eyes blazed over my greeting! A lively beginning for a prospective brother-in-law I will admit, but I can't say I regret it. If a fellow had only met her sooner, eh, and *she* were the uncle's favorite, what then? Nonsense! Of course, I do not mean anything of the kind. I wonder if Mary will appreciate my breathless dash up here to give her an hour or two of my precious time? And

I wonder if her sister will tell her of my mistake? I certainly shall not."

15. "KATHERINE SPELLED WITH A K"

Some of those last sentences need explanation. In order to give it, it will be necessary to return to the evening in which Mr. Kennedy was introduced to Miss Cameron. Arrived at his boarding-house after the social, he found his cousin Eustis Kennedy waiting for him. Eustis Kennedy was the son of a leading physician in the city, and was himself a lawyer of fair promise. Dr. Kennedy's uptown house was supposed to be too far away from business centers for his nephew's convenience; at least the young man was very willing to make that an excuse for finding other quarters during his stay in the city. The stately mansion where every-day life was managed in a dignified and methodical way was not at all to this young man's taste. He knew very little of his preoccupied uncle, and was not especially fond of him, and there were no young people except the aforesaid cousin. The two men did not assimilate very well, and by mutual consent saw extremely little of each other, though they were friendly enough when they chanced to meet. In view of this state of things, it was a surprise to Willis Kennedy to find himself waited for on the evening in question. It appeared that his cousin had just returned from a trip to a neighboring city, and had brought him a message of importance from his business firm.

"Still, it would have kept until tomorrow," laughed Willis Kennedy. "You need not have hunted me out away down here tonight for it."

"I should not have had time tomorrow to deliver it," replied his cousin, thereby showing in a single sentence the contrast between himself and his relative. Then he asked, "How do you pass your time after business hours? What do you do with yourself evenings, for instance?"

"Blunder around anywhere. This evening, for instance, I have been to a church social."

"Indeed!" Whereupon both gentlemen laughed.

"I have, on my honor," continued Willis Kennedy. "Got caught with a young fellow who runs that sort of thing, and couldn't civilly refuse. However, I am glad I went. I had a reasonably pleasant time, and made the acquaintance of an extremely interesting young woman."

"In this end of the town? Who is she?"

"A Miss Cameron, who seemed to be almost as much of a stranger as I am myself; although I believe she lives not very far from the scene of action tonight."

"Miss Cameron!" echoed his cousin. "What sort of a person? Tall and fair, with unusual eyes and a great deal of hair, and more than her share of stateliness?"

"That describes her very well; though she was friendly enough to me, I am sure she could be stately on occasion. In fact, I saw a little of it this evening, when one or two persons she did not fancy tried to talk with her."

"You are in luck, my boy. If she was gracious to you, I would suggest that you follow up the acquaintance. I know Miss Cameron by sight and by reputation. She can be decidedly stately, as you say. She is an heiress, or is to be as soon as a certain uncle resident in California dies. The interesting thing about it is, that she does not know it herself, nor do any of her family. It is a law secret which I am giving away. They live quite plainly, I believe, and have not too much of this world's goods. It is rather interesting to know that the oldest daughter will come into possession of something over a million before long. Romantic, isn't it? The uncle is quite old and feeble now, we hear. The revelation will probably come in a few months at the latest. It is quite a second-rate novel plot. He has kept his eye on these relatives, it seems, through all the intervening years, hardening his heart apparently to the amount of good his money might be doing while he is here, and waiting to astonish them at the end."

"What an extraordinary story!" said his cousin, deeply interested. "Are you sure she is sole heiress? And do you say that none of the family know of it?"

"Not one. There is an old family feud, I believe, which has kept them apart; and this uncle cannot make up his mind to be reconciled while he lives, but proposes to smooth everything over after he is gone. Oh, yes, I am as sure as a member of one of the firm having his business in charge ought to be. But it is a grave secret, remember. I do not know why I gave it away. I am not in the habit of gossiping about business matters, as you are aware. You took me by surprise mentioning the lady's name. I hope you will understand that it would make serious trouble for me if the story should leak out?"

"Of course," said the other cheerily. "I can be as mum as an oyster when I choose. I wouldn't mention it for a share in the Bank of England; it might jeopardize the millions. But, as you say, it is a very romantic story. What is the fortunate lady's first name?"

"Katherine, spelled with a K; there is another name, I believe, but I do not recall it. I remember thinking that Katherine Cameron had a euphonic sound."

"And she is the only daughter, do you say?"

"Oh, no! There are other daughters, half a dozen for aught I know; but she is the elect one. She bears the magic name which connects her with a memory dating seventy years back; so our chief says. Romantic to the end, you see; or rather to the beginning. Well, don't lose your heart for all that, if you can help it; for, 'there's many a slip,' you know. Good-night to you. Come up when you can."

Now Mr. Willis Kennedy's soliloquy after his meeting with Rachel Cameron will be understood. At the same time, I hope it is very plain to the reader that this young man was not that favorite character in a certain class of novels, a fortune hunter. Had he not become decidedly interested in Mary Cameron before his cousin Eustis gave that interesting secret into his keeping, it is by no means certain that he would have put himself out in any way to seek her acquaintance. But it occurred to him as a very romantic thing that he should have been spending an hour with the lady, and should have felt more interested in her than in any other lady of his acquaintance. He had asked and obtained permission to call upon her, and had fully meant to do so, before he heard of her prospective millions. The day came when he liked to emphasize this fact. As the acquaintance progressed, he tried to put the millions out of his thoughts entirely. He told himself angrily one day that he wished he had never heard of them. It would be an extremely awkward thing for him if Mary should ever learn that he had known about her fortune long before she did. He avoided his cousin, wishing to hear no more, and being scrupulously anxious that he should not know how well the hint given in jest had been acted upon. He carefully avoided all reference to the Cameron relatives, and tried to look utterly indifferent when Rachel Cameron was mentioned, and it was announced that she had been with relatives in California. He could not help a gleam of satisfaction as Mary explained to him one day, when he was marking handkerchiefs for her, that the K stood for an old-fashioned family name which had a history.

"All our names have histories," she said, smiling. "Father and mother keep up the family traditions." He tried to appear interested only in the corner of the handkerchief which should have the initials; but as he carefully fashioned the K it was impossible to put away the sound of his cousin's voice, "Katherine spelled with a K."

He did not believe, not even in his inmost soul, that the consciousness of what was to be had hurried his intentions towards Mary Cameron save as, of course—as he told himself—any sane man would know that he could not in his present circumstances support a wife. There were days when he went over these things carefully, and explained to himself with almost painful reiteration that he cared more for Mary Cameron, a great deal more, than for anyone else in the world; and at such times he was almost sure to add that that little witch of an Emilie Cameron would drive away the blues from any house; and that the Cameron girls were all charming. He and Mary would, one of these days, give them the surroundings they deserved.

Much of this soliloquizing went on after he had returned to New York and taken up again his regular round of duties and pleasures. He was not a young man who devoted himself exclusively to business. The claims of society were always loyally acknowledged by him, and it was not to be supposed that because he was engaged to be married he should therefore become a hermit. Instead of that, he must think of his future wife, and hold for her a place among his friends. He reflected with no little satisfaction that he claimed as his acquaintances some of the first people, and that as a married man he would, before a great while, be able to "hold his own " with the best of them.

Meantime, Rachel Cameron was trying to find her place in her father's house and settle into it. To leave home as a little girl with all the plans and memories of girlhood, and to return to it a young woman with every plan in life changed and every memory dimmed, is a bewildering experience. Nothing was quite as she had thought it. She roomed with Emilie, and that exceedingly bright and exceedingly giddy girl bewildered her quite as much as did her elder sisters. How strangely the child was bringing herself up! For nobody seemed to be trying to bring her up. This was the mental comment of the sister not quite three years her elder. One subject, which since Aunt Eunice had become a member of the family was often a bone of contention, was brought up one evening when they were gathered in the back parlor. This was no other than Emilie's extravagant fondness for dancing. She was urging the importance of being allowed to attend a dancing party which was to be given by one of her school friends; and her mother and Mary were both opposing it, each on different grounds.

"I do not understand why you want to accept Nettie Baker's invitations," Mary said. "The family are not in our list of acquaintances at all, and the young people do not go with our set."

Then Emilie: "Oh, 'our set!' I hate those words. We haven't any 'set,' so far as I can see. We have dropped out of our old one since we came down here to live, and for my part I am glad of it. I don't believe in 'sets.' When people are nice, and you like them, why is not that enough?"

"Emilie," interposed Lucia, "I am surprised at you; you should remember the honor of the family now. Are we not at last about to have an alliance with money as well as family? Think of Mary, and choose your associates with care."

This reference drew from Mary only a good-natured laugh. She liked to remember always that she was soon to be in a position to give advice to those younger sisters, as an autocrat, and to lighten her father's burdens. Let it always be remembered that she was sure to put this thought in the fore-front. Still, she felt it sometimes necessary to moderate their expectations.

"You should not be too sure," she said to Lucia. "Because Willis is a Kennedy, and belongs to the great firm of Kennedy & Kennedy, is no reason why he should have a great deal of money at present. Remember he is a young man."

Emilie nodded her head in that sage way she had as she said, "I'll risk the money part; he has enough of it. Doesn't he waste it awfully all the time?" And she glanced effectively at the diamond ring which gleamed on Mary's finger, and flashed its brilliancy in a thousand reflected sparkles. "That's the largest diamond I ever saw a lady wear. He might just as well have chosen a smaller one, and saved his money if it was scarce. And then think of that box of Huyler's very best—a great big box!" This was mixing the grand with the ridiculous to such an extent that there seemed nothing but laughter for the whole family.

"Emilie would rather have the candy than the diamond ring, I believe," said Lucia; and Emilie nodded instant assent. "Of course I would; I can divide that with my friends, and I couldn't the ring. But never mind either of them just now; let us settle about this party. Mother, why do you say I can't go?"

"It is a question of dress, child. You say you have nothing suitable to wear, and I am tired of telling you that we cannot afford to spend a cent for dress this quarter. We have even less than usual to depend on."

"Of course," said Emilie, with another of her nods. "It is always 'less than usual;' and there are always 'unusual expenses,' aren't there? I know that story by heart. But I can furbish up my old dress, I suppose, and wear it if I have to. All I shall want will be some gloves and slippers and a few flowers."

"But even those are out of the question, Emilie. I cannot consent to your asking your father for a single penny this quarter for anything but absolute necessities. You must see how harassed he is."

Then Mary sighed, and could not help wishing that she had in her pocket-book the hundred dollars which her ring must have cost; and she could not help thinking of the time when she could with great delight supply Emilie's small needs. It would certainly be pleasant to look after her in this way. While she was thinking these thoughts Aunt Eunice was talking.

"I don't see what you mean by letting her go on in this way. If she had a hundred pairs of slippers and gloves, and was my girl, she wouldn't go to any dances. I can't, for the life of me, think what her father is about. He wasn't brought up to be so careless. It's a disgrace to the family name. None of the girls of his mother's family went to a dance, any more than they would to a smallpox hospital."

Emilie was never other than amused over her aunt's tirades. She responded to this one in the utmost good humor.

"Aunt Eunice, what harm is there in a dancing party?"

"What harm! A girl of your age is old enough to know the harm without asking. Wasting your time and strength in skipping over the floor and simpering with the men. Supposing you were to die at a party, just while you were hopping around in that silly way?"

The girl replied only by a merry laugh

"Emilie!" said Mrs. Cameron reprovingly.

"Well, I can't help it, mother; it is too funny. What has dying got to do with it? Suppose I should die while I am washing up the lunch dishes for Betsey? It would be an equally inappropriate time, I am sure."

"Oh, you can make fun of even a death-bed," said Aunt Eunice angrily. "I am perfectly aware of that; but I knew of one girl who died on the floor of a ball-room. She went against her father's will, and she was brought home a corpse; now, that is the truth!"

Emilie had much ado not to laugh again. She could not see what that incident, solemn as it was, had to do with the subject.

"But, Aunt Eunice," she began again, "if we had to choose all our occupations and amusements with a view to possibly dying in them, a great many things would look inappropriate. Don't you think so?"

"I think in a world like this we have no time for simply amusing ourselves. It's a sick and dying world; full of trouble and suffering of every kind, and isn't going to last long for the youngest. We ought to be busy about other things; and dancing is just one of Satan's devices for leading souls to ruin. No respectable girl ought to have anything to do with it; and if I were your mother, my lady, you wouldn't, if I had to tie you up at home."

"Aunt Eunice, how glad you and I ought to be that you are not my mother!" This was as far as the argument had extended, when the door-bell interrupted them, and Professor Landis was announced.

They made room for him in the family circle, apologizing that the wind blew in just the wrong direction and the furnace declined to have anything to do with the front parlor. He had hardly time to express his pleasure at being welcomed to the cozier room, before Emilie pitched her question at him. "Professor Landis, do you think it is wicked to dance?"

"Oh not at all!" said the professor, regarding the bright-faced girl with amused eyes. "Why should there be anything wicked in that?"

"I don't know, I am sure. Aunt Eunice, you hear what Professor Landis says; and he is as religious as—oh, a great deal more religious than the minister—some ministers, anyway."

"Well," said Aunt Eunice, with firmly set lips, "I have seen a great many different kinds of religious people. I'm glad I'm not that kind *myself*."

Professor Landis, with his mirth-beaming eyes still fixed on Emilie, continued: "There is a charming little dancer at the University. If you will call upon me some morning I will get him to perform if he is present. He is not a regular student, you understand, and cannot be depended upon as to hours."

"A student at the University! That is a queer place for dancing. What does he do it for?"

"For his living. He earns it regularly in that way; at least most of his extras; mince-pie, and matters of that kind, you understand. Somebody whistles, and he dances in perfect time; then we throw him a bit of pie, or a bone possibly, from our luncheon, to show our appreciation. He can dance on two legs, and hold out the other two for the aforesaid pie. He is accomplished."

"Oh!" said Emilie, pouting a little while the others laughed. "You are talking about a dog. I was in earnest. Aunt Eunice thinks we ought not to dance, for fear we might die while we are at a dancing-party. What harm would it do if we did? I mean," she added, in response to her mother's reproving look, and Aunt Eunice's exclamation, "it wouldn't be the place one would choose, of course; but why does that prove it wrong, any more than it would prove it wrong to go on a journey because one might die on the way; and one certainly would not want to?"

"It does not," said Professor Landis, perfectly grave now. "In my judgment it proves nothing of the sort."

"That is what I think," said Emilie, waxing more earnest; "and all those things they say against it—that it takes time, and is frivolous and unfits one for study—so do croquet parties, and tennis parties, and musicales, and all sorts of things, if people attend them too often, or stay too late; and yet people who are good Christians go to them and frown on dancing. I don't see any sense in it. Allie Fenwood's mother won't let her even *learn* to dance; and she lets her play at musicales, and stay later than I do when I go to a dancing party. I think it is inconsistent and silly."

Professor Landis regarded the pretty girl with kindly eyes, and said gently, "May there not be a reason back of all these, of which you have not thought, that emphasizes the disapproval of some persons for this form of amusement?"

"I am sure I do not know what it can be," said Emilie with energy. And then the guest looked at the mother. The thought in his heart was: "What can that mother have been about while her beautiful young daughter was budding into girlhood?"

16. Being Weighed

"Mr. Landis," said Mary, who decided that about this time a change of subject would be wise, "how is our friend Ben prospering? I have not seen him for several weeks."

It was surprising, to those who did not understand it, how entirely Mary Cameron's manner had changed toward their neighbor. The certainty that there would be no further occasion for teasing her at his expense seemed to have sweetened all her thought of him, and no one of the family welcomed him more cordially than did she. Lucia and Emilie were outspoken as to their pleasure in his society, and even Aunt Eunice had admitted that he was "well enough." It cannot be said that the two families were intimate, for the sister, Dorothy, seemed the busiest of mortals, and had little time for society; nor had the young ladies of the Cameron household met her friendliness with such abundant cordiality as to lead her to earnestly desire their companionship. But there were occasional evenings when she was at her interminable classes, in which Professor Landis seemed to have leisure for his friends; and at such times it began to be natural for him to "drop in" next door.

The family were not yet intimate enough to ask questions. Even Emilie had to content herself with surmises; but she commented on them as freely as though they were known facts; for instance, after this fashion:

"I should think Professor Landis would hate awfully to have his sister teach in the evenings as well as daytimes. I suppose she wouldn't have to do it if she didn't take time to keep house for him. Why don't they board, I wonder? Shouldn't you think it would be cheaper for them? Anyhow, I'd find something to do, if I were he, that would make money enough for her to rest in the evening. Almost all men are selfish, I believe. Mary, don't you hope that Mr. Kennedy will be a delightful exception?"

Over Mary's question concerning Ben, the Professor looked grave, even disturbed.

"I am afraid I cannot give you an encouraging account of him, Miss Cameron. I feel more disheartened and troubled over him now than I have since his first entry into city life. He has developed some dangerous tastes of late, especially for a boy of his temperament. I do not know how it will end."

Immediately Emilie was curious, also sympathetic. "Oh, dear me!" she said. "How sorry I am! I like that boy, and we had real fun together, playing Halma. He is just as bright! Mr. Kennedy gave him some hints one evening, skillful hints, such as I do not know enough to give, and after that I had to watch with the greatest care or he would beat me every time."

Professor Landis did not smile; instead, his gravity deepened. "He has natural tastes in those directions I fear," he said, "possibly inherited tastes, I do not know."

"What, for Halma? How queer! I did not know that people inherited such things. Why do you fear it, Professor? There is surely no harm in playing Halma, if there is in dancing."

"Emilie," said Mrs. Cameron, "one would think that you were a 'Professor,' and our guest your pupil. Why will you ask so many questions?"

"I am only in pursuit of knowledge, mother. What is the harm in Halma, please?"

Thus pressed, he admitted that he was not thinking of Halma, but of other games less innocent.

"What games?" Emilie immediately asked. She was fond of games, she declared. Was there a new one, and was it really wicked, or only a trifle dangerous? She believed she liked things that were just a little bit dangerous; it gave them a sort of spice, didn't he think? What was this new one?

He was speaking of nothing new, he told her. Ben had learned to play cards, he was sorry to say; and they fascinated him, as they had many another stronger than he.

"Cards!" exclaimed Aunt Eunice, dropping her knitting to lift up her hands in a gesture of dismay. "Then he is lost! He is just the kind of boy to go to ruin fast. I could see it when he was here, playing with Emilie. I don't believe in any kind of games, myself; they are all luck and chance, and they lead folks down to ruin. I've seen it time and again. I shouldn't wonder if your Halma was the beginning of it, Emilie."

"No," said Professor Landis quickly; "or at least Miss Emilie is in no sense of the word to blame. It was very kind of her to give up her evening to Ben's amusement. No one could have foreseen that he would make the jump from the quiet home game of skill to the public card-table."

"He was very fond of Halma," said Emilie, a little touch of apprehension in her voice. The Cameron family had been brought up to have a horror of cards. Their father, who had had a bitter lesson in his youth, had been pronounced on this subject, if no other. "I noticed how eager he was to win. Did he go directly from that to cards, Professor Landis?"

"He was invited to do so, Miss Emilie, and was carefully taught the first steps. It was done in kindness, I fully believe, without so much as a thought of the possibility of evil consequences. But Ben is already weary of a game in which there is nothing to win but success, and plays for a cigar, or a ticket to the theatre, or any trifle, just to give spice to the game, he says."

"Who could have been so mean as to have started him?" said Emilie, in sharp indignation. "Almost everybody with sense knows how boys away from home are ruined in this way. There is a girl in school who cries half the time because her brother keeps losing at cards, and getting them into frightful trouble. Now I suppose Ben will go and make his father lose his house, after all. I think it is horrid!"

Mary Cameron bent over her work as if absorbed in it, and said not a word, while the others talked on about Ben Reeder, his prospects and his dangers; and Emilie questioned, but received no light as to who had started the boy on his downward way; but Mary knew. Her cheeks glowed as she recalled the fact that Mr. Kennedy had been exceedingly kind to the boy, and had taken pains to put him in a way to make his evenings less dull.

"I had him come into the club-house with some of the young men whom I know pretty well, and taught him a game we are fond of, just to help keep him out of mischief. He is really a very bright boy, worth looking after. My friends were good to him, and he had a 'real jolly time,' as he expressed it, and was surprisingly grateful. He hasn't happened to strike a great deal of kindness in this world, I fear."

This was the way Mr. Kennedy had put it to her; and she had admired him for his kindness, and said within herself that he had been more practical in his efforts than Professor Landis, who seemed to have nothing better to offer for the boy's entertainment than church socials! She had thanked him for the interest he took in Ben, and had felt that he did it to show her how entirely he was ready to further any efforts of hers.

But he had spoken only of a "game they were fond of." Why had he not said "a game of cards"? Was it accident or design that he had not? Moreover, was he a card player himself, a habitual one? If so, and her father knew it, what would he say? What had she to say herself? It seemed strange, seemed almost like design, that neither he nor Ben should have mentioned the word in her hearing; although Ben had told her of the "jolly" evening which Mr. Kennedy gave him, and had said he was what he called a "brick." If this were really an attempt to deceive her so early in their acquaintance . . . her eyes glowed at the thought. But she rallied instantly, and began to upbraid herself. What nonsense it all was! Why *should* he have mentioned cards? He probably merely happened not to do so. Everybody played cards, she presumed, except ministers and men with old-fashioned ideas like her father, and occasionally a fanatic like Professor Landis. She scarcely knew any young persons besides themselves who did not play at home for amusement. That was different from going to saloons and gambling-houses to play, of course. Mr. Kennedy ought to have been more careful, and to have remembered that Ben Reeder was away from home and friends. But because her father's young brother had been a most ruined with cards years ago, and he therefore had had a horror of them ever since, it was not necessary to pounce upon the world and try to bring it to that level. People had been ruined by fast horses before now, but that did not make it a crime to drive the best one could afford.

So, while the talk flowed on about her, she heard it but dimly, and patched up a peace with her heart and conscience, and was glad her father was not there. He might question even more closely than Emilie, and he had troubles enough now.

When she gave attention to the talk again, it was still about Ben Reeder and cards. Emilie was saying:

"But, Professor Landis, that is shocking! Mary, do you hear that? He says Ben played all night last night, and went to the store without any breakfast or any sleep. At that rate he will get sent home in disgrace. Perhaps it would be a good thing for him if he were. I wonder if they would be good to him? I wonder if fathers and mothers out of books are ever real good to their children who come home bad? Do you suppose they are, mother? How would we all treat Rod or Mac if we were ashamed of them?"

"Emilie!" said her mother with such sharpness and yet such pain in her voice that the thoughtless girl paused, looked at her wonderingly, and said:

"Why, mother, I am only supposing a case. But, Professor Landis, really, can't anything be done to get Ben away from that place? I'll help; I'll play Halma with him every evening for a month if that will do any good. I don't want him to go back to his mother, spoiled. He told me some nice things about her."

"Can he not be persuaded to take the Lord Jesus Christ for an intimate friend? Then he will be safe from temptations of every sort." It was Rachel Cameron's clear voice which asked this question; asked it simply,

225

naturally, as though it were the most reasonable possible solution of a difficulty. Professor Landis turned eager, almost hungry eyes upon her, and spoke quickly, while the others stared as though she had used a language unknown to them.

"Miss Cameron, you have struck the only force which I believe will do my poor Ben any good. I know something of the power of that disease called gambling, when it gets hold of a boy like Ben; and he has seized upon it as though it were the thing his life had been waiting for. If he would but allow himself to be introduced to Christ and accept his friendship, all would be well. Is it not the marvel of marvels that a young fellow of fair sense otherwise, should reject such a friendship?"

"Nothing is so strange to me in life as the fact that men and women everywhere are doing the same thing," said Rachel Cameron, with a note of pathos in her voice, which made it very expressive. Emilie looked from one to the other curiously, and could not resist the temptation to ask another question.

"What do people mean when they talk like that? How could joining the church, and going to prayer-meeting, and things of that sort, help Ben Reeder, for instance? Keep him from wanting to play cards, or do anything else that some people thought he ought not?"

"Miss Emilie, have you never met, intimately, people who found in Jesus Christ such an absorbing fellowship that they desired above all things to frequent the places where he could be met, and do the things in which he could join them? Who, in short, found him satisfying?"

"No, honestly, I don't believe I ever have. I know ever so many church members, of course; lots of the girls in school are, and they do not seem to me to have nice times at all. That is, I mean their nice times have nothing to do with their religion. Sometimes they say: 'Oh, dear! I suppose I ought to go to prayer-meeting tonight, I haven't been in three weeks;' and they speak as though it was an *ought* and not a comfort. No," she said, meditatively, "I don't believe I know one person whom it makes happy. Father is a church member, has been for ever so many years, but he is as unhappy as he can be. All sorts of things worry him. And Aunt Eunice is a church member; but you aren't happy, are you, Aunt Eunice? You know you said only this morning that it was a cross-grained world, and you were sick and tired of it. I don't think there are any such people as you are talking about, Professor Landis; and I don't understand how that kind of thing can do a boy like Ben Reeder any good."

The slow color mounted to Aunt Eunice's very forehead; but, contrary to the habit of her life, she answered not a word. Professor Landis looked at Rachel Cameron, and smiled a slight, grave smile.

"We are being weighed in the balances of a keen observer," he said. "Is it possible that we shall all be found wanting?"

The color went and came on the girl's fair face. She felt like a stranger in her own home; more of a stranger than was this next-door neighbor. Yet ought she to let such a challenge as that pass in silence? There was a moment of intense stillness, no one seeming to know what to say next, even Emilie the irrepressible being apparently subdued. Then Rachel spoke again:

"Emilie, dear, though we are sisters, I am almost a stranger to you. I hardly know how to say it, because my life may not match my words; will not, indeed, because, though I love Jesus Christ and try to copy him, I know only too well what an imperfect copy it is, after all; but I do want to tell you that he satisfies me. I do not reach out after anything that this world can give, if it must be had at the expense of an hour's separation from his approving smile; and I do know that if that young man should give his life up to Christ's keeping, he would keep it for him, and make it a joy and, in the truest sense of the word, a success."

"Amen," said Professor Landis. "Let me bear the same testimony throughout. I do not wonder that you find it hard to understand, because of the many poor imitations which we make; but in your fancy work you do not quarrel with the perfect pattern, do you, because of the mistake you make in working by it?"

And then Mr. Cameron's night-key was heard in the door; and some of them at least were glad that this conference, which had taken such an unexpected and embarrassing form, was over.

But Emilie began it again, when she and Rachel were in their own room.

"I liked what you said," she announced, as she stood at the dressing bureau, twisting her hair out of shape for the night. "It sounded interesting, somehow, and you looked as though you meant it; but I don't understand it. If things are as you and Professor Landis think, why don't we see more results? Why isn't poor father, for instance, helped and rested, instead of being tormented half out of his life, with the struggle to live? I'll own that sometimes I feel as though I would *steal* a little money, in a sort of respectable way, you know, just to help him out. You have no idea how he is harassed month after month with bills and things. He is doing his very best; why doesn't his religion come in and help him?"

"Are you sure it does not?" asked Rachel gently. "Perhaps his weight of care would be too much for him but for that help. But, Emilie, I cannot speak for the experience of others, only my own. I know I have been helped to live and to endure some things that else would have been too hard, because I was sure that my dear Lord Jesus sent them to me, and knew all about it."

"What hard things can you have had to bear?" asked Emilie, turning and bestowing a curious, searching look upon her. But finding that there was no reply to this wonderment, her mind promptly traveled to another subject.

"Well, I know I don't understand such things. What is the use of talking about them? There is one thing I do understand, however, and that is dancing. Can't you contrive some way for me to get to that party? You are quick-witted, I fancy; and I am just dying to go. It will be the event of the season for us 'young things,' as Aunt Eunice calls us. Don't you dance, Rachel? Well, now, why not?" as Rachel with a quiet smile shook her head. "You don't believe all that rubbish that Aunt Eunice gets off, I know you don't; you have too much sense. Even Professor Landis doesn't believe it, and I don't know a more particular person than he. What did he mean tonight by a 'reason back of all that,' looking as wise as an owl when he said it?"

"Emilie, dear," said the sister, drawing closer to her and resting a hand on her plump shoulder, "may I ask a few questions which may sound strange to you?"

"Of course," said Emilie, brushing her frizzes vigorously, "ask anything you wish; and I can be solemn, too, if there is occasion."

"Then, don't you think that there may come a time in your life when you will have a friend whom you will love more than any other person on earth; love enough to marry, I mean, and go away from home and everybody, if necessary, with him?"

"Why—I don't know," said Emilie, laughing now. "Perhaps I shall be an old maid. I would rather like to be, only I should want to represent a different species from Aunt Eunice. Still, of course, I may possibly marry; what of that?"

"Then do you not believe that when that time shall come you will feel humiliated to remember that you ever allowed passing acquaintances, perhaps almost strangers, liberties which should belong only to that one chosen from all the world?"

Emilie's cheeks flamed. "What do you mean?" she asked abruptly, even sharply. "I may be a very giddy person, as Aunt Eunice declares fifty times in a single day that I am; but I allow no one to take any liberties with me. I cannot imagine what you are talking about."

"My dear little sister, have you not in the dance allowed privileges that if offered outside the dance, under any other circumstances than that of engagement to marry, would have been considered insulting?"

"I do not waltz," the child said almost sullenly; "father won't let me."

"No, and I presume that is your only reason. You are young, and have not thought of these matters yet. You ought not to be expected to, perhaps. Others who have had experience of life should think for you."

This called forth a burst of laughter. "Such as you!" said Emilie. "You are so aged and experienced—almost nineteen!"

Rachel laughed and blushed. "I know, Emilie; but I have had an unusual experience. Aunt Katherine was a wonderful woman; and she had some wonderful children. Emilie, if I should tell you some things which my Aunt Katharine told me once, when I had great need of help, you would be shocked beyond measure."

"Tell me, then," said Emilie, "I like to be shocked. I should think it would be a delicious sensation."

Was there any use in trying to talk seriously with such a volatile creature? Rachel dropped her hand from the white shoulder, and turning away began to make preparations for rest; adding, after a moment, this sentence:

"I will tell you only this, Emilie, and I am sure of it. If any pure-minded girl could hear how men, *bad* men, talk about the dance, and even the most innocent and child-like among the dancers, she would never allow her name to be mentioned in connection with this amusement again."

17. "Just Once"

Yet, despite all that had been said to her, Emilie went to the party. When she lay down that night beside Rachel, she supposed that she would not. She was vexed with Rachel, angry indeed, and only half believed what had been said to her. How should Rachel know so much? She was only a little older than herself. Mother did not think dancing was such a dreadful thing, nor did father, or they never would have allowed her to learn to dance. Of course, one must choose one's companions with care; didn't she always? Wasn't their set just made up of girls and boys whom she knew almost as intimately as she did her brothers and sisters? Some of the girls went to dances that she did not care to attend, and chose companions whom she wouldn't; but what of that? Was she to give up her fun because somebody else did something wrong? What a charming world that would make! It was hateful in Rachel to say such things to her. If the world was as ugly as that, she did not want to know it. Rachel must have met some strange people out in that horrid California where she had spent so much of her life; she had always thought of the people there as only half civilized, and this proved it. Still, if Rachel felt so, perhaps others did. Perhaps Professor Landis thought—

She did not finish the sentence, but even in the night and the darkness her cheeks glowed with shame. Did Professor Landis really think that it was indelicate to dance, the kind of dancing that she did? How could he! She did not want to do anything indelicate, this young, gay girl; she did not want people to think she did; especially people whom she admired and respected.

She dropped asleep saying to herself that she would not go to this party; it was larger than any to which she had ever been invited, and there were to be some strangers present, Bertha Foster's cousin Richard among the number. She had been quite anxious to meet Bertha's cousin, because everybody said he was so handsome, and such a splendid dancer. She was the best dancer among the girls, they all knew it; but perhaps it was just as well that she could not go. By morning she did not think it was well; and by the time she had returned from school, she was sure that her sister Rachel was a Western-bred prude, and Professor Landis a narrow-minded crank, and that it was "just too dreadful" that she could not have "fresh gloves and slippers and things," when she was willing to wear her old dress.

Mary had thought so much, of late, about the time when she could bestow trifles of this kind that she could not resist the temptation to experiment, just to see how it would seem. There was a certain five-dollar gold piece in her possession, which she had almost spent a hundred times, and then had drawn back, resolving to hold it a little longer. Why? The answer to that question would have been very hard for Mary Cameron to have put into words. There was no sentiment connected with the giver, a stern-faced uncle who had felt compelled to bestow, because of many disagreeable duties which she had done for him.

At first she had kept it because she liked the gleam of gold in her pocket-book. Then, as wants grew more numerous, she could not be sure which of many needed things to bestow it on. It was a sort of extra, and had a right to be treated as such. Then there had come an evening when, as Russell Denham and she sat together in the parlor, she had occasion to hunt through her pocket-book for a certain card, and he had seen the gold piece and asked about and handled it. Was it a treasure piece? Was it charmed? Did she know there was an old legend about pocket pieces that were charmed by the giver, to the everlasting happiness of the receiver? Did she suppose he could charm that for her, so that whenever she looked at it his image would appear? There had been much nonsense and laughter, but Mary had admitted to herself when he was gone that he had charmed the gold piece. She could never see its gleam afterwards without seeming to see his handsome face reflected in it. After that, nothing which could be bought with money was to be exchanged for that gold piece.

Now, however, the time had come when all this ought to be changed—was changed forever, Mary Cameron assured herself with a firm set of lips. Russell Denham was nothing to her. She did not wish to remember him. Nevertheless, she had no desire to spend that particular piece of money about anything connected with her wedding outfit. It might be folly; probably it was, but the feeling was there. She wanted to be rid of the gold piece. The thought which came to her at last in its connection she believed was an inspiration. It should buy slippers and gloves and a bit of fresh lace for Emilie, and the child should go to the party on which her heart was set.

Emilie was radiant. Certainly there was pleasure in the bestowal of the gift. She danced about Mary in a perfect abandonment of delight, and assured her that she was a "blessed old darling," that she should never forget it of her, *never*. Then, growing serious, at least as serious as Emilie Cameron ever allowed herself to be, she assured her sister that she had never seen anybody in her life improve so much as she had since her engagement. She had never imagined that it could have such an effect upon character as it evidently had; and now if Aunt Eunice could only get engaged, too, they would be a comparatively happy family.

She came home from the party in the gayest spirits. Everything had been "perfectly lovely." The company was large, the refreshments more elegant, the toilets more exquisite, the dancing more superb, than at any previous time in her long experience. She had much to say about the greatly admired "cousin Richard."

"He is magnificcnt, Mary; handsomer even than Mr. Kennedy, I do believe, and a gentleman like him. He says little nice things all the time that he does not mean. Well, don't you all know what I mean?" as a shout of laughter greeted this statement. "Just pleasant nothings which make you feel as though you were a little nicer and prettier and more interesting than anybody else; and yet that you know he will repeat to the next girl he dances with, and you don't care if he does. Though he didn't repeat them very often last night. He confined his attentions chiefly to me; that is because I am the best dancer among them. It is queer, too, when I don't practice half as much as the others. Some of those girls go to a party or a rehearsal or something of the sort nearly every evening. Mary, Mr. Forbes knows your Ben. He says he saw him at the Club Rooms; and he says he is a little country simpleton, and is losing all his earnings, playing games that he does not understand. Besides, he thinks some of the fellows cheat him just for amusement, because he is so much in earnest and gets so excited. I told him what I thought of it all, and he agreed with me. He says boys who have their living to earn, and who are excitable and ignorant, ought not to meddle with cards at all."

There were reasons why all this talk troubled Mary especially. Was it possible that her first effort to help in the world was to result disastrously? If Ben Reeder had not been noticed by Mr. Kennedy he might have escaped cards; and but for her sake Mr. Kennedy, she felt instinctively, was not one to trouble himself about a boy like Ben. Then, too, Emilie was so excited, so—almost reckless. Were these late evening parties just the thing for her? It is true she had not opportunity to go very often; but was she not, like poor Ben, too excitable to indulge in such things at all? If she had looked worn and jaded, and been irritable, Mary thought it would be almost better, because then she could see for herself the evil effects. But she was, on the contrary, more wide awake than ever. She talked and laughed incessantly, was in royal humor with the world in general, and perfectly sure of one thing: that she would go to another dancing party as soon as she could.

"I danced seven times with Mr. Forbes," she confessed to the girls in the privacy of their own room, "and he begged for another; but I was as firm as a rock. Then he said if I would not dance with him I must promise not to with anybody, and I promised willingly, because I was tired by that time and there was nobody there worth dancing with after him. That was one of the nice little nothings I told you of. He didn't care two straws, of course, whom I danced with; but it was fun to hear him pretend that he did."

Over this confidence all the sisters looked troubled.

"I thought," said Lucia, "that it was not considered good form to dance so frequently with the same person."

"Well, it isn't," Emilie admitted frankly; "that was why I refused him for that last dance; though, of course, we young girls do not follow excessive etiquette about such things as the people do who are really in society. Besides, he is Bertha Foster's cousin. That made some difference. I am quite intimate with Bertha. She coaxed me to waltz with him; she said he was the most delightful waltzer!"

Then Mary spoke indignantly. "Emilie Cameron, you don't mean that you *waltzed,* and with a perfect stranger, after all that father has said about that!"

"Yes, I did; just once," said Emilie, pouting a little, yet evidently relieved that she had confessed the truth. "What is the harm? The girls all do it with their special friends, and I feel really peculiar in always refusing. It looks as though I was afraid of myself in some way. It was Bertha, though, who coaxed me into it. She said she wanted her cousin Richard to see that the girls here were equal to the New York girls that he had been raving about. You needn't look so disgusted, Mary. I don't mean to earn my living by waltzing, nor to do it again— perhaps. I forgot all about what father had said, for the minute. The music made me wild! They were playing just the *loveliest* waltz; I couldn't keep my feet still, and Mr. Forbes stood waiting, and all I thought of was how lovely it would be to be flying around keeping time to that music; so I just went. I shouldn't think there was any harm in it, if it weren't for father's notions; or—well, yes; I should, too;" she colored and corrected herself. Emilie Cameron was, like her sister, honest by nature. "I don't think it nice for girls to do it with everybody, nor very often with anybody, perhaps; but—oh, dear! I don't know what I think; I just *couldn't help* doing it last night. But I don't mean to again, ever; and if you girls go and be cross and hateful, I shall be sorry I told you." Then the excited child lost all self-control and cried bitterly. And Mary Cameron wished she had used her five-dollar gold piece in some other way, and wondered what sort of a person this "Cousin Richard" was.

Also, the more she thought about it, the more did her heart grow sore and anxious for Ben Reeder. Perhaps her pride was somewhat piqued. Professor Landis had been so grateful for her kindness to him, and now he had probably discovered that indirectly she was to blame for this sudden descent of the country boy into the pitfalls of city life. Was there nothing that she could do to help Ben? At this point in her thoughts she reflected almost indignantly upon Mr. Landis and her sister Rachel. If these two believed there was a power which could take hold of Ben and save him from himself, why did they not do their utmost to bring it to bear upon him? Well, did not she herself believe in this power? Certainly she did; but— and then she put her thoughts as far away from that subject as she could. Since she had not settled it that she was going to do, herself, what she believed to be a reasonable thing, and eminently important for Ben, the less she considered it, the more comfortable she would be. But she would not forget Ben.

She met him on the street a few days afterward, and took special pains to stop and talk with him. Where had he been this long time? Emilie was anxious to annihilate him in a game of Halma; and she had a song, a new one, which would fit his voice, and his mother would be sure to like it. When could he come and try it? Would he have a leisure hour this evening? Certainly Mary Cameron could be gracious and charming when she chose.

But Ben was non-committal. He didn't know; didn't believe he could come this evening. No, he couldn't come tomorrow any better than tonight; and he laughed, a half shame-faced, half sullen laugh, over this admission that he was simply making excuses. What was the use? he asked; he was no singer, never would be; never would be much of anything; and—here he turned his face away that Mary might not see the feeling in it—he didn't believe he should try it any more.

"Oh, yes, you will!" said Mary cheerily. "You will try this new piece, and like it better than any you have seen. It was sent to me on purpose for you. Why, Mr. Reeder, when I tell you that you have a good voice, you ought to be polite enough to believe me for I am a very fair judge of voices, it is said, and I always speak the truth. Will you come this evening? I want you to promise, because Professor Landis says you are sure to keep your word."

"He is mistaken." Ben's voice was husky now. "He thinks a lot of things of me that are not true. I'm not to be depended on for my word, or anything."

"Prove the falseness of that by promising to come to us at eight o'clock this evening," she said gaily, "and being there at the stroke of the clock."

He would not promise, and she had very faint hope of seeing him; but he came, promptly to the moment. Not in genial mood, however. He looked sullen and miserable, and was evidently going to be hard to entertain. He declined almost roughly Emilie's gay challenge to win a game from him; told her there would be no great honor in that; he was easy to beat, and used to being beaten; he wished he had never played a game of any kind in his life; and Emilie for once was silenced, and looked timid and distressed.

The song did not fare much better at his hands. He was persuaded to try; it but his voice broke utterly in the middle of a line, and he refused to make any further effort, declaring it to be the "meanest air" he had ever "struck."

Rachel Cameron made earnest attempts to second her sister's efforts, but did not get on at all with Ben. He would not be interested in anything she proposed, and was altogether so sullen and rude in his manner that, but for the fact that it was all the evident result of some inward misery, Mary would have lost patience with him. As it was, she had a yearning to help him which she could not have explained even to herself.

To the relief of those concerned, he made his stay very short; muttering something about having to get back, and going out so hastily as almost to omit the usual leave-takings. Her father was not present; and Mary accompanied him to the hall, wondering, as she went, whether Professor Landis would have let him go away so evidently wretched, or would have been able to do something to help him. While she was considering, he turned suddenly, and held out his hand, his lips quivering as he spoke.

"I hope you will forgive me; I hope they all will. I've acted like a fool, but I couldn't help it. I oughtn't to have come, but you seemed to think I would, and you have been—"

There he stopped, aware, apparently, that his voice would carry him no further.

"What is it, Ben?" Mary asked, holding the boyish hand in hers, and speaking as few knew she could speak. "You are in trouble of some kind, and away from your mother and all your home friends. Cannot I help you in any way? I should like to."

Then Ben snatched away his hand, and sat down suddenly in one of the hall chairs, and hid his face, and let the tears come. For a moment she was too distressed to speak. She had never seen her brothers cry; she had not realized that boys had tears to shed. Just then she heard her father's step on the walk. What would he think to find Ben Reeder in his hall, weeping bitterly, and she standing near him dumb! She pushed open the dining-room door. "Come in here a minute, Ben," she said, "and tell me, won't you, what is the matter? Cannot I be one of your sisters for the time? I have brothers, you know." But no persons would have been more astonished than her own brothers to have heard such words from her.

Ben struggled with his tears and gained the mastery. But he followed her into the dining-room, and dropped into the chair she indicated.

"I hope you will forgive me," he said again; "I don't know what is the matter that I act so like a baby. I'm not used to giving myself away in that fashion. It all seemed to come over me, somehow: it was that song made it worse. The fault isn't in the *air,* Miss Cameron. Those words struck at me; they made me think how much I had meant when I came here, and what mother was expecting—and father, and what had come of it, and it broke me down. Miss Cameron, that friend of yours who was kind to me—he meant it all for kindness, and I am a great baby to have let it get hold of me as it has; but I wish I had never seen him. Maybe I wouldn't have got hold of my ruin so soon, if I hadn't; but I don't know; it would have come anyhow, I suppose, if it is in me."

Mary stood like one paralyzed, looking down at him. But the unutterable misery, even desperation, in his voice, reached her very soul. She roused herself to speak.

"You mean about cards, Ben? He taught you to play? I, too, am sorry. I wish he had not done it. Still, as you say, it was in kindness. He does not think about these things in the way that some do. But, surely, you are not going to let that one circumstance ruin you! If you find that the game you have learned to play is an injury instead of being, as Mr. Kennedy intended it, a rest and amusement, why not give it up at once and forever? People do that who are much older and much more fixed in their habits than you. I had an uncle who played cards incessantly for months, even years, until he was almost ruined; but there came a day when he resolved never to touch another card, and although he was a famous player, and was sought after, he never did."

Ben Reeder shook his head. "I can't do it, Miss Cameron. There is a difference in folks, I suppose. I used to think I could do what I had a mind to, but it is a mistake. I haven't been playing with cards a great while, and I haven't had such good luck as ought to make me hanker after them; but I *can't* let them alone—I've found that out. I promised myself, and I even promised Professor Landis last night, that I wouldn't touch them again; and he thinks I keep my promises! I used to think I did; but I went straight from him and played the worst game I ever had, and got myself in such a place that now I must keep on. And then I had a letter from mother, and—"

Here the poor fellow broke off again, and bowed his face in his hands. He made no outward sound, but his strong young frame shook; and Mary's heart was wrung with sympathy.

18. A Troublesome Promise

W hat should she say first? There came to her an
almost overwhelming sense of the importance
of her words just now. She could but realize
that this was a critical moment for Ben Reeder, and she
was not used to dealing with souls in danger. She took
time to mentally rebuke Mr. Kennedy, and that with a
degree of sharpness which would have greatly startled
that gentleman, for his share in this misery. Why had he
not let the boy alone? People who did not know how to
help others wisely should not attempt it. Well, then, why
was she attempting it? Surely, no one knew less than she
about such matters, but the boy was manifestly leaning
upon her; she must say something.

Mary Cameron had never asked for the help of the
promised Spirit; but does He not sometimes help those
who are in dire need, and are too ignorant to ask? Her
first word was a question, gently put.

"What did your mother say, Ben?"

For answer he fumbled in his pocket for a half sheet of common note-paper, and handed it to her without raising his head. It held only a few lines, written in the cramped hand of one not much accustomed to writing.

Mother's dear Boy,

You know I wrote you a long letter only a few days ago; this is just a line because I cannot go to sleep without saying it. Joshua Knowles has been here this evening. He just came from the city; and he thought he ought to tell us that the report was that our Ben had got to playing cards, and was friendly with a set of sharpers, and was getting into trouble. I smiled on him and thanked him for the pains he had taken; but says I, "We hear from our Ben every week, and know all about him." Ben, dear, Mother doesn't believe one word of it; you know that, don't you? Mother trusts her boy through and through; so does father; but we are getting old, you know, and fidgety. You write a line as soon as you get this, to say that it is some other Ben in trouble, not ours, and I'm sorry for the boy, and for his poor mother; but, oh, so glad it isn't our boy! Just say so, won't you, for mother's sake? God bless my dear, dear boy.

Mary read the lines slowly, with a great swelling in her throat the while. She could almost see that old mother, sitting up to write her words of trust, with the painful doubt creeping in between the lines in spite of her. No wonder that Ben's heart had broken over it.

"Ben," she said, "if I were you, I wouldn't disappoint such a mother. I wouldn't indeed! I would show her that I was the boy she thought me, and that I would be the man she dreams of. Mothers think *so much* of their boys, Ben."

"You don't seem to understand," said Ben in a broken voice. "I tell you I *have* disappointed her. They never said much about playing cards at home, but I know they didn't think I would do it. They would as soon have thought of telling the minister not to. And I've disappointed them."

"But, Ben, begin again. Why, dear me! You are so young, and have just begun life away from home, you can't have gotten very far wrong in so short a time. Even if you had, what is to hinder your turning squarely around and being the man your mother and father expect to see, and that you planned to be?"

Ben slowly shook his head. "I don't know what's in the way," he said. "The devil, I s'pose. They say he is after everyone, and I guess he is. I know he is after me. Something has got hold of me. I've always been a good, steady boy, and always meant to be; but, down there at the clubroom stylish fellows go, you know, and I thought it was a fine thing to have them notice me. They were good-natured and kind, I thought; but I guess they are sharpers. They like to get hold of a green fellow like me, and lead him along by inches. Some of them don't mean anything, but the others do. They like the fun of seeing folks tumble, I guess. And I'm in for it now. I owe two of them, and unless my luck changes I can't pay them; and I can't get away until I do. Don't you see how it is? I'm caught."

Poor Mary's heart stood still. Her father's horror of cards made her wiser about their dangers than she was concerning many other things. Ben had evidently been playing for more than a "cigar."

"How much money do you owe them?" she asked abruptly. Ben shuddered. "It is only a matter of twenty dollars," he said, "not worth noticing or thinking about, they say; but of course I *have* to think about it; and unless my luck changes it will soon be more. I don't know how it is; I used to have good luck at first, but it seems to have deserted me. There's a stylish chap named Forbes, who lent me five dollars last night, and I lost it in five minutes."

Mary drew her breath hard. Forbes was the "Cousin Richard" with whom her young sister had danced seven times, to say nothing of the waltz. "Only twenty dollars!" But it might as well be a hundred so far as her ability to help him was concerned. If she had but kept that five-dollar gold piece! Might it not much better have been spent in this way, both for Ben's sake and Emilie's? The thought crossed her mind that Mr. Kennedy, who had been instrumental in this result, might appropriate some of the money which he tossed about so freely, to helping poor Ben out of the net. But she shrank utterly from asking his help, although she felt sure of receiving it. How could she explain the situation so that he would understand? She was not yet sufficiently familiar with him, by letter, to write freely. It was not to be thought of. But Professor Landis—why did not the distressed boy go to him? It is true he was probably poor, his salary could not be very large, and he had a house to support and a sister to help. Still, perhaps he could manage so small a sum. Why, she felt certain that he would manage it in some way; and she did not stop to analyze the feeling which made it quite possible for her to ask his help when she could not ask it of the man whom she had promised to marry.

"Ben," she said, "if I will secure the twenty dollars for you—lend them to you, you understand, until such time as you are quite able to pay—will you promise on your honor that you will give up this amusement and go no more to the Club House, or to any other house where they play cards?"

The slow crimson rolled over Ben's face and neck as he raised his eyes for the first time. "I could not think of taking money from you, Miss Cameron; I never dreamed of such a thing."

"It will not be my money," she interrupted him. "I have none of my own. If I had, I would lend to you in a moment; but I have a friend who, I am sure, will let me have it. Will you promise, Ben?"

"I told you that I couldn't," he said, almost with impatience. "Haven't I promised myself a dozen times already? It seems silly to you, I know, to say that I can't keep my word. It sounds silly to me. Only a few weeks ago

I would have called a fellow a muff for saying it, but I've proved the truth of it. I used to believe I could do what I liked, and I've found I can't."

Nothing more utterly hopeless than Ben's tone can be imagined. It was very different from the careless way in which that word "cannot" is often on the lips of youth when it means "I will not," or at the most, "I do not care to try." This was the cry of a heart which had lost faith in itself and was near despair. Mary Cameron stood appalled before it. The boy was in danger. Her Aunt Eunice had been a prophet when she said, "Then he is lost!" If ever a soul needed the interposing Hand, surely he did at this moment. Oh, for the sound of her neighbor's voice just now! Was not this the very moment to point the despairing one to the Power who *could?* But Professor Landis was not even at home, if she had had any way to summon him. She thought of Rachel, but Ben had repelled her kindly advances so rudely it was not probable that she could influence him. Then who was there? A curious longing to be able to do it herself, to be the instrument for saving this soul in peril, came surging into the girl's heart; but of what use was it? Could she, who did not know the way, attempt to point it out to another? Yet something must be said.

"Ben," she began, trembling, hesitating between each word, "there is a—there are people—Oh, Ben! Don't you *know* that God is ready to help people who cannot? He could keep you from falling into this dreadful way and breaking your mother's heart."

"Why doesn't he, then?" asked Ben, almost fiercely, from behind the hands in which his face was again hidden.

There was no help for it; she who had herself turned her back upon Him must explain the strength and sweetness of His way to this floundering soul.

"Oh, Ben! You cannot really mean that question. Would you have been made like a lump of earth which must be turned over whenever the spade pleases, and must grow whatever someone else drops into the soil, whether it be seeds of flowers, or weeds? Would you not much rather be the one to choose, to decide, as God has planned that you may be?"

Why had she used just that figure? She could not have told had she been asked, save that she had stood that morning and watched a florist at his work among his plants, and something of the kind had floated idly through her mind. But Ben's early life had been spent much among the clods of earth, overturning them with his spade. It made some things plainer to him than they had ever been before. Presently he dropped his hands and looked at her.

"You mean," he said, "that while I honestly cannot keep myself from going to the bad, I can choose Him for a leader and He will keep me?"

Mary bowed her head. She trembled in every limb, and could not have spoken. Here she was in the darkness, yet guiding a soul. Suppose she should start it in the wrong path?

Ben Reeder kept his eyes fixed on the floor, after that, for so long that it seemed to her he would never speak again, and she dare not. At last he said:

"Miss Cameron, I believe I begin to understand what Professor Landis is always driving at. I never got the hang of it before, but you make things plain to a fellow. I'm going home to think about it. If I can settle it tonight, I will; and I want to know if you will pray for me. Mother prays for me every day, I know; but I can't tell her about this, it would scare her so, and she has trouble enough. I've *got* to have help from somewhere right away. I feel that. I've always known about such things a good deal. Mother doesn't say much, it isn't her way; but she lives things. I knew she was different from other folks, but I never felt the need of it myself. I always thought I could take care of myself and make out first rate. Then when I found I couldn't, I felt kind of mad against God because he didn't do it for me, as I thought he ought to; but I begin to understand that I've got a part. Now, if I can see daylight about that part, why, I'll do it; but you'll pray it out for me tonight, just as mother would. Will you?"

Was ever one in a stranger dilemma? What was she to say? She opened her lips to confess that she never prayed, did not know how to pray; but no, this would not do; it might be a fatal injury to a soul in peril. And the boy stood waiting for his answer.

"I will try," she faltered at last, he being too busy with his own thoughts to note the strangeness of her manner. Then he went away at once, and Mary returned to the back parlor like one in a dream.

"Where have you been?" Emilie questioned curiously. "What did you say to that cross boy? Wasn't he horrid tonight? I hope the next time he feels as ugly as he did this evening he will stay away. He gave me the blues."

Then the family proceeded to discussing poor Ben and his prospects for making a wreck of life. Aunt Eunice and Emilie together essaying to answer Mr. Cameron's questions concerning the boy. Mr. Cameron looked even more troubled than the others over his story.

"I am sorry cards have gotten hold of him," he said gloomily. "He hasn't enough moral power to withstand their influence, I am afraid."

"And he began them in your own house," said Aunt Eunice severely. "I hope that is a comfort to you!"

In the somewhat excited debate which followed this disagreeable statement, Mary Cameron took no part. In fact, she heard very little of it. Her mind was in a whirl of excitement of its own. What had she promised to do! The poor foolish boy to suppose that her prayers, even if she could bring herself to try to offer them, would do him any good! But she *must* pray; she had promised. "A Cameron always keeps his word," was one of the proud sayings of this family, which had come down to them from a famous old great-uncle who kept his word under trying circumstances. Assuredly, if she never prayed again, Mary must try tonight to pray for Ben Reeder.

How should it be accomplished? Lucia would be in the room all the time, and would be talking probably. She generally chose that hour to chatter about anything which had interested her during the day. Could she say to her that she desired to be quiet because she wanted to pray? The very idea of such a thing sent the blood flowing swiftly through her veins. She might go now to her room while Lucia was helping Emilie to prove that there was not the remotest connection between Halma and poor Ben's gambling propensities, but she shrank inconceivably from doing so. She would put off the strange duty as long as possible. She set herself to try to plan what she would say; words of prayer were such strangers to her lips. Visions of her childhood floated before her, and she could seem to hear herself repeating in grave voice the old formula:

> "Now I lay me down to sleep,
> I pray thee, Lord, my soul to keep;"

but there was nothing in that to help Ben. She knew "Our Father," of course; and she let her mind run swiftly through with its various petitions, to make sure that there was nothing there exactly adapted to Ben's case. Then she grew almost irritable. What a ridiculous idea! Why should he need praying for, to help him decide so simple a question? If he could not stand alone, and wanted to stand, and believed there was One who could help him, why, then, wasn't the way plain?

Ah, Mary Cameron! Haven't you resolved at least a dozen times during the last few weeks that you will curb your impatient tongue, and say only words which the members of your own family can remember with pleasure and comfort after you are gone out from the home forever? And have you succeeded for even a single day in standing by that resolve? And do you care to stand? Well, then, isn't the way plain? But of that side of the question she refused to think. Life was too busy just now for her to take up any new line of work.

The end of it all was that she compromised with her conscience in a miserable way. Lucia lingered over her preparations for bed in an exasperating way, replying to Mary's impatient attempts to hasten her that she need not wait; there was the bed before her, and the road to it was certainly plain. At last Mary went to bed, and covering even her face from view, murmured her shame-faced prayer, "Oh Lord, help Ben Reeder tonight!"

She had not an idea that such praying would be heard—deserved to be heard; but when one had made a wretched promise, what was one to do?

19. A STARTLING WITNESS

Rachel Cameron had been several weeks at home before she succeeded in getting to the mid-week prayer-meeting. Surrounded by people who were not in the habit of attending, it was surprising how many obstacles they heedlessly threw in the way of one's doing so. At last it was Aunt Eunice who, as she expressed it, "set her foot down."

"I'm going round on Smith Street to the prayer-meeting tonight whatever happens, and you needn't any of you plan to hinder me. I never lived so much like a heathen as I have since I came here."

"Why should she think we would want to hinder her?" asked Lucia with surprise. But she was equally surprised at being invited to accompany her, and promptly declined; so Aunt Eunice and Rachel went away together.

The prayer room was fairly well filled, and a notable feature of the audience was the large number of young people. Rachel looked about her with kindling eyes. She had felt almost alone since her home-coming, but this gathering for prayer betokened that there were many kindred hearts right around her. Yet she was disappointed in the meeting. The singing was hearty and enjoyable, and the minister's address was certainly very fine, and in a sense helpful; but it was an *address,* not an informal social talk, like the family talks to which she had been accustomed in her aunt's church. Nor was there much praying. Two gentlemen being called upon, offered long, formal, entirely proper prayers; and Professor Landis prayed without being called upon, and this was all. Not a youthful voice was heard during the hour—that is, not distinctly. They whispered a good deal, especially those seated in the back part of the house; not in a defiant or daring way, but as though their interest in something was too great to allow of longer silence; and their interest was evidently not in the pastor's address. Nor could Rachel wonder at that. For the most part they were young people who, while intelligent, even keen in their natures, had not been trained to think closely, perhaps, on any subject; certainly not on the fine, scholarly theme which was engrossing Mr. Edson. Certain of his auditors, however, listened and appreciated; occasionally they nodded their heads in approval, and they said one to another when the service was over:

"Wasn't that a fine thing he gave us tonight? So intellectual; such a command of language. That will do to print. He is destined to make a stir in the city. I don't know a D.D. among them who could give a more polished address nor one involving more scholarship."

Mr. Edson was prompt in shaking hands with those very people, and, to judge by the sparkle in his eyes, was getting his needful mental stimulus from them. Meantime the young people were shaking hands with one another, talking almost too loud for the church, and exchanging bits of social life eagerly. They seemed not to look in Mr. Edson's direction, nor he in theirs. However, he saw one person who interested him. He caught Mr. Landis by the arm as he was passing with a bow and smile.

"Professor, do you know who those two ladies are who stand near the south door, back of Deacon Watson?"

Mr. Landis looked and explained.

"The young lady is Miss Cameron, one of a family living on Durand Avenue. I gave you the name a few weeks ago, you remember. The other is her aunt, whose name I do not recall; a guest, I believe."

"That is not the Miss Cameron who was at the social at Kinkaid's?"

"No; a younger sister who has but recently returned home after a long absence."

"Ah! I was sure I had not seen that face before. Introduce me, Professor."

Emilie would have had no cause to criticize his greeting. Nothing could have been more cordial. He walked down the aisle with the strangers, talking eagerly. He was very glad to see them in prayer-meeting.

Perhaps they could come often, the church was so near their home. Would Miss Cameron permit him? The streets were really almost dangerous just now; such treacherous bits of ice here and there.

It was not Rachel's hand which he drew deftly through his arm as he spoke, but the much subdued and bewildered Aunt Eunice's. Emilie's chatter had not prepared her for receiving such kindness and courtesy from this minister.

She was emphatic in her opinion of him, expressed as soon as they were at home. Such a pleasant-spoken man, and so friendly and thoughtful! It wasn't every young man who would have thought of offering his arm to an old woman like her to keep her from slipping. Emilie listened in surprise.

"I think better of him," she announced. "He is the sort of man whom I shouldn't have expected to know that there were any old people in the world, nor young people either, except a certain few which fit his pattern."

Mrs. Cameron called her to account. Why had she of late adopted such a strange way of speaking of ministers? It was not refined; people should respect the profession more than that.

"Why, I do," said Emilie. "That is what is the matter with me. I respect it so much that I do not like to see him ill-treating it. Really, mother, what is the harm? He is only a man, and a young man at that. Besides, I'm not saying anything very dreadful about him. Perhaps he will grow better as he grows older. There is room for improvement, I am sure." Then, as she felt that she was every moment making matters worse, the child stopped, laughing, and blushing, not at her mother's reproving look, but at the gravity on her father's face. Did it trouble her father to have her speak so of Mr. Edson? He had old-fashioned ideas about ministers.

"I don't mean anything in the world but talk," she began again. "I don't know Mr. Edson, of course; but I *will* say that he acts as though he thought more of rich people and cultured people than he does of common-place ones. I don't know why he shouldn't, to be sure; I do. But one resents it in ministers, someway. Don't let's talk about *him*. Tell us about the meeting. What is the use in people going to prayer-meeting if they cannot help the folks at home to do good?"

But Aunt Eunice had become strangely silent. She took her knitting as usual; but neither about the meeting nor the various other topics which came before them did she advance an opinion. It was not until the family had separated for the night that she came across the hall to the room occupied by Rachel and Emilie, and so astonished the latter, that, as she confessed to the girls in the morning, she "might have been knocked down with a feather."

"Let me come in a minute," Aunt Eunice said, tapping at the door, then opening it herself; "I want to talk to you both. I guess what you said the other night, Emilie, hasn't been out of my mind more than a minute at a time, since; and it's true enough, I may as well own it, but I want to talk about it."

"Dear me!" said Emilie, much startled. "What in the world did I say? Whatever it was, you mustn't mind it, Aunt Eunice. Nobody ever pays any attention to what I say, least of all, I myself. I know it is not worth it."

Her aunt made no reply to this, but dropped into the low rocker which Rachel pushed forward, and motioned her niece to another. "Sit down, both of you, can't you? I've got something to say. I tell you, it is quite true that my religion doesn't make me happy. It isn't the fault of religion, I know that; for I've had lots of trouble in my day—not much besides trouble you may say—and I know I should have gone crazy a hundred times over, if it hadn't been for what religion I had. Many a time I have prayed my way out of dreadful scares of one kind and another, and lived through things that I thought I couldn't, and I know as well as I want to, that the Lord heard me; but that is neither here nor there. I haven't been made sweet-tempered and patient and all that, by my religion. It is good what there is of it: but there doesn't seem to be enough of it to reach, somehow. I've felt it more or less for years; but I don't know as it ever came home to me so sharp as it did the other night when Emilie was going on, and Mr. Landis said that about being weighed in the balances. I'm not true weight, and I feel it. Your kind, Rachel, seems to be different. How did you get it? And what is the matter with me?"

Rachel opened her troubled lips to enter a protest, but Aunt Eunice waved it off.

"Oh, there's nothing for you to deny! I don't mean that you are forward, or conceited, or anything like that. There isn't a hint about you that would lead anybody to suspect that you knew you had a different religion from some; but it is plain all the same. I saw it the very night you came; saw it plainer than I have on any other face in years. There was a face once that carried it around just as you do all the time, and I envied it then, and felt half mad about it; but that one has been buried a good many years, and my conscience hasn't been troubled by the same sight often. I've thought of it more or less since the night you came; and tonight when that man prayed I saw the same thing in his face, and felt it in his voice."

"Who?" asked Emilie, unable to restrain curiosity even now. "The minister?"

Aunt Eunice made an expressive gesture of negation with her hand.

"No, child, no! The minister's religion is about like mine. He's got it; but there isn't enough of it to shine through on his face, and color all he says. I mean that Mr. Landis. His prayer just seemed to give me a heartache. I'd give anything in this world if I could speak to God in the way he did, and mean it."

"Aunt Eunice," said Rachel, letting fall the hairbrush, and dropping herself in a little white heap in front of her aunt's chair, "if I were to try to explain the difference between your experience of life and mine, I should say that you were energetic and brave and strong, and had shouldered a great many burdens and borne them yourself, and taken only the hard ones, which you did not know how to manage, to the Lord; while I am young and weak, and feel my ignorance, and am afraid to go a step alone, or do the least little thing without the direction and help of Jesus Christ; so that I walk as with him beside me, and look for his approval of each word I speak."

Aunt Eunice was watching her face, listening with the keenest interest to every word; but her eyes had a perplexed look as of one who did not understand.

"I don't know how you could," she said slowly. "'Every *word!*' Why, our words are not of consequence enough for him to listen. They have to be about such homely, every-day things, most of the time."

"Ah, but, Aunt Eunice, that is just what I mean. Haven't you kept the extra words for him, and planned the homely, every-day ones yourself? I cannot do this; I am sure to go astray if I attempt it. I have to take him at his word, and remember that the very hairs of my head are numbered by him; therefore nothing is too trivial for him. Besides, when we remember that the simplest words may do good or harm to a soul, they become important enough for even him to have their ordering."

Still that look of perplexity. "I don't suppose I can make you understand," Aunt Eunice said at last with a weary sigh. "You are young, as you say, and have had a quiet life, and not much to fret you; and I have been tossed about in a way which you could not even imagine, and my tongue has got so sharp that it cuts when I don't want it to; while you, I suppose, never had a temptation to say anything but nice, pleasant words. My tongue has always been the worst of me; and yours is, maybe, the very best of you."

The rich color flowed into Rachel's cheeks, and she bowed her head a moment on her aunt's knee, asking guidance; then she said: "Aunt Eunice, as a witness of His I must tell you how mistaken you are. So far from my tongue having never been tempted, I will confess to you that it was my bitterest enemy. Mother will tell you that as a little child I was inclined to be rude in speech, and, when excited or angry, impudent. The only time my father ever punished me was for saying very angry and improper words to mother when he was present. After I went away from home I did not outgrow this sin. I think sins are rarely outgrown; mine gained in strength, I know, with every day. My Aunt Katherine endured, oh, *so much* from me! Sometimes it almost frightens me, even now, to think how I used to speak to her, not as you would imagine it possible a self-respecting girl could speak to any person, to say nothing of its being one whom I loved, and who had shown her love to me in so many ways. After I became, as I now believe, a Christian, to my dismay this habit of quick and saucy speech did not leave me. I could control it for a time; but the moment something enraged me, all my good resolutions were forgotten, and my tongue was steadily increasing in its power for evil. One night matters reached a climax. My aunt had been talking with me for being in the society of a person whom she did not approve, and I was trying to justify myself and him. I grew, oh, fearfully angry! God only knows the wicked words I said—he has mercifully let me forget many of them—and then, losing every particle of self-control, I seized a great glass pitcher which stood near filled with water, and flung it at my aunt's head."

"Oh, my patience!" exclaimed that part of her audience which was curled on the foot of the bed.

"Mercy, child!" said Aunt Eunice, "you might have killed her."

"I might; and I almost did. The glass shivered in a thousand pieces; and some of them struck her on the temple, and cut; and one struck her eye. She suffered agony untold, and it was thought for a time that she would be blind; but God was good to me, and spared her sight. Oh, Aunt Eunice, if I could describe to you the horrors of that night which I spent alone in my room, with my aunt in the next room groaning at every breath, and they bending over her in an agony of fear! At first I could not pray; could not think; I could only cry out, 'O God, let me die! Kill me! Kill me right away! I am too wicked to live any longer.' After a little I knew I *must* pray or lose my reason. And I—I don't know how to tell you about it—but I cried to God as I never had before. I told him all of my resolutions made and broken hundreds of times, and then I just gave myself to him in a way which I had not before; gave my tongue into his keeping to be used by him, to speak his words and only his."

"Well?" said Aunt Eunice, after a silence; she spoke almost sharply in her keen desire to hear the rest.

"Well," Rachel repeated, with a little tremulous smile, "he took me at my word."

"And you didn't get mad after that, and say things you didn't mean?"

"I never did. My aunt lived two precious years after that; and I never once, to her nor to my cousins nor to the servants nor to anybody, spoke words which I could wish afterwards to have recalled. In truth, Aunt Eunice, I was another person from that hour; and I could truly say as Paul did, 'Yet not I, but Christ dwelleth in me.' He kept me; keeps me. What I have often thought about since, and what I want to say now, is, that, of course, it was not necessary for me to disgrace him so utterly with my besetting sin, before he would give me grace to overcome it. What if I had gone to him with my temptation at the very first, being sure that I *could not* rule my tongue, and depended on him to do it for me; would he not have been quite as willing? The mistake I made was in feeling that I could manage myself, and resolving to do so; and when I failed, consoling myself with the thought that I must not expect to overcome great faults all at once, but that by degrees I should get the mastery. It was all 'I' instead of all 'Christ.'"

They would have formed a group for an artist, sitting there: Emilie on the foot of the bed, with her white robes tucked around her, too interested a listener to remember to go to bed; Aunt Eunice with her worn, anxious face, about which the gray hair hung loosely, as she had suddenly left it after having begun her preparations for the night; Rachel with her long brown hair sweeping the floor, as she knelt and talked.

After Emilie's one dismayed exclamation, she had been awed into silence. Watching her sister, she recalled the words of a schoolmate to the effect that her artist brother thought Rachel Cameron ought to sit for her portrait as an angel, because there was nothing in her face that suggested earthliness. It was a strangely pure face; yes, and a calm one.

"I cannot imagine her as being angry," thought Emilie. "Fancy her throwing a pitcher of water at anybody's head! She must be dreaming, and yet, of course, it is true. How strange! I wonder if there is really such power in religion? I wonder if it would make a great difference in me? If it would in Aunt Eunice, I might have some hope for myself. Poor old Aunt Eunice! She means it, I do believe. It is queer for her to come in here and talk to us as she has. Oh, dear! What ought I to do now, I wonder?" For now the two whom her fascinated eyes were watching had knelt together; and Rachel with one soft white hand was clasping the wrinkled, bony hand of her aunt, and was praying aloud.

It would perhaps be difficult to convey an idea of the impression which this made upon Emilie. She had never before heard a woman's voice in prayer. At first she was mainly occupied in deciding what she ought to do. Would it be proper to kneel as they had done?

"But I don't know how to pray," said this honest young soul; "and I *won't* make believe."

At last she slipped softly into bed, deciding that that would, on the whole, be the most proper thing to do. At first she covered even her head with the bed-clothes, resolved upon giving them all the privacy she could. Then she decided that she would listen; there was no harm surely in listening to prayers. But before that simple, tender, strangely earnest prayer was concluded, she had covered her face again, to hide her tears.

"If that is the way to pray," said this gay young girl to herself, "I almost wish I knew how."

20. The Shadows of Coming Events

There was a breath of spring in the air. Emilie, on her return from school, reported the first robin of the season. She also complained of her heavy flannels, and wondered if her last year's gingham dresses could be worn this summer. Mrs. Cameron noted that the curtains at the sitting-room windows began to look dusty and winter-worn, and sighed as she thought of the spring house-cleaning and the endless needs it would bring to light.

House-cleaning and all other work would be heavier this spring than usual; for in early June would come the day set for Mary's marriage, a time looked forward to by father and mother with mingled feelings. Both realized how many expenditures such an event involved, and none knew better than they how empty was the family purse. Moreover, the first real break in the family was coming in this way. So great was the grind of what they unhesitatingly called poverty, that this thought was somewhat swallowed up by it; still there were times when they realized that their eldest born was soon to cease to look upon their home as hers. After the spring fairly opened, the sixth of June would come swiftly. Of one thing they assured themselves: when the wedding was over and Mary gone, they would begin those long-thought-of retrenchments which were every day becoming more necessary. "We cannot do anything until after Mary goes," became a sentence much in their thoughts and confidential words; and so great was the need for doing *something* that there were times when it was inevitable that this going away of the daughter to a luxurious home of her own must be felt as a relief. Meantime the household settled into busy quiet.

Emilie, for reasons of her own, watched Aunt Eunice curiously for a few days, half expecting a wondrous change to come to her, like unto that which she had heard reported in Rachel's sympathetic voice on that never-to-be-forgotten evening. But no such marked experience came to Aunt Eunice. Her tongue was still quick and keen; and though a close observer could certainly detect a change in her—could discover times, many of them, in which she opened her lips to speak, then closed them resolutely and knitted hard and fast, with the color rising on her face—still the change was not great enough to satisfy Emilie.

"There is a difference," she told herself frankly. "The poor old thing is trying real hard to be good. It isn't natural to her; and she would often rather box my ears than try not to; but it is honest effort, and one cannot help respecting her for it. I suppose it is unusual at her age, and she will never be like Saint Rachel. How I should have enjoyed that scene with Rachel and the water-pitcher! I wonder if she ever told mother about it?"

Whether she had or not, Emilie never knew. She kept her own counsel regarding the episode of the night visit, answering Mary's and Lucia's questions concerning it with only the vaguest generalities.

By this time the Cameron household were becoming accustomed to Aunt Eunice's presence, and beginning to feel it less of a cross to have her with them. There was much sewing to be done in view of the coming wedding, and Aunt Eunice could sew as well as knit; also, she could contrive, and get a respectable garment out of an apparently impossible quantity of goods. There was a bare possibility that in these busy days she might become invaluable.

One experience in the hurried life which Mary Cameron lived during these days must not be forgotten. One morning Ben Reeder met her on the street. He crossed the street, indeed, for the purpose of meeting her, his face radiant the while.

"I've been wanting to see you ever since," he said, not considering it necessary to be more explicit than that. Evidently their last interview stood out vividly in his memory, as indeed it did in Mary's. "I've been trying to come around to your house, but have been too busy; we are keeping open nights this spring, you know. Well, Miss Cameron, I *did it!*"

The triumph in his voice must be imagined; it is beyond description. He waited for an answer, but receiving none went on eagerly:

"I followed your directions just as well as I knew how, that very night; but nothing came of it, because I didn't know how, very well, after all. I can see now that I was saying, 'If the Lord will give me strength to get out of these scrapes and keep out of them, why, then, I'll belong to him.' That isn't the way, I take it; but I thought it was. I went to the store the next morning feeling *awful*. I knew the boys expected me to go that very evening to a place where I was sure I would be tempted to play, and would want to do it; and I knew I had no money to play with, and was in debt, and couldn't see anything but ruin before me. I hadn't slept much the night before; and I got up late, and didn't have a chance for breakfast, and about noon I began to feel downright sick. Just as I was wondering if I could get away for some lunch, the foreman of our department came to me and said he, 'Reeder, you are wanted in the little back room where the carpenters have been at work.' I went down there, and they told me Mr. Rhys, one of the firm, had dropped a piece of money, a gold piece, and knew it must be among the shavings, and I was to hunt for it while the men were gone to their dinner. I felt so dizzy and faint and horrid that it didn't seem to me as though I could do it, but of course, I must. While I stood there steadying myself, and making up my mind to begin, Billy Wilcox came along. Billy is a good-natured fellow, and he boards at home, and his mother puts him up a prime lunch every day to bring to the store. Said he, 'Why, Ben, what's up? You look as though you couldn't stand on your feet. Here, take a drink of this; it will give you some strength.' He had a mug of good, home-made coffee in his hand—he brings it in a bottle, and heats it on the gas. Well, I don't know why it should come to me as it did, but like a flash I thought of it. Suppose I should say to Billy, 'If the coffee will give me strength enough to go and find that gold piece so I can get out of here into the air for awhile, why, then, I'll drink it.' And he should say, 'Well, it will, for my mother made it herself, and it's prime coffee. Drink it down, old fellow.' And I should say, 'No; I want the strength first. Let it give me the strength I need, and then I'll promise to drink it!' Billy would think I was a fool, said I to myself; and I guess I am; that is the way I'm trying to manage about the help *she* said was sure if I would take it. I don't know why it was, but everything got as plain as day to me. I swallowed the coffee, and thanked Billy; and then I shut and locked that office door, and got down on my knees—to hunt for the gold piece, you know; but before I began to hunt, I just leaned on the shelf the carpenters had been building, and says I: 'O Lord, here is Ben Reeder; he gives himself up. He has made a failure of living, and disappointed his mother, and got into scrapes, and isn't worth a *shaving*; but here he is.' I said a little more, you know; but that is the gist of it. Well, I suppose you know what happened?"

He stopped in the street and looked at her, a great yearning in his big brown eyes; but Mary Cameron had no response ready. After a moment he went on in a more subdued tone:

"It isn't easy to tell that part, is it? I don't suppose anything happened that a body could see; in fact, I know there didn't; but I felt exactly as though a great, strong arm swooped down and got hold of me and said, 'Ben Reeder, my boy, lean on *me* forever.' And I said out loud, and with as much meaning as there is in me, 'I *will*.' And He did the rest! I found that gold piece twinkling at my feet the first time I looked down. That was queer, wasn't it? They said they had been hunting it for half an hour. There are a good many more things to be told, but I mustn't hinder you now. Perhaps I ought not to have told you this on the street; but I felt in a kind of hurry, and I thought you would be glad."

She tried to look and appear glad, this bewildered girl; but she knew no more what to say to him than as if he had been talking in another tongue. She would doubtless have been interested could she have heard a conversation which was held not long afterwards.

"She didn't seem quite so glad as I thought she would," Ben Reeder said, leaning over his counter to talk confidentially, while Professor Landis selected handkerchiefs. "I stopped her right on the street to talk, and perhaps that wasn't the thing. Do you suppose it could have offended her?"

"Oh, no!" said the Professor quickly; then he considered, while Ben turned to answer the question of another customer. When the handkerchiefs were selected and paid for, their purchaser had decided what to say.

"Ben, you were wishing yesterday that you knew some person well enough to be very deeply interested in praying for his conversion. Why not take Miss Cameron? She is not a Christian."

"Not a Christian!" repeated Ben, utter astonishment, not to say dismay, in his voice. "Why, Professor Landis, how can that be? She promised to pray for *me*."

"I trust she kept her word; nevertheless, she does not profess to belong to Christ. I believe she is thinking about the matter. At times she thinks seriously, but no decision has as yet been reached."

Ben stood, change in hand, too bewildered for the moment to deliver it. Then a sudden, settled purpose showed itself on his changeful face and he said:

"I'll do it. Why, I'm sure I can pray for *her,* different from anybody else. Next to mother and the girls she is the best friend I've got. I thought she was—why, everything! I thought that was what made her so good to me. You are quite sure, Professor? Then I'll never leave off praying for her until she *belongs*."

Mr. Landis went away with his heart more at rest about these two friends. It was good for Ben to have a soul in which he was deeply interested to center his energies upon, and it was good for Mary Cameron to have a boy like Ben praying for her. Making a Christian of him had not detracted one whit from his natural energy. Ben did with all his heart whatever he undertook; and he had entered the Christian life with an idea that its work was as important as any in which he could engage.

Among many other pressing interests of life during these days was one which Emilie Cameron at least did not ignore. That was the growing intimacy of Mr. Edson with the entire Cameron family. Not two days after the prayer-meeting which Aunt Eunice and Rachel had attended, he called, and made himself so entirely agreeable that Lucia said she could not imagine what Emilie meant by her reports concerning him. A company of chattering school-girls, she supposed, had become offended with him because he was not always thinking only of them. Certainly nothing could be more gracious and deferential than his manner to Aunt Eunice, and she was neither rich nor learned. Emilie admitted that he was very much "nicer" than she had supposed, and her respect for him increased with greater knowledge. He had evidently determined that the family should have every opportunity for knowing him well. After the first formal call, which in itself was too friendly and genial to be described as such, he dropped at once into the friendly stage—running in with a paper containing an article about which he had been talking with Mr. Cameron, with a book of which Lucia had spoken, with some very early strawberries to tempt Aunt Eunice's appetite that he had heard her say was poor, with a dainty spray of orange bloom to remind Rachel of her California home—there was really no end to his ingenious devices for stopping in a moment on his way up or downtown. By degrees it was becoming apparent, at least to Emilie, that the orange blooms had been his choicest gift, and that he had selected their owner carefully.

"People can't cheat me," she remarked sagely. "I've read too many books, and watched too many couples when they didn't know I was watching. That young man wants to add a minister to our family. He did not choose orange blossoms from all the other flowers that grow in California, for nothing. Well, I don't think I object; he is really very nice indeed. I had not imagined that I could like him so well. And Rachel is exactly calculated for a minister's wife. She is a great deal better than he; but women nearly always are—that is, when they are good at all. Dear me, we are really getting famous, with two weddings in prospect."

But Rachel showed such decided and painful dislike to being good-naturedly rallied by her gay young sister that Mrs. Cameron peremptorily forbade such amusement in the future.

"Rachel says there is absolutely no truth in your surmise, and that if you persist in talking about it she will have to make herself conspicuous by refusing ordinary courtesies at his hands, such as he offers her in common with Lucia and Mary. Under such circumstances it is very rude and disagreeable in you to keep noticing his attentions. Remember, I will have no more of it."

Emilie nodded that very wise head of hers, and spoke with decision:

"I'll keep still, mother; but that won't prevent me from using my eyes and my common sense. I just want you to remember, when it comes, that I warned you. It isn't Aunt Eunice that attracts the minister, nor you and father, though he is so thoughtful of you all. He gave even me a great bunch of spring violets yesterday, and said I was to divide. That was because I told him one day that Rachel couldn't pass the window where they were. But I'll be as silent as an owl—and as wise! I think we would better begin to go there to church regularly. It will be less embarrassing to do it now than later."

Into the quiet bustle of preparation which now began to fill the house, there came one day, a distraction. Mr. Cameron, contrary to his habit, came home at luncheon time; but instead of appearing at the table where the family were gathered, went directly to his room.

"Your father cannot be well," Mrs. Cameron said with concern in her voice, and she went to him almost immediately. Later, Emilie was dispatched to the business house where he was employed to say that a severe headache which had almost blinded him would prevent his return that day, but he hoped to report as usual in the morning. Numerous were the questions with which Mrs. Cameron was plied as she went back and forth, carrying tea and toast which were untasted, and getting pounded ice to apply to the aching head. Her replies were unsatisfactory.

"Yes; his head was very bad, but easier now than at first. He is not ill otherwise."

"He will not have the doctor called; he has been positive about that from the first."

"Emilie can by no means go up to see him; he needs to be quiet."

"No, I do not consider it necessary to send for the doctor. I think he will be better soon."

In all these responses there was a sense of reserve knowledge which to Mary's anxious ears was apparent. Something had happened to induce such a severe headache; she felt sure of it. Perhaps because her mother naturally leaned somewhat more upon this eldest daughter than upon the others, and perhaps because she already knew what the others did not, Mrs. Cameron's reserve gave way when the girl followed her upstairs with a beseeching, "Do, mother, tell me the whole truth."

She laid her head on Mary's shoulder and cried. Only for a moment, then she brushed away the tears hurriedly. "I don't want him to see that I have been crying. Oh, it is nothing so very terrible, only he will worry so! Yes; it is the boys again. He has a letter from President Force— really a very kind letter—nothing to be so distressed about. I tell your father so; but he will not listen to reason. His head is so bad that he cannot. These headaches trouble me the most of anything. They are increasing on him, I think. Why, yes, you may as well go up, if you can keep the others from wanting to go also. Your knowing about the other matter makes it seem different to tell you. Perhaps your father would be quieted by talking it all over with you."

So Mary went up to the darkened room where her father sat holding his throbbing temples with both trembling hands, and thinking his troubled thoughts. He seemed relieved rather than otherwise to see Mary; gave her the President's letter to read, and tried to discuss the situation with her.

The letter was, as Mrs. Cameron had said, most kind. The President had taken the trouble to write in person, because he was peculiarly interested in these young men. They were talented young fellows, both of them, in some lines even brilliant. They had gotten into some little financial difficulties, which, noised abroad, would create unpleasantness not only for them but for their friends. A mere trifle as those things went. Probably a hundred dollars would make everything straight and avoid publicity, which last was of all things to be desired. He would not enter into particulars, as he judged that the sons themselves would prefer to acquaint their father with details. They had, however, been glad that he was willing to write, seeming to consider that their parents might be inclined to be too severe in their estimate of the deeds of young men. He would not deny that the boys had been foolish—boys were quite apt to be. We must not expect too great wisdom, especially in money matters, from these young heads. But he thought he might venture to hint that the difficulty in which the two found themselves would be a lesson for the future. He would suggest that the money, say a hundred dollars at this time, be sent them as promptly as possible. In fact, it might be well to send it to him, and he would undertake to see that none of the class of boys, who liked to make much out of little, sometimes, got hold of details. Of course, it was due to him, the father, to have details, and undoubtedly his sons would so understand. Meantime there was really nothing which need cause him very serious anxiety; all would come out well in the end, he hoped and believed. Such was the tenor of the letter, carefully guarded, so that one could not read distinctly between the lines. Mr. Cameron pushed aside the wet compress to see what his daughter thought of it.

He frankly confessed to her that so far as his present ability was concerned, a thousand dollars might as well have been called for as a hundred. He not only had not half that sum, but knew no way to raise it. He was in debt now, as she knew; and his next quarter's salary, although not due yet for nearly two months, had been anticipated almost to its full sum. He confessed that it was brooding over the existing state of things which had brought on one of his headaches, even before this letter was received.

Poor Mary found it hard to keep her voice low and soothing. She was angry with President Force. Why need he write at all if he had nothing but smooth hints to give them? What did the boys mean by going to a stranger, instead of writing home for themselves, if they had gotten into trouble? What was the use in saying that the money *could not* be raised? Of course it must be raised. They ought to see to it this very day! On the whole, she succeeded so well in bringing on another paroxysm, that she was presently banished, while her mother wrestled with pain.

21. "DON'T ASK ME ANY QUESTIONS"

The headache yielded at last, and by midnight the Cameron household was as quiet as usual; though Emilie announced the next morning that there must have been ghosts haunting the house. She certainly heard one in Mary's room, and nobody seemed to have slept well. Mr. Cameron came to the breakfast table looking old and worn.

"These fearful headaches are sapping his strength," his wife said, looking after him with a heavy sigh, as he moved feebly away towards a car.

"What is the cause of them, mother?" Emilie asked. "Don't you think he ought to have a doctor?'"

"He ought to have rest!" said the mother; and she sighed again. It was not until the morning was well advanced that Mary had an opportunity to ask her mother privately what father had decided to do.

"I am sure I don't know," she said wearily. "He did not sleep until toward morning, though the pain was subdued before midnight. He lay perfectly still and I did not speak, in the hope that he was resting; but every once in a while he would draw a sigh *so* heavy and hopeless that it went to my heart. At last he said aloud, 'It *must* be managed somehow.' Then I said, of course it must. We could not afford to ruin the prospects of our boys for the sake of a hundred dollars; and I added that I should think a man as well known as he might borrow a hundred dollars of somebody. I am sorry I said that; he has such a horror of borrowing. This morning he had nothing to tell me beyond the fact that he had decided to raise the money in some way."

It was a long day to mother and daughter. The necessity which they felt laid upon them not to talk about their trouble, or to betray unusual anxiety, made the strain greater. Both of them were watching all day for— they hardly knew what. At every sound of the door-bell they started nervously and their eyes sought each other, each mutely asking, "Is that a message from or about the boys? And what does it reveal?"

"I believe you two have some dark designs or expectations," said the observing Emilie, late in the afternoon. "Every time the bell rings your faces get red and then pale; and you look as though you expected a policeman to pounce in upon you. Mother, you haven't been aiding and abetting Mary to steal white silk enough for a wedding-dress, have you?"

They laughed off the charge as best they could, and tried to be more careful, and did not know whether to be relieved or fearful when at last Mr. Cameron came slowly

from the car at the usual time. Both met him in the hall;
Mrs. Cameron saying eagerly that she must see how
"father" had borne the day, and Mary coming swiftly from
her room whither she had retired to watch for him.

"It is settled," he said quickly. "I secured the money,
and telegraphed President Force a money order. He has it
by this time. Now, don't ask me any questions, nor let me
hear any more about it;" and he passed them and went to
his room, where he locked himself in. But he came to
dinner as usual, and looked no paler than might have
been expected in a man who had borne such pain but the
day before.

Wife and daughter breathed more freely, feeling that
the mysterious cyclone which had threatened to break
over their heads had passed, after all, leaving them
unharmed. Had they spent the day with Mr. Cameron
their hearts would have been less light. When he left
home in the morning, he had no definite plan of action,
and had arrived at only that one decision: somehow or
other he must raise a hundred dollars before the day was
done. His excited imagination had brooded over the letter
from the President until it seemed to him that the very
lives of his boys were in some way in peril. Their father
must rescue them. How? Of course he had thought of, and
rejected, a hundred different ways. His wife had been
silent to her eldest daughter with regard to one bit of
conversation.

"I suppose if I should ask Kennedy to lend me a
hundred dollars for a few days, he could do it without the

slightest inconvenience," Mr. Cameron had said; and his wife had replied quickly:

"Oh, Edward! Do not think of it. Any way rather than that. It would humiliate Mary to the dust. She is very sensitive now about her poverty; and then think what a precedent it would suggest. He would conceive of you as a man who would be always borrowing his money."

And then Mr. Cameron had shuddered, and evidently turned at once from that possibility. So he had from any other which suggested itself; and was sitting at his desk trying to add a column of figures, and feeling like one on the eve of some desperate act, when young Clinton, the son of a member of his firm, stopped before him.

"By the way, Mr. Cameron, accounts are in your line, I believe. Here is one not connected with the firm, but I wish you would attend to it for me. I promised to meet Mr. Louis Stevenson here this morning at twelve, and let him have a little money which he wants to use. He is not here on time, and I must go. When he calls, will you hand him this, and take a receipt? Just count it before I go, that we may be sure we agree. There should be a hundred dollars."

A curious photograph of himself counting that money had been present in Mr. Cameron's mind all day. He knew his hand had trembled so visibly, that young Clinton had asked kindly if he was not well; and on hearing of his day of suffering had added that he ought to have rest. Then he had gone away with a word of thanks for the accommodation, and left that hundred dollars with a man who felt that it was able to save his sons from public disgrace and ruin. He locked it away out of sight, and watched eagerly for Mr. Stevenson; he longed to get the bills into his hands. He would not go out for luncheon lest he might miss the man. Besides, he wanted no lunch; the thought of eating was offensive to him. Meantime he made desperate efforts on his own behalf. He asked a fellow-clerk who had occasionally accommodated him, and whom he now owed fifty dollars, to lend him a hundred. The man replied coldly that he was himself embarrassed, and had no money to lend to anybody; the tone said, "Least of all to you."

He wrote a note to a well-known money-lender, offering payment in three months at twelve percent, but he had not the required security; and the day waned, and he had not raised the one hundred dollars. He looked up at the clock. In another hour it would be too late to have it delivered as a money order that day. What might *not* happen to the boys? By this time he had worked himself into the belief that a few hours more of delay would be fatal. And Mr. Stevenson had not come; and as often as he had need to open his desk, that roll of bills stared him in the face. At last two men waited at the desk while he ran over their account and verified it. While they waited they talked.

"Did you see Stevenson this morning?"

"No; did he lunch at the Club?"

"Oh, no; he was off before lunch time; took the eleven-ten. He's a lucky fellow; I wouldn't mind being a relative just now."

Mr. Cameron passed over the account, and asked this question: "Were you speaking of Mr. Louis Stevenson just now? Has he left town?"

"Yes, sir; went this morning, to be absent several weeks."

"I expected him to call on a matter of business," explained Mr. Cameron. "That is why I asked the question."

"Well, he went unexpectedly; that is, he did not mean to leave until midnight; but he had a telegram which hastened him. I presume that is why you have not seen him."

Then Mr. Cameron looked at the clock again, and put on his street coat, and explained to the proper one that he had had no lunch, and went out quickly with the roll of bills belonging to Mr. Stevenson in his hand. By the time he returned, President Force had probably received his telegram.

Mr. Cameron had *borrowed* the money; that was all! He explained it carefully to himself a hundred times during the next two hours. He had borrowed money before, but never in this way. He would say nothing to anybody about the way. The young man who had left the bills in his care was not in the store twice a month. Even if he came, all that he needed was a receipt. Meantime, of course, long before Mr. Stevenson's return, the hundred dollars would be ready for him. It *should* be raised somehow. This was the history of Mr. Cameron's day, about which he did not want to be questioned. His wife worried much because he ate almost no dinner, and slept but little that night, and restlessly. How could he hope to endure the strain of the spring work and care if he went on in this way?

"I wish I knew how he raised the money," said Mary anxiously.

"So that it is raised, what does it matter? You can trust your father, I hope!" The mother's tone was severe.

"Why, of course!" said Mary, opening her eyes wide. "But I mean I am afraid he has had to do it in a way which adds to his anxieties." Yes, he had, but nobody suspected the way. A *Cameron* could not do anything dishonorable!

What life was to Mr. Cameron during the weeks which followed, it is well that one has not to describe. Has anybody ever succeeded in describing the condition of a man who has lived half a century of honor, and then suddenly fallen in his own sight? As for the boys, this last prompt action on the part of a father whom they had dishonored, brought them to their senses. They both wrote very grateful letters. Father should see that his kindness was not undeserved. They had gotten into unexpected trouble, but had learned their lesson; he need never fear a repetition of it. They had learned some things now that they had not known before. They were going to work hard, and carry off all the honors. When they came home there were many details connected with the affair which their father should know; but they would not take his time nor try his patience by writing them. In fact, their letter, in its way, was as much a success at *not* telling, as was that of President Force. Father, mother, and eldest daughter studied it, and tried to be content. The father, indeed, told himself bitterly that *he* was not one to inquire too closely into what had been done; but Mary was, for a time, indignant. The mother was so glad to see the handwriting of her boys that she cried over it, and after that was happier than she had been for months; for the boys took to writing regularly again, letters which she read and re-read, and wore next her heart. Meantime, the young man from whom the hundred dollars had been borrowed, kept away from the store, and the borrower tried by every means in his power to raise the money.

Despite the many duties and cares connected with her approaching marriage, Mary Cameron found time to be harassed by nameless fears in still another direction. These were connected with her gay young sister, Emilie. The pretentious party which Mary had helped her to attend as a rare treat was by no means the last gathering of the kind at which she found herself. Indeed, this one glimpse of the bright world which had heretofore lain beyond her reach seemed to have bewitched the girl. She said no more about clothes, being willing, apparently, to appear in her old ones, if only she might *appear*; and, on one pretext or another, succeeded in getting permission oftener than she herself had imagined to be possible. At first Mary had laughed, and counseled that she be allowed to go. "The child will soon have enough of it," she said, "with no pretty finery to show off. Girls of that age go to parties chiefly for the sake of showing how sweet they look in their new dresses. Besides, it is innocent amusement enough; just girls and boys of their own set. What harm?"

But there was harm coming, and Mary was the first to rouse to anxiety. No, Rachel was the first; but she had discountenanced the parties from the beginning, and Emilie had bitterly resented what she called her "interference." It was bad enough, she declared, to be managed by her eldest sister; but to have Rachel, her next in age, attempt it was insufferable. So Rachel could do nothing; but she asked Mary if she did not see how the bloom was wearing from Emilie's life, and pointed out certain subtle changes which even the preoccupied mother had not noticed. Moreover, the objectionable "Cousin Richard" who was thought to have returned to New York, was discovered to be a person of distinction at the parties.

Mary, being interrogated, said that she did not know anything positively harmful concerning him, except that he played cards; but so did all the young men of that class. And he drank wine, at weddings at least; but so did many others—estimable young men. At the same time, she did not like to have Emilie associated with him. He was a great deal older than the company he affected; and the child was too young anyway to think of such things. But Rachel remembered her own bitter and dangerous experience, and knew that "children" did "think of such things."

Finally it was Ben Reeder who sounded the note of alarm—Ben Reeder, who belonged to the class that must give peculiar satisfaction to the Lord Jesus Christ. It is of such persons one instinctively thinks when one reads the verse: "He shall see of the travail of his soul and be satisfied." Ben Reeder had been made over by grace. To him the Lord Jesus was everything; he did his daily work at the store with a view to honoring him; he spent his evenings where he could be sure Jesus Christ would accompany him and make no inconsiderable part of the enjoyment. He spent his money exactly in the line in which he believed Jesus Christ would have done had he walked the streets in person.

"In short," said Mr. Landis, trying to describe the change to the Camerons, "the boy makes one think of the old life whose history is embodied in a single sentence: 'This one thing.' I have rarely seen grace do so much in so short a time as it has done for our boy Ben. I like to think of his father and mother when he gets back to them."

Ben Reeder came to Mr. Landis one day with a troubled face. "Professor," he began, for although that gentleman earnestly desired to be called plain "Mister," and was gradually so impressing his friends, Ben clung to the title; "Professor, do you know anything about the Vane Street Theatre?"

"Quite as much as I care to know, Ben. I am glad that neither that theatre nor any other interests you."

"Well, but we have to think about such things sometimes. There is a difference in theatres, I suppose; and you wouldn't choose the Vane Street one to have your sister attend, even if she would go to some of them, would you?"

Mr. Landis dropped the essay he was glancing over, and gave full attention to his companion.

"Ben, my boy, what are you getting at?"

"Why, Professor, I suppose they would think it wasn't any of my business; but they have been awfully good to me, and that little girl especially did her best to help me; and I wondered if—they *can't* know what kind of a place it is or they wouldn't have her go there; and they can't know what kind of a man he is, or they wouldn't let him take her—there, or anywhere. Couldn't you do something?"

"Ben, you are not given to such bewildering statements. What 'little' girl and what 'man' are interesting you?"

Thus called to account, Ben explained, not without an earnest parenthesis to the effect that he did not want to seem to be intruding or interfering, that little Emilie Cameron was occasionally seen entering the doors of the Vane Street Theatre, in company with Mr. Richard Forbes.

Mr. Landis was dumfounded. Not a friend to theatres of any type, because he had carefully studied them from the standpoint of a thoughtful, well-informed man, it had not occurred to him that respectable people would venture inside the Vane Street house; and it made his blood boil to think of the gay, sweet child being carried thither by a moral wolf whose sheep's clothing was of the flimsiest character. Of course, none of the family knew of these visits; but how were they managed? He thanked Ben, gave him a caution which he did not need, and began that very evening to "do something."

His relations with the Camerons were now those of a trusted friend. His sister Dorothy had gone home for a vacation, which gave him somewhat more leisure; and he chose to devote many pleasant half-hours to the Cameron home circle. Everyone welcomed him; but with Mary, especially, his relations seemed to be more that of a brother in whom she trusted. She frankly asked his advice on all sorts of subjects, and followed it often; always carefully, however, holding back from the subject of momentous importance which he tried to press upon her for decision. Sometime, she assured him, she was going to give serious attention to this matter, and really meant, when she had *settled down*, to order her life by the principles of the Bible. He knew that she meant after she was married, and he longed exceedingly to have her settle the whole matter before that time. When he thought of Mr. Kennedy's influence upon a soul who still held the claims of Jesus Christ in abeyance, he trembled for the result. But on all other subjects Mary Cameron was frank with him; so he had no hesitancy in asking at once where

Emilie was this evening. He asked it in low tones, as he was arranging the music on the piano for Mary to play for him.

She had gone to spend the night with her particular friend, Bertha Foster, Mary explained. Why did he ask? Had he any special message for her? Instead of replying, he asked if she often spent the night with Miss Foster; something in his tone making Mary look up at him anxiously.

Why, not very often. Father had old-fashioned ideas about such things, and liked to have the children at home at night. Still, Emilie went oftener than the older ones used to be allowed to. Being the youngest, it had seemed natural not to be so strict with her; and, now that she thought of it, perhaps she had been quite frequently of late to the Foster's; Bertha was a silly sort of girl, too. They wondered at Emilie for being so fond of her. Why did he ask the question?

He asked still another: Would she pardon him for inquiring if Emilie had been given permission to attend the theatre with her friends?

Oh, no, indeed! Father had never approved of their attending the theatre. The older ones had gone but rarely; and Emilie had never been allowed to go, save with her brothers once or twice to very exceptional plays. Wouldn't he *please* tell her right away why he asked? Was anything wrong?

Mr. Landis looked behind him at the family group gathered around the drop light, then bent his head and spoke lower still.

22. A Persistent Friend

Mary was at first inclined to be indignant with poor Ben. The idea of their Emilie being seen going into the Vane Street Theatre! It was absurd. Some other girl who resembled her had doubtless misled him; but he should be more particular than that. Why, it was almost as much as a girl's character was worth to have such things said about her! Mr. Landis was not relieved of his anxiety by all this. He had questioned Ben carefully, and knew him well; he was the last boy to be mistaken about such a thing. Gradually Mary's indignation changed to anxiety. She stopped the song in the middle of a verse to cross-question Mr. Landis; thereby calling from Lucia the remark that interludes occurred in very unusual places apparently. Did he not think it possible that Ben might have mistaken some other girl for Emilie? Or the child might have been standing near the entrance for a moment, speaking with some one. Surely the Fosters would not allow Bertha to attend such places. Then Mr. Landis frightened her still further by asking if the Fosters were not somewhat careless as to where the cousin took Bertha and her friends.

"Not that I should suppose they would be careless," he added with a gravity that was almost stern. "I cannot think of another person, found sometimes in respectable society, whom I would not rather choose for companionship than him; but people are often unpardonably careless where there is relationship."

"Is he so bad as that?" Mary asked, her face paling. What if Emilie were in his company at this moment! She had not thought of his being always with his cousin. The song ceased altogether, and the two conversed in low tones for some time. Then Mr. Landis came forward to bid good-evening to the family group, explaining that an important matter of business had occurred to him, which would take him away at once.

"Somebody ought to write to Mr. Kennedy," said Lucia, after he was gone. "If he had seen those two so absorbed in themselves as to forget all about the music they were pretending to learn, I am sure he would have been jealous, if he has any of that article in his composition. Mary Cameron, whatever other faults you may have had, I *never* thought you would develop into a flirt!"

She meant the merest nonsense, such as Mary had, of late, been able to laugh over; but this evening she was too nervous.

"Oh, *don't!*" she said, with something of the sharpness which used to greet such teasings; and Lucia was silent, and filled with wonder.

Mr. Landis's "business" was none of the pleasantest. He had promised to learn, if he could, just who Emilie's companions were this evening, and to bring Mary word again, if there should be ground for anxiety. She had assured him that these anxieties must be kept from her father if possible; for he had had a very serious strain of late, and was so far from well, that they were in daily fear of the consequences. Mr. Landis went away in some doubt as to how he should fulfill his commission. He had not even a calling acquaintance with the Fosters; but there was a matter of business which he might transact with the mother, although he would have preferred to choose another time.

He made his call much briefer than he would otherwise have done; having learned incidentally on his first arrival that Bertha and a friend who was visiting her had gone out with the former's cousin. He tried to shape his inquiries in a way to learn where they had gone, but failed in this; it would not do to excite wonderment over his curiosity. He took a downtown car while trying to decide what step to take next, and was busy studying the problem when Ben Reeder touched his arm.

"Excuse me, Professor, for interrupting your thinking; but I'm awfully anxious about something." Mr. Landis made room for him, and the boy went on. "You know what I was talking to you about this morning? Well, they are going there tonight; and it is one of the worst plays in the lot, that comes on tonight. I *don't* think he can know where he is taking her. He has been drinking."

"How did you learn of this, Ben?"

"I found it out by what folks call accident. I had to stay after time tonight, and had no dinner; so when I got a chance, I slipped into that restaurant around the corner from us; and at the table in front of me sat Mr. Forbes and another man. They had a bottle of wine; and while they drank it, they made their plans and talked pretty loud, and I listened. Mr. Forbes was to bring his cousin and Emilie Cameron down to the square; and there the other man was to meet them, and take the cousin somewhere, I didn't find out where; but Emilie Cameron was to go to the Vane Street play with Mr. Forbes; and afterwards they were to meet again at the square at half-past eleven, so that Mr. Forbes could take charge of both ladies. I thought maybe you would know something that could be done, and I've been hunting about for you here and there. I stood at the corner thinking what to do next when I caught sight of you in this car."

"What is this we are passing?" asked Mr. Landis; "the St. James? Then I will stop here. And, Ben, thank you very much. Be entirely silent about what you have told me; I will attend to it."

Drawn up near the St. James were rows of carriages, into one of which Mr. Landis stepped and gave his order:

"To the Vane Street Theatre."

Arrived there, he directed the driver to wait, adding that he should not be long gone. Then he stepped boldly to the office and secured a ticket, the first he had ever bought at that place. It was early yet; the play could hardly have commenced; but he must know whether the ones he sought were in the audience. Comparative stranger though he was, he recognized some faces that he had not expected to meet, and there were elbows nudged and whispers of astonishment exchanged over his entrance. He remained long enough to be sure that Emilie Cameron was not in the house, then went back to his carriage with a direction.

"Drive a little out of the line, to that side, and wait. I shall not be detained long." Then he took his station near the main entrance. He had not long to wait. Tripping airily from the car, with her pretty gloved hand resting on Mr. Forbes's arm, was Emilie, her bright face aglow with excitement and anticipation; too ignorant of the world to understand how low a world she was being taken to.

As they reached the sidewalk, Mr. Landis stepped forward and addressed Mr. Forbes.

"Excuse me, sir; I have a message for this young lady from her home. She is wanted there immediately."

Emilie gave a faint little scream of apprehension. "Oh, Mr. Landis, is my father ill? Please tell me, quick!"

"It is not illness, Miss Emilie; I will explain as we drive; come with me to my carriage."

"I beg your pardon, sir," said Mr. Forbes loftily; "the lady is in my charge, and I cannot engage to release her on such short notice. If no one is ill, what in thunder is the matter that you are acting the part of policeman?"

"One thing that is the matter," said Mr. Landis coldly, "is that you are partially intoxicated, and not fit to have the charge of a lady. Will you let her go quietly, or must I call a policeman?"

"Oh, let me go!" said Emilie. "I want to go with him, Mr. Forbes; I do, indeed; he is an old friend." As she spoke, she snatched her hand from her companion's arm; and Mr. Landis, without more ado, hurried her to the waiting carriage, gave the Camerons' street and number, and took a seat beside his charge—almost the worst part of his duty being yet to come. By this time Emilie was sobbing bitterly.

"Something dreadful has happened at home," she murmured, "and you will not tell me what it is."

"Nothing has happened to them, Miss Emilie," he said. "The 'dreadful' part all rests with yourself. Do you know what sort of a place you were being taken to this evening? Can it be possible that you have ever been there before?"

Emilie's tears were stayed, and her eyes began to flash. "Is there really nothing the matter at home? Then, what right had you to interfere with me? Who sent you?"

"I had the right of a man who would protect a lady from insult. Did you not know that the person with whom you were had been drinking so freely that he hardly realized what he was doing? And, when I tell your father where I found you, will he blame or thank me for my interference?"

Then Emilie began to cry again, and to exclaim between the sobs, "Oh, Mr. Landis, don't tell my father! He is so worried now over other things that he is almost ill. We are afraid, all the time, that he will break down; and I did not mean anything bad. I went to stay with Bertha; I did not know at all that Mr. Forbes was to be there; he asked us to take a ride downtown; then he said we would go in there just a little while to see some of the fun. It is nothing very dreadful; other people go there; nice people. Father does not approve of theatres, I know, and I would not go often; but just for a little while."

"Have you not been to that place before?" The questioner could not keep his voice from being stern; he was ashamed of the silly girl. She winced visibly, yet was angry.

"You need not speak to me as though I was a child and you my guardian; I am not under your care. I have only been there once before—or twice—for a little while."

"And you saw and heard nothing of which you did not approve?" The girl hesitated; it was her nature to be truthful. "They do things at all theatres that are silly," she said at last, "and that people don't like; yet they attend them. I have heard the girls talk. Some of my schoolmates, no older than I, go twice a week regularly, and a few of them oftener. Why, their *fathers* take them."

"Your father did not take you. Would he be willing to have you there? Would you like to explain to him just how often you have been, and just what you saw and heard?"

But he could do nothing with her. She cried again, and begged him not to excite her father; and almost in the same breath accused him of being cruel and hateful, and interfering. What business of his was it where she went, or how often? In the midst of this, her eye caught some familiar object outside, and she started up with a new excitement. "Where are you taking me? I *won't* go home; they don't expect me; I am to spend the night with Bertha Foster. I want you to tell the driver to take me directly there."

"You are going home," he said sternly. "It is much the safest place for you; and unless you have womanliness enough to protect yourself, I shall consider it my duty to warn your parents against allowing you to have such persons for friends. Mrs. Foster either does not or cannot protect her own daughter. How can she be expected to care for others? Miss Emilie, I am sorry to appear harsh, or to persist in an unwelcome service, but it is clearly my duty to see you safe tonight under your father's roof. I believe you are too young and innocent to know what you have escaped. There are degrees even in theatres. That play tonight was one which no person of respectability ought to want to see and hear. I know of no man so low, that he would take his sister to it. I do not believe even the person with whom you were, would have insulted you by doing so, if he had not been too much under the influence of liquor to realize what he was doing. Miss Emilie, you force me to ask if your father knows that you go *anywhere* in that man's company?"

And at last he succeeded in thoroughly frightening poor Emilie. With all her keenness, and her boasted knowledge of the world, she was really as ignorant as a child. There was a grave sense in which she had come up, instead of being brought up, thus far. Her mother, busy with the weary problem of life, trying, ever since her children had been old enough to suggest it, to do for them what she could not do—namely, give them all the advantages of dress and surroundings which people of wealth and leisure can command—had been too busy and too harassed to give careful attention to those sacred lessons which only mothers can teach. The result was that Emilie, being of a different temperament from her sisters, was more keenly susceptible to all the witching influences of worldliness, and knew only in the vaguest way what harm might come to her, and why she should hold herself in check. Mr. Forbes had been interesting to her chiefly because he flattered her, treated her in what she called a "grown-up" way, and offered her the attentions which she supposed belonged only to those older than herself. In truth, some of them belonged only to those who had little self respect; but Emilie honestly believed that Mr. Forbes was simply showing her the ways of the gay and cultured circles in which he moved. When he told her that some girls were prudes, and were not noticed by people in society, because they had queer "country" ways of looking at things, she believed him. When he offered to show her a charming bit of comedy, and she demurred, and was afraid her father would not like it, he replied that of course her father would not want her to go frequently, nor with all sorts of persons; but he was old enough, he presumed, to be trusted, and he had looked after sisters and cousins innumerable. Also, he told her that of course there were portions of the plays which were "not quite the thing;" but that sensible people must learn to discriminate between the good and the bad, and enjoy the good; just as they had to do in books.

It sounded reasonable to this silly, ignorant girl; and she let him take her whither he would. She would not ask her father's permission, because he was so worried nowadays, and so unlike himself that he would be almost sure to refuse her anything, and he ought not to be "bothered." She would not mention at home her fine times because Rachel, if she was an angel, was a very ignorant one so far as this world was concerned, and would be sure to think that everything done away from home was wrong. Of course she would not go often anywhere with Mr. Forbes; he was not to be here long. Such, in general, was the reasoning, so far as it can be said to be reasoning, with which the girl had comforted her conscience. None of her acts had looked very startling to her, until seen in the light of Mr. Landis's stern eyes, and until she found herself in a carriage with him being whirled toward home as a culprit.

There were some minutes of painful silence, during which Emilie cried quietly, and Mr. Landis considered. Presently he spoke again.

"Miss Emilie, I have no wish to make things harder for you than is necessary. I shall certainly take you home, for I feel sure that is the place for you tonight. Moreover, your sister Mary expects some word from you. There are reasons why she grew very anxious about you. Providentially she learned something of your late associations. I shall make what explanation ought to be made to her, and she and you can plan as to how much or little of all this should be revealed to your father in his present state of health. It may be that if you decide, after careful thought, to be the wise and prudent young woman whom I am sure you can be if you choose, it will not be deemed necessary to trouble your father with the matter. I need hardly tell you, however, after the very plain way in which I have spoken this evening, that it rests with yourself to decide how much or how little I shall interfere in the future. You were good enough to speak of me tonight as an old friend; be sure I shall not stand quietly by and see any friend of mine led toward ruin."

Then the carriage stopped, and Emilie was at home. She had stopped crying, but her pale, frightened face was pitiful. She appealed to him as a child might.

"Mr. Landis, will you not see mother and the others for me? Tell them—tell them anything you please, only let me go upstairs away from it all." Saying which, she ran away at full speed, leaving her companion no alternative but to make what excuse he could for his second appearance. Betsey had retired the moment she had admitted them, naturally supposing that Emilie would wait on the guest. The situation was certainly embarrassing. But for his promise to Mary, Mr. Landis would have felt like letting himself out and going his way, leaving that foolish girl upstairs to explain her presence as best she could. He hesitated a moment, trying to plan as to his best course, then quietly opened the door and advanced to the family circle. "I am becoming very unceremonious, you observe," he said; "at the same time I beg pardon for the intrusion; Betsey evidently thought I knew the way. I have brought Miss Emilie back with me, Mrs. Cameron; I had occasion to call at the Fosters', and she decided not to remain there tonight. She went up to her room."

It sounded like a very feeble explanation. Mr. Landis did not wonder that the mother half arose in alarm. "What could have happened to Emilie?"

He wished he could say something which would give the girl upstairs a few minutes alone. He glanced at Mary, but the hopeless anxiety on her face warned him that he must expect no help from her. Then Lucia unconsciously came to the rescue.

"She and Bertha Foster must have quarreled at last! I have been expecting it; it isn't in human nature that those two should remain excellent friends for very long. Confess, Mr. Landis, Emilie cried most of the way home, and deserted you in the hall, like the child that she is, because her eyes were red."

Mr. Landis smiled, much relieved. "I will not deny that there were some tears shed," he said, "and I fancy that Miss Emilie desires of all things to be alone for awhile."

"I was sure of it!" said Lucia in triumph. "And I must say I am not sorry; I only hope the rupture will last. I don't think an intimacy with Bertha Foster is a thing to be desired."

Mr. Landis had already turned to Mr. Cameron with an item of news which he had gathered on the street. Meantime, he was asking himself, "What next?"

Mary was still very pale and seemed unable to ask questions, or give him a hint of help; yet she must know about Emilie; and perhaps that father, who looked ill enough to be under the doctor's care, ought not to know, for that night at least. He resolved upon a bold move.

"Miss Cameron, may I have five minutes of your time? I would like to explain that matter of which we were talking, and make myself understood."

Without a word, Mary led the way to the farthest corner of the front parlor. Presently the murmur of his voice could be heard in the other room.

He told Emilie's story without reserve. Mary Cameron was the eldest sister; it was presumable that she would know what ought to done. If the father was as ill as he looked, it would certainly not be wise to rob him of his night's rest; but for tomorrow she must decide. At all hazards Emilie must be kept from having anything to do with the person named Forbes.

"The man is rotten to the core," he said earnestly. "You must stand between him and your sister."

Poor Mary! She did not know how to do it.

In the back parlor, Lucia was saying: "Things are really getting very serious! Don't you think so, Aunt Eunice?"

But they supposed that Mr. Landis was talking to Mary about the matter of personal religion.

23. Borrowed (?) Money

With the first days of May, Mr. Kennedy fluttered down upon the Cameron family, bringing a flurry of good cheer. It was impossible to withstand his genial, free-hearted ways. A nameless anxiety, which had been hovering over the household for weeks, lifted insensibly with his coming. He came unexpectedly, unheralded by so much as a line; Mr. Kennedy was the sort of man who always did unexpected things. Business called him within twenty miles; and he hurried it, and stole a day, and here he was. He had an errand also; this was to try to hasten the wedding by a week or two. He pleaded his cause skillfully, but Mary was inexorable; it would not be possible for her to get ready before the day appointed, and which was now so near at hand. Even now she felt hurried, almost appalled at times, at its nearness.

She did not tell Mr. Kennedy what was the main reason, perhaps, for refusing to be hurried; which was that her father was not to have one straw added to his anxiety. She knew he was striving in every possible way to raise money. Of course, it was in view of the coming wedding; he had actually grown pale but yesterday, when her mother had reminded him that it was time to see about the fruit-cakes and other articles for which they must depend upon Alburgh.

"So soon!" he had murmured, and she was sure he was thinking of the money which must be raised. It was hard enough at the best; he should not be hurried more than was necessary. Let it be taken note of, in passing, that this young woman who had an honest desire to help her father in his difficulties, who spent many an anxious hour in his behalf, had not so much as thought of one way of helping; namely, by having no wedding fruit-cake, from Alburgh's or elsewhere; and by dispensing with a hundred elegant and expensive trifles which were necessary accompaniments of a wedding-feast that Alburgh, or any of his tribe, managed. That is, the thing which the Camerons could not in honor do—prepare an elegant collation and bid their friends to it, on the occasion of their daughter's marriage—they were as steadily preparing to do as though it were a part of the marriage ceremony itself. How could they help it? People in their set always made weddings for their children.

Of course, they could not do anything great or expensive; but a few friends they *must* have in, and there must be a collation. These matters really did not need to be talked about; they were foregone conclusions. But Mary felt the bitterness of it, and began to long for the time when she could write letters home, and slip in a bank-note for a birthday, or holiday, or anniversary token. She carefully counted up the days which on some pretext or other could be marked in this way, and rejoiced in them; but these were matters which she could not explain to Mr. Kennedy.

He, on his part, had thoughts which were carefully kept in the background. It would not have done, for instance, to have told his bride-elect that the uncle who had made her his heiress was very feeble indeed, and might be called upon any day to exchange worlds; and that for this reason it would be wise to hasten the marriage, that he might have all proper authority when very important business matters came to her for settlement. It was a perfectly reasonable and proper feeling, he told himself; his object was, of course, to watch over her interests. Still, it had to do with a matter which could not be mentioned. Why, as to that, it was a legal secret; and the remembrance of that fact relieved him immensely. He chafed under Mary's decision, and felt that someday he would explain to her how utterly unreasonable she had been, and what an amount of unnecessary trouble she had made. But outwardly he was genial, and lavished money even more freely than usual; taking Lucia and Emilie with them for a long drive in the most delightful portions of the city, and with as elegant a turnout as the best livery could furnish. Emilie, especially, appreciated it, and was royally happy.

She had not been so happy as usual of late, poor child. Her experience with Mr. Landis, and the interviews which followed it, had served to thoroughly sober her for a time. On the whole, Mary had assumed the responsibility laid upon her, and managed it fairly well. Following Mr. Landis's advice, she had been quiet, even gentle, in her dealings with the youthful sinner; and as a consequence, Emilie had told her in detail all that there was to tell. It was by no means so bad that it might not have been much worse; but still, to Mary's lately awakened eyes, it was bad enough. Then they took counsel together as to what should be done. Emilie begged and prayed that father might not be troubled with her. He looked so dreadfully pale and worn, and had such wretched sleepless nights, that if he had her, too, to worry about she was afraid it would kill him; and if mother knew it, father would have to, for she always told him everything. What was the need for anyone being told? She knew now how silly and wicked she had been, and she would never, *never* give cause for further anxiety. That hateful Mr. Forbes who had made all the trouble had gone back to New York; when he came again she would not even recognize him on the street. Bertha was vexed with her, anyway, because she went home that night, instead of coming back to their house, and so got *her* into trouble; so she need not have anything more to do with her; and indeed if Mary would just be quiet about it all, she, Emilie, would be angelic for the future.

This seemed, on the whole, the wisest thing to be done; especially as Emilie was unexpectedly meek, and showed herself willing to be advised by Mary to a greater degree than she ever had been before. There was no difficulty in keeping matters quiet, because of Lucia's theory about the break with Bertha Foster; confirmed when a messenger from the Fosters brought Emilie, the morning after the trouble, a very cold and formal note. It was so carefully worded that Emilie could even show it to her mother; and that unsuspecting lady read, and said: "So she went out in the evening with company and left you! I do not wonder that you preferred to return home. I would not be in haste to renew the friendship, daughter. Mary and Lucia do not seem to have a very high opinion of the Fosters."

Emilie blushed over this; she must keep silence, and allow her mother to think that Bertha had treated her rudely. This was one of the penalties which came of her wrong doing; but to speak would be to have Bertha blamed far more, and justly; so she kept silence.

Matters were in this state when Mr. Kennedy came to the rescue, and none were more glad to see him than Emilie. She had naturally avoided Mr. Landis since their evening ride together; and Mary kept such careful hold upon her that she felt herself almost a prisoner, and chafed under it, even while her face crimsoned over the thought that she had brought it upon herself, and perhaps needed just such restraint. On the whole, the girl had sense enough to realize that she had made a very narrow escape, and had reason to be grateful to Mr. Landis for the prompt and quiet way in which he had rescued her. Of Ben Reeder's very important part in the rescue, she knew nothing; Mr. Landis wisely judging that such knowledge would unnecessarily humiliate her, and could be of no use.

Perhaps the only one whose face was not brighter because of Mr. Kennedy's visit was his host. He gave him cordial greeting; but almost immediately the look of weariness and unrest, which were becoming habitual, settled back into his face, so that Mr. Kennedy noticed it, and asked Mary if her father had been ill.

"He has aged since I was here," he said, with true solicitude in his voice; and when Mary explained that he was harassed by business matters, and added frankly that it was very wearing to be poor, he made her heart thrill with gratitude by saying tenderly, "I hope you and I can soon do something toward making life brighter for your father." He smiled over her manifest delight, and assured himself that he would advise the most liberal policy toward the family. With so large a fortune as he had taken pains to inform himself there would be to plan with, nothing less than liberality could be thought of. But he felt generous all the evening over the fact that he meant to advise it. At the dinner table, Mr. Cameron roused once or twice, and exerted himself painfully to help entertain his guest; until Mrs. Cameron said anxiously, "Edward, why do you try to talk? You are really too weary to do so; Mr. Kennedy will excuse you, I am sure."

Then he murmured something about feeling more exhausted than usual, and sent his cup to be refilled with coffee, directing that it be made strong, as he had work yet to do tonight; he must go back downtown. The family exclaimed over this; Mrs. Cameron begging him not to do so; and Mary seeming so anxious and ill at ease that Mr. Kennedy at last asked kindly if it were not some errand which could be entrusted to him.

Mr. Cameron's negative was so quick, that he felt the immediate necessity for explanation. "It is a very troublesome matter of business with Mr.—" He hesitated as if the name had escaped him for the moment, and then added quickly, "Mr. John Welborne."

"Ah, indeed!" said Mr. Kennedy, "then, if I really cannot serve you, I consider it a very fortunate circumstance that you have business with that particular gentleman, because I shall ask you to serve me. I have a couple of hundred dollars in my pocket that are to be given into his hands tonight. I neglected to bring my check-book with me, so must depend on the bills; I leave too early in the morning to attend to the matter, and besides it is due today, and I like to be prompt about money matters, so I intended to tear myself away early enough this evening to do the errand; but if you must go, could you kindly hand this package to him? It will not take your time with explanations; the note enclosed explains itself."

Mr. Cameron took the package like one in a dream; he neglected to say that he would be glad to do the errand, or that it would not trouble him, or any of the commonplaces which belong to polite life; instead, he stared into vacancy and was utterly silent. Mrs. Cameron felt compelled to apologize for him.

"Your father is too tired to think, tonight," she said, glancing in a distressed way at Mary; and then Mr. Cameron arose, and said he must go at once; he ought not to have delayed so long.

Once on the street, he walked the length of two blocks before it occurred to him to signal a car. Never before was his brain, which had borne a great deal, in such a whirl of bewilderment as it was tonight. He had had a great deal to think about that day. Nearly four weeks now since a hundred dollars had been given him for Mr. Stevenson; and in that time, scarcely a day had passed but he had made some effort to raise that amount of money. And the efforts had been fruitless. There was absolutely not a man who was willing to lend him a hundred dollars without security; knowing, as all men did who had dealings with him, that his bills at stores and groceries remained unpaid, and that his family were preparing for a wedding.

"A sad case," one acquaintance of a lifetime had said, shaking his head gravely as the door closed after Mr. Cameron bearing away a refusal. "A truly sad case; a man of integrity weighted down with a family who are trying, every one of them, to do what they cannot; live and dress and act as though their father was a millionaire, instead of a salaried clerk. I hear that they are planning now for a fashionable wedding; I wonder if Alburgh will serve them on credit?"

And today Mr. Cameron had had a shock. Among the sea of faces that surged by his desk that morning, he had recognized Louis Stevenson's. Before the day was done, he would probably learn that a hundred dollars were supposed to be waiting for him, and come for them. What should be said to him? In point of fact, it was not Mr. Stevenson, but the man who had given the trust, who called him to account.

"By the way, Mr. Cameron, that hundred dollars I left with you one morning; Stevenson tells me he did not call for it; went out of town that day and has just returned. You have had it in trust ever since, I suppose? Sorry to have bothered you so long, but I have been away myself. I'll take it now, if you please; he is to dine with me, and I can give it to him myself."

Mr. Cameron wrote his name carefully on the voucher for which the cash-boy was waiting, before he made reply. Then he raised his head, and said slowly, "I haven't the money with me, Mr. Clinton; I never leave money in my desk over night."

"Oh, is that so? Then how shall we manage it? Stevenson must have it tonight; he goes away again in the morning."

"I will call upon you this evening," said Mr. Cameron; and wheeled on his stool to attend to an imperative demand. Mr. Clinton, finding him unusually busy and absorbed, scribbled his address and the time at which he could be seen, on a card, and handed it in to him.

"Call as near that hour as you can, Mr. Cameron; I may be out later. Sorry to give you so much trouble."

And then Mr. Cameron had gotten through that day as best he could; not without sundry feeble efforts to raise the hundred dollars; not without a hundred plans as to what he would do before night. He would go to the senior partner and beg a loan, and lose the situation which he had held for nineteen years! It had been sternly hinted at the last time he asked to anticipate his salary. He would tell young Clinton that he had been compelled, yes, actually *compelled,* to borrow that money, and would pay it just as soon as he could. And lose his situation! Young Clinton's father was the member of the firm least disposed to show mercy. He would telegraph his boys that they must raise him a hundred dollars, or disgrace awaited them. No; whatever happened, he must shield his boys and his girls as long as possible.

He went home to dinner, uncertain still what he was to do. He had promised to call upon young Clinton that evening, and "a Cameron always kept his promises;" but what should he say? Visions of an interview with Mr. John Welborne, the well-known broker, floated through his brain. He might give his watch as security, and raise a little; but it was an old one; he doubted whether he would be allowed more than twenty-five dollars on it.

When he announced at the dinner table that he must go downtown again, he had not been sure of any one thing, save that he meant to get into the street and the darkness as soon as he could. He had mentioned Mr. John Welborne's name, because it was the one which occurred to him, next to the name of Clinton; and he shrank in a curious way from mentioning that, as though the mere repeating of it might give the listeners an idea of his trouble. He *would* call at Welborne's, he told himself quickly, as soon as the name had left his lips; it could do no harm to ask for money; and he would make good his word.

The poor half-crazed man clung pitifully to that notion about a Cameron's word and a Cameron's honor, and shut his eyes to the idea that the hundred dollars had been other than borrowed. Did not people borrow, every day? Why should the thought of it distress him so? Why had he been careful not to mention it to any of his family? At last he bethought himself, and signaled a car. One and another acquaintance came in and sat near him, and chatted for a minute or two, and passed out; and one of them said: "Cameron is breaking, isn't he? Ages fast; seems to me I have never seen such a change in a few months' time as there has been in him. Pity he couldn't get away somewhere and have a rest; but I suppose he is hard pressed. He has an expensive family, it is said."

"Living beyond their means," said the other, "trying to accomplish the impossible. Half the people in this world are trying to do what they can't." Then they dismissed Mr. Cameron and his affairs from their minds, and the car brought him to Mr. John Welborne's door.

He walked up to it with steps that tottered, and rang the bell. He said to himself that he was going to give that money into Mr. Welborne's hands; of course he was; why else should he call? Then he felt for his watch, and remembered that there was a seal on the chain which must have cost quite a sum; his grandfather's seal. Did they lend money on such things? Then his ring was answered. Mr. John Welborne was not at home; would not be for two days. His son was at home, and could be seen at the office in the morning.

Mr. Cameron went down the steps again, and signaled a Grand Avenue car. He took the package out of his pocket and looked at it. It was sealed, but Mr. Kennedy had told him the amount enclosed; what if there should be a mistake? Did he care to pass over money that might not be just what it purported? That was not business-like; he would count it. What if it was sealed; was not Mr. Kennedy the same as his own family? There were two hundred dollars. There was also a note addressed to Mr. John Welborne; he put that in his pocket; it could not be delivered; Mr. Welborne was not at home.

In young Clinton's room two gentlemen chatted. Clinton looked at his watch. "It is just past the hour I gave Mr. Cameron," he said; "we must not wait long for him."

"Wasn't it a trifle strange in him to keep that money all this time and say nothing?"

"No; I think not," Clinton said thoughtfully. "He is a machine; he held the money in trust for Mr. Stevenson to call for it; Mr. Stevenson did not call, so he held it. Clockwork you see. Oh, he will be here this evening. He is the soul of honor; he came into my father's firm the year I was born. Perhaps that is his ring now."

In five minutes from that time, Mr. Stevenson had received and cared for his hundred dollars; and Mr. Cameron was on his way home. He did not go immediately home; he took a car which ran out away beyond the park, almost into the country. It did not make prompt connection at the junction and he walked along the river bank and took off his hat, and even tried to loosen his necktie a little; it seemed hard work to breathe. When at last he reached home, Mrs. Cameron was waiting for him, alarmed at his lateness. "I was afraid something had happened," she said. He felt like telling her that something had!

It was not until seven o'clock the next morning that she told him Mr. Kennedy had been obliged to take the six-fifty train. "He made me promise not to let you know," she said, "for fear you should think courtesy demanded your getting up to see him off; and he said he would not have you for the world; that you needed rest, and your worn face would haunt him, he was afraid. He is very kind and considerate."

24. "Mrs. Willis Kennedy?"

Mr. Kennedy continued to be "kind and considerate." His prospective father-in-law told himself that night when he walked upstairs, too ill in body and mind for any further effort, that the first thing in the morning he would have a talk with Kennedy, would tell him just how embarrassed he was, and just how he had disposed of one hundred dollars, and ask him to lend the money for a few weeks— only a few weeks. He would soon be in a way to straighten everything out, and to plan against such experiences for the future. He even meant to humiliate himself by pressing that point, that he did not mean to be in any sense of the word a drag upon his son-in-law. But before morning he learned that by Mr. Kennedy's considerateness he was to be spared from having to see him. This was better; he would write, instead of talk; and he would wait a day or two to give himself time to get rested and strengthened for the ordeal. There were times when he confessed to himself that it would be a terrible ordeal to own that he had actually stolen the money and appropriated it to his own needs! That was an ugly word, and he only on rare occasions allowed himself its use. He waited two days, then four, then a week. It seemed impossible to get nerve enough to write that letter. Then he told himself that it was too late; that Mr. Kennedy undoubtedly knew by this time that something strange had happened; he would wait to be written to, and by the tone of the letter he could judge how to reply. Meantime, he worked steadily every day, and ate little, and slept less; and frightened himself occasionally, of nights, by thinking that he had perhaps periled his daughter's happiness for life. What if Mr. Kennedy, in a fit of righteous horror at being allied with dishonor, should break with her!

What Mr. Kennedy did, when he received a letter from Mr. Welborne to the effect that he had not kept his word, was to whistle softly for several seconds, then address the wall.

"So that is your little game, is it, my beloved father-in-law that is to be? If you do much of it, I do not wonder at your haggard face. Poor old fellow! I feel sorry for you; I know what it is to be in debt; and I have the advantage of you; for you don't see your way out and I do. If that ridiculous girl hadn't been so obstinate, I could probably help you sooner. Well, I'll write to old Welborne that 'pressure of business,' etc., prevented, send him the interest, and renew the loan for a month or so; that is easily managed. After we get affairs settled, I think I will just quietly give the money to father-in-law, and say nothing; unless he bothers me about settlements; in which case I can give him a little wholesome advice. On the whole, I think I am rather glad that it has happened."

Because of this, no letter came to Mr. Cameron, and he went on expecting it by day and by night; living in a sort of nightmare of horrors; and the wedding-day drew on apace.

With the first breath of June, the boys came home. Handsome, well-developed fellows; full of life, and bubbling over with kindliness, and much shocked at the change in their father. What was the matter? they questioned. What had happened to age him so? Had they had medical advice? What did everybody mean by standing quietly by and letting him die before their eyes? Mary tried to explain; father was not really ill, only tired and worried. This constant pressure of money difficulties, she believed, was at the root of all his troubles.

But that was absurd, the boys said. He had a good salary; other men lived on less than that amount. They did not understand it; there must be mismanagement somewhere. And that very afternoon they hired a handsome carriage, and took Lucia and Emilie for a drive; coaxing the latter to invite that pretty little Puritan maiden, Dorothy Landis, to accompany them. They had met her but the evening before, and Mac, especially, was struck with her beauty. That evening he said gaily, "Father, have you any money about you? I am dead broke, I find. Your liveries charge enormously here;

I can get a two-horse rig at college for much less than I had to pay this afternoon. Give me a ten, father, if you can as well as not."

Mr. Cameron's fingers trembled as he singled out the bill; it was the only ten he had, and there were few fives to keep it company; but the boys had been gone so long, and they were such handsome fellows, and their mother was so glad and proud over them; what was he to do? It was reasonable that they should need a little money. Really, they were not reckless boys, only thoughtless. They had been brought up to ask for money when they needed it, to think little about spending it, to fancy that more could be had somehow when that was gone. They knew their father was not wealthy; oh dear, they believed that none knew it better or deplored it more than they. No large expenditures could be allowed them; and in all such directions they believed themselves economists; it was in the ten thousand little things that their money went; and in all little things, they spent as freely as though millions stood behind them.

They had been three days at home, yet that promised explanation of their financial trouble had not been given to their father. Truth to tell, with them it had retired into the background. It had never at any time been so vivid a pain to them as it was to their parents, living as they did among young men who thought nothing of such escapades. To have taken, on a certain evening, a little more wine than was good for them, and because of it to have been indifferent as to the amount of plate-glass they shivered, or the furniture they injured, was so commonplace a thing among a certain set, as to be worthy only of a passing laugh. There were times when they really felt quite virtuous because they had taken the trouble to secure President Force's kindly aid, and so saved their father from much that would have been disagreeable. Moreover, they had kept themselves remarkably free from college "scrapes" of every sort since that time, and, besides carrying off the leading prizes, had stood so high in their other classes as to be excused from examinations; so they were home in triumph, a week earlier than they would otherwise have been. On the whole, they felt that their father could afford to wait for those "details," especially since he really looked too ill to be bothered with them. He, on his part, showed no disposition to question them; they could not have understood how painfully he shrank from confessions of any sort. What was he that his boys should *confess anything?*

Those last few days went on swift wings; and on the evening before the wedding, Mrs. Cameron heaved a sigh of relief as she toiled up the stairs for perhaps the hundredth time that day. She was tired, but victorious. Through trials and perplexities such as none but those who have borne them understand, she believed she had arrived at last at the point where the most fastidious would have nothing to criticize. The embarrassments of that well-remembered luncheon party had not been without fruit. She had carefully shunned the rocks on which they were injured that day. No blundering Betsey, with a second-rate helper hired at the last minute, should have to do with this experience. From the first, Mrs. Cameron had been resolute; it might be more expensive, but it was necessary. They would not try to do great things; they would have only a few of their most intimate acquaintances, and they would have the simplest of refreshments; but what they had must be of the best, and faultlessly served. Thus much was due Mr. Kennedy. Because they were themselves poor, they must not forget that Mary was about to marry into a wealthy family; he must see that his wife's people were refined, and knew how to entertain their friends. The matter of the collation must be put entirely into Alburgh's hands, only stipulating that it was to be of the simplest character. She would undertake to see that the house was in order, and to see to everything, in fact, up to the hour when the collation should be arranged, but with that the family must have nothing to do. Alburgh must be responsible for extra forks, and spoons, and glasses, and whatever other extra was necessary to the proper serving of his order. This was the only way to ensure Mary against embarrassments. The probable estimate of expense had appalled them, even after Alburgh himself had condescended to go over the estimate with them, and, with an injured air, had obliged himself to erase entirely certain things which he deemed indispensable. Mr. Cameron had roused to more strength than he had seemed for some time to possess, and had walked the floor declaring that they *could not* do it; but Mrs.

Cameron had answered gently that she was sure he would regret it after Mary was gone, if he did not make everything as comfortable for her as he could; moreover, what would Mr. Kennedy think if they did not? After this was fairly over, she knew ways of retrenchment which would soon make matters straight. She had been talking things over with Rachel, who had a very clear head, if she was young; he would be surprised at her suggestions, and find relief in them. As for Alburgh, he had promised to wait for three months; she had told him, laughingly of course, that if his bill was not promptly settled then, she would give him leave to carry off the piano; and, as it was a very fine one, he was certainly safe.

The mention of Mr. Kennedy's name seemed to have a subduing effect upon her husband; a fact which Mrs. Cameron noted and made use of during these later days of preparation. Now, as I said, she was ascending the stairs, weary but triumphant. An all but endless task it had been to get the rooms in order. No one would have believed that she and Aunt Eunice and Rachel could have worked such marvels as they had. What with careful laundering, and turning, and darning, curtains and carpets, and the very upholstery of chairs and lounges, looked fresh and inviting. Nobody could darn more skillfully than Aunt Eunice; no one had been more persistent early and late with her needle and her skill. Aunt Eunice might believe that a great deal of it was utter folly, as assuredly she did; but she had taken a vow to hold her tongue, and she held it and worked away.

There was no harm in having things look as well as soap and water and skill could make them, and it didn't cost anything for her to sit and sew.

Emilie said the rooms looked really beautiful, even without the flowers; and when she and Dorothy Landis got them arranged, it would be a display fit for the bridal of a queen. She added that Dorothy Landis seemed able to fairly bewitch flowers; she had never known anyone who could arrange them so exquisitely; but that Mac was developing astonishing talent in that line, under Dorothy's tuition. This young woman's keen eyes had already discovered that her brother Mac was ready to take any sort of tuition at the hands of their neighbor Dorothy.

And so, through experiences manifold, Mary Cameron reached the evening of the sixth of June, and sat alone in her room taking leave of herself. Tomorrow at this time she would have been for several hours Mrs. Willis Kennedy. She said the name over aloud, looking grave. It had a very strange sound; a pretty enough name, but it seemed not to be hers. Some other girl in her shape was going to wear it; and she, Mary Cameron, would surely be there as usual, after that other girl, whose bridal dress lay at this moment on the bed, was gone.

A strange mood was hers for a bride. She wondered if all women about to be married felt so. There had been hours during that busy day when she had stopped over her packing, and stood quite still when someone called her to ask if she would take "that old cashmere" with her, and did she want "the long brown box packed in the trunk which was to go with them;" and, instead of answering, had said to her inmost self, "Going away with Willis Kennedy! Going, not to come back here, to my home, anymore! How absurd that is! How can they believe it possible?"

She had been left to the privacy of her own room for several days now; Lucia, with many seriocomic sighs and groans and hints of martyrdom, having betaken herself to Aunt Eunice's quarters; that good lady still had peaceable possession of the room which had been known as the boys', and they had settled themselves in an attic chamber which had heretofore been used as a storeroom. So Mary could sit with folded hands without fear of intrusion, and gaze at her past and her future.

She had had several calls this evening which had somewhat unnerved her. Lucia, who rarely showed to any person her inmost feelings, had broken down for a few minutes and cried outright, and declared that it was cruel and unnatural to separate families in this way; and she had not imagined that she should feel it so. Emilie had hovered about her eldest sister and kissed and patted her, and whispered, with her bright eyes dimmed the while with tears, that she should never forget how awfully good she had been to her, and she, Emilie, would really and truly be a comfort to father and mother, and do nothing to worry them. Mrs. Cameron had folded her in her arms and laid her head on her shoulder, and said not a word, but Mary had felt hot tears against her cheek. Even her father had helped to increase her bewilderment and pain.

"Well, Mary," he had said, meeting her on the stairs, and he had held out his hand, and tried twice to speak some other word, and then had turned away abruptly and walked downstairs, holding heavily to the balusters as he went. That experience made Mary feel in a hurry to be married. Why had she not allowed Willis to have his way? Then it would have been all over by this time, and she in condition to help her father; and he was failing so rapidly! It would have been a matter of interest to a curious student of human nature, to have known that Mary Cameron invariably thought of her married life as something which would be "over" when the ceremony was concluded, and she was fairly recognized as Mrs. Kennedy.

But one call she had had that evening which had shaken her nerves more than all the others combined. That was when Rachel, who had been at her side nearly all day, doing little last things which required taste and skill, doing them rapidly and deftly, turning from one to another with a thoughtfulness which she could never forget, tapped at the door with a "May I come in a moment?" and then had dropped in a little heap at her feet, and said, "Do you know, it seems to me as though I had just found my sister, after doing without and missing her all these years, and now I am losing her!"

Mary had been touched by this; she greatly admired, while at the same time she stood a trifle in awe of, her beautiful sister. She had been a new type of girl; firm in her convictions, unswerving in regard to what she considered right, and intense almost to narrowness, Mary thought, in her ideas of right and wrong; yet, at the same time, gentle and sweet and unselfish. They had grown to know each other better during the past two weeks, because Rachel found so many things which she could do to help, and discovered to her admiring sister many touches of skill and taste which it had not been known she possessed. It was hard to think that they, who had been apart so long, must separate again, and never belong to the same household anymore.

She expressed her sense of regret, and several little love words were exchanged, drawing the sisters closer to each other than ever before. Then Rachel had said suddenly:

"Oh, Mary, it is a foolish thing to ask, but are you *sure* that Mr. Kennedy is the one who, next to God, can be all in all to you? Of course you are, but I want to hear you say it. Marriage is such a solemn, such an irrevocable thing, and one should be so *settled*. You are sure it is all right?"

Mary had laughed at her wistful, almost pleading tone, and told her that she was a sentimental creature, much more so than she should have supposed. Then, finding that Rachel pressed the question, not in sentiment but in strange earnestness, she had said, "Of course it is all right, you foolish child. If it were not, what good would it do to talk about it now? It is quite too late."

"Oh, no, no!" Rachel had said, and begged her not to speak such words. If *she* should find, even while standing at the marriage altar, if she should have the least feeling that she might possibly be making a mistake, she should draw back even then. Such solemn promises as those given in marriage *must not* be taken on uncertain lips.

Mary had laughed again a little, and told her she must never marry; she was too nervous; and then had abruptly changed the subject. But now that she was gone, the bride-elect went over the conversation carefully, remembering with singular distinctness Rachel's every word.

Marriage meant more to Rachel, evidently, than it did to her. Mr. Kennedy was, of course, of more interest to her than was any other person, else she would not have promised to marry him; but she admitted that, after marriage, she thought with satisfaction of being left to carry out her own plans and schemes, leaving him at the same time at liberty to carry out his; always being the best of friends, and having pleasant hours together when they met, and being able to have pleasant hours apart. Was not this as it should be? Was not the intense feeling which Rachel seemed to think necessary, the senti-mentalism which belonged to extreme youth?

At that moment she thought of Russell Denham and the flutter of heart which his very footstep used to arouse; but she curled her lip disdainfully over the thought, and told herself that here was a proof that such feelings were mere sentiment. Now she did not even respect Russell

Denham; he had trifled with her. As for Mr. Kennedy, he had sought her out from all the world, and been kind and considerate not only of her, but hers. Of course she loved him. And when she was once his wife, she could begin to do all those things of which she had lately thought. She would make a safe, sweet, helpful home for tempted boys like Ben Reeder. She would have her own brothers with her much, and do for them in a hundred ways which had been suggested to her by hearing Mr. Landis talk. And Emilie—she could guard her young life, and at the same time enrich and brighten it. Then there was father—oh, there were so many things to be done! She had wasted her life; now she must redeem the lost years. Mr. Kennedy was a very busy man, but he would heartily second all her efforts. Hadn't he told her he would be delighted to see her at work? And didn't he most cordially endorse all that she had said about having Emilie much with her?

Isabella Alden

25. "A Nervous Shock"

Despite the fact that Mrs. Cameron had congratulated herself the evening before on everything being done, the morning found them very busy. It was not until nearly ten o'clock that even Emilie had time to wonder "why in the world" Mr. Kennedy did not appear. It had been planned, in view of the crowded state of the house, that he should stop over night with his uptown friends; and he had explained by letter that some "vexatious business matters " would prevent his reaching the city until late on the evening of the fifth. But it was presumable that he would make his appearance early in the morning.

"I thought he would come to breakfast," said Emilie "I hope he will not be later than twelve o'clock; we *couldn't* go on without him, could we? And for a marriage service to be even five minutes behind time is considered very countrified nowadays."

They laughed at Emilie's nonsense, as usual, and hurried their preparations; for the ceremony was to be performed at high noon, and, if they must not be even five minutes late, there was need for haste.

One person was looking nervously for Mr. Kennedy's arrival; this was Mary's father; he had resolved to take his future son-in-law into confidence that very morning. He was to be told briefly about the temporary embarrassments, and to be duly apologized to for "carelessness" in not acquainting him promptly with Mr. Welborne's absence, and in the subsequent temporary use of the money. Mr. Cameron liked the sound of that word, "temporary." He opened the door of his small private room at the end of the hall several times in the course of the next hour, to ask if Mr. Kennedy had not come yet, and to repeat the direction that he was to be shown in there the moment he arrived.

"What can father be going to do to him when he does come?" asked Emilie. "Somebody ought to be preparing to give him a lecture on tardiness. The idea! It is after eleven o'clock. Mary won't do it; brides have to smile and be pleased at everything until a few days after the ceremony." Then she darted forward to answer a ring; she would be the first to receive the belated bridegroom. It was the postman's ring, and she took from his hand a single letter addressed to Mary. "How curious!" she said, studying it. "It is Mr. Kennedy's writing."

"A belated letter," said her mother, coming forward to glance at it; "Mary did not get one yesterday, you remember. Take it up to her; it will amuse her while she is waiting; and do, child, put the finishing touches to your toilet before you come down again. It is almost time for the guests to arrive."

A little later it was Mary who came down the stairs with an open letter in her hand.

"Mother," she said, stopping half-way down, as she caught a glimpse of Mrs. Cameron's draperies by the back parlor door. That lady rushed out to her. "Why, my *dear!* Don't come down yet. What is it? Come back, dear, do!" in a hurried whisper. "Some of the guests have come, and of course you do not want them to see you yet."

"No," said Mary, aloud and calmly, "nor at all; I want them sent away; there is to be no wedding."

"Hush, child, *hush!*" said the mother, in an imperative whisper, drawing her daughter in nervous haste up the stairs. "You do not know what you are saying. What is it, dear child? What has happened?"

She had drawn Mary within her own room now, and closed the door.

"Has he been taken ill, dear, or is there an accident? Sit down, my darling, and let mother have the letter."

"There it is," said Mary, pushing away the seat into which her mother tried to draw her. "You can read it; it is not long; nothing has happened, only he has changed his mind. I wish he had let us know before—" She did not complete her sentence.

And Mrs. Cameron, scarce knowing what she did, read:

Dear Mary,

*Not that I have any right to call you so after this;
yet you are dear to me, so dear that I must shield you.
Mary, I am a poor man! Prospects that I believed
were sure, are utterly ruined. I have not a penny. In
view of these expectations I have lived freely; now I
have nothing with which to pay wedding expenses,
even if it were right to condemn you to beggary. I
have no home to bring you to, and no money with
which to pay our board; in short, I am utterly ruined.
The only honorable way for me is to tell you the truth,
and release you from all pledges to me, and to
promise never to insult you by line or word again.
What this blow is to me, I must leave you to imagine. I
have but one gleam of comfort; that is, that you never
seemed to care for me as I do for you. Good-bye.
From a miserable failure,*

Willis Kennedy.

Three times the poor mother read these lines with
brain so bewildered that she could not seem to take in
their meaning. Then she lifted her frightened eyes to her
daughter's stern ones.

"He must be insane," she faltered.

"No, he is only business-like. He has failed in some
desperate business venture which he thought was sure,
and has decided that he must marry a rich wife instead of

me. I wish he had discovered it before we had had so much trouble and expense."

But her mother interrupted her, weeping bitterly. "Oh, my darling, don't, *don't!* You are insane yourself; you will be, if you stand there so quiet and cold, and talk like that. You might better scream, or faint. Oh, Mary, my poor girl! *What shall we do?*"

"I don't think this is any time for fainting, mother. We have too much that must he done. All those people who keep coming must be sent away; or shall we let them stay and eat the wedding dainties? They might have their part, even though ours is spoiled; and my father must be told, and—and *comforted.*" Her face changed a little with this word. "Mother, stop moaning, and let us think and plan. Where are the boys? No, they could not do anything, it would break their hearts; and father must be spared." She had walked to the window while she talked, and had been watching the coming of guests. "There is Mr. Landis," she said, "he will do. He knows just how to manage everybody. Send for him to come up here, mother, and tell him the whole story. I will tell him myself. Then he will get rid of the people for us. It will be better than trying to depend on the boys."

The poor dazed mother! She looked at her daughter as one frightened; she believed her to be stricken with insanity. She felt as though she was herself insane. Mary turned at last from her pathetic bewilderment, and, stepping into the hall, sent Emilie to tell Mr. Landis she wished to see him immediately.

He came promptly, not surprised at the summons; he had been doing duty as intimate friend of the family for the last two days. Quietly, in a matter-of-fact way, Mary handed him the letter, saying simply, "Read that, and tell me how to act."

He read more rapidly than the poor mother had, and reached his conclusion sooner. "The consummate villain!" he muttered, between lips that he seemed to want to keep closed.

"Oh, no," said Mary again. "I told mother that he was only business-like. I think I understand him. Money, or the want of it, has held us all, always, from doing what we wanted to. Mr. Landis, will you send the guests away, and tell my father and the boys, and keep the boys from doing anything rash? That will be their first thought; to rush away and find him; as if *that* would do any *good!*"

Was ever a friend called upon to perform stranger service? How he got through with the next hour, Mr. Landis himself could not have told. He knew that in some way he made known to the guests that circumstances had so changed as to make their very presence an offence; and that he was closeted, afterwards, first with the father, then with the sons, and that he found the latter harder to manage; for while the father's utterly stunned condition had not yet passed, they were burning for revenge, and could think only of rushing away by the first train to shoot the villain who had deliberately planned disgrace for the household.

It was perhaps a providential thing for all parties that their attention was soon and sharply called to another matter. It came to pass that the poor mother, whose body and brain had been undergoing during all these months, even years, heavier strains than any of them realized, reached the end of her powers of endurance that morning. When Mary returned from her conference with Mr. Landis she found her mother in a dead faint. Being entirely composed herself, she was not alarmed; but did for her what she was sure were the proper things, only to find that she rallied but for a moment, then sank away again, her condition becoming each time more alarming. In point of fact, Mr. Landis's conference with the sons was interrupted by a sharp summons to them to go for the doctor without delay; and thereafter, for several hours, the bewildered family had need to center their thoughts on what had been suddenly transformed into a sick-room. It was Mary who received and made explanation to the doctor.

"She has had a sudden nervous shock, coming after unusual fatigue. It was on hearing the news which shocked her that she went into one of these faints, or spasms, or whatever they are."

The doctor, who had known the family professionally for years, and who had already heard what the "nervous shock" was, looked at his informant curiously. Had no "shock" of any sort come to her? She had certainly never been more entirely herself than at that moment. Not only then, but afterwards, throughout the trying ordeals of

349

that day, she maintained the same quiet self-poise. She gave careful attention to the doctor's orders, and took measures to have them carried out with promptness and skill. She directed the thoroughly frightened Betsey; listened to, and agreed with, Aunt Eunice's plans for her mother's comfort; and interrupted Emilie's tearful attempt at expressing sympathy for herself, with a composed, "There is no time to think about that now, child. Mother is very ill, and we must all think of her, and do everything we can to help."

Such a miserable family as it was which gathered, sometime toward the close of the day, to make an attempt at that belated feast which was to have been served so royally! The caterers had disappeared long since, carrying their extra spoons and forks and all manner of paraphernalia with them, and Rachel had struggled bravely with the problem of how to rid the rooms of all traces of festivity. But there remained the extra dishes which poor Betsey felt ought to be eaten, yet which, by their very unusualness, emphasized the situation. Even Mr. Willis Kennedy, taking his dinner gloomily and in silence in a strange restaurant, might have pitied the condition of the home whose comfort he had despoiled.

Mary Cameron stayed with her mother; and Mr. Cameron, after swallowing his coffee, and shaking his head at everything which Lucia and Emilie eagerly offered him, staggered away to his post beside his wife's bed. All other anxieties were for the present swallowed up in an agony of pity and remorse for the wife of his youth.

He was not accustomed to seeing her ill. The thought that she might die was terrible to him; not only in the sense of the desolation which would result, but in the thought that he had failed in most of the things he had meant to do for her when they began life together. Such a happy home as they had meant to have! And it seemed to him now that an imp in the form of Poverty came early, and sat grinning on their hearth-stone all through the years. Yet when he had married, on a salary of eight hundred dollars, he felt rich, he remembered. It was a strange and bewildering experience connected with this dreadful day, that those pictures of the past, and of what he had meant and had failed in, kept haunting his brain; so unnerving him, that the doctor said in a warning tone to Lucia as he left the house, "You want to look after your father, and shield him as much as you can; he is in some respects in a worse condition than your mother."

The hall clock was striking ten when Mary Cameron entered once more the door of her own room, and dropped into the nearest chair to think. Aunt Eunice had asserted her authority; the mother was quiet now, sleeping under the influence of opiates; and she, Aunt Eunice, knew as much about illness "as the next one;" and this was the time for Mary to get a little rest.

"You have been on your feet all day, and haven't eaten a bite. Go down now and get a cup of tea and a bit of toast. Rachel has some ready for you; and then do you go to your room and rest awhile." Such had been her dismissal.

Mary had smiled over the idea of the tea and toast. She did not feel the need of either; but she was willing to get away to her own room. She sat down in the chair which had held her but the night before. Was it the night before, or was it five, ten, twenty years ago when she was a girl and was going to be married? She felt like an old woman now; one on whom the cares and responsibilities of life had dropped suddenly years ago, and which she had met and borne. She glanced around the room curiously. It had been hurriedly reconstructed; Rachel and Emilie, between them, having gotten rid of bridal robes and belongings as much as possible; yet the great trunks, two of them, still stood there; one locked and strapped, the other waiting for those last things which were to have been put in after the ceremony. In the hurry and confusion, the girls had not been able to get rid of these; and the bride that was to have been, looked at them as something which belonged to that long-ago past.

This evening she had expected to spend in Albany, and to be introduced to certain friends as "Mrs. Kennedy." She had said over the name several times in the privacy of her room, trying to get accustomed to its sound. She said it over now with a curling lip, and wondered where Mr. Kennedy was, and whether he had carried out his part of the programme and gone to Albany; and was he at that moment entertaining those charming young cousins of whom he had told her? Then she pulled herself up sharply from this bewilderment of reverie, and tried to look her present and future in the face, and decide what to do with them. In the first place, was she a fit subject for the unutterable sympathy which had flowed about her all day, and been so prominent a part of her father's woe that he could not meet her eye, nor speak her name? She had felt almost like a hypocrite when poor Mac, in an agony of pity and pain, had held her in his arms for a moment that evening, and begged her to let him and Rod go together and rid the earth of such a scoundrel. She had put from her Lucia's pitiful attempt at sympathy, with a word about their mother and her needs. She knew they all felt that she had turned from their efforts because the wound was still too fresh and sore to endure their touch; she knew they felt anxious for her, and expected a sudden and perhaps terrible descent from this unnatural calm. So anxious were they, that there had been earnest expostulation with Aunt Eunice about sending her away, and an assurance that she might better be allowed to stay and busy herself with her mother; and Aunt Eunice had stoutly held to her convictions: "I tell you she will be better to get away by herself and cry. This kind of quiet ain't natural. I know all about it."

Mary had overheard these things, and faintly smiled at them. She did not mean to cry; she had no desire to do so. Back in the dim recesses of her heart, somewhere, behind all the shame and indignation and sense of having been wronged and made a public spectacle of, there lurked a dull feeling of relief. She was not married, after all! She was Mary *Cameron* still; free to remain so; and it was through no fault of hers. She had been willing to do her part in relieving her father of the burden of her support; and to relieve him in a hundred other ways which she had planned; and the opportunity had failed her. She could not feel that she was in any sense to blame; and the thought was a relief.

Had she, then, not loved the man she had promised to marry? Why, of course she had; at least she had supposed that she did. She had respected him always, and been grateful to him; he had chosen her deliberately before all others, though he was at home in high circles, and a man of wealth—or had posed as such—and she had been grateful to him. It had all been somewhat sudden, she remembered; but she had not meant in any way to deceive either herself or him. Afterwards, quite lately indeed, there had come to her a question as to whether it was all just as it should be; whether, for instance, she could live that entirely different life which she was resolved upon living— the life which people like Rachel and Mr. Landis thought alone was worthy—with Mr. Kennedy for her constant companion? She knew intuitively that he did not care for that sort of life, although he had been entirely respectful with regard to matters of religion; but he would at least be out of sympathy with it. Could she be what she desired to be, with him indifferent? But she had told herself, as she told Rachel, that there was no use in thinking about such matters now; it was too late; everything was settled. She had decided that she could and would live her own right, separate life; be what she had discovered every woman ought to be; and win Mr. Kennedy to her way of thinking if she could. If not—well, people *had* to go their own ways in this world. And she knew so little about God's real plan for married life as to actually suppose that this was probably as true a marriage as any!

She was surprised and ashamed at this undertone of relief which had oppressed her all day. A woman on the eve of marriage ought not to feel *relief* that circumstances entirely beyond her control had prevented it! She was sure of so much. But what was that feeling which lurked behind the sense of shame and indignation, if it could not be called by such name?

"I have lost my respect for him," she said aloud; and quietly, "It must be that which has changed my feelings."

Isabella Alden

26. "WIIAT'S IN A NAME?"

It is perhaps time that Mr. Willis Kennedy should receive some slight attention. Mr. Landis in his excitement had called him a "consummate villain;" but that is too strong a term. Mr. Kennedy was a victim of a weak will, a determination to please himself, and an education which had no firm moral foundation. Up to the evening of the third day of June, he had no more idea of failing in his appointment with Mary Cameron than he had of ceasing to live. On the contrary, he was anxious for the day to arrive, and shaped all his engagements and plans with a view to it. On the evening of the third of June, his Cousin Eustis dropped down upon him suddenly. It will be remembered that this young man was a lawyer; was, in fact, the junior partner of a very important law firm in the neighboring city. He had been absent for months in the far West on an extended business trip, and had not met his cousin since a short time after he confided to him that interesting bit of news about the Cameron uncle.

"So you are going to desert bachelorhood," he said, after he had been duly welcomed and refreshed by his cousin. "I was astonished to receive your cards; I had set you down as a confirmed bachelor. And to marry a Miss Cameron, at that! No wonder you were so much interested in my bit of news about Miss Katherine Cameron! You thought possibly they were relatives? I could have told you differently. Our firm has had to trace relationship to the third and fourth generation. It is a curious coincidence, 'Mary K. Cameron.' Does the K stand for Katherine, so as to complete the strangeness of it?"

Mr. Willis Kennedy stared; no other word will describe his gaze. "What are you talking about?" he asked at last.

"Why, man alive! I'm talking about the romance I spread before you the last time I saw you. Are you so much married already as to have forgotten it? You told me then of being introduced to a Miss Cameron, and I supposed it was the one our firm is managing."

"Oh," said Mr. Kennedy at last. "And when did you find out your mistake?"

"Never thought about it again until I received your cards and saw the magic name. Why didn't you go in for the heiress, Willis? It would have been more convenient for you. She has been here much of the season, and is here now."

"Here! In New York?"

"Yes, sir, in New York; within five squares of your club house. Are you thinking how much postage you might have saved if you had chosen her? But you are too late, old fellow; no use in breaking your engagement now. My Miss Cameron is engaged to a doctor here; he is poor, too, and struggling, but enterprising. He is fighting the tenement-house question down near the College Settlement; wants a row of shells hauled down, and some choice palaces put up; and he spends every cent of his hard-earned money in caring for his poor patients. They are to be married in the course of a few weeks, I believe. Think how that fortune will be squandered! She is of like mind with himself, I am told; and neither of them knows the first thing about the money. But it will all be out soon; the poor old uncle is done with life at last. A telegram from my chief is what brought me down this way, instead of going home. I am to call in the morning, and break the news as gently as I can, and escort my lady home, if she pleases, to meet her lawyers and her fortune. Only I presume the doctor will prefer to do that for her. Romantic, isn't it?"

"Very," said Mr. Willis Kennedy. After a few minutes of silence he began to ask questions, probing his cousin's knowledge to the utmost; showing such keen interest, indeed, that he was laughingly rallied about having so many questions to ask concerning another than THE Miss Cameron.

"What's in a name?" he said at last, rising with a yawn.

"So you don't know what the K. stands for in your lady's name? Probably it is Keturah, or Keziah; to have it

Katherine would be too strange a coincidence. You must take her to call upon the other one; they are so enamored of tenement-house people they won't be lofty in their ideas. Well, good-night to you, my boy. No, thank you; I have promised to spend the night with my friend Tremaine. When are you going down? Not until Tuesday night! You don't give yourself much holiday beforehand, do you? But, as a married man in prospective, I suppose you have to be industrious."

He was gone at last, and Mr. Willis Kennedy had time to think. What a bewildering problem was before him. Instead of millions, nothing! And on the eve of marriage with a young woman who had been brought up with expensive tastes and habits, and nothing with which to gratify them. Moreover, she had a father who was in such financial embarrassments that he had to resort to dishonesty to keep himself, probably, from exposure. Also, to come back sharply to himself, on the strength of his prospects he had been more than usually careless of money matters, even reckless. Only the day before, he had borrowed five hundred dollars to meet the expenses of his wedding-trip, and had promised to pay a startling rate of interest for the private accommodation. What did a millionaire care for the amount of interest to be paid on a paltry five hundred dollars!

His thoughts did not shape themselves logically in the young man's brain; they merely floated before him in a sort of vision. In truth, he was stunned by the magnitude of his disappointment. He had taken such pains to learn just the amount of the fortune to be inherited, and just the condition of the uncle whose feeble breath of life had endured so long. The only flaw in his work had been the taking it for granted that the Katherine Cameron whom his cousin described, and the Mary K. Cameron whom he knew were the same.

When at last he sought his room late that night, and made preparations for rest, wearily, like an old man, instead of one in his prime, he had not, even yet, so much as thought of proving false to his promised wife. He was to be married, of course; but what afterwards? How were they to live? He was not a member of any firm; only a salaried clerk. Through some heedless words of his, somebody had gotten the impression that he belonged to the firm; and he had not cared to deny it, even to Mary Cameron herself. What harm for her to think so? But his salary had never proved sufficient for his wants as a single man; the number and amount of his debts stared at him now as they never had before, and frightened him. He arose the next morning unrefreshed, and went about his duties like one in a dream. He still planned for tomorrow night, when he must start on his journey; but he began to shudder at the thought. Just when or how there crept into his heart a sense of pity for Mary Cameron and the life to which he was bringing her, he could not have told; but once evolved, he nursed it with care, until by night he had made himself into a monster for allowing her to sacrifice herself to such a poverty-stricken wretch as he.

It was in one of those moods that he wrote the letter which you have read. Not that he intended to send it; he told himself that he should do nothing of the kind; it was too late. Still, he carefully addressed, sealed, and stamped the letter from force of habit; but he did not post it, nor leave orders to have it attended to. He went to the store the next morning as usual, and received the sallies and congratulations of his fellow-clerks, and laughed with them over his "last day of freedom," and was unusually attentive to his work, and much slower about leaving than usual, until at last somebody asked if he did not intend to take the six-ten train? Wouldn't he be late? He looked at his watch then, and told himself that he was startled over the lateness of the hour. He left the store at once, and was surely not to blame because there was an accident and a blockade. Arrived at last at his room, he dashed hurriedly up the stairs, and consulted watch and time-table, only to find what he had feared—that the six ten was gone! There was not another train which would accommodate him until early morning; he could barely reach the city by noon; it would be an hour later before he could reach Durand Avenue. What a state of things!

Then he took time to glance about his room. The chambermaid had done her duty; everything was in order. He crossed to the table, and looked it over carefully. His letter was not there! He rang the bell furiously, and angrily questioned the bellboy, and sent for the chambermaid, and fiercely questioned her. She had seen the letter; yes, indeed; and had gone herself and mailed it, stealing time from her work to get it into the first delivery. Hadn't Mr. Kennedy thanked her twice before for doing that same thing, when he had forgotten his letters? How was she to know that it was not to go, when it was sealed and stamped, and everything?

As soon as he could, Mr. Kennedy sat down and considered. He called himself the victim of circumstances; he said it was all a wretched piece of business. Probably tonight, certainly by the first delivery tomorrow morning, Mary would have that letter. What was the use of trying to follow it? How could he explain? She would never forgive him for writing it, even though he had never intended to send it. She would not believe him, would not marry him. The least he could do now was to keep away from her. He had a holiday before him, and could plan his future in it. He need not waste money by leaving town; New York was large enough to take a holiday in, and meet no acquaintances. Will you not understand, and have a grain of pity mingle with your contempt for this despicable "victim of circumstances"?

For the two weeks following the shock which they had received, the Cameron family, especially the father, were kept mercifully anxious and fearful over the condition of the wife and mother. Long years of anxiety and care, during which Mrs. Cameron had lived more entirely for her husband and children than any of them realized until now, had called for their revenge at last. The peculiar fainting-turns, which were more like spasms than faints, were the beginning of a desperate illness, and for fourteen long days the battle between life and death raged fiercely. Even the boys put away all thought except that terrible one, that their mother might be going to die, and waited, taking their turns as watchers, and being invaluable in their help in other ways.

And at last the day came when the doctor, in answer to their mute inquiries, said, "I am really hopeful this morning that the worst is past. Given the most persistent and faithful care, I think she will rally; but it will require time and patience; and meantime, boys, you must look after your father. I am afraid for him."

He had left him but a moment before in his own little room at the end of the hall, where he was weeping like a child. Day and night he had hung over his wife, the most pitiful remorse mingling with his love and fear. He had been so busy, *so busy* with the burdens of life that he had not been to her what he had meant to be; and he had prepared for her worse burdens to bear in the future! Turn which way he would, his thoughts were as daggers stabbing him.

Meantime, they had had their blessings; Mr. Cameron's employers had been most kind. Mr. Clinton, the member of the firm who was supposed to have no heart, had called in person, and had assured Mr. Cameron that he was at liberty to stay with his wife until she was better. His place should be temporarily supplied, and his salary, of course, continued. Others had been kind; friends who lived so far away that they had not been seen for months, and who they thought had dropped them, directly they heard of illness, rallied around them with offers of help and sympathy so free and hearty that they could not be ignored. As for their next-door neighbors, Emilie voiced the feeling of the family when she declared that no brother and sister could have been more constant and self-forgetful in their helpfulness than Mr. Landis and his sister Dorothy.

On the whole, perhaps nothing could have helped the Cameron family so successfully through the embarrassments of this period as had illness. Anxiety for the mother was so sharp and so long continued, that it seemed natural and reasonable, when people called, to think only of her. Among themselves people talked and wondered. They supposed, they said, that some accident had detained the bridegroom—probably he was ill himself; and now, of course, the wedding would be deferred until the mother was well, perhaps until fall. Very soon the incident dropped into the background; two weeks is too long a time for people in cities to be interested in the affairs of others. Those who knew about matters kept their own counsel, and those who only thought they did, began to say, on inquiry, that they believed Mr. Kennedy was ill; and Mrs. Cameron being taken ill at the same time, they understood that the marriage was now to be deferred until fall. Somebody had said so; they did not remember who.

The doctor's advice to Mr. Cameron's sons to look after their father was evidently needed. No sooner was the strain of hourly fear for his wife's life relieved than his face told what that strain had been. It was apparent that if he did not get rest, bodily and mentally, soon, he must sink under it. Yet the severest strain of all he kept to himself, until one afternoon nearly a week after his wife began to mend. Mr. Landis had come to his little room to speak to him about an errand which had been done for him downtown, and was shocked with the haggard look on his face.

"My dear sir," he began, "you certainly are not able to return to your desk tomorrow. I am sure the firm would have continued the substitute a week or two longer, and will yet. If you will allow me to interfere, I will see them personally. I am acquainted with Mr. Clinton."

Mr. Cameron shook his head in earnest protest. Oh, no; no, indeed! He was quite well; and it was very important that he get to work as soon as possible. It was not *work* which was burdening him; there were reasons— Here Mr. Cameron came to a full stop, and, leaning his head on the table in front of him, let his whole frame shake with some overpowering emotion.

"If there is any way in which I can help you," began Mr. Landis, his voice made tender by sympathy, "I cannot express how glad I should be to do so."

"Nobody can help me," said the poor man, raising his bloodshot eyes, and looking at his caller. "I am a miserable man; I have ruined my daughter's happiness for life."

And then Mr. Landis was thoroughly alarmed. Surely this was a fancy of a distorted brain. He drew a chair beside the excited man, and tried to speak in low, soothing tones, without much regard to what he was saying, simply with the desire to quiet excitement. But Mr. Cameron interrupted him. He was not talking wildly, he explained; he knew exactly what he was saying, and had meant to say it. He had borne the burden alone as long as he could. He meant now to tell the whole story, and ask if there was anything which could yet be done. He began at the beginning of his troubles, when the boys first went to college; up to that time, by dint of perpetual straining and contriving, he had managed to keep almost even with the world, but that added strain had been too much. He talked rapidly, shielding the boys, shielding everybody but himself, whom he spared nothing, even down to that terrible evening when he appropriated Mr. Kennedy's two hundred dollars. But this time he used no smooth-sounding words.

"I stole the money, and used it for my own needs," he said firmly; "I have called it by other names, but I won't any more. It was stealing. And now, sir, you see why that man did not keep faith with my daughter. He would not ally himself with one of my dishonored name. I have ruined not only myself, but my family, and especially Mary."

It was an inexpressibly painful interview. In vain did Mr. Landis try to set before him the folly of a man deserting the woman he had chosen because her father had done wrong; he might as well not have spoken. The father had gotten where he could see only his own sin. All other wrong-doing was as nothing beside that. Still, by the time the talk was over, Mr. Landis felt that something had been accomplished. He had succeeded in convincing the almost insane man that his first step must be to get the two hundred dollars into Mr. Welborne's hands without further delay. It was at least possible that Mr. Kennedy did not yet know it had failed to reach his debtor, in which case matters might be so arranged that the story need go no farther. He had a couple of hundred dollars which he could spare as well as not, and there need not be haste about returning it. He was going past Mr. Welborne's office that afternoon, and if Mr. Cameron would empower him, he would leave the money, make all necessary explanations, and secure the proper receipt.

On the whole, the poor man was, almost in spite of himself, comforted. It was something to have told the whole painful story plainly; it was a great deal to have been met as the listener had met the tale. If he had only known what a friend this man could and would be, how much might have been saved! Not once, in all his struggle for help, had he thought of the poor professor next door. How good he had been! He had not spoken a reproachful word; neither had he tried to gloss over the sin which had been committed. In the state of mind he then was, Mr. Cameron felt that he could not have borne *that*. As it was, he watched Mr. Landis move rapidly down the walk toward a coming car, realized the errand on which he was

going, and felt that whatever came now, he had a friend;
one who understood the whole.

.

27. Soul-Searching

Several hours later Mr. Landis, disappointed in his search for Mr. John Welborne's son, who proved to be the one with whom business must be transacted, was trying to determine just how to pass the time until he might call at the Welborne office again. He felt almost as excited as Mr. Cameron; but from a different cause. He had no idea that the man whom he still called a "consummate villain" had broken his solemn troth because his prospective father-in-law had been guilty of a dishonorable and dishonest act. He had more fear that, directly the truth should become known, the man would take steps to publicly disgrace the family still further. Why not? A man who could do as he had done was capable of anything. He had chafed under the announcement that Mr. John Welborne was out of town, and had caught at the suggestion that all business could be transacted through his son, and had raged inwardly when the son was not to be found in his office nor his home, and none knew his whereabouts. In his excitement it seemed as though another hour's delay might be dangerous.

At the street corner he came face to face with Mary Cameron. It was the first time she had been downtown, since her mother's illness; but today some fancy of the mother's, which only she could satisfy, had sent her out. She was looking pale and worn, and Mr. Landis felt shocked to observe the ravages which a few weeks of trouble had made. They showed so plainly, now that he saw her again in street dress.

"Miss Cameron," he said, instinctively reaching out his hand as though she needed support, "how very weary you look! Have you been walking far?"

"Not very far," she explained; but she had overestimated her strength; it was so long since she had done any walking. Moreover, she had not felt like taking lunch before she left home, and had been detained longer than she had expected, and was somewhat faint she supposed.

He was all solicitude; she ought not to go so long without food; in her fatigued state it was really dangerous. He had just been considering the wisdom of lunching downtown, while he waited to do an errand later; and they were very near Schuyler's; she must come in with him and have something to strengthen her.

It was after lunching-hours, and Schuyler's was comparatively deserted. A waiter motioned them to a table near which sat two gentlemen, one of whom Mr.

Landis recognized, as he glanced back after being seated, as the younger Welborne, whom he knew only by sight. He resolved to send him his card with a request for a business interview as soon as possible, then gave his undivided attention to caring for Miss Cameron's needs.

She was very pale, and the hand which raised the cup of chocolate to her lips, trembled. Although she had met this man many times a day during the past weeks, she had never been for a moment alone with him since that morning when she had summoned him to read her letter and tell them what to do. It was not possible that either of them could help thinking of that morning; though Mr. Landis showed no sign, and talked the kindest of commonplaces, not obliging her to talk at all. Suddenly the attention of both was arrested by the gentlemen behind them.

"We've got a curious case on hand now," Mr. Welborne was saying. "A neat little scandal in quiet circles, where scandal seldom touches. That precious scapegrace of a Kennedy, from New York you know, has owed my father a couple of hundred dollars for some time, and promised as many times as there are days in the month to pay it without fail on such a date. Now he writes that he gave it to a Mr. Cameron—father of the girl he was supposed to be going to marry—six weeks or more ago; has the date down, you know; and declares that all the Cameron family are witnesses, it having been handed the father at the dining-table, for that purpose. Of course the money has never reached my father, and it is not likely that it was ever sent to him; but it will work up into a pretty little case, you see. Probably Mr. Cameron will deny ever having heard of such a thing, and there will have to be suit brought, and no end of interesting particulars will come to light; and the fellow himself will have to be unearthed as a witness. Do you suppose he thinks of that?"

If Mary Cameron's face was pale before this flow of words began, how shall it be described now? At the first mention of her father's name, the blood had rolled in waves to her very forehead, and then receded, leaving her wax-like in her pallor. She looked at Mr. Landis with wide, frightened eyes that had in them an appeal hard to resist. He took his resolution on the instant. Pushing back his chair, regardless of Mary's hand which had suddenly been reached out as if to detain him, he turned to Mr. Welborne and said, as he laid down his card:

"I beg your pardon, sir—that is my name and address—but since it has been impossible not to hear your words, you will pardon me for attending to business matters out of business hours. You are mistaken in some of your conclusions. Mr. Cameron did receive the two hundred dollars of Mr. Kennedy; and your father would doubtless have received the same that evening, had he been in town. But you may not be aware that since that time there has come very serious illness to the Cameron home, and all minor matters have been held in abeyance. I was, however, commissioned by Mr. Cameron, this afternoon, to bring you the two hundred dollars, and called at your office for the purpose, at the hour when you advertise that you will be in; but not finding you, I was obliged to postpone my errand, and have been unwittingly a listener to your 'little scandal.' Here is the money, sir; you will oblige me by writing a receipt in full which I can have forwarded to the proper person."

Just how they got through with that lunch which had suddenly become formidable, and got themselves away from Schuyler's, neither Mr. Landis nor Mary Cameron could have explained afterwards; they knew it was a relief to both when they found themselves on the street again.

"You are too weary for street-car riding tonight," said Mr. Landis. "I am going to call a carriage." And having placed her in one, he took a seat opposite, bidding her lean back and rest, and be as quiet as she pleased. Presently she dropped the hand which had shielded her face, and spoke earnestly.

"Mr. Landis, it is strange how you seem to be of necessity mixed up with all our pain and danger. You were so thoughtful for Emilie and for me; and now this! I cannot think how my father could have forgotten the money; but how terrible it was to be thought—"

"Do not think about it," he interrupted hurriedly; "there is no need. Your father explained the matter to me; I understand it perfectly."

"You understand everything," she said quickly; "and you are the one who comes to the rescue. I have never thanked you for helping me in my . . . rescue." She seemed to hesitate for the right word, and then to deliberately choose that one. Her companion noted it all carefully.

"There is no need," he said again, more earnestly than before. "I shall not even attempt to tell you how glad I am to serve any of you." Then he asked her to look out at the sunset, and said they would have another beautiful day, he thought, tomorrow; and, had she noticed how rapidly her mother was beginning now to improve? He could see changes each day. In this way he held her steadily to safe, pleasant commonplaces until they were at home.

"A carriage!" said Emilie, with wide-opening eyes, and a gleam of her old spirit, which had been wonderfully subdued of late. "That man is really getting extravagant!"

It proved to be an eventful day. In the Cameron parlor that evening a scene was enacted which had to do with vital interests. The caller was Mr. Edson, and the only one at leisure to receive him was Rachel Cameron. This had been quite as it should be in the minister's estimation. It was by no means the first time that he had so planned his visits or his walks that Rachel was of necessity his sole companion. On this evening, however, matters were certainly not going to his mind. He stood leaning against the mantel in the attitude of one who had received a shock, and felt the need for a moment, at least, of some outward support, and on his face was a look not only of pain, but bewilderment; while Rachel sat apart, deep distress apparent in face and manner. The actual fact was, that this man had just asked this woman to be his wife, and she had quietly but positively declined. He was bewildered. In all his imaginings such a thought had not occurred. He had been from the first of his acquaintance with her entirely sure of the degree of interest which he felt, and he had thought that she understood. Perhaps his distress was not greater than Rachel's; she could not help asking herself whether in her anxiety to show him that she received no such impression from his kindly attentions as Emilie absurdly hinted at, she had been careless, and so misled him. But it was nothing of that kind which had misled him; he had settled it almost from his first acquaintance that this young woman was the one designed by Providence for him, and the only one he wanted. It is true he had thought of others; it had crossed his mind, for instance, that the wealthy Miss Manning was not averse to his society, and that probably—but it had only been to smile over the folly of a man choosing her, when he knew Rachel Cameron.

He spoke at last in a low, constrained tone, "I do not suppose I have any right to ask, and yet I someway think you will allow it—are you—is there some one else?"

"No," said Rachel quickly. "It is nothing of that kind, Mr. Edson; and I wish I could make you understand how much I have esteemed your friendship, and been grateful for your kindness."

He made a deprecatory gesture with his hand. "Oh, *don't,* please! I beg your pardon, but how can a man bear *that?* I do not understand it. If you have enjoyed my society—and you admit that—and there is no other person, why then—I know I have been precipitate, have sprung this thing upon you at a time when you were just rallying from a severe nervous strain; I ought to have known better, and did. When I came here this evening I had not the remotest intention of saying what I have—not yet; if you can forget my words, and let me go back to where we were at the beginning of this interview, I will not take advantage of you again. I will give you ample time; I will wait as long as you may desire."

She tried to interrupt the eager flow of words. "Indeed, Mr. Edson, you do not understand! It is not that; I do not need time. I mean that time would not change my decision. It is not right that this thing should be; and therefore it must not be."

"Miss Rachel, you have not said once this evening that you did not care for me."

The ready blood mounted to her very temples at the words; and he was quick to see and take advantage of her evident embarrassment.

"I cannot but feel that I have a right to know more plainly than you have told me why my cherished hopes must be dashed from me. Why is it not right?"

"Because," said Rachel, her face paling again, "it is— oh, I *wish* you would not ask me! We are not alike in our views and plans; we could not work together as people should. We would not help each other in the best and highest ways."

The look of bewilderment deepened on Mr. Edson's face.

"I am farther from understanding than ever," he said. "I have thought that our fitness for each other must be marked even to outsiders. Your deepest interests seem to me to lie among those things to which I have given my life; and I believe that we could help each other to a degree that is very unusual. Will you not explain to me by what line of thought you have arrived at so strange a conclusion?"

She looked at him almost pitifully. "You force me, Mr. Edson, to say that which I have no right to say."

"On the contrary, you have every right; not only that, but I think I am justified in almost demanding it. This is very serious business to me, Miss Rachel." He left the mantel, and drew a chair, not near her, but in front of her, where he could study every line of her changeful face, and waited. He had to wait for some minutes; it was evidently hard for Rachel to speak.

"I do not know that I can make myself understood," she began at last; "but you oblige me to try. I have not denied that I am—interested in you. I do not wish to deny it; but with us it should be the interest of friends, no more. I did not think it was more, with you. We are not alike, Mr. Edson; we think and feel differently on the most important of all subjects. You have ambitions. You are a servant of Christ; but you are one who seeks distinction. You are scholarly and eloquent, and you know it, and pride yourself on it; you mean to fill high places in the church someday. You like, and you mean to cultivate, the wealthy and the cultured, rather than the poor and forgotten. In short, you seem to me to put Christ on a level with other interests, and to choose—sometimes—between them. If we were—if we tried to be very intimate friends, we should trammel each other. I want first and always to do Christ's work in the world—the work he did when he was on earth, the work I believe he would do if he were here again; and it is different in many ways from that which you mean to do. I should irritate you in a hundred ways, and do, every day of my life, things which would hinder your progress on the road you mean to travel; and you, in turn, would hinder me, come between me and my conscience perhaps, and—*I am afraid!* Oh, Mr. Edson, I can never explain it! Why will you make me say things that sound cruel and hateful?"

He looked at her every moment with keen, piercing eyes. When she stopped he suddenly leaned forward and buried his face in his hands, speaking no word, making no sound. He sat thus for what seemed to Rachel Cameron hours of misery, though in reality it was but a few minutes. At last he rose.

"Thank you," he said. "Do not feel badly about what you have told me; you could not help it. I forced you to it. Be sure I shall not forget it. Good-bye."

He let himself quietly out at the front door, and Rachel sat still in her chair. It was thus that Emilie found her an hour afterwards.

"Alone?" she asked in surprise, as she pushed open the door. "Betsey thought Mr. Edson was here. Why, you have been crying!" She studied her face for a moment, then stooped and kissed it. "Don't you go to crying, and being unhappy over anything, Rachel Cameron," she said earnestly, "or I believe, I really *believe,* I shall run away. What a dreadful family we are getting to be!"

Who shall undertake to describe the tumult of pain and shame in which the young minister went homeward? It seemed to him that he had been struck blow after blow that reached his very soul. He made all speed toward his study, and closed and locked the door. The gas was burning low, and he left it low. Darkness fitted his present mood. He began to walk up and down the room, almost clenching his hands in his efforts at self-control. What had she said to him—that one who was so dear, so *dear!* That he would trammel her in her work for Christ; hinder her from being such a follower as she ought to be, and wanted to be. That he put other things first, and Christ second! Was not that the meaning of it all? That his ambition and his scholarship and his love of culture had come between him and his Master. Was it true? Oh, *was* it TRUE! I call you to witness that here was a true soul, misshapen, dwarfed, almost smothered at times under pride of intellect and the triumphs of success; yet the thought which stung most, probed deepest, even at this moment, was that one, that it might, in a degree, be true.

Though he should live beyond even his four score and ten years, Mr. Edson will never forget that night. Until past midnight he continued the soul searching which Rachel Cameron's words had begun. Sometimes walking up and down his room, sometimes sitting quite still with face shaded by his hand. It was such a different evening from that which he had expected to spend! It was such an experience as he had hardly known was possible for a soul. Just as the clock in his own church tower struck one solemn stroke, Pastor Edson gathered himself up, and dropped upon his knees.

What passed between that soul and his Maker during the next hours, only they two will ever fully understand.

28. RECONSTRUCTION

Not many days after Mrs. Cameron had so far recovered as to be able to join the family at meals, there was a family council in the Cameron dining-room.

Aunt Eunice was for a time the chief speaker.

"The girls and I have talked it over, and looked it over on every side, and we are all agreed that it is the best thing that can be done; that is, if you will go into it like folks, and not grumble, nor sigh, nor anything." This was her concluding sentence, after a careful explanation which had followed a very bomb-shell of an announcement. The proposition, which had almost taken Mrs. Cameron's breath away, was simply that the Cameron home should resolve itself into a boardinghouse on a reasonable scale, with Aunt Eunice as housekeeper, and each daughter in charge of a distinct department. Many and earnest had been the conferences held, before the subject was brought to the notice of the heads of the house; so each daughter knew what she was saying, and stood ready to aid and abet the chief schemer, Aunt Eunice. She had a way of going directly to the point, and had made her statement short, it was not difficult to prove two facts.

First, that something must be done to clear them of the debt; and secondly, that Mrs. Cameron was not, and would not for a long time be, able to resume her duties as housekeeper. Aunt Eunice reminded them that she had been a housekeeper for thirty years, and served a careful apprenticeship at "making ends meet when there wasn't much besides odds and ends to do it with." She declared that she knew how to make good bread, which was more than could be said of Betsey—she refrained, from motives of kindness, from making her statement any broader than that—and she affirmed that having first-rate bread always on hand was "pretty near half the battle." She reminded them that the lodging-house around the corner was said to be always filled with a very nice class of people, all of whom were thrown out of routine by the closing of a boarding-house on the next square, where they had taken their meals. It was entirely probable that as many of these as were wanted could be secured at once. She affirmed that Betsey was as good a girl as she cared to have for the heavy work, that she was capable of doing as she was told, and "that was two-thirds of it;" and that *she* herself could cook, they would find, if they chose to try her, "as well as the next one;" and that, with the help of the girls, each in charge of a department, Betsey would be all the hired help they would need. That made the plan as plain as daylight; they had to eat, three times a day, now; and had to have a fire in the range all day, and go through just about so much work; it was only buying and cooking a little more of everything, and making a comfortable place for people to eat in, in return for which they would pay enough to support the table; and there would be no more house-rent, nor fuel, nor hired help than before; and when those three things were counted out, every housekeeper knew that the three great leaks in keeping boarders were stopped. Mary came to the front as soon as her aunt stopped for breath, and announced that she was entirely willing to try the experiment, more than that, she was anxious; they all were. Aunt Eunice had suggested their several lines of work, and they were things which they could do.

"Yes," said Lucia, with energy, "and therein lies a great advantage. I've been daubing at pictures all my life; and one little scrap that Dorothy Landis dashed off for me in a half-hour's time showed me that I had been struggling at something I couldn't do, and wasn't intended to do probably. Now, I *can* sweep, and dust, and arrange rooms, and keep things in order; and it will be a real relief to know that it is my business to do it."

Mrs. Cameron looked timidly toward Rachel, this newcomer of whom she was yet almost afraid; she had lived a life of luxury with her Aunt Katharine, what must she think of this descent into the commonest of prose? Aunt Eunice saw the glance and understood its meaning.

"You needn't look at Rachel," she said briskly, "she is at the bottom of the whole thing. Planned it out, and arranged what each one should do; and she is tingling with energy to her fingers' ends. She told me not to say anything about her, but I didn't promise to mind. All I said to start her was that I was sick and tired of sitting around doing nothing; that I had been used to working all my life, and that if I had the means to rent a house and get started, I'd go to keeping boarders; that I had done it before, and could again."

There was opposition, of course; chiefly on the part of Mr. Cameron and the boys. The father, it is true, admitted that any scheme which would give his wife a year of rest was worthy of consideration. He had made a failure at supporting the family himself, and perhaps— here he stopped, unable to continue, and the boys took up the word vigorously. They did not believe in setting the girls at work to which they had never been accustomed. They had a different plan. Let them both give up all idea of college, and get situations at once, somewhere, and help take care of the family, as they had always meant to do, just as soon as they could.

"And throw away three years of work?" said Aunt Eunice, with a toss of her head. "That would be economy with a vengeance! You don't do it, if my advice has any weight. I've seen one man upset all his life, because he couldn't get the education he ought to have had, and had to do things that he wasn't fitted for; and I don't want to see any more. You go back for your last year, and work hard at it, and then support as many families afterwards as you please; that's my notion."

She looked resolutely away from her brother as she spoke, and not a child of the six who listened knew it was their father who had been disappointed in his education; but the wife of his youth knew, and sighed. She *could not* have the boys sacrificed; even a boarding-house would be better than that. She could not help, however, one faint protest in the form of a reminder.

"I don't know what our acquaintances will say." This brought Mary to the front again.

"I don't think I care," she said, with cheeks aglow. "All our lives we have been trying to do what we couldn't; keep up appearances with acquaintances and so-called friends who were much better off than ourselves, and who thought by the way we acted that we were their equals in wealth. I am tired of it. Anything honorable I am not only willing, but shall be glad to do to help father. He has had too heavy a burden to carry; and we girls are largely to blame for it."

This was generous; the boys said nothing, but they knew they were the greater sinners. Such resolves as they each made that hour are certainly worthy of being carried out. As for the father, every word of tenderness, and especially every word about honor, were stabs. He could not get away from the thought that he had dishonored the Cameron name. What if his children knew all! It may seem strange to have relief come to a debt-burdened family through the medium of a boarding-house, that weak resort of inefficient, worn-out, and discouraged females the world over. Let it be remembered that those adjectives explain in great measure the reason for the failures; but none of them could be applied to Aunt Eunice. Inefficient she had never been; and so far from discouraged was she, that she sprang to the work as a horse goes to battle.

Before the summer was over, it had become entirely certain that she knew how to keep house. The heretofore much-blundering Betsey, who had been frightened almost to the extent of giving warning when she heard of the new order of things, discovered that Aunt Eunice could not only be alert and vigilant, but she could be patient with honest effort, and she knew how to teach the best and quickest ways of doing things. In less than three weeks after the new *regime* was inaugurated, Betsey's face was wreathed in smiles over it. To Mrs. Cameron, as soon as she was able to do it, was delegated the duty of buying the supplies.

"It will give her the daily outing she needs," explained Aunt Eunice; "and she knows how to choose good things. We want the best of what we do have, and plenty of it; if there is one mean thing in this world that is meaner than another, it is starving folks who are paying a decent price for their board."

So it came to pass that Mrs. Cameron went every morning on a pilgrimage through the great downtown market, stopping here and there to enjoy choice blooms or rare displays, and selecting with care and skill such articles as were on her prepared list. Some lessons she also was learning. Aunt Eunice had said that she was a good buyer; and so she was, after being told what to buy. But she had never been trained in certain lines of economy; and in the old days had been in the habit of buying spring chickens, for instance, when she saw some that she wanted, without giving so much as a thought to the fact that spring chickens were as yet fabulous in price; and the illustration will apply to many other eatables, and to all seasons. Aunt Eunice carefully guarded against such mistakes.

"Not yet a while," she would say grimly, in response to some delicate suggestion. "We'll give them good, honest food, and plenty of it; but we can't afford to feed 'em on gold-dust."

Mrs. Cameron took the hint; she had sometimes fed her family on gold-dust unawares. But the boarders in this reconstructed house thought that they were being fed, if not on gold-dust, certainly on something far better; such a change was it from the boarding-house around the corner, which had closed its doors because it could not make a living. They were for the most part quiet, busy young men—students, teachers, lawyers, just beginning life, and obliged to seek economical quarters. It is safe to say that never had they been so carefully, even daintily served. Rachel had charge of the dining-room, and saw no reason why everything should not be as carefully arranged as though they were expecting guests; even the flowers were not forgotten, but daily adorned the tables.

"They like them, too," Emilie announced. "That shy little clerk from the drug-store fairly devours them with his eyes, and I caught him in the act of slipping a sweet-pea into his buttonhole the other day. He said his mother was fond of them. I think we keep a very aesthetic boarding-house, anyway."

Meantime, some other things were very quietly happening—so quietly that only those immediately concerned, knew about them; yet they had to do with interests that reached into eternity.

The story of some of them the Cameron boys could have told. With them it began through Dorothy Landis, before she went home for the summer vacation. Both Rod and Mac admired her exceedingly, and during their mother's illness were so constantly coming in contact with her that they felt after a little like old friends. As soon as anxiety with regard to their mother was relieved, they began to contrive ways and means for seeing more of their next-door neighbor. They planned gay little trips which she and Emilie were to enjoy together under their escort, which trips she always spoiled by decidedly, though most courteously, declining the invitations. When this had occurred several times, and under such circumstances that it hinted at design, McLoyd, who was by nature outspoken, boldly accused Dorothy of not intending to accept their courtesies, and demanded the reason.

Was he sure he wanted to know? she asked, with some hesitancy; but when he said, "Why, of course!" she proceeded, without further urging, to amaze him. It was true that she had declined his and his brother's invitations from design. She was sorry to appear rude; but she had resolved long ago—taken a mental pledge to that effect, indeed—that she would not ride, or walk, or visit more than was necessary, with young men who used liquor ever so mildly, as a beverage, or tobacco in any form. What the world needed today, she believed, more than any other thing, was young people of principle and moral force enough to stand up squarely, even fanatically—if he chose to put it so—for the unpopular side of these great evils; and so far as she was concerned, she would throw every shred of influence which she might possess, on that side. She did not care to argue the question—not now at least—when he tried somewhat excitedly to draw her into argument; she was very far from desiring to force others to adopt her views— when he hinted that such was the case—she only reserved the right to choose her friends among those who stood for the principles which she believed were vital.

Something of this sort, McLoyd surmised had been said also to his brother. They were both angry, *very* angry, and from that time until Miss Dorothy went home, were severely polite to her from a haughty distance. Nevertheless, the thoughts she had aroused rankled. She was the most cultured and graceful and charming young lady that they had ever met. Was it possible that she represented others of her grade in society? People who were less outspoken, but who nevertheless were half ashamed of the young men of their time? They wanted nobody to be ashamed of them. They both intended to be leaders; and they began to consider more carefully than ever before in what lines they intended to lead, and what people it would be safe to have follow them. About this time, too, came up another interest which had much to do toward shaping their awakened thought.

The Smith Street Church was having an unusual experience. People, talking about it, said they did not know as they had ever before heard of a revival in mid-summer, especially in a city; but they certainly were having wonderful meetings at that church; and "dear Mr. Edson" was working himself to a shadow. How could he expect to endure it? Poor man! Meetings every evening; and he was here, and there, and everywhere, all day. What a remarkable young man he was! Had they heard how the interest began? The speaker said it was told to her in strict confidence by one who knew; that "one evening, away back in July, Mr. Edson had called the officers of his church together in his study, and told them that he felt himself to be such a sinner, he wanted them to pray for him. He hadn't done his duty in the church, or out of it; he had been ambitious and cold, and, oh, she didn't know what all. Just think! The dear man! When he had been almost a saint, always, she had heard. The church people were amazed, and distressed, and didn't know what to say or do; but they had met with him in his study, night after night, and prayed as he wanted them to, and, well—that was the beginning of the meetings, and really they were wonderful."

The Cameron family would have agreed with this decision. They were very regular in attendance even during some sweltering August nights. Mrs. Cameron voiced the feeling of all concerned when she said she did not know as it was any warmer there than it was at home. And when, on a breathless August night, she had actually heard the voice of her boy, Mac, *praying,* then indeed she would have gone, if the thermometer had been among the hundreds, instead of well up into the nineties! Yes, McLoyd Cameron had done that thing which he had never supposed he would do, risen for prayer in a crowded downtown church, surrounded by a great many "common people;" and afterwards prayed for himself with audible voice, pledging himself from that time forth to take the Lord Jesus Christ as his guide.

Ben Reeder's face was scarcely less radiant than was Mary Cameron's, that night. It ought to be said in passing, that she had, some weeks before, settled the question which had been pressing its claims upon her for so long. Before the revival commenced, as soon indeed as her mother's health would permit her attendance at church, Mary had explained to father and mother that she was going to unite with Mr. Edson's church on the following Sabbath, if they had no objection. She preferred that to the uptown church; it was much nearer home, and she wanted to work in the Sunday-school. Besides, some of the boarders whom she would like to influence were more inclined to go there than elsewhere.

Father and mother had no objections to offer. The father said he was glad; it was what he used to hope for. And the mother kissed her, and wondered if Mr. Kennedy's desertion had anything to do with the strange sweet change in Mary, and whether Professor Landis, before he went away, had urged her to take this step. None of them knew how Ben Reeder fell on his knees that Sabbath day, and actually cried for joy, because his prayer was answered; and then chose McLoyd Cameron as the next one for whom he would "never leave off praying until he *belonged*."

Oh, there were wonderful things taking place in the Smith Street Church!

That young man, Ben Reeder, is worthy of a chapter by himself, if there were but room for it. There are so many young men who might be like him, and are not. Having only a very ordinary education, almost without that mysterious force which we call culture, he was yet learning to have such an influence over certain whom he called "the boys," that there were mothers and sisters and Sunday-school teachers who were beginning to plan ways and means of bringing Will and Charlie and Fred into frequent contact with Ben Reeder, and not for Ben's sake. It was being discovered that the boys who associated much with him came home with new ideas about certain matters, with new subjects for thought, occasionally, even, with new plans and intentions. Nor does that sentence about culture do him justice. It would not have been named that, just yet; but it was a fact that Ben was growing cultured. He was associating much with an absolutely perfect gentleman, even one Jesus Christ. He was trying daily to shape his actions, his words, even his thoughts, in line with that One whom he so admired; and the law of our being held good here, as elsewhere—he began to grow, slowly, indeed, yet steadily, like the Object on which his thoughts and hopes were centered; and people began to feel the charm, as they always do, even though they may not always be well enough acquainted with the Original to recognize the likeness.

29. THE "NEXT SCENE"

Not Aunt Eunice herself was more constant in attendance at the meetings than was Rachel Cameron; and her influence, especially among the young girls, was kindred to Ben Reeder's over the boys. Much that she did was recognized and felt; and there may have been much accomplished through her influence which received no human recognition. During those days only her Father in heaven knew of the time which she spent on her knees, praying for the pastor of the Smith Street Church.

It was one evening early in September that Mr. Cameron walked away from the church service in company with the pastor to whom he was talking earnestly. When they reached his study, Mr. Cameron followed him in, leaving his wife to go on with the others.

The moment the door was closed, the gray-haired man began telling to the young minister the terrible and pitiful story of his moral downfall. He told it fully, with almost painful exactness and detail.

It is true everything had now been righted so far as was in his power; he explained that the only persons he owed were Professor Landis, who had insisted on lending his hard-earned savings, and taking Mr. Cameron's unendorsed note for the same, and his sister Eunice, who had lent the only fifty dollars she had in the world to help the boys in some college expense. He was careful to add that the boys did not know anything of this; it happened last winter, soon after she came to live with them, and he had never been able to pay her. He had much also to say about the unparalleled kindness of Mr. Landis, who had fairly forced upon him a loan sufficient to meet all his debts, and had probably trammeled himself in so doing.

"He shall be paid," said the poor man huskily. "I feel that every farthing of it will be paid. We have fallen upon better days lately, thanks to the sacrifices and the wisdom of my family, and I am sure we can do it. But the question which haunts me is, have I any right to go on in this way, posing as an honorable man, when I have so terribly fallen? You urge me to take my place in the church as I used to be, and take up again my outward duties; but ought I not first to make a full confession of just what I have done? There was a time when I felt that I could not do this and live. I am a Cameron, son of an honored father and grandfather; the name has always been above reproach; and it seemed as if it would kill me; but even if it should, I believe I am ready now to do it. If I know my own heart, I want *at last* to do only what is right, without regard to myself at all. Still, there are other people to be considered. I have prayed over this thing a great deal, but my brain is in such a whirl that I cannot be sure for any length of time what duty is; and I determined to tell you the whole, and be guided by your advice. You seem to me to live very near to God. I think he will tell you what to say."

Mr. Edson's young, handsome face was eloquent in its sympathy. He spoke quickly and with assurance, grasping his caller's hand as he did so. "God bless you, brother; I have been praying all the while you were talking. I am sure his word to you is, keep silence. You will wrong no man or woman by doing so; and by speaking you will bring needless pain to many. It is a matter which you have a right to settle with the one who knows the secrets of all hearts. I am sure brother Landis would agree with me if he were here to counsel with us. Come into the work, brother, with all your soul; and leave the forgiven past with God. We all make mistakes; some of us graver ones than you have."

All things considered, before the winter fairly set in, perhaps the Camerons might be looked upon as a reconstructed family. To outsiders, indeed, the only marked change was the presence of boarders. Of course, there were comments concerning these:

"The Camerons have gone down in the world since they lived at Clark Place, haven't they? I hear they are keeping boarders! And the oldest daughter has been deserted, it is said. You knew about that affair last spring, didn't you? For a time they gave out that an accident or something of the sort had disabled the man, and that the marriage would be postponed until fall, but there really wasn't any truth in it. Nellie Anderson knows him; and she says he is flourishing around New York as usual, going with all the stylish ladies who will allow it; he is getting rather fast for some of them. It is very sad, isn't it?"

The sentence is mixed, but the ladies seemed to understand themselves. Certainly they understood little about the matters of which they were talking. In point of fact, despite the boarders, every Cameron in the list believed that they had "come *up*" in the world. As for the statement about the "accident" and postponement of marriage, of course this was made out of the surmises of those who did not know the facts, and had nothing to do with the family. Those who were intimate saw other changes; for instance, the old-time family worship had been resumed, and remarkable indeed must be the circumstances which would cause them to omit it for a single morning. Sunday, too, had become a different day. There was no late sleeping anymore; for both Mary and Rachel were teachers in the nine o'clock Sunday-school, and the other members of the household went to church as regularly as the bell rang. Even the boarders, several of them at least, dropped into the habit of lingering after supper, and walking to church with the family. To some it seemed homelike to do so; and others thought that the Camerons were such churchgoing people it was only respectable to fall in with their ways occasionally. These belonged to the class who had known them only since they became their boarders.

When the University opened in October, and Professor Landis returned, he astonished the family by applying for board. His sister Dorothy had decided to remain at home during the winter; and he meant to sub-let his house, if his next-door neighbors would receive him as a boarder. Every member of the household was glad; no one more so, perhaps, than the mother. This man's unobtrusive yet persistent thoughtfulness of her during the long period of her convalescence had made a place for him in her heart.

"He seems almost like a son," she told herself half mournfully. "Mac and Rod could not be more thoughtful of my comfort." In point of fact, he thought of a hundred little things that Mac and Rod had never trained themselves to notice.

Sometimes Mrs. Cameron found herself looking regretfully at Mary, when her thoughts were on this man who was like a son. If only Mary had been interested in him, instead of in that man who had wrecked her life! But it was too late now. Nothing was more evident than that they had no such idea. They were like brother and sister together.

The boys had gone back to college; and as the year waned, there came only good reports of them. They stood higher than ever in their classes, were almost sure of taking at least one of the choice prizes at the close, and had kept their expenditures well inside the limit which their father had mentioned.

And keeping boarders paid! Mrs. Cameron was meekly astonished over this, but it was undeniable.

"It is a great mystery," she said one day, looking upon Aunt Eunice with respect and admiration, as she turned from the account book kept by Rachel's careful hand, and announced that they were thirty-nine dollars ahead this month. "It is a great mystery—I don't know how you do it. I have known so many who attempted to get out of straits in that way, or to support themselves, and made only disastrous failures. I always shuddered over the thought of attempting such a thing."

"There is no mystery about it," said Aunt Eunice in grim satisfaction. "We don't have to count out house-rent, nor coal, nor gas, nor help. And we have four young women who know how to handle their end of the ropes, and do it with a will; to say nothing of a first-class buyer always watching the market."

"Let us say everything we can about a faithful, efficient, responsible head who knows how to manage us all," returned Mrs. Cameron, half laughing, but wholly in earnest. She had come to look upon Aunt Eunice as the wizard who had helped in no small degree to give her back the husband of their early years, with his firm step and quiet face, and his days commenced and closed with prayer. "That is the secret, after all. As for the buying, I thoroughly enjoy it, now that I have a well-filled pocket-book, and am sure that no horrid bill which I cannot pay will be thrust in my face. The fact is, Eunice, you know how to do it, and I never did."

"Well," said Aunt Eunice, "I won't deny but that I think there is a knack in keeping house, and I believe I do know how. And you've got more than one daughter, let me tell you, who will know how, too. I must say I never saw Lucia's equal in the way of puddings and cakes and things. She fairly seems to bewitch them."

"You see, I've discovered something that I can do," said Lucia, looking up with a laugh from the dish of white foam which she was at that moment skillfully manipulating. "I wonder if everybody has something, little or big, in which they could excel? I wish mine had been painting—perhaps it might have been if I had had the opportunity; but since I hadn't, I'm glad I can make cake. Do you remember when you criticized my cows, Aunt Eunice?"

"Your time may come for daubing yet," said Aunt Eunice composedly; "you are not so very old."

The busy, quiet winter hastened away. The boys came home for Christmas, and pointed the contrast between that and the last year's holidays. Mr. Cameron, at the close of the first quarter's trust, put a sum of money into Mr. Landis's hands, larger than he had even hoped might be possible, and seemed to take on fresh strength and courage from that hour. At this rate he would soon be out of debt; and once out, it should go hard with him if he ever got in again.

"If ever I should get behind," he said to his wife, speaking with what seemed unnecessary energy, "I'll sell my watch and books and pictures, even my very clothes. I *won't* get into debt."

"It seems almost strange to me," said his wife serenely, "that you have such a horror of debt. You have never had any very disagreeable experiences of that kind. To borrow of Mr. Landis seems almost like borrowing of our own boys. But I suppose it is in the Cameron blood. Eunice feels very much the same, and I am sure it is a good trait to have. I don't think there is danger of our running behind again."

Mr. Cameron drew his breath in hard, and looked at his wife in a way that, if she had been observing him, she would have thought peculiar. *He* had had no very disagreeable experiences connected with debt! Then who had? Sometimes he felt like a hypocrite—felt as though he must tell her the whole terrible story. But she had never been quite well since that serious illness, and the doctor had assured him that he must be careful that she had no anxieties and no shocks. There were no shocks of any kind in these days.

Emilie's one sharp lesson of a dangerous world seemed to have been sufficient; that, and the strange experiences which followed, especially the shadow of separation from her mother, had toned her down. There were constant gleams of the old

403

Emilie; but they were followed by such airs of quiet dignity that Mr. Cameron, looking wonderingly at her one evening, said to his wife in a tone of utmost surprise, "That child is growing up!"

The unusual calm which had come to them as a family was occasionally the subject of conversation among the girls.

"I positively dread what is to come after this lull," said Lucia one morning when she and Mary were in the dining-room, putting finishing touches to the dainty breakfast-table. "This spring-like morning makes one think of it. What a whirl we were in last spring at this time! And what a whirl we had been in all winter for that matter! What change do you suppose will come? We don't seem to be made for long stretches of quiet. Don't you rather dread the next scene? We haven't moved in a long time—for us. I hope it won't be that, though I did hear that this house was to be sold. If there was ever any safety in predicting anything, I should say that Rachel would make the first break. She and Mr. Edson seem exactly suited to each other, I think; but nothing that any member of this family plans ever comes to pass. 'It is the unexpected that happens.' Mary, don't you wish we had some spring violets for this table? Perhaps we might venture to get some, now that Aunt Eunice is resolved upon dividing the surplus of each month between us girls. Dear old soul! Doesn't it seem strange that she should have been such a trial to us at first?"

"Aunt Eunice is very much changed," said Mary gravely.

"Dear me!" said Lucia. "That, of course. So are we all. I don't think, next to Aunt Eunice herself, that I ever saw a greater change in anybody than there has been in you. But I wish we had some violets. Horrid little things! I wonder I care for them. They were the very last flowers I tried to paint, and they stood up, every one of them, as though they were wired. I mean to ask Mr. Landis to bring some up tonight from that florist's on Park Avenue; they always have the nicest ones there, and he passes the door."

She ran after him from the breakfast-table, to give him this commission. Mary had already asked him to return a book for her at the library, and to bring that one of which he was speaking the other day. She came with the book, while Lucia was explaining about the violets.

"We trouble you with our errands, little and big, exactly as though you were our brother," said Lucia. "Half the time we forget, I believe, that you are not."

He smiled gravely on her. "Forget it altogether," he said. "I miss Dorothy very much, and would like to be adopted."

It was in the afternoon of that same day, as he was going for his violets, that he saw Mary Cameron in the near distance. He quickened his steps and joined her, very near the Park entrance.

"I have been thinking all day of what Lucia said this morning," he began quietly. "I find that while I am very anxious to be *her* brother, I have no such feeling in my heart for you—and cannot have; and yet, without your help, I cannot have Lucia for a sister. Is there any hope for me?"

The carnations he held in his hand were rivaled by the glow in Mary's cheeks. He looked at her carefully, and waited for his answer, which did not come.

"Am I not to have even a word?" he asked at last.

"I do not understand—" she stammered. "You cannot think—I mean—you cannot mean—" but the sentence would not finish.

"I have meant it, I think, ever since I first knew you," he said simply. "Let us go through the Park, while you let me tell you about it."

So the first break in the lull which had come to them was on its way while Lucia was dreading it.

"So strange," she said when she heard what the "next scene" was to be, "that I never thought of it. But he and Mary seemed so very friendly; so—just as they were while Mary was engaged to that wretch, that it never so much as entered my mind."

Actually they planned again for the sixth of June! That queer couple would have it so, Lucia said—they were unlike any other people who ever lived, she fully believed. One would think they would be almost superstitious about that date.

"No," Mr. Landis said, when she ventured something of the sort to him, "Mary and I feel alike about it, I find. There will always be some unpleasant memories connected with the date, unless we banish them forever by giving it a new setting."

"Oh, of course you think alike," said Lucia coolly. "You did as far back as before that date. I might have known."

It was very different planning from the last. No "Alburgh" was required this time. In fact, they would have no guests at all. Of Mr. Landis's friends, only Dorothy and a younger brother and sister could be present; as his mother had been ill and was unable to travel, and his father would not leave her. So it had been planned that the newly married couple should go at once to the old Landis homestead, where Mary would meet her new father and mother for the first time. There were many points requiring discussion, but it was finally agreed that a quiet home breakfast together would be a unique and pleasant proceeding.

"The fact is," said Emilie, "we are evidently resolved upon doing everything just as different from the way other people do it, as we possibly can. That is Mary's disease now; she used to want to do just as 'they' did."

30. "SPRING VIOLETS, AFTER ALL"

However, it came to pass that some of their arrangements had to be changed. It was Mr. Edson who proposed amendments. He called one evening on Professor Landis, to inquire whether he and Mary had serious objections to church weddings, and explained that there were so many young people in his church who would like to be present at their marriage, that he and Rachel had determined to gratify them by having the ceremony there. Moreover, although Rachel had insisted on talking a good deal about September, he had finally convinced her that June was the only reasonable month in which to be married. And didn't the professor think it would be pleasant for the sisters to choose the same morning, and stand side by side in the church? And such was the final arrangement.

"Two poor brothers, after all!" was Emilie's comment as she one morning gravely reviewed the situation. In view of my maneuvering to secure a rich one, it is rather humiliating. A minister and a professor! Eminently respectable, both of them. The very names give entrance to the best society; but think of the struggle for bread and butter and clothes which will have to continue in three families instead of one! And they can't keep boarders. Rachel will be too busy running the parish, and Mary never would be able to do it without Aunt Eunice, unless Dorothy will come and live with them; she could run a house, I believe."

"Dorothy is going to be an artist," said Lucia, to whom these half-serious, half-comic sentences were addressed. "Her people will manage after a while to send her abroad; I know, from some things she has said to me, that that is her hope, and she will become famous."

"Well," said Emilie with a pretended sigh, "there is some relief in that thought. Famous artists get rich, generally, don't they? We shall at least have a little reflected glory. The trouble with me is, I planned to be taken on journeys, and be given fine presents, by my brother-in-law. I had no hope of Rachel, but I really thought Mary would secure him for me; and so it is quite a disappointment, though Mary seems to be entirely satisfied. Isn't it queer, when one stops to think of it, that she should marry Mr. Landis after all? Here he was all the time, during the going on of that other farce. Why couldn't she have known her own mind in the first place, and saved oceans of trouble? I knew his mind ages ago. Why do you suppose she ever thought she cared for that Mr. Kennedy? He is so utterly different from the one she has finally chosen. Do you know, it used to worry Rachel. She felt all the time that Mary didn't think enough of him to marry him. I used to laugh at her, and tell her she wanted people to worship each other, instead of showing they had common-sense, as Mary did. But I suppose she was right all the time. Certainly Mary cannot be complimented on having much common-sense now!"

"The trouble with Mary was, that she wanted to help father," said Lucia gravely. "She thought Mr. Kennedy was rich, and that by marrying him she could do a great many things for the family, and so relieve father's anxieties. Of course, she did not deliberately plan to marry him because he was rich, and I don't suppose she knew at the time that such an idea had weight with her; but she has realized it since. She told me only the other day that it frightened her to think how nearly she had made a wreck of her life, through a false idea of helpfulness. And here we had the means for helping in our own hands all the while! We have all been idiots."

"And behold that creature wasn't rich after all—the wretch! What a trying disappointment *I* should have had, as well as Mary, wouldn't I? I'll tell you what it is, Lucia, my hopes center in you now. Keeping boarders is all very well; but it won't pay for journeys, and things, will it? And I am dying to go somewhere. Don't you *dare* to choose a professor or a minister. And the average artist is worse. I don't know what I shall do with you!" She sighed heavily, as one weighed down by responsibility; yet before

Lucia was done laughing at her folly, had turned to another subject.

"I'll tell you something that I worried over really and truly. You don't think I am serious enough to ever worry about anything, do you? I am sometimes. Do you remember that Mr. Denham who used to pay so much attention to Mary? Well, he worried me. I used to think she cared a *great deal* for him; and I didn't know but— never mind—yesterday I heard that he was married. Since he gave up that post-graduate plan, we have lost sight of him, you know; but it seems he married a cousin of one of the girls, and she told me about it only yesterday, and I was afraid to tell Mary. But I thought she ought to know, because she might hear it someday when it would take her by surprise. Don't you know that sort of thing often happens in books? I spent hours planning how to tell her carelessly, as if it was of no consequence, and yet do it when we were alone. At last I arranged it beautifully, while we were out on the back porch fussing over those flowers. What do you think she said?"

"I haven't an idea," said Lucia, much amused by this bit of confidence.

"Why, she said 'Oh, Emilie! Don't put any petunias among them; Cleveland doesn't like petunias. A queer fancy, isn't it? But he told me once they were the only flowers he did not admire, and they were really almost disagreeable to him. I don't want one of them. Excuse me, dear, you were speaking about some one being married.

Who was it, did you say?' I meekly repeated the name, and she said, 'Is he? Did he marry anyone we know? Oh, Emilie dear! I hear Cleveland in the hall talking with father, and I want to see him a minute; could you run and ask him to come out here?' So I carried all the petunias up to my room, where his lordship could not be disturbed by them, and I felt wiser than I had. People who are going to be married are past finding out! Mary wasn't silly the other time, but she is now."

They laughed gleefully over her evidence of "silliness," these two sisters, and privately rejoiced in it; surely this was as it should be. "If I were going to live in the same house with a man all my days, and meet him three times a day the year around, and be at his call at any time, and make use of his name, and all that, I'm sure I should want to think more of him than of all of the rest of the world put together," was Emilie's way of closing the conversation.

Moreover, one of the "lost" journeys over which she pretended to sigh in her whimsical fashion was being planned for her, and presently burst upon her, a delicious secret.

Rod and Mac were to be graduated two weeks after the marriage, and it had been joyously planned by the young people that father and mother should witness their triumph in person. It was a genuine triumph; not only prizes, but places of honor on the Commencement programme, had been awarded them. Aunt Eunice, with Lucia and Emilie, were to "hold the fort" at home, while

Mr. and Mrs. Cameron went on this rare pleasure-trip, to be joined on Commencement Day by their married children. This was Emilie's understanding of the matter; and it was not until the day before the wedding that the full programme was explained to her. Behold, she was actually to be of the bridal party! At least, she and Dorothy and the younger brother and sister were to journey together to the Landis homestead, starting three days later than the bride and groom, but reaching there by the same train which they were planning for; and afterwards she was to be taken to see her brothers graduate.

The new brother had planned it all, and insisted on paying the expenses of her trip. He had also invited Lucia, who had promptly declined for herself, urging that Aunt Eunice could not possibly do without her; but she had been eager for Emilie's outing, declaring that "the child," as they still called her, was longing to take a journey, and had never been a hundred miles on the cars in her life. It was all arranged at last; and Emilie, on the day before the marriage, found herself in a greater tremor of delight and expectation, outwardly at least, than were either of the prospective brides.

Albeit the child had her little anxious thoughts about it all, which she confided to Lucia, after this fashion.

"He ought not to afford it. I don't see why he does, wasting the money he has saved; but he really insists, so that mother says it would be rude to refuse; for which I am thankful. You ought to be the one to go, you blessed unselfish girl! I don't believe I ever could be unselfish; but I'll stay at home in a minute and help Aunt Eunice all I can, if you'll only go in my place."

This magnanimous offer being declined, Emilie continued: "One thing worries me. I'm afraid I shall not know how to be real nice to them all. You see, I don't know anything about farmers, only what I have read in books. I suppose they are just plain country people, and work in the fields, and have dinners together; the haymakers, you know, and all. That is the way it is in stories. And I shall want to do just the nice, kind thing, and act as if I were used to all their ways; and perhaps I shall make some miserable blunder that will hurt somebody's feelings."

Lucia laughed. "I wouldn't borrow trouble," she said. "Decide to be your own merry little self, and have a good time on your first outing. The people with whom Dorothy and Professor Landis have spent their lives cannot be very peculiar. Besides, these young people, Cora and Earle, are perfectly well bred in every way."

"Oh, yes; but they have been away at school; it is the father and mother, and the house, and all that sort of thing, of which I am thinking. Still, I shall do my best. I've read a great many books about the country, that is one comfort."

And so the evening of the fifth of June came to them once more—an anniversary which to Mr. Willis Kennedy had its horrors. He had lived to realize the bitterness of some of his mistakes. Too late the man had learned that what heart he had possessed had actually been given to Mary Cameron! If only his honor had gone with it, all might have been different.

In the Cameron home there was little time for retrospect; they gave a thought, indeed, to the past, but that was all. Everything was so different. The boys were at home; but they had only come that afternoon, and must rush back tomorrow. The responsibilities and honors of the coming Commencement filled their thoughts. The break in the family was coming; but Mary, though married, would be a very near neighbor, and Rachel would be the mistress of the manse around the corner. And father was well, and looked so rested, and at peace; and he and mother were going on a journey together. It was true that mother had to be watched, lest she should overdo, and she would never be very strong again; but there was always a smile on her face now-a-days.

"I do not feel as though I were losing two daughters, but gaining two more sons," she had said when a caller tried to sympathize with her. She had liked Mr. Kennedy in the old days; but Cleveland Landis was a son to love.

But, oh, the contrast that it was to Mary! She could not help recalling her past as she stood at her open trunk, laying in some last thing, and the hall clock struck ten. The same room, the same trunks, the same young woman, with her bridal dress lying on the bed; but the infinite difference!

"Going away with Willis Kennedy!" She remembered how she had said over the words, and had not understood the thrill of pain which ran through her at that thought; but had supposed it to be a girl's natural feeling on leaving her childhood's home.

"Going away with Cleveland Landis?" questioned her heart tonight, and received instant response. "Yes, anywhere! To the ends of the earth if he will, and forever! Oh, thank God! Thank God!" At the eleventh hour he had interposed and saved her from herself.

At twelve o'clock next day the Smith Street Church was packed to the very doorways, while before the altar gathered the bridal group. A ministerial friend and classmate of Mr. Edson stood beside Rachel, while the pastor pronounced Cleveland Landis and Mary Cameron husband and wife. Then there was a quick and quiet change of places, the attendant becoming the officiating clergyman; and Rachel Cameron and Robert Edson became one.

Will Emilie Cameron ever forget that perfect afternoon in June when the carriage which had met them at the station, wound around a broad avenue lined on either side with grand old trees, and drew up at last before an old stone mansion, whose wide piazzas luxuriated in easy-chairs and hammocks and genuine Persian rugs? Standing amid the luxuries, as one with them, was a beautiful woman who, but for the threads of gray in her abundant hair, and the matronly dress she wore, might still have been called young. But she held her arms close about the tall and dignified "professor," and called him "My dear boy!"

A "common farm-house!" Emilie thought of the forebodings which she had confessed to Lucia, and laughed. Her ideas of farm-houses, gathered only from books, had been very crude; but she had also ideas concerning palaces, and this great stone mansion, with its wide halls and long, wide, old-fashioned staircases, and its lavish display of beauty everywhere, might have passed with her for a palace.

The room into which she was presently shown as hers was more luxurious by far than any she had ever occupied; and a glimpse of Mary's bridal surroundings just across the hall almost took the young enthusiast's breath away.

Nor did the wonderment lessen when she went down a little later to the dining-room for the festive dinner.

Such splendid old heirlooms in silver as greeted her! And how the china, yes, and the napery, must delight Mary's beauty-loving eyes! And her husband accepted it all as a matter of course, only saying as he seated his bride, and took his place beside her, "Mother, can you think how good it is to be at home?"

Once Emilie thought of Ben Reeder, and the story she had heard of his bewilderment over forks and spoons. What would poor Ben do with all the appointments here? Yet he had told her once that he had "always felt at home, somehow, with Professor Landis."

She was glad that she understood the mysteries of forks and spoons, and all the belongings of cultured life; and then she remembered that she had wondered if they would use two-tined steel forks! And had much ado to keep from laughing.

Truth to tell, Mary, as well as her bewildered young sister, moved through the rooms like one in a dream.

Turn whatever way they would, from the large parlor and its companion, the sitting-room on the other side of the hall, and the library just back of it, which was lined from floor to ceiling with treasures, to the conservatory, where the choicest flowers vied with their humbler sisters in wealth of bloom, or to the wide-spreading velvet lawns, with their rustic seats and their fountains and their overflowing rose-bushes—everywhere evidences of highly cultured taste, not only, but abundant means to gratify the same, met their eyes.

They stopped at last under one of the magnificent old trees near the fountain—Mr. Landis and his wife, and Dorothy with her arm about Emilie. The father and mother, who had been showing their new daughter through her husband's old home, had been summoned away to receive a call; so for the moment they were alone.

"I am glad you like it," Mr. Landis was saying, in response to a murmured word of his wife, just as Emilie and Dorothy came up to them, "I have always loved every tree and flower about the old place. I was born here, you know. I have been away from it for many winters, but no summer has passed as yet that I have not been able to give a good deal of time to the dear old home. It has been one of my dreams that we might spend our summers here together. By the way, what is the look, larger than admiration, which I see especially in Emilie's eyes?" His own twinkled with amusement as he asked the question.

"Speechless amazement," said Emilie promptly. "Why have you always palmed yourself off as a poor man?"

"My youngest sister, is that a fair statement of the case? Did you not rather, very early in our intimate acquaintance, decide all these matters for yourself? Because I was a teacher, did you not infer that only for the sake of earning a living could one possibly indulge in such work? I discovered some time ago that not only you but your sister had the impression that I lived up to the limit of my means. I did not mean to convey that impression. In fact, I thought nothing about it until some words of yours, Emilie, enlightened me; it did not seem at the time an important enough matter to discuss. Later, I will confess, that I was afraid to state the truth, lest I should lose ground entirely with this lady." He looked at his wife as he spoke, with eyes that though brimming with amusement, had nevertheless a world of tenderness in them. She understood his meaning.

"I am glad you are poor," she had said to him one day, speaking almost passionately. "If you were not, I should distrust and hate myself. Poverty has been such a trial, such a snare to me; and now I want to conquer and enjoy it."

She remembered the words, and her face was aflame as he added, "I meant to confess sometime; perhaps this is as good an opportunity as any. And do you know, I cannot be sorry that the Lord has made me steward over a large portion of his money? I look to you to plan with me as to how he would have us use it."

The sentence commenced half in sport was ended so seriously, and with such inflection of voice, that the two girls moved away, instinctively feeling that here was a spot where they were not needed.

"But why did he teach?" asked Emilie, later, while she and Dorothy continued their walk in the moonlight, among the lovely shadows of those wonderful old trees, and Dorothy poured out her confidences.

"And, oh, Dorrie, why did you?"

"He teaches because that is his work, he says; his life work. He thinks he can reach boys in that way, and young men; and he does. I can tell you such lovely stories about what he has accomplished. He is good." She spoke the last words as if they covered all ground. Then, after a moment, answered the other question. "I? Why, child, I never taught anything; I am not like my brother. The only good thing about me is that I want to be like father, and mother, and Cleveland."

Emilie's great brown eyes seemed to grow larger and browner. "But what did you do all those times when you went out with books, and rolls of paper? We thought you taught drawing; and Lucia thinks you have such talent."

421

"Dear me! I was selfishly absorbing, all the time, being taught. I longed so sometimes to pass my lessons on to your sister; but I never dared. Oh, Emilie, I have something lovely to tell you; Cleveland said I might. I am going abroad to study—this very winter—and Cleveland is going to send your sister Lucia out with me. He has talked it all over with your father and mother. Oh, yes, your father understands, but he didn't, until a very few hours before the wedding; and my brother made him promise that he would not tell even your mother until after the ceremony. He said your sister—*our* sister Mary—was almost morbid about marrying wealth. Won't it be lovely for Lucia? I know she will succeed. She has done wonders, all alone; and she doesn't know that she has talent. She gave it all up so bravely. You can't think how we honored her for it."

Said Lucia, when, weeks afterwards, it was all explained to her, and she had had time to take in its greatness, "Perhaps, oh *perhaps,* I shall learn how to paint spring violets, after all! And cows!" she added after a moment's silence.

Then she cried.

BIOGRAPHY OF THE AUTHOR

Isabella Macdonald Alden was born in New York in 1841. Her mother, Myra Spofford Macdonald, was the daughter of a distinguished scholar. Her father, Isaac Macdonald was well-educated and an advocate of social reform. In her younger years, her father tutored her at home instead of sending her to public school. It was her father who gave Isabella the nick-name "Pansy" and encouraged her to write, beginning at a young age. At ten years old, Isabella had a story published by a local newspaper.

When she was old enough to leave home, she continued her education as a boarding student at the Oneida Seminary in upstate New York. There she met Theodosia Toll (later, Theodosia Toll Foster), who would become her roommate, life-long friend, and co-author (under the pseudonym, Faye Huntington). Later, Isabella attended the Seneca Collegiate Institute and finished her formal education at the Young Ladies Institute at Auburn, New York. After finishing her formal education,

Isabella took a teaching position at her alma mater, where she met her husband, Reverend Gustavus Rossenberg Alden. They were married in 1866 and had one son, Raymond.

Prior to her marriage, her friend Theodosia (or "Docia," as she was often called) helped launch Isabella's literary career. Docia submitted one of Isabella's novels to a writing contest (against Isabella's wishes). Isabella won the contest and in 1865 the winning novel, *Helen Lester*, was published under her pseudonym, Pansy. Isabella would use the Pansy pseudonym for all her published works.

As a new bride, Isabella devoted her energies to being the ideal pastor's wife. She called on church members, cared for the sick, taught Sunday-school, orchestrated ladies' prayer meetings and mission bands, and developed Sunday-school lesson helps that were widely used by Christian churches across the country.

With her husband, she instituted a weekly magazine for children, appropriately titled, "The Pansy." The magazine was wildly popular. Children from all over the country subscribed and devoured the stories that described God's plan for salvation and reinforced Christian behaviors. Producing the magazine was a family business, with each member contributing stories. Isabella's husband, son, father and sisters all wrote for the magazine, as did her best friend, Theodosia Foster.

Isabella was active in the Chautauqua movement of the late 19th Century. The movement was named for New

York's Chautauqua Lake, which was the site of the original assembly in 1874. John Vincent and Lewis Miller began the program as a training camp for Sunday-school teachers. Over the years, the religious focus of the program evolved to include nondenominational lectures and classes, concerts, plays and university-level courses. The program proved so popular that by the end of the century, hundreds of Chautauqua camps had sprung up across the country, offering similar programs.

Her Chautauqua experiences sparked Isabella's interest in the temperance movement of the time. She was an officer of the Women's Christian Temperance Union; and she featured the WCTU's work in her book, *Judge Burnham's Daughters*.

With all her activities and responsibilities, Isabella still found time to write novels. She was prolific, producing an estimated one-hundred books, as well as short stories and articles. Many of her books were based on personal experience or featured characters based on real people in her life. Her childhood friend, Theodosia Foster, was the inspiration for the main character in *Docia's Journal*. Her own life as a teacher and pastor's wife served as the model for Marion Wilbur in the Chautauqua Girls series. In *Wanted* and *Julia Ried*, her heroines boldly speak out in church—a direct and liberating reference to her own upbringing in which her father had a strong aversion to women speaking in public, especially in church.

Her books were translated into several languages, including Japanese, Armenian, Norwegian and French, and sold around the world

After Isabella's son and husband passed away in 1924, she lived with her daughter-in-law until her own death in 1930.

Isabella left behind a legacy of sincere, beautifully written books and stories that tell of Christ's salvation and the joys of living a Christian life with strength and conviction. In her memoirs, she wrote:

> "My very first little story books were written with a single distinct purpose in view, given over to the desire and determination to win souls for Jesus Christ. The longer I wrote and the older I grew, that was my central purpose."

> "I dedicated my pen to the direct and continuous effort to win others for Christ and help others to closer fellowship with him."

Isabella Alden accomplished much in her remarkable life. Most importantly, she accomplished her purpose and wrote to win souls for Christ through her inspiring stories.

You can learn more about Isabella Alden's life, read free novels and stories, and view a complete list of her published books at:

www.IsabellaAlden.com